Ever Rest

Roz Morris

Twenty years ago, Hugo and Ash were on top of the world. As the acclaimed rock band Ashbirds they were poised for superstardom. Then Ash went missing, lost in a mountaineering accident, and the lives of Hugo and everyone around him were changed forever. Irrepressible, infuriating, mesmerizing Ash left a hole they could never hope to fill.

Two decades on, Ash's fiancée Elza is still struggling to move on when her private grief has been outshone by the glare of publicity. The loss of such a rock icon is a worldwide tragedy. Hugo is now a recluse in Nepal, shunning his old life. Robert, an ambitious session player, feels himself both blessed and cursed by his brief time with Ashbirds, unable to achieve recognition in his own right.

While the Ashbirds legend still burns brighter than ever, Elza, Hugo and Robert are as stranded as if they were the ones lost in the ice.

How far must they go to come back to life?

Praise for *My Memories of a Future Life*

'Morris's hugely enjoyable novel includes a medium who channels spirits through her piano playing, a sinister spiritualist chatroom and a man who might be the reincarnation of Jack the Ripper – to name just a few – and knits them into a compelling, narrative. But the biggest surprise is how grounded the story is. Morris is a shrewd observer of the minutiae in people's lives ' *Indie Litfic*

'Ambitious. Enthralling.' *Critical Mass*

'Both romance and thriller, a first-class page-turner, strong and original. Elements of *The Time Traveller's Wife* with the spiritual charlatans of Hilary Mantel's *Beyond Black*. Kept me guessing right to the end.' *Fictionwitch*

'The canny cultural observations of Barbara Pym and Penelope Fitzgerald. Prepared to be surprised, mystified, and sorry it ends.' *Debra Eve*

Praise for *Lifeform Three*, longlisted for the World Fantasy Award

'Reminded me of *Never Let Me Go* by Kazuo Ishiguro, but much more joyous.' *Build Another Bookcase*

'Lyrically gentle, bold and disturbing. Deservedly compared with Margaret Atwood and Ray Bradbury.' *Juliette Foster, Surrey Life*

'Tightly plotted, nailbiting, evocative... a compelling tale of finding and keeping one's soul' *The Booklife Prize*

'With a richness and depth mimetic of authors such as Margaret Atwood, Morris has skilfully crafted a novel that uses science fiction themes such as artificial intelligence to start a deep and long lasting dialogue about what it means to be alive, and ultimately what it means to be human.' *Michelle Phillips, One Giant Read, University of Plymouth department of literature*

'Marvellous, powerful, beautiful. The characters are deeply moving. I am extremely picky about the books I finish, and I couldn't stop thinking about this one as I read.' *Kij Johnson, Assistant Professor of Fiction Writing at Kansas University, specialist in speculative fiction, Associate Director for the Center for the Study of Fiction, and multi-times winner of the Hugo and Nebula Award*

Also by Roz Morris

My Memories of a Future Life
Lifeform Three

Memoir
Not Quite Lost: Travels Without A Sense of Direction

For writers
*Nail Your Novel: Why Writers Abandon Books & How You Can
Draft, Fix & Finish With Confidence*
*Writing Characters Who'll Keep Readers Captivated:
Nail Your Novel 2*
*Writing Plots With Drama, Depth & Heart:
Nail Your Novel 3*
Draft, Fix & Finish With Confidence: Nail Your Novel Workbook

roz morris

EVER REST

a novel

ISBN 978-1-909905-88-7

Published by Spark Furnace, Cambridge House CB10 in association with Vine Leaves Press, Melbourne, Victoria, Australia

rozmorris.wordpress.com

Cover design by Roz Morris
Figure image © Owen Gent

The sound of the phone ringing in the flat would stop everything. Its sudden summons blanked her mind entirely. Nothing existed but the receiver and the slow advance of her hand to pick up.

This would be the call. A voice, a stranger's voice, would carefully say her name, her full name, to confirm she was the right person. And they would say: 'I'm afraid I have terrible news.'

But other people also called and sometimes it was him, saying he'd survived another day, still safe. One day, he'd be calling to say he'd done it, climbed to the summit and down again, and would soon be home.

She was in London. He was in Nepal, on a mountain.

When he first told her he was going away, she thought it might be a relief. He was constantly alight, giddy with the new, on a mission to amaze her. She was ready for downtime, to catch up with her own thoughts, for peace and silence. But now, each morning, she leaped out of bed to escape his absence.

Until this trip they'd never spent a day apart. She'd expected long separations would come, though, because of who he was. There was always a car arriving to take him to the recording studio, or to a photographer, or to an interview for a newspaper or TV. Or a person on the phone because everyone was waiting. He would tell them he was on his way, but then they'd say goodbye and that took its own time.

Still, she knew he belonged to everyone, not just her.

He had never climbed a mountain, but it was a time of amazing possibility. May 1994. You could board a train in London and go all the way to Paris. Nelson Mandela was beginning his presidency in South Africa. If these two miracles could happen in this one month, a rock singer could summit Everest and come back safely.

Even the air tingled with promise. Suddenly it was warm enough to leave the windows open. The breeze brought the balmy scent of blossom from Hampstead Heath, the peppery catch of pollen.

He'd been gone for seven weeks now. The last time he'd called was from Base Camp, via satellite phone. But now there was no contact. He had passed beyond satphones into the true ordeal of Everest.

They had read, together, about mountains.

If you could melt the immaculate snow, you'd uncover an archaeology of human daring, abundant as the fossils in the rock beds below. Metal ladders, heaved off their fixings by a shift of the ice. Ropes, bleached by the blazing light. Tents shredded to rags by the icy wind. Axes, crampons and ice screws. Oxygen tanks. The basics needed to shelter, walk and breathe.

And so many gloves, boots and down jackets. Easy losses, the slip of a moment, which might become frostbite, a ruined hand, or worse.

And the lost people. Hundreds of them, like exhausted passengers in a railway station, propped against a crag where the cold closed them down, looking towards the highest point on earth. Slipping out of a glacier or an avalanche, in the travelling gear of their year. Alone in a place no one would ever find, for the rest of time.

At the time she had shared his sense of awe. Now she faced these thoughts alone.

When Elza heard the shrill of the phone on the private line, when she whispered her scared 'hello', she knew she didn't sound like herself and the caller would ask if she was all right. I'm fine, she'd say. Usually she laughed. Yes, she was fine, now they weren't who she feared they were.

The next day, in sunshine, other calls came in. His manager reporting a deal for the new album. A commission for a Bond theme.

The manager knew Ashten would return. Elza should know that too.

She should be like Ashten's aide, who called to say he'd booked a tour of US radio stations. His tone was remonstrating, as if to warn her that Ashten must not forget, as he was now apt to do. Don't make me responsible, she thought. It's up to Ashten what he does. I haven't imprisoned him or lured him from his duties. We have fallen into a delirious state that's ripped up the rules. But thank you for requiring him to return, with appointments into next year.

A person like Ashten was not allowed to take risks. He would come back.

He would come back because he was so indelibly still here. Elza could find his voice any time she wanted, on a CD or a radio. She could watch him on a video, prowling a ruined warehouse, past rusty girders and clouded windows, telling the song to the camera in close-ups of his lips. Singing in a stadium, to a firefly sea of lighter flames.

He would come back because the press was fascinated. She wasn't from his world; she wasn't eligible and famous. Just a nineteen-year-old nobody dancer from Australia. He would come back because their romance was bare feet and lovebeads. Because people said she was a phase. Because he seemed to hear the secret heartbeat of the world and he had chosen her.

While he was gone, Elza had time to herself again. For dance classes every day. She received offers of film roles and book contracts, none of which she took seriously. Perhaps, she joked with herself, when he came back she'd have a full schedule and no time for him. She said it in case fate was listening, and thought she made too many assumptions.

Then the phone would ring. The two-bleat ringtone like the strike of midnight in a fairy tale, when she was alone with his absence.

One night she was woken by a heavy settling on the bed. She jack-knifed up. Was she dreaming? No, there was a definite shape, which she could see in the fan of light from the open door, and a breathing, male weight sitting on the mattress. She tipped towards him, with such relief and happiness, onto his shoulder. He smelled cold, like a cat's fur at night. And he smelled wrong.

Big hands lifted her gently away. Put the light on.

It was not Ashten. It was Ashten's bodyguard, who had a key to their flat.

He began to speak.

Ashten had fallen on the mountain. The body might never be recovered.

She had learned to be wary in crowds, especially in situations when people had time to look idly around. Waiting in a queue, riding up the escalator on the Tube.

These days, eighteen years on in 2012, being recognised was less likely. But it did happen, and it was a nuisance.

Across the check-in lines in an airport or supermarket. Past the packed heads and shoulders on a crowded Tube platform. They watched for where her attention was. If they thought she might notice them, they studied their phones or found something to read in the distance. Otherwise, they were on her, for as many moments as possible, as if she was a poster, not a person. Like the game Grandmother's Footsteps. Look at them – they were not interested, not in the slightest. Glance away and they gazed greedily.

She found it was useful to carry a big tote bag. If they were too close, or the crowd wouldn't herd them away, she could step aside and rummage, perhaps bend out of sight until they moved on.

Sometimes a person standing beside her would speak. Hello, how are you? Their eyes, flick-searching her face, said I know you, please jog my memory. She would smile and reply: 'I'm good. Nice to see you'.

Sometimes they knew exactly who she was. They said a bold, smiling 'Hi!' and used her name. Expecting her to make things comfortable, perhaps to entertain them. It wasn't comfortable.

When she met Elliot, he didn't do any of those things, and that was nice.

Elza met him when she was making a painting for an office in Shoreditch. She walked into the board room to measure a wall and photograph the lie of light on the bare bricks. A guy was doing something with a laptop. She called hello, not looking at him, and he said: 'Are you the facilities manager? I think that chair's broken.'

'I'm not,' she said, walking the tape measure down the room, writing in Evernote. 'I'm here to do a painting.'

'So sorry,' he said. 'I'll leave you in peace.'

On her next visit a few days later, she saw him in the kitchen. He was searching in the cupboards for a coffee mug. She was there to find a paint match for the lime green fridge, a colour needed in the picture.

She said: 'Broken any more chairs lately?'

He said: 'Sorry about that. I'm a contractor. I don't know who anyone is here.'

He opened the dishwasher and extracted one dirty mug and then a second. For her? A considerate thought, but was it all it seemed? He placed them in the sink with water and detergent.

'I'm Elza,' she said, because there weren't many Elzas, or Elzas of her age. After her notoriety there were Elzas everywhere. If names were a contagion, she was patient zero.

I'm Elza, she said, because then this guy might realise why he felt the urge to wash a mug for her as though he already knew her.

'Is that Australian?' he said, because of her accent.

'The name's Cornish. Short for Demelza. My mother liked the *Poldark* series in the 1970s.'

A detail about her that the newspapers reported widely. She'd done so little in her life there was nothing else they could write.

The guy didn't say, Oh Elza who... or You're surely not Elza who... He said: 'I'm Elliot. How do you like your coffee?'

He must wonder why she talked so much about her name.

It embarrassed her to set tests like this, but she couldn't stop herself.

...

She saw Elliot again, stepping out of the sandwich bar on the corner. She wasn't a person who instantly thought of a good thing to say, but with him she did. She felt unusually witty when she talked to him, and with no effort. He transformed her into an amusing, easy person.

One morning he held the lift for her as she pushed the painting through the foyer on a trolley, protected in bubble wrap and cardboard. He helped to steady it as they rode up the storeys, facing each other over the package, like neighbours over a fence.

'Finished?' he said. 'Or abandoned?'

'Finished,' she said. An instinct told her he wouldn't leave it there.

They met in a restaurant with dark charcoal walls and rows of white urns, as if Wedgwood had staged a production of Ali Baba. They talked about the films of *Skyfall* and *Cloud Atlas*, forgot to read the menu and asked the waiter for the special. He brought two plates of vegan beetroot pasta and tiny green legumes, which they didn't expect. They ate it, making a plan to get red roast pork in Chinatown afterwards, and talked about an art installation at the Barbican where you could walk through a room of rain without getting wet.

Then there was a particular quiet chime in her bag, more of a vibration than a sound, which changed everything.

3

At first, Elliot thought she must have seen something shocking across the restaurant.

No, it was her phone.

Her conversation was terse, and obviously with someone she knew well. Then she stood up and said: 'I'm really sorry'.

A pre-arranged getaway? A cynical person would think it could be. No, she looked too worried and impatient. She couldn't be putting it on.

He found himself rising too. 'Can I help?'

'No.' She laid a twenty on the table. Far too much for her share, and he said so, but she was walking, dragging her coat off the back of the chair, which scraped after her until an alarmed waiter set it free. Another waiter looked up as she reached the door and opened it for her with a bow, as if he hoped that small assistance might make all the difference.

..

A few minutes later, Elliot was outside. She was there, standing on the pavement, peering around the Friday night revellers and late-night shoppers for a cab, frustrated by their chatty amble and lack of hurry.

'Hey,' said Elliot. 'There might be one at the station. I'm walking that way.'

She looked relieved to see him.

A cab delivered them to a row of townhouses in Kennington. Elliot walked her to the door. He intended to get a bus home, but she asked him up.

Her flat was on the first floor. Every corner had something he wanted to look at. The kitchen cabinets were decorated with blackboard paint, which bore the rubbed-out ghosts of shopping lists. One wall was a collage of pictures of road signs at night, cut out from magazines. Red give-way and speed-limit signs. Yellow diamond-shaped warnings about kangaroos. Blue one-way arrows. Motorway signs to destinations in Italy, Nairobi and Ireland. Hazard triangles with the symbols for tunnels, pedestrians, birds, deer, boulders, gradients, windsocks. Some were scarred by wild environments – rusted or folded at one corner or pierced with bullet holes. All sizes, all nationalities, all surrounded by darkness.

Did she make this? She must have.

It made him think of a journey through an endless nocturnal continent. A punkish, apocalyptic aesthetic that wasn't his taste. He didn't know what to appreciate in it, but it expressed things he found intriguing about her. She seemed solitary; restless; defensive.

He should go home; he'd intruded enough.

She handed him a bottle of Wolf Blass. He was glad to open it, to have a thing he was certain of. He was glad she seemed to have need of him.

She paused at the kitchen window, studying the street through a gap in the blinds. Looking for what? When they came in, she had checked the neighbouring gardens before she crossed the path to the front door.

'Are you being chased by the Mafia?' he said. He hoped it sounded lighthearted enough. And that it wasn't the truth. From her watchful nerviness, anything might be possible.

She lifted an iPad off a shelf, set up the screen, handed it to him.

It was a story on the BBC news site. *Answer for Ashten Geddard's girl?*

Elliot didn't read celebrity news. Was Ashten Geddard a footballer?

Elza was watching him, wanting him to read. He read more.

Representatives of the band Ashbirds are today flying to Nepal to confirm whether a body recovered from the mountain is that of their front man Ashten Geddard, who went missing eighteen years ago in 1994 when he and his bandmate climbed the mountain. Today, Elza Jones,

Elza Jones.

Elza, right here, sliding a goblet of wine towards him. Tangerine paint outlining her fingernails. Keep reading, said her steady eye.

Elza Jones, who was his fiancée at the time, is holding a vigil beside the phone, waiting to hear. Has Ashten been found at last?

Elliot laid the iPad down. 'You're famous? Sorry, I didn't know.'

That sounded inane, or maybe rude. He really should go.

She leaned one hip on the counter-top, which gave her boyish body an unexpected curve. 'Elliot, have you never trashed your mind by reading gossipy papers?'

He hadn't. She was trashing his mind right now, though, by leaning like that.

'What music did you listen to when you were a teenager?'

Oh God, a test he was sure to fail. He was never into bands, or the world of bands.

'I knew Ashbirds a bit, but when all that happened I was fourteen. I was head of choir. I sang in a barber shop quartet. I wasn't cool.'

Her cheekbones lifted in a smile. 'You are adorable.'

Adorable. The word hit Elliot like a wave, an actual visceral reaction, though she must have meant it as a throwaway expression. 'Adorable' was a word that matched the amused lilt of her accent. She might say it of a pair of gloves, or a vintage chair. He wasn't sure what to do.

He looked again at the iPad on the counter. There was a picture of a young couple leaving a restaurant. The man was heroic looking, with a tousled mane of hair and a loose shirt, like a classical actor. You instantly knew him, even if his name eluded you.

Beside him was a slender woman with long hair like a sheet of silk down her shoulders. This woman, standing now in front of

Elliot. Hair shorter now, shaggy and blonde. But the same face, with a neat tip of chin and an expression that scrutinised what you were thinking.

Elza Jones, who was his fiancée at the time, is holding a vigil beside the phone...

'That's you?' A silly question. She didn't seem to mind a silly question. He risked another. 'So how do we hold a vigil?'

The doorbell rang in three short bursts. A key turned in the lock. The click made him jump. She had a flatmate? Partner? And why the warning code on the doorbell?

'It's okay. That's Steve. He was Ashten's bodyguard.'

Steve entered the room. He had close-cropped hair that looked military. He was tall. Elliot could imagine him shepherding a normal-sized person easily through a crowd, walking behind them like a protective exoskeleton, parting the masses with his arms. A belly swelled over his waistband. This did not make him look soft. Quite the opposite.

Elza introduced them. Steve grasped Elliot's hand to shake it and stared point blank at his face. Making sure he'd know him if he saw him again.

'Don't text or email her,' said Steve. 'It can be hacked.'

Her phone might be hacked? 'Don't you use a secure password? I can show you how.'

It was an automatic answer for Elliot. But it didn't make any impression on Steve or Elza. And this wasn't his techie world. It didn't have any rules he understood. The wall crowded his sightline with signs, directions and warnings. That's what he needed: a sign to show him what to do. Instead, it posed a bewildering slam of options and told him to be careful of all of them.

Steve walked Elliot to the door.

..

Elliot caught a bus. It took him away from Elza's street and her world. He wouldn't run into her again anyway. Her painting was finished. And he had a fresh start too, in another office.

But she ambushed him anyway. News websites and papers continued the narrative from the moment he left her. He saw a picture of her house in Kennington, the house he had been to. That place belonged to his personal history.

He saw a picture of her at the BBC studios. Was it really her? She was dressed like an expensive lawyer, in a sombre shirt, skirt and court shoes. But the Elza he knew wore construction boots flecked with paint and a sweatshirt tied around her waist. Indeed, he noticed she often tied things in knots to change their shape. It looked like a personal ethic because, he now recalled, she did it to bag handles too. It was a detail he liked, a statement that she would not accept things the way they were. Her dress when they met for dinner was appealingly scruffed with knots in the shoulder straps.

He didn't intend to google her, but nobody had got her right.

He was unprepared for what he found. Pictures of her aged nineteen as a studio-styled icon. Her face looked unformed; an oval of pale skin with glowering eyes and serious mouth, a child. In a biker jacket. Or wearing candystriped leggings and satin pointe shoes, poised against a wooden stool, her hair scraped in a severe bun. She had been a dancer.

There was a precision in the way she moved, even in construction boots. He'd noticed that.

Here was a picture of Elza with Ashten Geddard at a film premiere. A crowd of clones in diva gowns and dinner jackets. Elza and Ashten were dressed like clones of each other, in tailored black suits, sparkling jewels in their ears. Her jacket was knotted into a rosebud at the navel.

Elliot saw, many times, the photo Elza had shown him, leaving the restaurant with Ashten. Their hands were clasped, both caught, by luck of the shutter, in an identical pose. The right knee pulling forwards. Their heads at the same querying angle as they looked into the distance. It seemed the quintessence of young love, joined in hearts, hands, thoughts and stride. What was it like to lose that person? And so young? Here she was now in the *Standard*, still being asked to talk about it and when he might come back, her life a tossed coin in the air, never coming down.

He found a recent picture of Elza that was true. Her cautious eyes were exactly the way she'd listen as you talked, suspecting you intended more than you were saying. At first he'd thought she disliked being talked to, or specifically disliked him. Then suddenly, he found talking to her was easy. Very unexpected.

It became a habit to check if she was in the news, decide if he thought it was accurate. Despite hardly knowing her. He appreciated this was absurd.

He noticed when the media reported, a week later, that the body found on Everest was not Ashten Geddard.

Time to stop.

At the beginning of the summer, Elliot had moved to a house in Battersea with a small yard garden. It had a population of squirrels in the surrounding trees. He liked watching their alien grace, their gait, hooping and hurdling one moment, paused and wary the next. He left peanuts on the flagstones while he drank coffee at the open window each morning. One day, a squirrel arrived on the fence post and sat, its tail a flicking question-mark over its back. The next morning it came again, or another did. It stayed until he went indoors. Soon this was his morning routine. He set out the nuts, a squirrel arrived, and they both sat. Its eyes were hole-black, the black of limousine windows that let nothing out while the occupants watched, looking for dangers he could only guess, which would not be dangers for him. He didn't hope it would come closer or eat from his hand. Its distance was part of its nature, and also its dignity. He didn't talk to it, not even to say 'good morning'. But there seemed to be an understanding when they coincided, which he liked.

He was busy. He joined a choir that rehearsed twice a week. He helped a friend renovate a house. He built IT systems, sang in the choir, he plastered and painted. He had coffee, sometimes, with a squirrel.

4

Robert sat at a mic in a BBC radio studio, in headphones that made his voice sound raspy and very close when he talked. The lighting was dimmed, like a restaurant, for a conversational mood. Across the desk, the ponytailed presenter was introducing him in her smiley voice.

'My next guest is part of music legend. I can't tell you how excited I was last month when the news came that Ashten Geddard might have been found on Mount Everest. As we all know now, it wasn't him, but if you're as old as I am you'll remember when...'

Robert had been the bassist on the third Ashbirds album. In those days he was known as The Rib. Now he went by his real name, Robert Speed, and had a quiet life making jingles for commercials. But today he was speaking for Ashbirds.

'Robert, you're looking fantastically well.' That was his cue to say 'thank you' and begin chatting. On the presenter's screen with her notes was a picture of him from Ashbirds days, which she'd put on the show's website. Sinewy in a headband, rearing up his instrument, a T-shirt pasted to his chest muscles. He'd sent a recent picture as well, but she'd chosen the old one, so no one would believe he was looking fantastically well. They'd think he wasn't fit to be seen.

He might not be seen, but he could be heard. Beside him was a Laurence & Nash upright piano, a mic dipping into each end of the open lid, ready to rock.

The presenter went to a music track. Ashbirds, naturally. While their mics were off, Robert reached for the piano lid. 'All right if I try the action?'

She was skimming emails on her screen, making thoughtful noises as she read, a tic she must have learned to avoid the mortal sin of dead air.

'A few questions have come in from the listeners. We'll do those next. Sorry, what did you say?'

'I'm playing in the next segment. So I'll just try the keys.'

The presenter looked confused.

'Your producer mentioned it in the email.'

'Did she?'

Yes, she did.

'That's a shame. We just had Jem from the Thought Bicycles and he played, so that's our live slot today.' She was wearing a Thought Bicycles T-shirt too, the traitor.

'I could play "Air Tigers".'

The presenter put her hand on her chest as if her heart might burst out. Good, he'd surprised her. 'You played on "Air Tigers"?'

'Not on the original. It was before my time. But I can play you the piano part.' The bass wasn't his only instrument.

'We'll get you back on. When's your next album coming out?'

He hadn't got an album coming out. If he had the chance, he could leave the Thought Bicycles gasping in his dust, but nobody would want a solo album from him.

Robert returned his visitor pass to reception and pushed out into the street. The BBC buildings rose around him in the darkening sky, illuminated towers like a city of circuit boards. His interview gear was zipped into a rucksack and he now wore a high-viz jacket, leggings and a helmet. Streamlined for the rush-hour scrum. He jogged to the yard by the church where he had chained his bike.

His bicycle was gone.

The U-lock was open and lying on the cobbles.

Robert snatched up the lock.

How? The spot seemed secure. Several other bikes had also been chained there. Were still there.

He checked each bike in case he'd made a mistake.

No mistake. His bike had gone.

The bike next to his was still there. A Sirrus Expert; a high-performance thing with a carbon fibre frame that was probably worth twice as much as his.

Someone must have seen the thief. Or CCTV must have clocked them.

He couldn't see any CCTV.

What was this, an amusing ironic theme for the day? First, the Thought Bicycles bum his live spot. Then a scumgit steals his wheels.

In the street behind him, a group of Japanese tourists walked past, wearing rucksacks in cutesy kindergarten fabric. In their yammer of language he identified the word 'BBC'. They took pictures. They should watch out. Someone might snatch their cameras.

The Sirrus Expert had the same lock as his did. He knew how to break it open. He'd done it once when he lost his key. He could do that now, with this bike. If he did, would anybody notice?

He walked to the carbon bike, shrugged his backpack off. Surely someone must see what he was about to do. He drew a ballpoint pen from the side pocket, rammed it in the U-lock, which sprang apart. He pulled it free. No sirens sounded. Nobody cared. The lock was flagrantly open on the ground and nobody cared. He reversed the Sirrus away. Surely he'd be stopped. There were enough people dawdling past, admiring the towers, calling 'Look, BBC'. Would anybody notice him?

..

Robert powered the bicycle through the bumpy paths, over tree roots, through mud feathered with the tracks of other tyres, the jigsaw cleats of walking boots, the bubble prints of dog paws. His heart felt big and open and strong.

He was still riding the Sirrus Expert, the bike from the radio studio. It had been three days now. Nobody had come for him. Robert had googled the bike, once he'd got it home, and had nearly fallen over. It cost about five times as much as his.

He hadn't decided what to do about it. But a person who could afford that bike would insure it. They probably already had a new one.

His phone buzzed in his back pocket. He braked. His feet hit ground too soon, unused to the bike's size.

He checked his phone.

Ari Markson. Manager of Ashbirds.

Okay, that was worth answering.

'Robert, I hope you're sitting down. We have a backer for an Ashbirds fourth album.'

Every now and again this came up. Robert asked his usual questions. What kind of backer? How much? When?

It sounded surprisingly good. A small studio for the rough mix, a week in a prestigious studio to finish, session musicians as needed, PR consultant, distribution deal. A bung to charity to get the Ashbirds name from the remaining original band member, who had quit music in all respects except to be a legal obstruction. This deal could be serious.

'Are you in?'

'Markson, you'll write that offer in your own blood?'

'I'll write it in yours if you don't do it.'

'I'm in,' said Robert immediately, gratefully, loudly.

A woman was walking past him with a waddling dachshund. She gave him a startled look. Yes you stare. If you ever did anything this amazing you'd shout so loud that sausage-dog would sprint up a tree.

In Robert's ear, Markson laughed. 'Right, so we need the songs.'

'Yeah,' said Robert. 'When we get the band together.' Why was Markson even asking this?

'It's a bit unorthodox,' said Markson, 'but our investor wants to hear songs before he signs. He's a longtime fan. What have you been working on?'

Robert had scraps he'd started, but no time to work them up. Markson never got him songwriting gigs, even though Robert asked him often enough. Instead, Markson kept him on jingles for ads. The safe money. I write real songs as well, Robert told him. Did Markson now think he had a string of hits hidden under his hat?

'How long have I got?'

'Oh a bit of time. A week.'

Robert must have been quieter longer than he intended. Markson spoke again. 'It was hard enough to make the investor wait that long. Here's what he's like – he told me he once heard an interview where the Bee Gees said they wrote four Number Ones in an afternoon. I've put him right, but he wants to spread his cash right now, and he's crazy about your Ashbirds connection. If he hears some strong singles, we've got him. It's your time, Robert. Dust something off. Make it your best.'

'No problem,' said Robert. He ended the call.

A week? Did Markson have the faintest clue what working life was like?

Think. Think. Actually, he did have something.

It might be complicated. It might be a shade illegal. But it might be perfect. Depending on what anyone remembered.

..

Nearly twenty years ago. It was 1993. Robert was working sessions in a London studio. He was about to cycle home and had gone to the kitchen to refill his water bottle.

There, in the seats at the far end of the room, beyond the ping-pong table, was a guy. Arms crossed. A questing, provocative stare like a contacting signal through outer space. Talk to me.

That face was everywhere. On the cover of NME, Rolling Stone, the Sunday Times colour supplement.

Ashten Geddard sprang to his feet, snatched up a ball and tossed it. In reflex, Robert grabbed and by luck got the ball in his hand.

'Time for a game?'

'Sure.'

Ashten Geddard talked as they played. How are you? What are you working on?

He hadn't bothered with introductions. He assumed you wanted to know him, so he acted as though he already knew you. This was irritating. Robert felt guarded. Really, was this who he thought it was? A mistake would be mortifying. Robert looked for clues as they trotted the ball across the net. This man was tall, with an easy pantherish muscularity that made you watch him. He wore tight, faded jeans that fitted to the millimetre. A lumberjack shirt with cut-off sleeves that showed capable shoulders, which looked like they could hassle a punchbag. If he wasn't a star, he had star-grade training and styling. A thin metal chain glinted between the dark hairs in the open collar. The same chain in Ashten Geddard's bare-chest shots in Rolling Stone.

Ashten Geddard let Robert stare, kept count of the points, made polite noises when Robert told him his name and who he was working with, called him 'Jim' on one occasion and 'Owl' on another.

Robert guessed that Ashten was waiting to be asked what he was working on, so Robert asked.

'I'm making a solo album. It's for Elza.'

It's for Elza. That swaggering familiarity. I don't have to explain who Elza is. Everyone follows my story. Irritatingly, they did. Even Robert was curious about Elza Jones. She was a scowl-faced dancer from Australia with a pulled-back ballerina hairstyle that made her look twelve years old. Previously, Ashten Geddard dated supermodels with racehorse haunches and flicky manes. Robert could not see the appeal of Elza, except that she might make Ashten look serious, like a pair of prim spectacles.

'A solo album for Elza?' said Robert. 'Sounds good.' He tapped the ball over the net.

Ashten Geddard caught the ball in his fist, knocked it on his breastbone. 'These are really from deep in my soul, these songs. The kind of music that brought me up. Y'know?'

'A solo album,' said Robert. 'You usually work with Hugo Bird, right?' Hugo Bird was the other band member.

Ashten did not answer the question about Hugo Bird. He made the next serve harder, though, as if to prove something.

That was interesting. Was the solo album going badly? Was that why he was out here playing ping-pong, cooling off, showing off?

'The songs start with me, then I put my energy with another artist. I like to be stretched. I'm not one of those guys who thinks they can do it all.'

Bullshit. He was in trouble.

He probably needed a musician. Hugo Bird was usually the tunesmith, writing to Ashten's lyrics. But this was a solo album.

Tock-tock-tock, went the ball. What was the score? They'd both lost track.

Was Ashten Geddard looking for a partner? Surely not. He probably wasn't even making a solo album. Any moment, Hugo Bird would sweep in, ready for vocals, and they'd laugh for the rest of the day about the guy in the kitchen, who thought he was going to work with the singer of Ashbirds.

But what if it was true? What if Robert walked away and Ashten Geddard pounced on another person who wandered in to make tea, and they had the guts to say I'll write your music. Rely on me.

Robert said: 'I do a little writing. I could help.'

How could he be so brazen? He might as well have propositioned a prince. But here they were, at ping-pong.

'Are you free tomorrow?'

Yes, said Robert. Yes he was.

Please, God, don't let Hugo Bird come crashing through the door, calling Gotcha.

Ashten Geddard caught the ball. 'Best of three?'

..

It was the first time Robert dealt with Ari Markson. Markson's office drew up a deal. There would be a session fee and co-writing royalties once the album was released. And this would be huge. Ashbirds' other two albums sold ten million copies worldwide. Each.

Work began.

They used the tiny studio in the basement. There was a mixing desk, a keyboard and guitars hanging on the walls. Ashten hadn't been a slouch. He had an album's worth of demo tracks with keys, vocals, a simple drum pattern and synth strings.

They all sounded roughly the same. Ashten used a limited series of chords and melody lines. The verses and choruses were so similar they could be swapped between songs and no one would know.

Placeholder melodies. Robert wasn't surprised. That was why he was there. But the lyrics were placeholders too. Many were just fragments. Ashten repeating a phrase he liked.

'Sometimes I put down a single idea,' said Ashten. 'Then we find the edge.'

If edge was there, Robert couldn't hear it.

Robert was truly surprised. Ashbirds songs had a stylish and savvy strut that made you feel wiser, bolder, mysterious. But Ashten's demos were self-indulgent celebrity stuff about the trial of being him, the lovelessness of promotion, the loss of his illusions and how nobody saw his sensitive side. Robert didn't even find them convincing, because from what he'd seen, Ashten Geddard had no difficulty with his confidence or happiness.

As they listened, there were two interruptions for meetings with journalists. Several lyrics on the demo were about hating interviews, but Ashten returned with an afterburn, a magnified gratitude in his manner, as if thanking everyone for being a great audience. Robert knew other artists who had true fragility, who burned themselves alive for their music. Ashten was not one of them.

As each new song started, Robert prayed to hear a special vibe, a strong hook, a distinctive signature. Or a randomly spewed lyric with accidental depth.

What was he going to say when the tapes finished? These songs wouldn't even make album fillers. They were B-sides at best. One of the very worst was a rap about his personal trainer.

'I'm going to record them in Spanish, Italian and French as well,' said Ashten, 'for when I play in Europe. Don't you hate it when performers sing in a language you don't know?'

'Totally,' said Robert. Inside he felt like he was strapped on a guillotine, waiting for the blade. Was Ashten serious about these songs? If Robert gave his honest opinion, would he be sacked, probably by Ashten's aide, while Ashten went back to ping-pong and gave the job to someone else?

Robert wanted this.

But God, he could see how important Hugo Bird was in the partnership. Ashten didn't write a damn thing. Not music, certainly. Not even lyrics. Furthermore, Robert noticed that nobody had mentioned Hugo. Mick, who was operating the desk, occasionally made bland, encouraging remarks, but never spoke about Hugo, or even about previous Ashbirds hits.

Ashten must be serious about these tracks. Serious about doing them without Hugo.

Robert could be his new Hugo.

If he told the truth and Ashten fired him, what would that do to his reputation?

The last tired track strummed down to a fade. Ashten turned to Robert: 'What do you think?'

Ashten sat in a peculiarly supplicating pose. His elbows were on his thighs, propping his chin so his eyeline was below Robert's. He looked up in a way that appeared humble. And was not.

At the desk, Mick concentrated hard on the controls as he rewound the latest tape. He wasn't going to say a word.

Ashten's brown eyes seemed to swallow all the light. They said: 'I am yours'. I'm sure you won't be, thought Robert, if I tell you.

Robert opened his mouth. 'Obscure,' he said, then realised he had started the sentence at the wrong end, and, moreover, he could not lie. The brown fabric on the walls seemed to be vibrating, or his nerves were, because nothing in the room held still. Except Ashten with his trick-or-treat expression.

Robert said: 'The lyrics were perhaps too obscure and unrelatable.'

Ashten's face held a magnetic stare. He must have learned it for camera lenses, for interviewers. It was patient, but also made you feel you shouldn't keep him waiting.

More words arrived in Robert's brain, tripped over each other and fell out of his mouth. 'The chords could be made more inventive.'

Ashten remained still. I'm dead, thought Robert.

Then Ashten launched to his feet and clapped Robert on the shoulder, like a football coach. 'It's great you can do that. This is a new departure for me. Just tell me what you need to make this a great album.'

Robert felt the sweat spread over his back in a big, cold butterfly. He hadn't been thrown out. He still had the gig. Behind Ashten, Mick smiled. Good job.

'Okay,' said Robert. 'What music are you listening to at the moment? Any influences you'd like to explore?'

'I want something different,' said Ashten.

'Such as?'

'Something with a bit of story.'

'Shall I find us some stuff to listen to?'

Ashten opened the door and went out of the room, up the little staircase. Robert thought he'd gone to fetch something. He didn't come back. He'd left for the day.

..

The next day, Robert cycled to the studio with a stack of CDs. He'd start with smoky jazz vocalists who could tell a story with their voices. Concept albums by Iron Maiden, Willie Nelson, Marillion, Tony Banks and Styx, to explore narrative. The soundtracks to some musicals as well.

He arrived to find Mick in the studio. He had set up a couple of mics and a drum synth. When Ashten arrived, Robert was ready with the CD player.

'I thought we'd listen to a few things. To sort out some ideas.'

'Listen to what?' said Ashten.

Robert handed him the CDs.

Ashten began to look through them, then put them on the chair as if the task was too difficult. 'They're cliches,' he said, and picked up the vocals mic.

They began work. Ashten started to sing. They were nonsense

lines about a wolf. They were embarrassing but Ashten intoned them so gravely, walking around, they seemed like messages of sacred importance. And somehow, with the straightness of his back and the size of his baritone in this small room, he made you believe them. *'The wolf is, the wolf isn't.'*

Okay, they'd rewrite later. Robert tried a variety of licks with a jazzy feel.

Ashten put the mic down, left the room and didn't return. Mick gave a sympathetic look. Robert suspected he had seen this pattern before. And before and before.

The next day when Robert arrived, Mick said: 'Ashten wants you to hear this.' A beat came through the speakers. It was brooding, shrewd. Just drums, but drums that took care of you, told you to surrender. A total hit.

'When did you do that?' said Robert.

Mick squinted with his left eye. He punched the CD player in. The drums came up with vocals and keyboards. Mick had sampled the opening of 'I Had Your Dream', from the first Ashbirds album.

'He just needs to get comfortable with you,' said Mick.

..

After the session finished that day, Robert rode his bike to Ari Markson's office in Soho. Markson took him to Whistlers, a wood-panelled dining club, and ordered them both an aperitif made from vodka filtered through tobacco. Robert didn't drink his.

'Chill out,' said Markson, sipping the vile liquid that to Robert smelled like a nightclub floor at a groggy and self-disgusted dawn. 'He's worried you won't do his music justice.'

'He won't let me do anything with his music,' said Robert.

'He's pleased with you. He calls you his Rib.'

'His Rib.'

'Yes, he said that to me. A structure on the inside, invisible on the outside. A piece of body, roughly near the soul, from which he could be made.'

He thinks he's TS Eliot, thought Robert. Yes, that's exactly what he'd say.

'He doesn't trust new collaborators immediately,' said Markson, signalling the waitress and pointing at his glass. 'Just give him time, Rib. Do you want another of those?'

..

Eventually, Robert weaned Ashten away from the Ashbirds sound and they got four strong demos.

The album would be called *Superstring*. Each song would be a facet of love. The sound was skippier than Ashbirds, but the demos would be good singles. Robert thought they were like early Beatles; simple but catchy. There was 'How Long', a straight poppy ballad. Then 'Strung Out'. Then 'Souled Out'. All with that string theme, which Robert was pleased he'd thought of. But he was most proud of a track called 'A Shebird'.

Okay, 'A Shebird' wasn't entirely his own work. The stand-out lyric started with a bitchy remark by Robert's lodger, a 17-year-old pianist called Paul Wavell who was working in a call centre while he tried to break into the business. He saw Robert as a mentor and listened with reverent attention to his anecdotes of recording, especially Ashten's notable absences. Paul, who thought of every-one in terms of how much sex they might be having, decided these must be for nooky with Elza.

Robert and Paul were jamming in the flat one evening and Paul blurted out 'A shebird' with a lewd cackle and a sultry rumba on the keys.

Robert's entire spine turned to glitter. 'Do that again.'

Paul did, and also invented a set of lyrics and melody. Right there, out of nothing.

Robert tidied it – it needed discipline, but it was holy gold. It followed the tradition of rock songs inspired by women. Clapton, Harrison, eat your hearts out.

The following day Robert played it to Ashten.

'I love it,' said Ashten. 'It pays homage to the old line-up and looks towards the new life. A perfect circle.'

He thinks he's Dylan, thought Robert, but things could be worse.

They now had four songs for the demo of *Superstring*. They burned them onto a CD to play to the label executives and a bunch of influential DJs and critics. Robert remembered that day was a

Wednesday. He wouldn't usually drink on a Wednesday, but he and Mick went for cocktails. Paul Wavell came too. He was just discovering fashionable nose powders. They all had many, many cocktails.

The following day, Robert arrived at the studio. In the control room he expected to find Mick or even Ashten. Instead it was Ari Markson. Alone.

Markson's expression made Robert suddenly aware of his hangover. His senses felt like cardboard.

'Come and sit down, Robert,' said Markson.

Markson only used people's names if he wanted to be extra persuasive.

Markson leaned across the desk, searching the faders for the master playback. He found it, next to a label in black Sharpie made by a condescending engineer. 'Ashten wants a sax part for this.'

From the monitors, a lilting piano began, shimmering with reverb. At the very first chord, Robert felt a peculiar and exquisite twist. The melody was commanding and melancholy, exactly what they had been striving for all these weeks. The figure repeated, then Ashten came in with a vocal, sailing high over the piano line. His range sounded amazing; much higher than Robert had ever dared push him. When the song hit the chorus it made you feel like you were on a precipice, the brink of something that would change every atom of you irrevocably. *'It's coming, when you hear the roar, it's coming.'*

The song was called 'Hurricane'.

When it ended, Robert could not speak. His throat was full of rising pressure. With his hangover he felt removed from his centre of control. He yearned for a bump of coke to pop the dimness in his mind. The room seemed unfamiliar, as if he had been abandoned there and was growing smaller. For weeks, they had worked, struggling with phrases and beats and lyric lines and a stubborn fog of nothing. Now here was this soul-splitting, startling song.

Robert felt liquid heat in his eye. He touched his face to stop it spilling down his cheek.

There was no need to get so emotional. It was the damn hangover. It made him feel he was in a private space, like a dream. He checked he wasn't naked.

Markson was watching him; Robert couldn't show how much

this song had unmanned him. Their own work was sharp and solid. But they'd played it too often. They knew the tawdry tatters it was built from. If he'd heard 'Hurricane' that many times, he probably wouldn't react to it at all.

He supposed they would have to include 'Hurricane' on *Superstring*. It took charge of your emotions, changed your molecules, like all the classic Ashbirds tracks.

Robert spoke. 'Is this going on the album as well? Where did you get it? Did you buy it in? Who's on the keys?'

He knew, though, that the track wasn't bought from a commercial hit-writer. And the pianist was not a session player. Some of the notes were fluffed. Session players were not so slapdash.

Markson said: 'It's Hugo Bird!' He gave a bright smile that said everything was fantastic.

Of course it was. The playing fitted Ashten's phrasing tightly, as though they operated from one soul. It knew his best notes.

'So that's an old recording, then?'

'No!' Again the smile.

Robert felt a horrible sensation, a sense that he had been fooled. Had Ashten been secretly working with Hugo Bird alongside their sessions? Was that why he was absent so much?

They couldn't have written that song in the space of a few hours.

'So "Shebird" is now the second single, is it?'

Markson said: 'Now that's the thing, Robert. The boys have come up with this so we're rethinking our plans for the album.'

The boys.

Robert said: 'What are you rethinking?' It was an odd way to phrase the question, he knew. He still felt like he was speaking in a dream and could only use a word if it had already been said to him.

Markson smiled. 'There's going to be a third Ashbirds album. And there's a place for you, Robert. Ashten is used to working with you. You're his Rib.'

There was a place for him. Another dreadful flush of heat in his eyes. It was the hangover, it made him feel like an infant. That and the emotion of the song. He swallowed. 'So what's happening to our songs?'

'Ashten's not going to record your songs.'

Your songs. Not 'our songs' or 'the songs you spent these last weeks creating together'. They were his now, placed at the door like garbage.

'Okay,' said Robert. 'What's happened to the demo?'

'It's wiped. We don't want to keep rough stuff and workings. They get into the wrong hands. The boys don't want any confusion.'

The boys. The boys were always indivisible, always would be. And the boys had wiped his songs.

Robert went home and told Paul Wavell. They were going to use the song we wrote, he said. Imagine that. But then Hugo Bird told Ashten not to. That's what this industry is like. As your mentor, I have to show you the reality.

Robert played on the 'Hurricane' album, which was called *Hush*. The album swiftly took shape in the studio. 'Hurricane'. The lead track: 'Hush'. Then came 'Hunger'. 'Hurry'. 'Hustle'. 'Human'. Hugo Bird built the entire first side from pieces titled with the first two letters of his name. Grinding it in. Me, me, me, me, me, me. Never forget whose album you're making. The second half was a concept called *The C Side*. Robert couldn't be sure that wasn't also code, though he never figured out what it was code for.

They offered Robert the tour, but he'd had enough of them. Besides, he had an offer from a band called Whistlefish, with co-writing credits. He gave up the lease on the flat. Whistlefish never charted higher than number sixty-eight, despite being promoted until it became embarrassing. Of course, Ashbirds came to an unexpected end and there was no tour, but if Robert had been signed to it he'd have had an insurance payout for the cancellation.

He saw Paul occasionally in studios over the years, going through the motions to a piece of pop pap, playing with a lobotomised sneer. Paul was with a boy band called Laser, but seemed to spend all his time sagging on people in nightclubs while he put his earnings up his nose. The last Robert heard, Paul was working the cruise ship circuit.

..

That was 1993. Nearly twenty years ago. How many people ever heard those *Superstring* songs? Ari Markson might have. Hugo

Bird might have. Were they ever played to the label execs and critics?

Markson never gave Robert an explanation. Robert didn't ask for one. He was the new guy. He didn't think he'd get the truth. And he didn't want to blow the deal he'd got. But what really went on? Did an exec tell them to bring Hugo back? Did Hugo get arsey when he was replaced? Was Robert a convenient fall guy in their political game? Did anyone give his songs a fair crack? Maybe nobody ever heard them. Hell, the album was even called *Hush*. Hush it up.

'A Shebird' should have stayed in the charts for months. The song was sweet genius. It should have headed a blockbuster romantic movie. It should have been a top single that year, in every radio station's hall of fame. It would have paid out for ever. 'Hurricane', by the way, would never have been made. It was probably written in spite, so Hugo Bird could jemmy his name into Ashten's legacy. So no one ever erased him.

The biggest question: who might make trouble if those songs surfaced now? The label execs and critics? Fat chance they'd recognise a demo from nearly two decades ago. Fat chance they were still in the business, actually. Musicians were more of a problem. If Robert heard a song once, he'd got it for ever. He still remembered Ashten's agonising solo dirges. That meant there was one person he had to worry about, who might know those songs were rejects: Hugo Bird. But Hugo had been out of music so long. He climbed mountains now. Didn't play a note. After everything he'd done to stay in the band, he had no interest in it. What would he care?

Fuck it, fuck them all, use the songs.

There you go, Markson. Four strong singles. 'How Long'. 'Strung Out'. 'Souled Out'. 'A Shebird'. While those got ink on the deal, Robert would write some fresh songs that were totally his own with no dubious history. He'd take his time, show what a musician he was now.

Robert swung his leg over the crossbar, found the pedal, hitched his rear on the seat. He pumped along the paths, heart like a furnace. Actually, did he have to hide the songs' history? That history was also a distinguished pedigree. His blood was rising to the possibilities. People went nuts now for mega-bands of their youth. The summer of 1994 was the great fan migration of mourning, when everyone came to London with funeral wreaths, florist bouquets, dandelions from the roadside, CDs, teddy bears. *Superstring* was a treasure from that wonder time. It was Ashten's unreleased soundtrack for his muse Elza Jones. For what should have been.

This is what Robert would do. Work on the album, with old songs and new. Once it was well advanced he'd drop the facts on Ari Markson. Did you know I wrote some songs with Ashten years ago? Think of how great it would be if we used them. The great lost romance: what Ashten wanted to say to Elza. From his own heart, with a bit of help. Can you clear the way? Robert would watch Markson do the sums with that big banana smile and it wouldn't matter that the songs were rejects. There might be a toot of white powder to ride the magnitude. Markson, that is. Robert didn't do white powder. Not since that time.

A briar caught around Robert's legs. It clawed through his leggings and into his skin. He skid-stopped. It was a wild rose, a skinny cable of stem and thorns. He pulled it off and launched away again, chasing down the tracks of previous bikes, slicing the footprints of ramblers and dogs. His mind was running a version of 'Hurricane'. *It's coming.* No, I'm coming. Hear the roar.

..

Robert had a meeting in an advertising agency behind Russell Square. An art deco block, painted meringue white. He was a few minutes early. Just time to check in with Markson.

'How's that investor? You can tell them I've got four songs and can make a rough demo by next week.'

'Hang fire. They've gone quiet.'

What? But Markson had been sure.

No, Robert should never have believed that. This was how it always was. Even with assurances in blood. 'So should I bother with the demo?'

'I told them you were on it, but … Look, I think they've forgotten they asked. You've got some songs?'

'Four.'

Markson swore. 'Sometimes I hate this business.'

Robert looked into the distance. Across the street was a post-war block of flats with a row of shops at pavement level. The shops were the depressing kind. A bookie. A laundrette. Someone was coming out of the laundrette, making a mess of it. A fat guy trying to angle himself and a fat child and a fat bin liner of clothes out of the swing door. He was pushing, not getting anywhere. It was the simplest thing, walking through a door, and it was a fat struggle.

Markson swore again.

'Yep,' said Robert. 'Anyway, I've got a meeting.'

'I'll chase them again.'

No use. The moment was gone. Robert ended the call. He looked up at the advertising agency building. A stack of white, with balconies and railings. It made him think of those cruise ships where many musicians he knew had ended up, including Paul Wavell. Floating prisons where they played middle-of-the-road oldies for people who had never been alive to real music. No, they were never properly alive at all. He at least was in London on dry land. He would have this meeting and then he would be out again, back on the pavement, walking away to wherever he wished. But first, he was going to talk about jingles for cat food.

5

Elliot and Elza spent their first Christmas in the Lake District hiking through rainstorms. Afterwards, she moved to Elliot's house in Battersea. They converted the conservatory at the back to a studio, fixing panels over the glass walls, keeping just the light from above.

She worked a lot and seemed to enjoy it, even the clients who changed their minds several times or interfered and spoiled a work. She had uncommon tolerance, more than any other freelance contractor he knew. If she couldn't talk them round, she shrugged and said: 'it's not what I'd do myself'. After a while Elliot realised it wasn't patience. It was a robust sense of proportion. Whatever clients did, it was hardly the end of the world. She'd actually come through the end of the world.

So what art did she do herself? That was an interesting question.

Elliot had seen plenty of her client work, but only one piece that was personal: the collage of nocturnal road signs in her Kennington flat.

She destroyed it. He went to help her smarten the flat for lodgers, and found her stripping the collage off the wall.

That's a shame, he said. Can't we preserve it?

Time for a change, she said. She soaked it with a steamer and skinned it off in wet strips. She seemed pleased to do so. Shredding it, like a sensitive document. Then she went back to her studio, to make art that was not the end of the world, or even close.

She shook off the collage, but not its spirit. She remained on that nocturnal journey, travelling warily, not settling. She didn't have people she rang or emailed or met just for fun. Although she'd lived in London for two decades, she'd collected just one longtime friend: an ex-flatmate, Gina. And Elliot suspected that was mostly Gina's doing.

Elliot liked Gina. Her instant, welcoming warmth told you it was easy to become her friend. From the moment she learned your name, her door was open.

Gina's husband, Robert, was more difficult.

The first time they met, Gina made the introductions and re-marked that Robert was a musician, currently composing music for a major brand of cat food.

Elliot said: 'I'm so impressed by people who can make a living out of an art.'

Robert stared accusingly and said: 'Even if they have no ability?'

Wow, thought Elliot. I meant it genuinely. What nerve did I tread on?

Then Robert smiled. 'I'm just messing. What'll you have to drink?'

So Robert liked to throw people off balance, to watch what they'd do.

Mostly, Robert was energetically entertaining, but Elliot never shook the idea that there was something fierce and provocable in his core, like a breed of dog that might turn.

Gina never seemed fazed. She seemed to enjoy Robert's spirit, as though he was a difficult horse that set a little fire in her. Elliot admired her for it. He also admired that she worked as a registrar of births, marriages and deaths. He could imagine her conducting these times with a sure touch, especially the deaths, knowing when to give comfort, how to give it, and when to leave a person to themselves.

Gina was a bridge back to Elza's early years. She had been a girlfriend of Steve, the crowd-parting bodyguard. Like Steve, she seemed to maintain a protective watch over Elza. At the first dinner party, Elliot felt he was being evaluated. He caught Gina looking at him thoughtfully, as if considering questions she'd like to ask in private. When the main course was finished, he volunteered to help.

As he rinsed plates for the dishwasher, Gina leaned close for a confidential word.

'Remember, it's been tough for her. I'm sure you know.'

Elliot didn't want to dismiss Gina's concern, but he also didn't think Elza needed special handling, like people at times of life and death.

Gina seemed to sense the awkward note. She smiled, as if to start again. 'Have you managed to get a photo of her yet?'

That made Elliot laugh. When they met his friends, Elza was adept at sidling out of frame, raising the wine list or turning so her hair veiled her face. Elliot teased her about it, which she took easily, but no one could snap her unawares.

'We were at a wedding last weekend,' said Elliot. 'Not one person got a picture where she was looking at the camera. She has spider sense.'

'If you ever need to talk anything over,' Gina said.

'Thank you,' he said.

'What's happened to her... isn't something you get to the end of, like a tunnel. It's with you for life.'

'Okay,' he said. What he meant was: we're okay. We talk to each other as much as we need to. Just like everyone does. We don't need a special manual or guidebook. Though it wouldn't surprise him if Gina sometimes wanted a manual for Robert.

If Elza thought he needed to understand something, she would tell him.

Although there were times when the past blew doors open behind her.

If he was delayed on his way to meet her and couldn't call, which happened quite a lot on the Underground, he'd arrive to see her searching the crowd with eyes full of blame and black lightning. She'd master it when she saw him, but he could see she was recovering from actual, mortal fear. Later, she might say: 'If you're late, call me. I don't want to be imagining awful things.'

'I will if I can,' he said.

'I know you will. I used to be worse. You wouldn't have liked me then.'

..

For their next Christmas, they didn't go away. London emptied for the holiday. They went to concerts and movies and galleries, walked the South Bank, among people who were relaxed, unrushed, friendly. A secret enchanted season, right in their own city.

..

On an ordinary Wednesday in February, Elliot and Elza were preparing supper. After that, they would settle to *Game of Thrones*.

He heard her answer her mobile. Hi Gina. Then a startled question. 'When?'

He knew what it would be, just from that.

She stepped away from the worktop, phone pressed to her ear. Elliot turned off the water bubbling for rice so she could hear more easily, but she was striding out of the kitchen down the passageway to her studio. She called back to him. 'Steve has messaged.' Then to Gina: 'No, we haven't got plans. We'll be here. Yes, the weekend too.'

Actually, that wasn't true, but she didn't know. Friday would be Valentine's day and as a surprise he had booked a hotel on a moor in the West Country.

She might come back from her studio, relieved, saying there was no need to worry and they now deserved wine.

She didn't.

He went to the lounge, picked up his own phone and emailed the hotel to cancel.

He glanced out of the front window. The streetlight showed a shiny gleam on the gate. A bunch of flowers in cellophane, hooked to the top spike. It wasn't there when he came home, though such things appeared from time to time. Had somebody heard the news already or was this one of the routine tributes?

Elliot called up another address. A jeweller in a town near the hotel. Elliot had commissioned a piece from him, copying a set of Elza's abstract paintings. She had been reluctant to part with them. Elliot sent pictures of them to the jeweller, who made a necklace of coloured enamel discs and silver. What's more, Elliot arranged to text the jeweller so that the necklace would be in the window as they walked past.

Another email, about that.

From the studio he could hear Elza, talking to Gina, quiet and professional, preparing for the coming days. Sometimes he said to her: Gina and Robert are great, but we could also get to know other people. She always laughed and said 'You're the person I want to spend time with', as though he had made the comment to seek reassurance that she wasn't bored with him. Thus she slipped deftly out of the question, just as she slipped out of photos.

Also, he only thought to say it at moments when it would be totally wrong, like now.

6

Steve was at the gate for a flight from Heathrow to New Delhi, first leg of the haul to Kathmandu, where a body was waiting in a hospital morgue. Staff in red Air India uniforms were standing by the front desk, having sham conversations to look busy until they could start everyone boarding.

Steve had quit bodyguarding years before. He now owned a gym in London's East End. Occasionally a dead climber was found on the mountain and everybody got excited, and sometimes there was a fund to send Steve to Nepal and pay for his time. A crazy waste of money, though he wasn't going to refuse. So he was still Ashten Geddard's fixer and bodyguard, which, in the circumstances, had a certain black humour.

He needed humour to deal with the other people. Elza Jones always let him know his call had ruined her day, or her date, or whatever.

And now he was about to make another Grim Reaper call, to Ashten's former bandmate, Hugo Bird.

Steve dialled Hugo. He waited for the phone to parse the number, spark up some rusty remote switches through the intercontinental lines. Sometimes they never made it. Hugo Bird didn't live in places with reliable comms.

Some rock musicians retire and buy a country pile. Others invent a designer cheese. Or become a UN ambassador. Hugo didn't even own a house. His chief property was a lock-up in the Everest foothills, full of ropes and axes and arctic clothes, and a trunk that went around the world with him like Dracula's coffin. He had gifted most of his music royalties to charities, but his philanthropy wasn't very logical. He could have plugged into Kathmandu's music scene, run charity projects from there, made more albums to keep them funded. Instead, he nuked that life and spent his time clinging to frost-blasted crags.

Steve was glad he no longer took care of Hugo's safety.

To Steve's surprise, a voice said hello. Rough; as if yanked from a hundred-year sleep.

Hugo probably had been asleep. Usually, that was the only way to catch him.

The passengers in the departure seats were absorbed in phones and books, but Steve couldn't risk being overheard. He pushed through the doors and out into the corridor, which stretched both ways into the distance like a spaceship.

'Hugo, which country are you in? It's showtime.'

A gulf of intercontinental delay. Or monumental reluctance. 'Steve, I can't. I'm not at Base Camp. I'm flying to South America.'

Steve knew that already. He still learned the routines of people he'd have to meet at short notice. Hugo's routine was predictable because of the climbing seasons. Now, in mid-February, he usually joined an expedition in the Andes. But with luck, he hadn't left Nepal yet.

Indeed, Steve was now sure Hugo hadn't, from the way he answered. Hugo was too honest to lie. Most people would pretend they were already beyond reach. They'd tell you they were stuck in the departure lounge, couldn't get out, such a shame. Hugo instead hoped that if he sounded extremely unkeen, you'd back off.

Steve took no notice.

He knew Hugo's likely route. 'So you'll be flying from Kathmandu. That's where the body is. It's been airlifted to the teaching hospital at Tribhuvan University. I'll be there early evening your time.'

'Wait wait wait.' A spike of surprise. 'Who's paid for an airlift?' Not a trace of sluggishness in Hugo's voice now.

Steve couldn't answer his question. Or the questions that followed, outraged and accusing. Who's been on the mountain? Who raised the money? They didn't send us a picture to check before they went up? Which newspaper is behind this?

It could be a newspaper. And if he and Hugo refused to cooperate, that would also be a story.

In the lounge, the red-uniformed stewards unhooked the barrier. The passengers rose immediately to their feet, as if about to sing a hymn.

Steve started walking. 'I don't know, Hugo. But the body is the right age and European. This could be over. It would be nice if you were there for a picture. Finish it properly. Your charities might get some sales. I'm boarding in one minute. Gotta go.'

..

Kathmandu was never kind to the nose. The air was a drench of dust, car fumes and human smells. Sweat, fragrances, soap, breath, hot staleness. Steve sat in the back of a cab and watched the city pass in a sandy scrum of motorbikes, taxis, trucks, chorusing horns and headlights, whose beams showed the apocalypse of dust he was drawing into his lungs.

He stepped out of the cab at a concrete building that bore a sign in two languages: the hooks and curves of Nepali; the block capitals of English, both blurred with sooty pollution like smoky eyes in rain.

Tribhuvan University Teaching Hospital.

Under the sign, Hugo was waiting.

He had a tan, which Steve never got used to. In the band days, Hugo was pale as a geisha. Now, the contours of his face had tightened on his bones. He wore shorts and sandals. Back in the day, Hugo was an indoors creature, living mainly in the studio or darkened auditoriums. He wore trainers that never went training. They stayed as nerd-white as his skin.

Hugo was chatting to a policeman. By the look of their smiles, they were already on first-name terms. It was a habit Hugo had, to ask people's names. To Hugo, no one was just a doorman or a roadie or a receptionist or an assistant. Steve liked him for that.

Steve clapped Hugo's shoulder. Hugo clocked the swell at Steve's midriff. 'Good advert for your gym.'

'That's not fat, it's experience,' said Steve.

They walked into the hospital building, away from the blare of the city and its olfactory assaults, into a stringent tang of disinfectant. They followed the policeman's pale blue back through a tiled corridor. Echoes lapped around the walls.

'What about this body?' said Hugo. 'How was he found?'

'Don't know.'

'How many legs has he got?'

Viewing bodies was not the kind of thing you got used to. Although the cold stopped decay, the environment did not treat them kindly. Some were hard as glass, preserved as the day they went in. Others were mummified scarecrows, teeth bared like wolves, a Gaudi arch where a nose had been. Sometimes they had fallen to their deaths, or been tipped into the void when another climber found them dead and could not bring them down. Such falls did not respect the proper arrangement of limbs.

'What about these sponsors? What do they expect from us?'

The sponsors would want what they always wanted. A picture of the body if possible. Hugo wasn't seeking an answer. He asked the question to register his disgust.

The policeman led them past bilingual signs pointing to other departments; X-ray; outpatients. A doctor passed them. Steve glanced at Hugo as they both thought the same thing. They listened. Yes, there it was. The pause in the footsteps and the comically indiscreet snap of a camera phone. Knowing what they had come for. Off to tell Twitter, perhaps. Perhaps to go viral, perhaps to fall into the tealeaves with all the other unnoticed reports of everyone's days.

Ahead was the sign for the morgue. And the smell. Rotten.

Sweet. The sour-spirity reek of the chemicals. Steve always needed a long shower afterwards. In his pocket he had freshening towels from the flight to use as masks. He gave one to Hugo.

Hugo struggled to grip the packet, as though it was tiny and he was wearing massive gauntlets. Then he opened it left handed, though he wasn't left handed.

'Frostnip?'

'Tweaked a tendon. It should get better in time.'

Once again, Steve was glad he no longer looked after Hugo's safety.

Steve held the scented towel over his mouth.

The scent now reminded him of morgues.

A man in pea-coloured scrubs was waiting in the doorway. The mortuary assistant. Steve introduced himself with a handshake and got the man's name; Abiral.

'In here,' said Abiral. Steve heard the catch in his voice, his awareness that he might be in possession of the world's most famous dead man. The policeman, whose name was Lakshman, stayed at the door.

Abiral led them into a long tiled room. In the middle was a row of steel taps arching over a line of metal tables, which were punched with holes for sluicing.

'Glad to see you cleared away,' said Steve, not for the first time. He and Hugo had joked that one day they'd be faced with a hollowed-out autopsy or a grisly accident victim, and wondered how many seconds they'd last if they were. But today, as on the other occasions, the steel was scrubbed clean.

One wall of the morgue was a bank of metal drawers like filing cabinets. Abiral paused there and spoke. 'The body is in pretty good shape.' He described a few injuries and blemishes. Minor things they wouldn't see. His voice was steady now. He was in everyday territory.

Abiral put his hand to a drawer. As he did, he gave a smile. Steve saw him try to disguise it, obviously thinking it was unprofessional. The smile would not be extinguished. It became broader.

This was one of the strange things people did in the presence of someone who was very famous. They smiled all the time, very widely, and seemed alarmed that they could not stop it. An animal thing. A smile from the chimp brain.

Steve smiled back, though he had to put most of it into his eyes, over his hand. He saw Hugo's eyes crease as he did the same.

The drawer was open now. Inside was a shape wrapped in a blue tarpaulin. It was completely, disconcertingly still. It might have been a disassembled tent. The face was covered.

Steve rapidly took in the rolled shape. Noted with relief that everything seemed in a decent place.

Abiral lifted the tarpaulin. It crackled. He folded it down, framing the face, like a bouquet of flowers.

The face had its nose and cheeks and was pale as stone. This was also a relief. Sometimes the wind shrivelled the flesh. Frostbite turned the nose and ears to sticky, blackened pulp. The intense UV burned Caucasian skin to the colour of coal. This disturbing transformation, they had learned from one mortuary assistant, indicated the person had lain alive and helpless for some time.

Steve and Hugo allowed themselves a longer inspection. But the brain recognises a person in an instant, more rapidly than the processes of thought can catch.

Steve looked at Abiral and shook his head. 'Same time next week?' he said, into his hand, into the moist perfumed towel.

'Don't hold your breath,' said Hugo.

7

Elliot pushed the front door closed, shutting out a photographer's lens. Being doorstepped by them was a curious and disembodying experience. The photographers called out his name, but when he looked at them, which he could not help doing, they didn't look at him. They watched his image in their camera screens, as if he was their tiny avatar in a videogame.

Elza had put up a curtain a few feet inside the front door to stop them sneaking a shot of the house's interior. As an extra piece of rebellion, the curtain was stitched together from patterned fabrics, a fussy multicoloured background she said would infuriate picture editors.

Elliot pushed past the curtain. Elza was on the sofa, curled against a cushion. They did their usual hello smooch. She passed him her phone.

An email. From Steve.

I've got pictures, but to save you looking, it's not him.

'It just arrived,' she said.

The wait was over already. Were they celebrating or commiserating?

Her phone rang.

'It's *Hello* magazine. I quite like them. Shall we give them the scoop?'

Sometimes she spoke her thought processes out loud, as though she wanted his help with the decision. He had nothing to contribute, but she seemed to like to offer him the chance. 'Good idea,' he said.

Elliot walked into the kitchen. Looked in the fridge to decide if there was something he should marinate for this evening. A red and a green pepper. A duo of chicken breasts. Was that equal to the situation?

What was? He'd spent much of the day wondering what these next hours would bring. Work should have taken his mind off it. He was training a client on a new system and that usually meant a challenging time trying to understand why they couldn't grasp it. But they wrapped up by early afternoon. On the Tube journey home, the newspapers were in a fever of anticipation. The *Evening Standard* carried mocked-up pictures of Ashten Geddard, speculating how he'd look if he'd continued ageing. The *Mail* made a romantic picture of him in the ice, the world's young sleeping prince, his lashes sparkling with frost. For Valentine's Day.

Elza talked in the other room. 'Yes, I've got time for a short statement. How nice of you to ask.' Her tone was grateful, as if she wanted them to feel they were doing her a favour, but Elliot didn't fail to notice the underlying grit. Behave yourselves or no more statements.

They deserved wine tonight. Elliot went to the rack in the utility room. Elza's desk was just beyond, in the passageway that led to her studio.

Steve's email had also come through on her laptop. He could see it. The pictures of the body were there, in thumbnails. A face, pale as porcelain.

Elliot felt an unavoidable compulsion to look. He sat down, clicked a picture open.

His heart clenched. The face had a mark over one eye. A blemish of decay? Elliot scanned through the other pictures. The mark wasn't on them. Not decay, then; a shadow. Probably a person getting in the way of the light.

A sudden, high-pitched noise. Jolting, like an alarm.

Not an alarm. His phone.

'Elliot, it's Gina. I tried Elza but she's busy. How's she holding up?'

'She's fine. She's just making *Hello* magazine happy.'

'Don't forget, if it gets too much, come round and hide with us. Just call.'

'I appreciate that. I think Elza's fine. She seems to know what she's doing. She's quite the trouper.'

'But you as well – how are you doing?'

'I'm sitting here looking at pictures of a dead guy.'

A sympathetic noise. 'That's not something you forget in a hurry.'

'Do we ever find out who they are?'

'No, we don't. Look, I mean it. If either of you get wobbly or need an escape...'

Thanks, he said to Gina, and put his phone down.

He could hear the reporters outside. He couldn't discern their words, but the tone was patient, timekilling. They did not yet know.

The press attention was manageable. He'd seen this before. Once they were told it was a false alarm, they'd lose interest quickly.

But these pictures. The dead stranger released by the white Everest darkness. Somebody might receive news of his arrival. Begin a process. The same process that would one day come to them.

This was what Elliot had been bracing for.

But for now, it was nothing after all.

8

Aconcagua, Argentina; highest peak of the Andes. Right now, it looked like a travel brochure. The guides were starting back down the trail to the lower camp. Three figures in jellybean colours, the noble sun-brushed mountains behind. Earlier the wind was so violent they couldn't see each other in the whiteout and had to abandon their summit attempt.

Hugo was about to pack up his own tent and follow them. There'd be more snow tonight. The light was opaque and heavy.

A patter of scree from the slope above the camp. He looked up. He didn't think there was anyone else here.

A female silhouette. On her own.

She was moving slowly, at a jerky sleepwalking stumble. Something was wrong.

Hugo called out, grabbed a trekking pole and sprint-pegged up the slope. 'Stay where you are. I'm a guide.' Diagnostic possibilities raced through his mind. An injury? Could explain why she was moving carefully.

She leaned on him. Her breathing was fast and deep and uncomfortable, like she'd been running hard. But she was barely moving. 'Are you in pain?' he said.

She shook her head, lips pinched together. She was about to be sick. At that moment, she fell onto her knees on the stony slope, so violently she nearly turned him over like a judo throw. She stayed there, on hands and knees, her back heaving.

Nausea and shortness of breath. Altitude sickness. How bad?

He knelt by her, one hand on her convulsing back. 'You're near my camp. Let's get you down.'

Sitting in the entrance to the tent, he got her name: Charmian. Also the expedition she was with. Noted she didn't have immediate danger signs. Her lips weren't blue. She was able to focus her eyes on him as he unfastened her boots. Her accent was French in the words that croaked through her half-closed lips, then she dived away again to crouch miserably over the ground.

'I was taking pictures this morning. Until the whiteout. Felt great. Think I overdid it.'

She'd overexerted in the thin air. Overestimated how fit she was.

His radio, in an inner pocket, called. His group were worried. He explained; he'd be here overnight because Charmian couldn't walk down. They laughed. Oh bad luck. You're missing the party. It was the birthday of one of the other guides.

She had normal co-ordination. She was able to crawl into the tent and move a stuff sack to lie against. He asked if she had any pain. A headache, she said. Could be a sinister sign if it became severe. He offered her a choice of ibuprofen or paracetamol. She was alert enough to understand the question, though she looked defeatedly at the pills on her palm as though swallowing was out of the question. He positioned a sick bag next to her. Thank you, she said. If I hadn't found you.

He set up his head torch, dangling from the tent's ventilation flap, and, in the boot area, a butane stove to melt snow. Night fell. The light in the tent grew warmer and bigger.

They sat in sleeping bags top to tail. He ate boil-in-the-bag stew. She couldn't eat. He made her drink hot water and hydration salts. He filled hot water bottles for later. The wind was swelling, like an ocean, flexing the tent walls.

The warmth settled on them. Charmian's voice became small and slurred. Despite his tiredness, Hugo watched her. Was she slurring from natural weariness or was she getting worse?

He kept her talking. What did she do in the outside world? She was writing a book. What books had she written? Would he have seen them? She said she wrote for adventure magazines. What was her book about? Women on the Seven Summits, she said. 'If I ever get to the top of this one.'

If she could joke, if she could laugh without becoming breathless or collapsing in a spasm of coughing, she was probably safe to sleep.

Hugo turned his head torch off. The moon was bright, made grainy by the textile of the tent. Other forms took shape and he tried to identify them. The hulk of the mountain, or perhaps a phantom from his imagination. Outside, a loose piece of metal dinged on a tent pole, a tiny speck of sound in the roaring Andes night.

He woke to a buzz. The roof of the tent was grey, lit by the reflection of lunar light off the high slopes of snow. The moon itself had slipped behind the mountain. The wind was still feisty, bumping at the walls.

The buzz was his satphone.

Not many people had the number. He found the handset flashing in his backpack.

The caller was Ari Markson, who still managed Ashbirds. Hugo wanted to ignore it but was now wide awake. He answered.

'Hugo! I've been trying to get you for days.'

Markson's cheery tone set Hugo on edge. Perhaps the man was just an extrovert, but he called only when he wanted to persuade Hugo into something, such as advising on a script for a movie about Ashbirds, or to endorse a fourth album. Hugo only considered these requests if there was a worthwhile donation to his charity. The projects themselves usually fell through.

'Hello, Ari. I've been out of range.' In the lower areas of the mountain, the satellites had trouble making a connection. Unlike here, in the peaks and clouds.

Markson's end sounded like London. Chattering voices. A mumbling snatch of saxophone.

Markson spoke. 'Which mountain are you rocking at the moment?' His voice had a performing tone. Did he have an audience for the call?

Hugo could have said he was in the Andes, but instead he said Aconcagua, exaggerating the local pronunciation. So that Markson would have trouble repeating it to his people.

Markson wasn't fazed. 'Hugo, when are you finished with Anaconda?'

Definitely laughter in the background. A fluttering sax. They were so incongruous to Hugo, here in a dot of toughened nylon on the side of a mountain.

'Ari, what do you want?'

'A collector wants to meet you next time you fly back. He has items he'd like to verify belonged to Ashten. Set lists from the *Surface Tension* tour. His guitar case.'

This also seemed absurd, for so many reasons. Hugo picked just one. 'Ash couldn't play the guitar.'

'So that's one of the things we need you for. To put it straight and certify them. He's offered to donate a thousand pounds to your charity.'

A thousand pounds? Hugo didn't know what Ashbirds artefacts sold for, but that seemed low. Right now, he was trying to sponsor the climbing school near Everest Base Camp, where local Sherpas could learn techniques to work safely as guides. A thousand might buy a few ropes, bolts and harnesses. Hardly worth it.

'Are you still there, Hugo? Obviously, a thousand isn't enough. We had a talk and he'll pay ten thousand.'

Hugo could hear the grin in Markson's voice. This was irritating, but the guy had done a good job. 'All right,' he said.

The call finished. Hugo zipped the phone into his pack and lay back in his sleeping bag. Night-time Soho was gone and he was here, drowsy and warm, in the cosmic emptiness of the mountain.

..

He opened his eyes. The stove was hanging in the open vestibule, hissing under a pot of water. The unzipped flap showed stars outside, but the darkness was blue, not black. It must be nearly dawn.

Charmian must be better.

He heard a click. He sat up. A lithe figure in black thermals and a skinny hat was poised over him in a ninja crouch, with a camera.

Another click.

She laid the camera on a cushion and passed him a steaming mug of tea. She now had sparkling eyes, in laughing creases. An open smile too, ski-slopes white in a rugged tan.

'I can't believe it's you. Come on, let's watch the dawn.'

The previous night, she was gritted, sunk in nausea. No longer. God, she must be tough. You'd think she'd never been ill.

The warmth of the mug was welcome, but he would prefer another hour's sleep.

He would prefer not to be photographed.

Hugo was rarely recognised and he liked that. Climbers did not wonder about him because they were focused on summiting the mountain. Besides, his face had never been widely known. Occasionally, if someone was sufficiently curious, they might work it out.

Perhaps Charmian had heard him on the satphone. He'd mentioned Ash's name. Perhaps she wasn't as exhausted as he'd thought.

She slid on her knees across the tent floor and out of the zipped entrance, steadying her mug in two hands.

She hadn't mentioned the photos. Or asked if he minded.

Beyond the slit of the tent, far away in the blue-black sky, the horizon was starting. A faint flare of sun.

Charmian turned to him again. 'Please. Come out. You're missing this beautiful dawn.'

Her restored smile was still surprising. Her appeal was hard to resist.

Hugo pulled on a warm layer and joined her. The air beyond the tent was a sheet of sharp cold. The steam from their cups was thick and white.

In the distance, a bronzed line of peaks was now appearing, on a spreading glow of light.

Charmian looked out. 'Ashbirds formed me when I was a teenager. "Hurricane". It's my compass. It saves my life. It reminds me not to forget who I am. Who I should have been before life got complicated, and I had to make rubbish decisions.'

'What decisions?' It seemed he had to ask and he knew she wouldn't hold back.

'I became pregnant too young. Before then, I was going to be an adventurer. I lost my way for a while. I settled for the conventional life.'

Sometimes Hugo felt like a priest or an analyst. Would she talk like this to any other stranger?

'But now I see amazing things and meet amazing people.' She butted her mug against his with a conquering, ice-mint smile. 'Do you still write music?'

There were some questions he didn't answer. One didn't stop writing music. It still formed in his mind, as readily as language, even if he no longer played it.

The sun was spilling the horizon wider, a luminous band around the visible world, flaring on a peak in the far, far distance.

Charmian said: 'What was Ashten like?'

Hugo replied: 'He'd have liked you.'

This answer usually ended the conversation. It was what the fan dreamed of hearing. Charmian gave a gasped laugh, wriggling her toes inside her socks, her mind inside this thought. She was a teenager again, helpless in her emotions.

She spoke again. 'You lost him. How do you cope with that?'

Teenagers weren't worried whether they should ask.

Another question he never answered.

The wide, sprawling saddle of Nido de Condores was starting to become visible, full of contours and folds. He could see the weathering of Charmian's skin more clearly too.

' "Sacrophiliac". It's raw life in three minutes. And "Blood Noise".'

There was a change in her. He felt it like the heat of an approaching fire. 'Sacrophiliac' and 'Blood Noise' were Ash's most smouldering sex-god performances. He'd argued with the label about them, wanting them to be singles. The label said they'd never get airplay. Ash knew that. He just wanted to have the special meeting where they tried to explain this, reading the lyrics to him in a dead, admonishing voice.

Now there was nowhere for Charmian to put her blood noise, except into the hand she placed with suggesting weight on Hugo's, the face she turned towards his.

Hugo said: 'Would you do something for me?'

'Name it.'

'Delete the pictures you took of me.'

She held his gaze in challenge. Did he mean it?

He meant it.

She twisted away and crawled into the tent. He heard the rasp of zips. She was packing, briskly, angrily. Whatever request she hoped for, that was not it.

He heard her call her camp on the radio to say she was on her way. He heard a series of electronic bleeps. A person deleting pictures. He counted the pattern. It repeated six times.

Six pictures? He remembered just two. How long had she been crouching over him before he woke up? He had rescued her, stopped her stumbling into a lonely, freezing night and probably a lonely, stupid death. He had stayed awake in case she became dangerously ill. She had watched him sleeping and taken secret pictures.

She crawled out again, padded in more layers, goggles tilted upwards on her hat, ready for use. She placed the camera in his lap, then turned away to her boots and overboots. 'I've deleted them. Look.'

Hugo checked the camera. There were no pictures of him. Just scenic shots for her articles and book. He should erase some of those. He didn't.

She slipped the camera into an inner pocket and stood up, goggles in position over her eyes. He held her pack while she hooked her arms in and fixed the straps. The sun was fully up. The snow was white and brilliant.

'You know, I could help you tell your story.'

'I don't have a story.'

She walked a few steps, stamping her feet into the rind of snow. 'I have the structure already. You rescued me with your music, then again last night. Two rescues – beginning and end. It would make a great book.'

Was that supposed to be 'thank you'?

'Be careful,' said Hugo. 'Don't go up again until you've acclimatised.'

She glanced back at him. In her glossy lenses he saw a tiny panorama. The coloured bobbles of the tents, the soaring mountain, his arm, waving her on her way.

9

Fans remembered every detail about Ashbirds' work, performances and interviews. They were perplexed when an actual Ashbird didn't recall these details at all.

Steve was with Hugo. They were at a faux-Regency mansion in Sussex, meeting a collector of Ashbirds memorabilia. The first item he showed them was a towelling sports headband. Hugo didn't touch it. Steve did, and hoped its ossified texture came from its age, not from the sweaty head that once used it. But whose sweaty head?

Hugo was no help. The collector suggested names. Hugo looked at the headband, and at Steve, helplessly. Drills made a dentisty wail in the house's upper storeys, a whine like the rising desperation in this room. The collector dabbed his phone and found a picture of a guy under supernova stage lights, grappling with a guitar, wearing the headband.

'Aha, it was Rib,' said Hugo. 'Sorry, it's been a while.'

'No problem,' said the collector, but Steve could see it was.

The collector's name was Oliver Jared and he was nervous. Twitchy as a grasshopper when either of them spoke. Eager to do everything right. Flummoxed that Hugo couldn't get it right at all.

There was also the way Jared stared at Hugo. Steve did the chit-chat and Hugo was almost mute, but Jared looked exclusively at Hugo. Gazed at him. Hugo shifted uneasily.

Ashten had never minded that scrutiny. It put his lights on. But Hugo seemed like he would prefer to put Jared behind a locked door.

'What else have you got, Oliver?' said Steve. If he didn't get this moving, Hugo might bolt.

Oliver Jared led them at a bustling walk through empty rooms smelling of wet plaster, apologising for the dust as he'd just done a refit. He showed them into a high hallway with a granite fireplace. The hall was as big as a barn and the fireplace was tall enough to stride into. No wonder this guy could spend ten k for Hugo to certify his memorabilia.

He surely, please God, had something better than a crusty headband.

On the black, twinkling hearth was the collection, organised like a haul of archaeological finds. Gig detritus: plectrums like scales from psychedelic snakes; torn packets from guitar and bass strings; drumsticks darkened by use. Oh, Oliver, those could be from any band. There was concert merchandise: programmes and T-shirts. They were more provable, though it was hard to remember if they were official. More importantly, none of this was rare or special enough to warrant a ten-k certification. Steve could see worry in Hugo's hunched posture as he looked at it all.

But there was a stack of handwritten set lists. Steve nudged Hugo. Hugo fell on them, clearly relieved.

'These are definitely us. That's my writing. And this –' A bag containing a yellow microphone windshield. He held it out to Steve. 'That's his, isn't it?' The foam was crumbling to a polleny smear where it touched the plastic. On it was a letter in black pen: *A*. 'Ash marked his gear so no one else used it. He was paranoid about getting colds.'

'He used to gargle with that brown stuff,' said Steve.

'So did I. It tasted of vinegar and pepper.'

'Nobody cares what you did,' grinned Steve.

Oliver Jared looked like he cared what Hugo did, and disapproved of Steve for teasing.

'So he's actually called Ash?' said Oliver Jared.

'Only Hugo calls him Ash,' said Steve. Again, Oliver Jared looked worried. To cheer him up, Steve pointed across the room. 'I think Hugo should look at that.'

Oliver Jared stepped around the hearth and lifted a white guitar case so it stood up. It was daubed in energetic graffiti. 'I hope this is genuine.'

'Jackpot,' said Steve.

'For real?' Oliver Jared looked so suddenly happy, Steve wanted to hug him.

Hugo went closer. 'This case probably belonged to one of the session musicians, but that writing is Ash's.'

Jared gave the case a long, almost mystical look, as though seeing a morphic resonance of Ashten in the lavish loops and underlines. 'Do you know what it means, what he's written? Is it lyrics he was working on?'

If it was lyrics, Ashten was hardly on top form. *My place, my being, I'm alive, my world world world.*

'Just stuff in his head,' said Hugo. 'He was a tomcat. He liked to mark his territory. You've got yourself a good piece there.'

'I'm alive. It sounds like he knew this would happen to him, don't you think?' Jared quoted the lines again, earnestly, with a musical beat. It was awkward.

'Oliver,' said Steve, 'is there any more, or shall we do the paperwork?'

..

Jared led them to a kitchen fitted with acres of white quartz, like a kitchen for a filmset of heaven. A line of folding windows looked out onto a patch of ground that would presumably become a garden. Right now it was heaps of earth, scalped and furrowed by construction traffic, turning to mud in the March drizzle. Further back was a hardstanding of fresh tarmac, where a helicopter stood, its blades in a drooped position.

Steve looked out of the window. 'Nice machine, Oliver.'

'It's my indulgence. I can fly to Paris for lunch. Ari Markson mentioned you were going up north to do some visiting. My pilot can take you if you like.'

'We're good for this trip, thanks,' said Steve. 'But if you make that offer too many more times...'

Jared looked instantly happy again. Hugo gave Steve a look that said No.

This was what Ashten was needed for. To spray his essence like tiger musk. To receive the homage and never flinch.

Jared handed Hugo a pen and an inventory, with pictures and descriptions. 'Amend as appropriate. I know you can't verify those strings and stuff. I just like to imagine where they might have come from.'

While Hugo initialled down the list, Jared laid a cheque on the counter. Ten thousand pounds, the payee name blank for Hugo to complete. 'Will my donation help the search for Ashten?'

'Not really,' said Hugo. 'Looking for him isn't like dredging a pond. But it will make a real difference to the local people who work on the mountain. It'll get them proper training, better schools, medical support.' He folded the cheque and slipped it into his wallet. 'I'm deeply grateful.'

'You're welcome,' said Jared. He looked at the list. 'Your hand-writing. It's changed.'

Hugo had relaxed. Now his eye had a wary distance again. Would this guy never stop noticing things, like a psychoanalyst, and wanting to talk about them?

'Your writing is bigger on the set lists,' said Oliver Jared. 'More open. Is that because you don't play so much music? I suppose that must make a difference.'

Steve chuckled. 'It might be because he's older.'

'Do you still play music? At all?' said Oliver Jared. He sounded indignant that Steve was dismissing a serious question. He was gazing at Hugo again, and Hugo again looked like he wanted to run behind a door.

Time to get out of there.

10

Robert's phone quivered in his pocket. He was on City Road, walking to the Tube after a meeting. The caller was Markson.

'Robert, it's your time,' he said.

Robert hadn't the dimmest idea what this was about.

'I hope you've still got those songs for the Ashbirds album.'

Ashbirds. The name was an instant sting of adrenaline. Wait, calm down. If the Ashbirds album might be on again, really on, he had serious questions.

What serious questions? God, he hadn't thought about this for a while.

Markson was talking. 'I know it's ancient history, but...'

Ancient history? The last time they talked about this was autumn 2012. Now it was spring 2014.

Markson talked more. All the boxes were ticked. There would be publicity, tour possibilities. The backer was ready to sign. Was Robert ready with the songs?

'Well, I've got some other work on,' teased Robert, and Markson called him a crude name and they both laughed.

Markson said: 'Now we just need Hugo Bird on board.'

Hugo Bird? 'I thought Hugo was sorted. We pay him and he lets us use the Ashbirds name.'

'My investor just had a meeting with Hugo. He wants Hugo on the album.'

Hugo Bird on the album? Whatever for? This was what investors did, though. They brought some idiotic condition you had to grapple with. For God's sake. 'Does your investor know Hugo hasn't played or written music for years?'

Robert realised there were people pushing past him. He happened to be near the bus stop. A woman in a pink version of a Rupert Bear scarf was glowering at him, as if he was in her way. He was not in her way. She could walk around him.

Her interruption gave Robert a reality stop. Markson couldn't be serious about Hugo Bird on the album. 'You really had me going there, you bastard.'

'There's more. The investor wants a video feed of you all together.'

'Markson, quit messing around.'

'No he does, unfortunately.' This was said on a sigh. 'For his private collection, he says.'

'He wants... he does realise we spend days playing moron stuff before we find anything good. We can't show him that.'

Markson laughed.

Robert knew Markson's laughs. This one was a smug laugh that said you'd just let him prove he'd been clever. 'Robert, I'll explain you work behind closed doors. I'll offer him short drop-ins where you jam "Stairway to Heaven".'

'And Hugo's not on the album. That's a wind-up.'

'I can get rid of the cameras but not Hugo.'

Questions made a pile-up in Robert's mind. If Hugo got involved, he might trample all over the writing. If Hugo left all the writing to Robert, the *Superstring* songs might be tricky. Or they might not. They might never be a problem. If only someone had told Robert the full story, exactly why they were junked and whether anyone bothered to listen to them. Instead, he had to guess. Should he ask Markson's advice about this? But Markson might confirm the songs were off limits, and he didn't have any others right now.

'But Hugo doesn't have to be in our studio, does he? He can stay in Timbuktu or the Bat Cave. We can mix him in.'

And maybe not mix him in.

'The investor feels strongly about this. He told me he had an uncle who fought in the Falklands war, then couldn't readjust so he went to the Yorkshire moors and lived in a tent. Quite tragic, apparently. Our investor thinks Hugo's got survivor guilt, and wants to bring him back to where he should be. In a studio in London, making an Ashbirds album.'

Another pause. Not to dodge bad-tempered commuters, but to digest this astounding idea. 'Are we making a prestigious comeback with an international reputation or a third-rate piece of therapy?'

'Hugo's original Ashbirds. If he's on the album, you sell a hundred times more copies. You make way more money, even splitting the royalties. You get a chance of a stadium tour. Hugo can be there when you're writing. He can listen to the production. He's your Linda McCartney. Get a triangle. Or a theremin; they're retro. If he does something that's rubbish, overdub it later. But he has to breathe on the tracks. That's the backer's bottom line.'

'Markson, who is this backer?'

'Robert, think of all the time you've spent trying to get a solo deal.'

A bus lumbered past, roaring through whatever else Markson was saying. But Robert had the gist. Think of all the time you've spent on crap. This afternoon you had a meeting to discuss jingles for juicers.

'Good,' said Markson. 'We hope to get the request to Hugo today. He's not in the country for long. We'll need you to get onto that.'

Silence. Had he lost the call? 'Markson? Are you still there?'

'Still here. We'll need you to get onto asking Hugo.'

Silence.

A deliberate silence. Markson did it when he made an offer. The yes-or-no silence.

'You expect me to ask Hugo? Haven't you done that?'

'Robert, I have no cred with him. For years I have asked him to bring his scrawny arse to a studio while someone makes an album to put his name on. He won't listen to a money man. We're "not about the art". But you are. Tell him you want to work with him. I've sent you his number. Talk to him, Robert. I've got another call now.'

'That's your job, isn't it?'

'It's your album, Robert, if you want it. Theremins are cool. Ciao.'

The bus arrived. The crowd's heads moved like a shoal of fish, watching where the doors would be as the vehicle stopped. It was close to the spot where he was standing. If one more person tried to walk through him, he wouldn't answer for his actions.

11

'Is it a bad time to call?' said Gina.

'No,' said Elza. 'I'm looking at clouds.'

'Sounds proverbial.'

Elza had spent the last few hours framing a painting, which was her least favourite job. There was always one stubborn speck of dirt under the glass when she'd finished. So now she was standing in a street near her house, letting her mind drift, studying the light in the clouds. The smoky underside. The white fluff in the sunny top layer where a plane might cruise. The spectrum of mid-greys that gave body and contours.

'What's up?' she asked Gina.

'I had a stupid row with Robert yesterday. You know what he's like.'

Elza certainly did. Robert was lively company, with a performer's impatience to keep everyone surprised, but he also scared her. Elliot said the same. There's a thing Robert does, said Elliot. If the conversation dries, he doesn't start a new one. He waits for you to. Yes, and it feels like a test, said Elza. Don't leave me alone in a room with him. Likewise, said Elliot. How does Gina cope? Nothing seems to faze her.

Today, Gina was fazed.

'We're cool again,' said Gina, 'but there's a big bad thing we can't talk about. Do you know about this new Ashbirds album? I'm sorry, I know you don't like being asked about this.'

If you needed to learn extreme tact, you could watch how Gina sought permission to talk about subjects that might be difficult. She must do this all the time, in her work.

Elza hated being asked about Ashbirds albums. Did nobody realise she wasn't in music? People thought she had influence, but she didn't. She never had, even at the height of everything. But people still angled for her to pull strings for their band, or their album, or their friend's band or album. She'd been a visual artist for at least a decade, but nobody asked her for favours there. They defined her by a guy she dated twenty years ago.

Gina surely wouldn't expect her to pull strings for Robert, but Elza nevertheless felt wary.

She said a few noncommittal things. Great. So Robert's doing the album? Good luck to him.

'That's the trouble. I don't think Robert will do it. And he damn well should...'

A car with L-plates was slowing with exaggerated care for the mini-roundabout. And Gina was trying to drive this conversation with the handbrake on. She wanted to ask Elza something. And she didn't.

Elza felt a need to ease the strain. 'Yes, obviously it would be good.'

'But it looks like the album won't happen. I think it's connected with the other guy from the band.' Gina gave another checking hesitation, then said a name. 'Hugo Bird.'

This was also something that everyone did; an awkward pause when mentioning Hugo Bird. Hugo had survived Everest; Ashten hadn't. Therefore, his name was assumed to be politically delicate, for the rest of time.

It wasn't politically delicate. But the pause was.

Every time Elza heard it, genuflecting, hesitating, asking her permission, she wished they'd get on with it, spit out what they had to say.

Gina probably didn't mean to make her uncomfortable. Elza studied the clouds, hoping to feel patient again. She noted that some clouds had crisp edges. Others faded like breath into the upper band of blue. 'Tell me more,' she said.

Gina explained a muddled situation about an investor, and some kind of antipathy between Hugo Bird and Robert.

'I tried to talk sense into him,' said Gina, 'but I ballsed up. I don't suppose you know what's behind this?'

'Not a clue, I'm afraid.'

She'd lost her mood for contemplating clouds. She turned and walked back towards home.

'Knowing Robert,' said Gina, 'he probably doesn't know himself what it's about. I'd better go. Thanks for letting me vent. Men get in the way of themselves, don't they?'

Elza didn't believe in typically male or female behaviour. But Gina laughed as she said it, a capable, cheery sound. It made Elza want to believe it. Life would be so easy and breezy for a citizen of Planet Gina.

'They certainly do. Take care, Gina. Bye.'

Email alerts hopped for attention on her phone display. There was an interesting message from Stevens Hotels, who she recently sent a pitch to. She walked in a fast spurt, keen to get to her desk and follow up. But the conversation with Gina chafed at her. She'd done it badly. She should have been supportive. That's what Gina would do if she was upset; put the world back together and make it manageable. She'd use Planet Gina theories and Planet Gina solutions, which Elza wouldn't believe in, but they would help. Instead, what had Elza done? She'd agreed how peculiar and unreadable and impossible Robert was.

Well, he was. Look at Gina. This fight had torn the stuffing out of her.

The email from Stevens Hotels shuffled an idea into her mind. Perhaps there was a way to help. Ask Steve, bodyguard Steve, to send Hugo Bird's number to Gina, then Gina could talk to him directly.

She typed Steve a message.

Her phone rang. Of course. Steve rarely replied with an email. He liked your ears and voice.

'Do you want Hugo? I have him here.'

Talk to Hugo Bird? God no. 'No need for that, Gina needs to –'

'Don't talk here. Let's have a meeting.' Steve's East London twang came through a texture of noise. He must be in his gym. The squeak of trainers on a sprung floor. The drummy bounce of gloves on a punchbag.

A meeting? 'Steve, all I need –'

'We'll come to your place tomorrow. Is that good?' Steve called an instruction for ten uppercuts. An answering doof of blows, close by.

She supposed tomorrow was good. Steve knew how he liked to do things. Ears, voices. Faces. Closed doors. She suggested a time. It probably won't take long, she said. You'll hardly think it's worth the bother.

Tell us when we see you, said Steve, and asked for two straight punches and a hook. The fists came in a fast, aggressive trio. Those fists might be Hugo Bird's.

She opened the front door, tossed her keys in the bowl and trod the backs of her sneakers to pull them off.

So Steve and Hugo were coming tomorrow.

It would probably be over in ten minutes. Hello, she would say. I've brought you here for nothing. Gina needs a word. Here's her number. They'd leave again. Leave her alone.

12

Hugo had never properly met Elza Jones. He'd encountered her through the press as Ash's latest accessory at restaurants and film premieres. He'd met her voice when he phoned Ash at home and she answered. On the phone, she sounded exactly the way she looked in photos. Suspicious, serious, daring you to mock her – though what for? He had no wish to mock her. He just wanted Ash in the studio.

After Ash was lost on the mountain and the first body was found, the record label flew him to Kathmandu to view it. He later learned that the authorities didn't automatically recover bodies because it was so dangerous and so expensive, and that the label had bank-rolled the entire operation, but the albums were selling millions. Hugo arrived at Tribhuvan airport to a firing squad of reporters. As Steve ran him to a car, the long barrel lenses spied a delicious new target. Elza Jones, shepherded by minders, quivering like a spring-bok, in a fitted white suit that a stylist must have put on her. As if this ordeal wasn't bad enough by itself, was he expected to wait for her? View the body with her? A female journalist with a thick Spanish accent put a microphone in his face. How did he feel at seeing her, she said, in a tone razored with blame. That lovely woman mourns in white. She is the frozen bride.

After that, Hugo told Ari Markson: if she's there, I won't be.

Now he was with Steve, looking for her address in Battersea.

'Any idea why she wants to see us?'

'I guess we'll find out,' said Steve. He was on alert. Observing a man climbing out of a black BMW. A woman in striped wellies who was jogging faster than she intended behind a bounding Alsatian.

Hugo looked just as carefully at the neighbourhood, reading its appearance. A street of small houses transformed into big ones. Basements; wings of architectural glass. It was prosperous. Profes-sional. That was Elza Jones now. She might have children.

Steve stopped. A black gate of curly iron. Chessboard tiles on the path to a front door of nouveau grey.

Hugo gripped the gate. 'You talk to her. I'll wait here.'

'You can't wait here, Hugo.'

'There's a cafe on the corner. That's where I'll be.'

Steve stepped away from the gate. 'I'd better come with you.'

'Steve, it's 2014. I'll be fine.'

Steve took out his phone. 'I'll call Elza.'

Hugo put his hand over Steve's. 'I'll sit where I can see the exits and I won't talk to strangers.' He prepared to cross the road.

'If you don't go in,' said Steve, 'I don't go in.'

Across the road, the BMW driver raised a phone and scrutinised the screen, taking a picture. It was pointing at Hugo. Hugo pivoted.

'He's taking a picture of his car, isn't he?'

'Might be; might not,' said Steve. 'Shall we?'

..

Steve hurried them both in and closed the door.

And here was Elza. She was still thin, wearing a big white shirt hitched with a knot at the hem. Steve folded her in his fleshy embrace.

Elza turned to Hugo. No embrace. A formal, offered hand and a hello. He noticed crescents of bright blue paint around her cuticles.

She was now a commercial artist, Steve had said.

She turned. They followed. The hanging shape of her shirt gave an aura of serenity, like an apostle. He remembered she had been a dancer. She used to wear her hair very long or scraped in a chignon, as though she was about to place one hand on a barre and hoist her leg up to her ear. Now her hair was a springy cropped ponytail. It was blonde. Blonde ponytail seemed too frivolous for her nature.

Everywhere he glanced were clues for interpreting her. The house was restfully dark, like a hotel. He glimpsed a lamp that looked like origami. A floor-standing vase of dried flowers. The home of someone who was busy and had regular visitors, not chaotic and reclusive, which is how he remembered her. On a small table was a set of photos in frames. Selfies with a man in hiking gear, rainy hills in the background. Any children? None that he could see. The hiking gear looked fresh, not scuffed from years of use. Bought recently. Bought together? A recent partnership?

He should not be surprised by this. It was only the press that thought she was forever damaged, forever in recovery.

'Where did you park the helicopter?' she said.

'Battersea heliport,' answered Steve. 'Just a short walk.'

'You really came in a helicopter? The rockstar life.'

'Depends what kind of rock,' said Steve.

'That's what I meant,' she said.

She didn't do jokes very well.

'The helicopter is borrowed,' said Hugo. His first words since 'hello'. He did not want her to think he swanned around like a superstar.

'You borrowed a helicopter,' said Elza.

Perhaps that was worse.

The first words she had directly addressed to him.

'Since you're here, can you help with this?'

She led them to a corridor. Down one side was a washing machine and a desk with a closed laptop and a stack of trays with papers. Lying on the floor was an antique grandfather clock, its corners padded in rippled cardboard and bubble wrap. 'I need to get it into the studio. I was making room for it when you arrived.'

Hugo was carrying a shoulder bag. He took it off and set it on a chair, then walked to the head end. A clock face was visible under the strips of packaging. Not a real one. Painted. The hands were at five to 12.

Steve went to the foot. 'So this old thing's back.' He looked at Hugo. 'It's from the play.'

'Were you in a play?' said Hugo. He hadn't known Elza was an actor.

'It was years ago.' Her tone let them understand exactly when.

Her conversation contained a sense of effort, as if her friendliness was forced, like the joke. This was how a voice would sound if it had plastic surgery.

'Do you still act?' said Hugo.

'It was a thing people wanted me to do. I was Miss Havisham. She has a clock stopped at the moment... they found out the time it should be set at. That was the whole point, really.'

Here it was, the reason he knew her. The reason she knew him. Had he thought they might avoid it and talk politely of other things? It wasn't avoidable now. A clock stopped at the time she got the news about Ash.

'Could you bring it into my studio,' said Elza. It was not a question.

Steve took the foot end of the clock. Hugo lifted the head. They walked it into a high, light space; a conservatory with the glass walls panelled over. After the mud-mink mood of the rest of the house, this was colour anarchy. Canvases leaned on the wall; primary blues and reds next to paintings of brooding shadows. Paper plates were spread with oozes of paint. Brushes with finger-marked handles stood in jam jars. A powerful pigment smell took him back in time. He was smelling the art room in his school.

Elza pointed to a space she'd cleared next to a paint-scuffed plan chest. Hugo and Steve tilted the clock up to a standing position. Beside it was an easel with a blue canvas, the blue on her skin.

Hugo's phone buzzed. He sent the call to voicemail. It took longer than it should. The stiffness in his fingers was like wearing heavy gloves. He saw Elza had noticed.

'You don't play music much now, do you?'

'Music was a long time ago,' said Hugo. 'Was that what you wanted to talk about?'

Let's get on with this. I've no idea why I'm here.

Steve pulled out his phone and moved to a discreet distance.

Elza said: 'I don't suppose you'll be doing this fourth Ashbirds album? I've heard there's financing for it.'

'A fourth album? Nobody listens to albums any more.'

'Precisely,' said Elza.

A surprise. Hugo was used to people trying to persuade him to help with a book, a movie, a concert. No one gave up before they ever asked properly. What did she really want?

Elza looked at her blue-rimmed fingernails, choosing her next words. 'Sometimes people ask me to perform. I haven't danced for years and I couldn't. Or they ask me to act, which I could never do properly anyway. These days I'm wise enough to know when to say no. There are a lot of things we agree to do because it makes people happy. Or we get away with them because the public want to be nice to us, or nice to their own fond memories. It might have worked when we were young. But now it would be grotesque.'

Her voice flowed honestly now. He could hear the difference.

'I can't argue with that,' said Hugo. The clock behind her, in the unforgiving light of the studio, looked crude and fake. The numbers were outlined in black so that the time – that nearly fairytale time – would be visible at the back of the audience.

'Right,' said Elza. 'We can't coast any more on the things people remember we could do. They still think we're like the videos on YouTube. We know we're not.' She turned away from the clock and walked out of the studio.

Behind her, Steve put his phone away and followed. The interview, such as it was, had ended.

Now they were in the front room again. Traffic moved in the street outside. Elza said: 'Lots of people must envy your life in the mountains.' A distant police siren wailed. 'It's surely more peaceful than this.'

This was the friendliest she had sounded yet. When she was telling him he must be pleased to leave.

He picked up his bag. A sharp edge inside it caught his hip. The frame of a picture. He'd had it printed the day before, thinking he should bring her a gift. It was a photo he'd taken on the trail to Everest Base Camp, of a stone inscribed with the Buddhist mantra, *om mani padme hum*. Was he thinking he might make a diplomatic offering, perhaps a fresh start after all the other pictures she'd had to see? There was nothing diplomatic to be done here. She was showing them out, and she couldn't disguise how happy this made her. The picture went out with him, still in his bag, by his side.

13

From the window, Elza watched Steve and Hugo. They crossed the road and passed the bus stop. A woman was waiting there, minding her own thoughts, watching the two men absently. Her expression was desolate, and probably not deliberate, but she looked as if she blamed Hugo for something.

Elza closed the blind. That blaming face lingered in her vision, a reproach from her own past, from the most embarrassing, shaming moment of that time.

In the early, raw days, she was a soft touch for anyone who offered the chance to talk. Nothing existed as urgently as the questions and sensations that told her every hour that Ashten was not here. Each time, it was as if he had only just gone. You think that person crossing the street is him? It's not and you will never see him cross a street again. That's him singing from the radio but you will never hear him speak a new sentence to you. The rest of the world passed by as if on a screen, an experience that seemed devised to lull her to forget and then shock her with it again, in case she thought she might ever get used to it.

There was a journalist. He didn't seem like a person, merely a voice to send her chasing thoughts, like the conversations that never stopped in her own darkness. Out loud or silently; she barely knew the difference.

What do you think when you see Hugo Bird? It must be hard. You can't help but think it's hard. He went up a mountain with Ashten and came back without him. You wouldn't be human if you didn't think about that, and you are so human, Elza love. You don't want to say anything; I understand. But the boys didn't always get on, did they? The band split up. There were court cases. No, of course you don't think there was an argument while they were up there. What happened was an unfortunate accident. But accidents have causes, and somebody did something that led to something else, and you're left wondering. What if one thing in that chain was different? You wouldn't be sitting here like this. Here, love, I know you're going through hell. I think you need a good listener today. Tell me from your point of view. What do you think when you see Hugo Bird? No, of course it's off the record.

It wasn't off the record.

But now she'd met Hugo Bird again. In her house. This was her in 2014. Not a cell of her was the same as in 1994. They had talked. She'd made a joke, though the joke could have been better. She'd said sensible things too, because it was no longer 1994. She hadn't expected she'd have so much to talk about or that she'd mention the new album herself. She hadn't planned any of the things she'd said about dancing and music and that old life. Those ideas fell out when she had to explain the clock.

Hugo and Steve had listened seriously when she talked about

the album. Now they must be laughing it off, especially Hugo. Hey, Elza has some interesting opinions. Then they'd shrug and talk about something else. Ashbirds didn't need the approval or help of anyone. Ashbirds was its own sovereign nation. She was an occasional visitor, bound by their customs. For arranging meetings, for considering a dead body.

She hadn't mentioned Gina. Actually, would it have made any difference? Gina's opinion and wishes against the Ashbirds mafia?

Anyway, now she had the problem of this clock. After the play closed, a fan bought it and presented it to her as a gift, which caused so much trouble. She and Gina were sharing a tiny first-floor flat in Lewisham. The clock was too big to carry up, so it lay like an unfinished piece of DIY along one side of the staircase, getting bashed whenever they walked up with shopping bags, and sometimes bashed deliberately because it was there. She wanted to sell it. She dearly wanted the money. But Steve warned her not to sell because the fan might find out. She loaned it to exhibitions, hoping it would never come back. Occasionally, it went missing. Occasionally it was found and returned.

And here it was. Still too big, in every way. She'd ask Steve to find someone who'd adopt it. It was an Ashbirds problem.

14

Elliot climbed into the van. Elza was in the centre seat beside the driver, sunk to her ears in a scarf and puffy jacket, as she did with the duvet on cold nights. It was four in the morning. The sun wouldn't rise for another two hours.

The driver pulled out. 'Gatwick airport?'

London was empty as a game board waiting for pieces. The driver took them through roads lit for no people. The other vehicles were navigators of the night: taxis, buses, delivery drivers. The driver didn't talk, not even about where they were flying to.

Steve had arranged it. Elza said he'd arranged getaways in the past when she needed to escape.

There had been an incident recently. A week ago, a paper published a picture of Steve entering their house with a former Ashbirds musician. The headline said: *Ashten's bandmate visits Elza to seek forgiveness*. There was also a graphic of a front page from the paper twenty years before, and that was much worse: *Broken Elza says 'I don't blame Hugo'*. This was a finely lawyered interview with her that did as much blaming as possible without actual libel.

Elliot thought he'd come to terms with the press, but this? To secretly photograph their visitors and dredge up an old piece of sensationalist tattle? It was like a burglary. Elza had simply said: 'I'll call Steve. I needed to talk to him anyway.'

Now, the driver swept the van up the slip road, gunning to the motorway. Behind the seats, their suitcases shifted. They were wedged beside a set of mirrored doors. The van belonged to a property developer from Steve's Ashbirds clan. There was also the hideous sham clock with Ashbirds connections that Elza needed to discreetly get rid of. It lay in the back, wrapped in cardboard. Buying their getaway, perhaps.

The M25 unwound ahead of them. A few cars were crawling up the lanes, their speed diminished by their smallness, following the giant curve of the tarmac, into the paling sky.

Steve would live in their house and handle the press. And they were flying to a remote island in Scotland for their delayed Valentine break.

Probably they could have made the arrangements themselves but Elza seemed to take comfort in the old precautions. And actually, now, so did he.

15

Robert loved the transformation as he walked through the doors.

From the outside, the building was a row of lock-up garages. It stood next to a stump of bruised-looking concrete that had tried to be a skyscraper until its builder went bust. Inside the garages, you found a hushed warren of rooms lined with mixing desks, instruments and racks of equipment, all alive with sound. From semi-armageddon to secret lair.

He was here to start the rough mix of the album. Everything had worked out. Markson said Hugo had quit. He was letting them use the Ashbirds name if they promised his charity a hundred grand, and he was buggering quietly off. Who'd have thought that could happen?

In the studio, a big guy pulled him into a footballer's embrace. Gil, the drummer from the third album. They talked. There had been life changes. Gil was now a father and had started a drumming academy on YouTube.

They settled to work. Robert sat at the Steinway. He played 'A Shebird'. He hadn't rehearsed it, except in his mind, but it flooded out of him, note for note.

The music made its own zone of brilliance, like spring weather, the kind of weather that filled you with new purpose, cleansed your bad luck. Gil felt it too. After Ashbirds, he'd played in a novelty pop group based on characters in a children's TV show. He wore a giant foam suit on stage, he told Robert, which made him sweat like a hog. He cut a hole in the back so he wouldn't suffocate, and was nearly fired for it. They swapped tales of doubtful times, of disappointing work they'd had to take seriously. They laughed at themselves, because Ashbirds were flying again.

Robert finished a rough guide track of keyboard and vocal. Then Gil wanted to work on it alone, so Robert went out to the reception area, the only part of the building that had a window, and checked his calls.

A message from Gina about an invitation for the weekend. Robert left a reply, holding the phone in the corridor so his voicemail caught the piano and drums. She'd be so excited. Right now, Gil was trying a ticking woodblock mambo, smart and sultry. The song was sounding fantastic.

They'd need more like this, though. Robert's other songs, 'How Long', 'Strung Out' and 'Souled Out', were solid but not storming. He was working on a fresh idea, but every melody or line sounded too much like the others. As if he was running in a maze, down a path that seemed new, but always dumped him in the same stale place. He was out of practice with longer form.

Any other band would buy songs in. Their backer had nixed that. Ashbirds didn't use other writers, he informed Robert, with total assurance because he was a builder, not a musician. Robert had a name for this scenario, when money men told him artistic rules as though they were holy writ. He called it confidunce. The backer, Oliver Jared, had confidunce in bucketfuls.

Robert could smuggle in a bought song, but Oliver Jared would see the payment in the accounts. And the extra name on the credits.

From the studio, 'A Shebird' continued. Mamboing and evolving. A sweet, foxy pulse.

Robert's heart gave an anxious cramp. How would he write another like that?

He needed time to get back to it. But they might not have time. Oliver Jared said he'd be visiting the studio regularly, to hear what they'd done. Once they'd laid down his *Superstring* four, he needed more.

He went outside to think, away from the music, to the streaked concrete stump of the abandoned tower block. Walked to the main road, watched lorries and cyclists duelling in the six lanes past the warehouse town of New Covent Garden.

What were his options? He could write if he volleyed with a partner. Look what he'd done with Paul Wavell.

Paul Wavell. Of course, it was obvious. He should find Paul. Paul might still be working, and if he was, he'd be perfect. They needed a pianist, too, and Paul could do the style. Moreover, Oliver Jared would accept him because he could be sold as the Ashbirds blood-line, if a bit removed. Robert could still lead the writing, and he wanted to. But Paul could kick up ideas. Start him off.

If there was more time, Robert could find his own way. But he needed insurance, in case Oliver Jared got worried that the brilliant songs weren't falling out of the sky fast enough. Robert knew the type.

The phone was in his hand. In the distance a tower crane turned, sweeping the seconds onwards.

He dialled Ari Markson. 'Hi Ari. Could you track down a session player for me? His name's Paul Wavell.'

...

Markson could not find Paul Wavell.

Robert did some sleuthing of his own, searching for Paul's name. A musician couldn't disappear entirely, from the whole world.

He must be somewhere, on the credits of an album. Maybe he was now a teacher, like Gil. He'd have a web page. A profile on Soundcloud. A Twitter account?

Robert could not find him.

Markson must know how to find people. Maybe Paul had changed his name.

Markson got an assistant on it.

Markson's assistant said: 'I can't find him. Look, if you want a pianist, I'll find you one...'

Robert knew a detective. In the early days, he, Gina and Steve had hired her to investigate Elza Jones's potential boyfriends. Elza was guileless and clueless when she started dating again. She chose beaus who then blabbed to the press, so the detective warned her off the ones with debts, media friends, expensive dependents, anything that might make them snitch.

Robert's detective found Paul.

'He's working in a call centre.'

Paul was working at a call centre? He was doing that when he was seventeen, when Robert first knew him. 'He isn't in music?'

The detective said: 'Do you want me to find that out?'

Robert didn't. He'd already dropped two hundred and fifty on this, and that was with a discount for being a previous good customer.

Paul was working in a call centre. Robert's one hope of making the album was no longer a musician.

..

Robert was walking down a corridor in the back warrens of the BBC television studios. Gil was walking ahead of him. Their first interview as the returning Ashbirds.

Also with them was Oliver Jared, the builder. Pride glimmered off him as he fingered the visitor pass with the BBC logo that swung in a wallet around his neck, as his eye caught the red recording light over the set of studio doors. That light, that pass, this fuss was for Ashbirds. And Ashbirds were here because of him.

'This way,' said the production assistant, and in front of them was the studio, with a circular desk under a halo of light as though guests might beam down from a starship. Oliver Jared sent Robert to the hot seat with a clap on the shoulder, and in that touch Robert felt all Jared's hopes.

The presenter was in Robert's eyeline. Questions would come about the new songs. The only possible way to answer them, to the presenter, to the watching nation, was to know he would have Paul, his partner in brilliance.

He'd call Markson. Tell him to make Paul an offer.

..

Paul agreed to meet. He nominated a cafe in Canary Wharf, at lunchtime.

Robert felt laughably out of place. Everyone in the café wore shirts, ties, suits. Their hairstyles were office neat. Not one pony-tail, except on the women. Was this now Paul's kind of place?

It was. Paul wore suit trousers, plain shirt and a dark parka. He was plumper than Robert remembered.

The Paul he remembered, in the studio days, wore denim dunga-rees on a bare chest, or singlet vests that showed a lavish sprout of underarm hair. At the time that was too displaying for Robert's tastes, but Paul now walked towards him in an anonymised office uniform. That troubled him.

Paul set a tall cup of something green on the table and put his bottom heavily in the chair. The drink looked radiant with vita-mins. Robert remembered Paul as a big-time swiller of less nutri-tious fluids.

'Rib,' said Paul.

'It's Robert. I haven't been Rib for a long time.'

Paul looked at Robert as if trying to decide whether to dislike him. 'So you still have a manager. Getting to play much?'

Condescending bastard. Paul always had a low opinion of every-one.

'Are you still playing cruises?' said Robert. An insult for an insult.

'No. I still play. But not sessions. I work for a call centre.'

Should Robert look surprised? Pretend he didn't know? No. Bullshit wouldn't work on this slumped, weary-eyed Paul.

Robert said: 'I thought that call centre stuff was in India.'

'This is CallMe. You must have heard of CallMe?'

Robert hadn't heard of CallMe. Why would he?

'You're a session player and you don't know CallMe? We employ members of Equity and the Musicians' Union. They work for us while they're resting and we give them time off for auditions and jobs. You should sign up. You'll never know when you need us.' Paul barked a laugh.

His laugh hadn't changed. It was still smirky. It relished the sour. And yet, if stirred the right way, this acid bitch could blurt out 'A Shebird'.

Robert would rather cut off his own fingers than register at CallMe. No matter how desperate things got, he'd always done music.

Paul looked defeated. Despite the drink of Dr Broccoli and the crisp shirt, he had the air of someone who had pulled out of an exhausting race and hoped no-one would kick him back in. Robert found that shocking; unexpectedly so. 'But you're a good player, Paul. If things had gone differently, you'd have been keyboards on Ashten Geddard's solo album.'

Robert didn't usually offer praise. This urge was surprising to him. But he didn't often see a person with such little regard for their talent. He saw plenty of the opposite.

Paul shrugged. 'Come to our office. We've got people who played on all the classic albums.' He took a sip, which lined his lip with green before he licked it away. 'So what are you doing?'

'I'm writing the fourth Ashbirds album.' Robert felt a giddy tremble.

Paul hardly reacted. His mouth had a downward turn, like the mouth of a fish.

'You must have seen us on *Breakfast TV*.'

'I start work at seven in the morning.'

'Instead of that, what about working on an album?'

Paul looked at his drink. His lips and cheeks made small movements as though words were forming in his brain and mouth. It was impossible to tell whether they were positive or negative.

'Ari Markson said you wanted to offer me work.'

'That's right.'

'On the Ashbirds album?'

Paul was being slow to understand. And Robert could scarcely believe it himself. He was the spokesman of this band, its front man, empowered to grant this opportunity. 'I'm offering you work on the Ashbirds album.' The words filled him with a bright rush. He could change the world. He'd start with Paul.

Paul remained silent. Figuring it out. What was there to figure out?

'You said you get audition leave?' said Robert.

'I do payroll and accounts. I'm not one of the shift workers.'

Paul had a permanent job. So he'd been out of the business a long time. That might present an immediate, practical problem: his playing would be weak.

It might not matter. His mind would still be napalm.

'But they know you're a musician, right? Do you get leave like everyone else? For sessions and auditions?'

'You want me to play? You can't find a pianist? I'll send you twenty.'

'This is the thing. We want people from the original line-up. You said you still play?'

'What about Hugo Bird?'

'Hugo Bird is not in Ashbirds now.'

'But he's still alive? I heard he topped himself.'

The way Paul said that. As if suicide was ordinary, logical, inevitable for everyone. As if his own inner life was closed down, like a person who has spent years on Death Row.

'Hugo's not playing any more,' said Robert.

'So where are you getting the songs for the album?'

'I'm writing them.' Robert felt the rush again as he said it. A rush that had a chilly anxious edge, like a swab before an injection needle.

Paul gave him a look. A memory stirring? Of good days? Come on, Paul.

Robert pulled a string of earbud headphones out of his pocket, cued a soundclip on his phone of 'A Shebird', recorded for Gina. Slid the phone to Paul.

Paul looked at it as if it was faintly offensive.

Listen to it, you lifeless sap. I'm here to rescue you.

Paul took one earbud. As the music kicked in, he gave a little jump. When the excerpt ended, he played it again.

Good man. And now, was the offer still so impossible?

Paul slid the phone back to Robert. 'Those were good songs. But we got shafted.'

No, no. Paul, of lightning fingers and vinegar tongue, Paul must not stay here, stewing himself to death in M&S suits and vitamin hyperslime. In a bloody call centre. 'Things are different now, Paul. I'm Ashbirds.' Surely the most mighty sentence ever uttered. It tasted like fire in his mouth. So did this: 'You can be Ashbirds too.'

'We know how that went last time.'

'We're older and wiser,' said Robert.

'Older, wiser, younger, stupider. Doesn't make any difference. Come and meet the gang at CallMe.'

CallMe was the problem. No wonder Paul thought about people topping themselves. His clothes looked recent and neat, but he made them look borrowed. In his soul, he was sitting on a sheet of cardboard at Waterloo, waiting for the rain to pour. Robert wanted to kick him. Get up. Join the human race again.

'Paul, Hugo Bird is gone. Come and hear the song properly.' If he got Paul into the studio, that would change everything.

'Rib, you're killing me.'

No he wasn't killing him. He was dragging him into the dawn. 'Robert; I'm Robert now. It's time you took some leave for a big break.'

Paul looked away. Enough, thought Robert. Enough pressure for now. Robert steered the conversation elsewhere. They talked about keyboards and war-tales from the studio. With each anecdote, Robert saw Paul's knowledge come back to him, of music, of playing, his cocky sureness in his ability. He hadn't completely stopped playing. He taught students. They were too mediocre, all of them. He proved it to them by being a tyrant, making them study famously hard pieces by Liszt and Ravel. If you can't play this like I can, you won't work, you're not the real thing, you haven't got it.

Paul took another sip of the grass cuttings elixir. 'It would be a shame to see that song go to someone who couldn't play it.' He put the glass down and his hand shook. A birth tremor. The birth of the old Paul. 'You're a good man, Rib.'

'Robert,' said Robert.

16

Everest's landscape of snow and ice seems perpetual, changeless.

It is not.

Base Camp was wakening. Hugo became aware of booted feet passing his tent at a dreamy pace, a person emerging from sleepy warmth into the morning chill. Other sounds were beginning. The ting of cutlery, the bubble of water on stoves, the hiss of showers, the spreading chatter of human noise. The rumble from the mountain as snow and ice shifted in the upper reaches. All was entirely usual.

And then: a crack that split the air. A roar.

A roar that didn't stop. Not for several long seconds.

When it finally did, all voices, all footsteps had ceased.

Then, like somebody falling a great distance and finding they are still alive, the camp snapped into response. Feet moved, at speed. Hugo twisted out of his sleeping bag, seized clothes. He heard a clamour of rising voices.

Hugo stumbled out of the tent. The sprawl of Base Camp was tinted pink with the dawn. People were staring up at the mountain, padded in jackets and hats, tall in their high, strapped boots. The Sherpas were working up there, depositing supplies for the expeditions that would climb that season.

On the upper white slopes, where the noises came from, the snow had settled again. All looked smooth and peaceful. But nobody thought it was. Those sounds meant a massive avalanche.

..

Hugo worked with the expedition doctors. He pressed pads on bleeding wounds. It wasn't a clean avalanche, a fall of snow that buried. It was a wedge of ice that sheared off a glacier and smashed into shards that fractured bones and tore through flesh like shrapnel. He helped to strap broken limbs for airlift to hospital.

Gradually the work became grimmer.

The helicopter came into view. A tiny black fly in the fierce blue sky. Its rotors made a snare beat that rattled off the jagged mountain, stirred the prayer flags strung on the tents, a warning for what it brought. On a long line hanging from its fuselage was a person, in helmet and boots, hanging slack in a harness, sliding towards them like a travelling fish. Hugo and a doctor caught hold, dodged the swipe of the crampons, guided it to the ground, released the clips. Sometimes, that glimpse was all the doctor needed. They covered the dead man with a tarpaulin and, as the helicopter lifted away, lay across him to stop the downdraft taking the shroud. Hugo kept his eyes on what was above him, the craft getting smaller, a diamond of white light in its red belly, the freed rescue line trailing back to the mountain.

They did this twelve times, until, at two in the afternoon, no more bodies were recoverable. Four men were still missing. They wouldn't make it.

Hugo returned to his tent. His fleece was streaked with blood. He took it off to put it in the laundry bag. In the orange light of the tent it looked worse. A black scorch.

His phone rang. An unfamiliar number. It might be somebody elsewhere in the camp, looking for him. He answered.

It was Oliver Jared. The guy from the UK who collected Ashbirds stuff. He'd seen the news. The avalanche. Wanted to check Hugo was all right.

'Still alive,' said Hugo. He laughed. How did he manage that? He didn't feel like laughing.

'The album's going well,' said Jared. 'I wanted to let you know.'

'Good,' said Hugo. How was anything good? He was looking at a fleece stained with blood.

Jared said: 'I wanted you to know because the album will have to work harder than ever, right? For your charity? We'll do our best here.'

'Sixteen people have died,' said Hugo.

Silence. Then: 'We have four songs on demo already. I can send them to you. Ari Markson says you have some sort of satphone connection for getting soundfiles via Dropbox?'

'Yes,' said Hugo, not intending to access it at all. But he recognised Oliver Jared's intent to help. 'Thank you.'

'I'll let you go. Take care of yourself, Hugo.'

Hugo changed and went to the dining tent. Three of his clients were there, drinking tea or Tuborg beer. The orange tint of the tent walls made them like images in a photographic darkroom, defined by their eyebrows, eyes, mouths, mountain beards.

Each person had a story. Where they were when it started. One had seen a block of ice as big as a mansion plunging off the mountain. Hugo told of waking to the sounds of the morning, then the splitting crack, then the roar and the silence. More climbers came to the table, sat heavily, stared, shared what they could. One had climbed to the impact zone and found a man she was unable to dig out.

Hugo was exhausted but he didn't want to leave. He wanted to be with survivors, rescuers. People who had navigated this terrible random day and made it through, whose lives went on, who therefore made life itself go on. Darkness fell. The tea became beer, wine, rum. The group grew.

One of the climbers was wearing a peaked cap and dark wraparound glasses. He kept his face turned away from the light that hung from the ridge pole. As the hours wore on his face shivered with pain. Snow blindness. Hugo fetched eye drops for him.

..

A new day. All the dead were from local Sherpa villages. Their team mates queued at the morgue tent, carrying sleeping bags to take them home. Hugo, the doctor and two other volunteers helped zip each body in, wrapped it in tarpaulin and rope, carried it to a helicopter. Some of the survivors walked away immediately, to trek home on foot. More bodies were brought from the mountain, gliding below a helicopter on a long line.

Hugo returned to the dining tent. Everyone was impatient for a task. What should be done? Would anyone risk going up to stock the higher camps? Might the season be cancelled? Did anyone's opinion mean squit if they hadn't personally lost a colleague or family member? Discussions began energetically. A new angle. A new idea. Hit a dead stop.

They talked about what they had seen. The same camp-fire tales from the previous day, repeated in identical words like accounts of an epic battle. They listened as though they had not heard them before.

Hugo returned to his tent, done with talking. It was late. In other tents, the voices continued.

A soft thud came from far above. More ice and snow on the move. The camp was instantly silent. Before yesterday, nobody would have noticed.

Hugo lay down. He could not sleep.

He checked his phone. A text from Oliver Jared. The Dropbox link.

A message from England. It felt almost dear to him; a thing from a safe, tame place, like a letter from a grandchild where all was smiles and blitheness.

The murmured conversations began again. Around the great bowl of the camp, in all the languages being spoken, the question would be the same. What happens now? What can be done?

Here in his hand, Hugo might have an answer. This phone connected to a world where Band Aid and Live Aid were born. And the situation here didn't need a rescue on that scale. If those guys in their studio had good tracks, if they got in the major festivals, they could pre-sell a tour and make a difference here. It was possible. Very possible.

Hugo looked for headphones.

..

Hugo pulled off the headphones. Before he listened, he was full of hope. Perhaps he had hoped too much.

There were four tracks. Three of them seemed to belong together, like a set of table mats. 'How Long.' 'Strung Out.' 'Souled Out.' They were laborious and lifeless, as if constructed by an algorithm. Robert Speed, the guitar guy who used to wear the headband, was singing. His voice was thin and characterless, though there were ways to fix that if they had to.

Worst of all was the fourth song. It didn't fit Robert's plodding pattern, so he must have had help. It was a ballad called 'A Shebird'. Hugo listened to it twice. Why did he dislike it so thoroughly? The concept was a blokey fantasy where the singer admires a girl who's being eyed by all the guys in the room. Without the right playful touch, it could easily be seedy. They'd surpassed seedy; it was sneering and sinister. Pleased with itself. And that title. What were they thinking? How to wreck a reputation in one foul release.

He chucked the headphones down. This would not be Band Aid or Live Aid. It was sleazy has-beens singing a stinker. In his name.

There was an answer, of course. Go to London, to the studio, and sort it out.

No. That was a place he did not go back to.

The phone was still in his hand. On the news app, an Everest expert was explaining that a hanging cliff of ice had fallen off the western shoulder. Ice that must have been there for thousands of years.

The scattered conversations from around the camp drifted to him, still going on, still seeking answers, solutions, still coming round to nothing. Towers of ice that have stood for thousands of years can tumble. If that could happen, what could any of them do? Talk in futile circles; that was all. For a brief time, in the minutes when he prepared to listen to that music, he thought he'd found something better.

..

Twenty-four hours later, Hugo was on a plane, bound for Heathrow.

Above the hum and swell of the plane engines, and the quiet tap of fingers on laptop keys, someone was laughing. Across the aisle, Hugo saw a passenger whose head was bent over a book. His face split like Mr Punch drawn on a crescent moon. His laugh rattled out, unstoppable as a sneeze. The plane cradled the seated people through the clouds over India, then Europe, towards London, the city he was going back to. And Punch in the moon would not stop laughing.

17

Robert took off his cycle helmet. From the main studio came the ripple of piano. Paul Wavell was already there.

Robert had hoped he was early enough to be alone.

It had been going well. Four tracks were on demo. Paul was sharp as a bite. His years of teaching, or persecuting students for their lack of talent, had kept him slick. He was sober as a parson, too. Now, just last night, Ari Markson called and everything turned rotten.

The investor had decided, on an inexplicable whim, that he didn't like the demo songs.

'He's a builder,' said Robert. 'What the fuck does he know about music?'

'Ask his bank account,' said Markson.

'Do we even need him? We could go to Kickstarter.'

'You won't have the Ashbirds name. How much money will you raise without it?'

'So we need to scrap those songs? That'll put us back.'

'Good news,' said Markson. 'You're going to need a theremin.'

Now on the Steinway, Paul Wavell was amusing himself with an embellished Chopin piece. He looked like an urchin gatecrashing Harrods, sitting at the elegant instrument in a green T-shirt, vandalising the Chopin with unauthorised extra notes. Making the keys smile.

Robert went into the live room and waved to get his attention. Paul grinned and played a rumbling, Scott Joplin run of the riff of 'Shebird'.

Robert told him.

Paul's bravado switched off. Completely. Like a tap. The guy thought he'd been fired.

'Relax,' said Robert. 'You're still needed. Hugo doesn't play. He'll need your hands.'

'But not our songs?'

'It's changed now,' said Robert. 'I'm going to take a shower.'

He walked down the corridor to the men's changing room. Bolted the door. In his mind he saw Paul's homunculus face, accusing him, and had the horrible feeling Paul might follow him. Holding him responsible. Why aren't they using our songs? Now we won't get the publishing royalties.

That's the business, Paul. I've had this for years.

Robert stripped off his rucksack and his sweaty cycle Lycra. He stood under the shower, full blast, the water like nails.

Oliver Jared must always have intended to bring Hugo in. But at least Robert was prepared for this. For Paul, though, it was tough. He'd only been here a week.

When Robert came out of the shower, calm and presentable in jeans and a shirt, the piano was quiet again. He could hear people in the back half of the building, the other studio. A guitar and husky-girl vocals, briefly as a door opened. A duo called Where's Rosie were at work there.

In their control room, an internal window showed the live area with its tranquil lighting. It had a sanctuary feel. For concentration. The Steinway bench was now empty. But the room was not.

A figure was standing there, hands tucked in the pockets of a jacket. He stood very still, the way fans stand when they've seen someone who gives them a special pause. Needing time.

This wasn't a fan.

It was Hugo Bird.

Robert inspected Hugo. Very swiftly, in case the moment broke and he didn't get another chance. Hugo looked averagely urban. A padded waistcoat with jeans and walking boots.

Hugo remained still. Robert slowed his mind and took in the details. Arms sheathed in tight black sports fabric. He adjusted a canvas bag on a strap across his body and Robert saw the swell of biceps and a well-capped shoulder. Muscled like hard rope.

Hugo moved. He passed along the rack of guitars and basses, slowly, as if it was a lot to take in. The saxophone, reflecting a liquid mercury gleam, hanging from its strap. He glanced down, as if only now remembering to watch for leads, mic stands and other toe-tangling hazards. He walked to the drumset, spent a while looking at it and the patterned red rug it stood on, the way you'd return home after a long absence, look at the curtains and know them for the first time.

Hugo returned to the Steinway. He studied the keys. His gaze scanned up and down the notes.

He lifted the strap of the canvas bag over his head and off his shoulder.

He was going to sit at the Steinway.

Paused, the bag dangling from his hand.

Go on, thought Robert. Let's see you play.

Hugo laid the bag on the floor. He sat on the stool. The black body of the instrument hid Robert's view of the keys, but he could see in the set of Hugo's shoulders, his downward eyes, that his hands were poised over the notes.

Robert stared hard through the glass. Give us a noise, Hugo. Show us what you're made of.

The door to the studio opened. Hugo stood up. Gil barrelled in like a bouncer, moving in a hurry despite his thigh-chafing bulk. There were hugs.

'Good to see you, Hugo. You look damn well.'

'So do you,' said Hugo.

Robert would have to go in.

Both men turned as he did. Hugo advanced, with welcoming face. Took Robert's hand in a brisk, hard grip. His fingers, when he let go, were crooked and thickened, like a glove worn by a construction worker.

Ruined for playing the piano.

A murmuring bustle made Robert look at the control room window. A crowd was in there now, standing at the console and peering in. A couple of engineers. The two girls from Where's Rosie, giving an insolent teenage glare from Cleopatra fringes. And Teri, the hoop-earringed receptionist who sometimes doubled on backing vocals.

Robert was certain that Hugo flinched when he saw them. The tough guy had a hard time with attention.

Paul Wavell entered. Introductions were made, with more handshakes. Robert saw Paul take a long, noting look at Hugo's bricklayer hands.

Hugo bent to his bag, opened the flap and slid out a laptop. 'I'll leave the playing to you guys. I've got some ideas we can build on.'

A beat sounded from the monitors. In the control room, someone had put on a track. Four steely twangs on a guitar, shimmering with echo. A spare beat, like a man tapping a tin can alone on a rooftop. It repeated, then shook into a brittle, plangent riff.

Just those few notes changed every face in the room. Then two voices began. Hugo and Ashten. On the same instant. In perfectly matched timbre. They sang a verse. Breathed at the same time, phrased identically. Their voices slid and twined as though they came from the same throat. A pause for the guitar to throw back a metallic response. The tin-can rooftop tick of the percussion. Ashten sang the opening phrase again. '*She did not turn.*' Hugo echoed. '*Did not turn.*' Pause for the guitar to jangle across. Into the next verse and onwards. Their voices warm and close on the parched, percussive backing.

They listened to the complete track, all the way to the fade.

In the control room, one half of Where's Rosie took a picture.

'That's going on Instagram in a minute,' said Paul, and he made it sound like a warning.

'That's good, isn't it?' said Gil. 'Get the word out.'

Hugo moved to the control room. In the live room, Gil went to the drumkit and bumped his bolster thigh deliberately against the stool, checking the height, then sat down, took his sticks and gave four wooden clicks. Before they went on stage, that's what he'd do. Four taps to align them: from here, we serve the music.

Work began.

..

After two hours, they took a break.

In the lounge, Robert saw the early edition of the *Evening Standard* on the table. The front was a montage of pictures. Ashten Geddard, forever youthful. Hugo, flight-worn in a Heathrow corridor. And the Instagram studio snap by Where's Rosie; four guys wandering among mic stands and a piano. Their unguarded wow-I'm-back-here expressions and the soft lighting made them look bemused and young, so it wasn't as bad as it might be. The headline read: *Back to life – Ashbirds reunite for 4th album after 20 years.*

Hugo glanced at the paper. ' "Back to Life" wasn't even our song.'

Paul was checking his phone. 'It's trending on Twitter. There's nasty stuff.'

There was. Robert was sweeping through it. *Why aren't you dead, Hugo? The wrong one came back.*

'Take no notice, Hugo,' said Gil. 'Twitter is just –'

Hugo was also looking at his phone. 'Gil, we do have Twitter where I come from.' He left the room.

Minutes passed. 'I'll see if he needs help,' said Gil.

Gil came back. 'Hugo's happy working on his own.' Gil's tone was jovial. It suggested his conversation with Hugo had been much more ripe and forthright and he was choosing to laugh it off. Gil settled to read a book on his phone.

Paul didn't take the waiting so well. He walked around the room. He looked in every cupboard, at the shelves of mugs, plates, beer glasses, packets of cornflakes and tubes of lethal chilli sauce. He opened the fridge, which was stocked with beers. He sat with his phone, swiping through a parade of faces on a dating site, but he looked more frequently at the closed door of the fridge, reckoning with the bottles he'd seen with their necks towards him, pullable like organ stops.

Don't start that, Paul. Not after it's been going so well.

Gil read out a text. It was from Hugo. They weren't needed any more today.

A text. Helluva way to make your band feel good, Hugo.

Paul stood immediately, as if he was on a spring, and left without saying anything, not even goodbye.

Robert grabbed his gear, unlocked his bike and caught up with Paul on the potholed track to the main road. Paul walked, his mouth in a sullen line.

'If I'd known we'd sit there with nothing to do,' said Robert, 'I'd have brought a guitar out and we could have worked on something. We should do that tomorrow.'

'Rib, you please yourself. I'm going back to my job tomorrow.'

He surely wasn't quitting? 'Give it a chance, Paul. This last week's been great.'

'It was, but I can't do days like this.'

Oh yes, drinking the fridge with your eyes. You could just learn self-control. Robert tried to sound encouraging. 'There won't be more days like this. We'll work. On new songs. Like we planned. Hugo might piss away the studio time today but the backer won't let it continue. He'll need new songs and they'll come from us.'

'You write the album. I might go back to my job.'

And leave me alone? Do you not think you owe me a bit of faith? And gratitude? For the past week, you've been sitting at a Steinway in a studio where anything is possible. Where were you before that? Rotting in a call centre.

'You have a job here, Paul.'

Paul was silent.

'You said CallMe would keep your job open.'

'Yes, they'll keep it open.'

Ah, a doubting note. He was worried. That open job was a jail cell. He didn't want to go back.

'So you don't have to make a decision yet.'

Silence.

At the road, they turned left towards Vauxhall station. Cranes hung over a line of tower blocks, laboriously moving girders. It looked like a task devised as a hellish torment to take for ever.

'Paul, what does your Wiki page say? *Paul Wavell had one hit with a boy band called Laser*? Is that what your talent amounted to? What will it say if you make this album?'

Robert meant to be encouraging. His own Wiki page was hardly more impressive, but he took that as a spur.

Paul did not look spurred. He looked like he was screaming, inside his mind, *shut up.*

They were at the subway entrance to Vauxhall Tube. Bare bricks, brown tiles, exactly like a public convenience. Paul raised a hand and walked down into the guts of the station. As he went, Robert felt a sickening lurch. He saw himself at his guitar, scratching for a melody, trying to believe that drab chords might turn to gold. Hating everything he played. Pushing on, watching the clock to see if he could stop for the day. Another day with nothing. And now they couldn't even use the *Superstring* songs, which had been his safety net. And Paul, who, if he chose, could blurt a blinding hook as easily as spitting, was walking down the steps.

'See you tomorrow, Paul,' called Robert. Turn around and tell me you'll be back.

Paul raised a hand again, as before. What the hell did that mean?

18

Elliot enjoyed opera. He knew Elza was less keen, but she didn't mind small doses. That's why he'd chosen *Dido and Aeneas*. Less than one hour long. And it had the lament, 'When I Am Laid In Earth', famous well beyond opera buffs, the most aching piece ever written for a voice.

Elza did not seem to feel the magic. She hardly looked at the stage. She gazed at a middle distance of shadowed backs and heads, picking the paint painstakingly and lengthily off her fingernails, which she did when preoccupied.

'Everything okay?' he said as they got up to leave. Fine, she said. It wasn't a good place to ask, crowded against strangers' shoulders and backs in the theatre's bordello-red staircase. But nowhere would be.

Theatre trips could sometimes make her irretrievably introspective. The dark auditorium forced you to wrap in solitude, and if her attention drifted from the action in front of her, she didn't come back afterwards. Whether it was a creative problem with an artwork or a troubled negotiation with something older, in the hour or hours of a theatre or cinema performance, she could get so far down a thought-hole that she'd hardly notice him calling from the surface.

Riding the escalator into the Tube station, standing close on the train, he knew she was hardly noticing what he said to her. Her face had an inward look, as though he wasn't next to her, but seeing her from far away, through a telescope.

Locking the front door, hanging coats up, she said: 'I'll be up in a bit.' He knew 'a bit' meant 'eventually'.

'Everything okay?'

A kiss that said emphatically yes, then she walked down the passageway to the studio.

He knew there were things she'd never told him, and troubled moods she never talked about, and that was fine. They did not need to know every drop of each other's pasts. But had he somehow provoked this? It would be useful to know. Then he wouldn't drag her to events she'd have to suffer through. They could both have a good time.

There was a good reason why he found opera so relaxing. Although it was artificial, it was also candid. The rich, high voices; the sinuous underline of Baroque violins; the limited gestures. Arms spread expansively to explain a point; a hand on the heart to emphasise a truth. The witchy women with black hag robes who demonstrated their evil natures in coarse singing and hunchback postures. Easy to read. With opera, you knew exactly where you were.

Was she going to her studio now to be deliberately alone? Or was she simply sorting out a problem with a work she was making? Why not just tell him, because there was a big difference between those options and if it was work then he wouldn't wait up, wondering and worrying. He'd get some sleep.

19

In her studio, Elza spread a bedsheet on the paint-smeared floor, tore a bin liner off a roll, and opened the lowest drawer of the plan chest.

She pulled out a sketchpad.

At some point, she'd thought, I will throw this away. But she'd always put it back in the drawer.

It dated from the first year that Ashten went. The press kept asking for statements. She hoped art might be less troublesome than interviews. She found a tutor and showed him sketches. Your work is a marvel, he said. Elza was relieved not to be told she was a deluded idiot. But were her first attempts really so amazing?

The tutor had been recommended by Gina. Elza made enquiries about his background, which she should have done beforehand. He was actually an art therapist, whatever that was. Of course. She was a therapy case, not a person studying art. She asked him not to come again. She didn't look for another tutor. And anyway, who did she think she was? Yoko Ono?

Tonight, she would throw this sketchbook away.

It contained ideas for art installations – rooms with stick figures, video projectors and loudspeakers. A series of shadows falling through white space, a glacier of visions. Student stuff. The world would never need it. Especially these days, when everyone could do it themselves on their computer. Recently she'd seen a fan video of Ashten apparently stirring in the ice. It was made from a studio photoshoot, where he stood against a white background. A series of pictures joined to make a film in which he appeared to make minute, eerie movements.

She didn't actively look for these things. The computer offered them to her when she looked at websites, because it knew her age. She was used to it.

This evening was one of those situations. *Dido and Aeneas*, specifically the lament, was part of Ashbirds legend. There was a video of Ashten performing it at a charity concert. '*Remember me,*' he sang, to the crowd's candles, in a counter-tenor that could rend the heavens.

The fifty minutes in the theatre, waiting for this song, sorting herself out afterwards, was fifty minutes to reflect, properly, on clutter from the past that she could ditch.

The sketchpad went in the bin liner.

Next was a leatherette portfolio tied with a ribbon.

This was an item she had never shown to anybody. Certainly not her therapist-tutor.

It contained portraits of male faces. Some were bearded. Some had their eyes closed, some had their eyelids half lowered, as if in meditation.

In the early days, there were a lot of photos. The first were prints, developed in a private lab with strict security, brought to her personally by Steve. Later, they came on a password-locked file-sharing site. Then on passworded email. Once the bodies were confirmed not to be Ashten, they seemed to be forgotten. Men with their skin sucked back on their face bones. Open mouths, as though they had roared their flesh away. Men who didn't look dead. The freezing of photography blurred with the freezing of life.

She set up a darkroom. She worked on them, using contrast and retouching to smooth away their horror. To get used to what they represented. To be with their strength and their frailty. To share their state of waiting. To send them on their way and set them quiet in her mind.

All these men, found in the ice and brought to her. Some weren't through official channels. People found the secret routes to get pictures directly to her. Steve traced their sources. Many weren't from Everest, or even the Himalaya. They were from the Alps. Why did people send them? Because the world was full of cranky fans with obscure motivations. It was senseless and cruel, but so was everything. She kept them, studied every face. Even if they were not from the same mountain where Ashten lay, they came from the same strange land.

Once you started a practice or a collection, it became a routine. The reasons were not always clear, except you felt you must. That was part of artist life. Before you knew it, you had all the dead men, stretching back through the years, brought to you like an endless task in a fairy tale. A duty to do for ever.

When Steve sent her the picture recently of the man in the Kathmandu morgue, she opened PhotoShop, studied and adjusted him, printed him for the collection.

It might be therapy. It might be a burden. Unless you consciously stopped.

This was where she would stop.

She stacked the pictures, knotted the ribbon around the binder and slid the collection into the bin liner.

How should this be done? Put them out with the rubbish? A reporter might choose that day to forage through the coffee grounds and putrid salmon wrappers.

She could burn them. The house had a working fireplace. No, imagine the flames consuming the faces.

If Elliot helped her they might laugh their qualms away.

Elliot would not want to burn photographs. So she would have to explain about them, and convince him that burning was the right thing, and let him look at them, and answer his questions, of which there would be many.

Elza texted Steve the next morning. Good, he could meet her. Actually he was at an address nearby for the next couple of hours.

Steve was the best option for getting rid of the portraits, though it felt like she was asking him to dispose of a murder victim.

What would Steve do with them? He'd probably have to burn or shred them. She said an apologetic prayer for the toll on his nerves.

She checked the address where Steve was. Just a ten-minute walk.

Spring was really coming. Bluebells were clustered at the foot of the tree at the end of the road. There was an energising chill against her shirted arms. A milky sweetness in the breeze.

Steve's directions took her to a renovated townhouse. It looked squeaky new, fresh off an architect's laptop. The windows were clear as sheet water. The flagstones on the front path were sharp and exactly square, not yet shifted by the trek of feet. The ground-floor windows were masked with unusual shutters of frosted glass. They held her attention, those shutters. They must have been expensive.

The door was opened by a big-framed fleshy man. His gasped smile told her she didn't need to introduce herself. She asked for Steve, and the man clasped her hand in both of his, said it was so good to meet her. He called her Ms Jones, like the director of that play had.

The house's interior was blank white, like a new sketchbook. She could hear Steve in another room, talking, maybe on a phone. This portfolio under her arm might be catnip to this excited man, so she kept an ear on Steve's voice. She looked for a subject for neutral chat until Steve could come out. She remarked that she liked the glass shutters.

The man said he'd just installed them, but would probably sell the house and never get the pleasure of them. You could use them in another house, she said, and he said he couldn't because they were a non-standard shape. I shouldn't have put them in, he added, but they were beautiful. She recognised the type, like the clients who enquired about a painting for their boardroom, then got carried away and commissioned something wildly personal that could never work for their business. She gripped the portfolio, sealing its open edge between her fingers.

But she did like the shutters. Plumped with light by the morning sunshine, they filled the white chambers with luminous tranquillity, like a swimming-pool.

And what was that against the white back wall?

The Havisham clock.

So this large-girthed bear was Steve's friend, the builder.

'You helped with our holiday, didn't you?' she said. 'Thanks. Thanks for taking the clock too.'

'I like the clock.'

She liked it too, seeing it here. That surprised her. Its theatrical fakery was softened by the shutters.

She remembered his name now. Oliver Jared.

In his house, this clock had been given meaning and gravitas. Might Oliver Jared also understand this artwork she held? That would be nice, before Steve disposed of it for ever.

'Would you let me try something?'

'Of course.' Jared answered, too instantly.

He was nervous. So was she. She set the portfolio on the wood floor. 'These were never for public viewing. But I hoped one day to show them to someone.'

She spread the portraits over the boards.

The faces with their ice-sprinkled eyelashes, their expressions defiant and serene. The tarpaulin shrouds. The house's glacial light was perfect. She might have had it in mind when she made them.

Oliver Jared knelt beside her. 'They are like angels.'

'You do realise what they are?'

He did. His silence said so. 'What will you do with them?'

'They're a bit eerie to keep at home.' She tried to excuse them with a joke. But there was no need. Oliver Jared accepted the work for what it was. Without suggesting interpretations of her mental state or her progress through recovery.

She heard a footstep. Close behind. Looked round.

It was Hugo Bird.

He was lost in the sound from a pair of padded headphones, but then she saw his attention refocus. On the spread of portraits.

No, they were not for anyone else to see. Not accidentally. Not without context. And especially not Hugo Bird.

She saw the jump in his eyes. She reared to her feet.

A strong pair of arms grasped her.

Steve. He gave her a hug, a good-to-see-you hug. 'How are you doing, Elza?'

Steve, the bodyguard still. Saving them all from themselves.

'Where are your manners, Oliver?' said Steve. 'You haven't so much as put the kettle on.'

Hugo spun and walked away, fast, into the next room.

20

Steve rushed Hugo out of the house, *prestissimo*. Oliver Jared's Jaguar was at the kerb. Across the road, a man in a paint-smeared sweatshirt was looking at a phone. Taking a picture? A nanosecond check. Steve decided he was not.

In the car, leather-lined doors and black windows sealed them into privacy. Nigel, the driver, eased the vehicle into the road.

Hugo stared shock-eyed into the seats. 'She is worse than any fucking tabloid. What are those photos? A shrine to go in the house?'

'She asked me to help her get rid of them,' said Steve. 'She's not going to exhibit them.'

Hugo looked into the traffic through the dimmed windows. Let his head tip against the window. His breath clouded the glass. 'When will she let up? She still acts as if Ash would come back and marry her. She does know, doesn't she, that she was a shag you picked out of the crowd?'

Oof. 'Now you mention it, H, I've not found the right time to tell her.'

Long ago, one of Steve's duties was to prowl the queues before the concert for girls to invite backstage. Elza's origin was more dignified, a little. She was an exhibit at an art student's degree show, painted like a statue with tiny electrical resistors stuck all over her body. Steve saw her having a cigarette break at the back of the gallery, scowling as she toked on a Silk Cut, perched on a fire escape in her contoured make-up. There was a strange energy about her; a gamine fragility that belied the futuristic sass of her outfit, like a nervous creature kidnapped for a circus. He gave her a pass for the concert after-party. She came in her cyborg costume and one ballet pointe shoe, walking on its tip with one foot, walking flat with the other, a lop-sided rise-and-fall gait she somehow made graceful. Ashten couldn't kidnap her fast enough. Unusually, he didn't send her home afterwards.

Hugo slammed his hand on the leather seats. 'She thinks she was The One. Ash had hundreds of Ones. She blames me but hasn't she done well from this? She's an international celebrity queen of pain, with a lifetime ticket to be anything she wants.'

He looked into the traffic again.

'Nobody's to blame, H. She was very young at the time.'

'And the rest of us weren't?'

21

Hugo grew up in a quiet town in Shropshire called Bonnet. His parents ran a house clearance business. When old people died, Bird & Co arrived with a van and took away the chaos.

From this, Hugo learned that stacks of old newspapers get infested with a species of bug. That paperback spines break like hard caramel. That shoes, chairs and mattresses keep a three-dimensional memorial of the bodies that used them. That Bakelite turns yellow if left in sunshine. That Tupperware containers fray with age. That taxidermy cats never look convincing, and fur hats eventually look like taxidermy cats.

He also learned that old photographs in frames went unclaimed. You could open a drawer and find letters, diaries, all the writings and moments a person had thought important to keep, and no one came for them.

Bird & Co reconditioned the furniture, crockery, clocks, curtains and collectable clothes, and sold them in a shop next to the Bonnet Post Office.

Bonnet was a crop of red brick streets in the shadow of an ancient hill whose official name was the Long Mynd. To Hugo it resembled a giant sleeping rat behind the town. Holding them there with its long mind.

The owner of the hiking shop retired and sold the business to new people, the Geddard family. They came from a more ambitious place. They put leaflets through the doors of the other local businesses, suggesting they form a commercial guild.

That was how Hugo met Ashten. Mr Geddard invited the Bonnet businesses on a team-building hike on the Long Mynd, to outline his plans for the guild.

'I expect,' said Hugo's father, 'that Mr Geddard is one of those people who wants to be in charge of something.' Despite their scepticism, they were willing to give it a chance. The Bird family believed in giving people a chance.

On the day, just two cars showed up at the car park on the top of the Mynd; the Geddards and the Birds. Hugo watched his parents trying to make up for the poor turnout by being super-pleased to meet them.

Ashten was fourteen, like he was. He knew this because the adults discussed it and said that was nice, they'd get on. Ashten refused to look at Hugo. He stared down, his hands rammed hard into his pockets. He wore a faded, oversized army camouflage jacket with sergeant stripes painted in yellow emulsion on the shoulders, a clear naff-off to catalogue-fresh hiking gear.

They chose a footpath. Ashten walked in an aggressive, stamping silence that said, I'll speak to you if I choose to. Hugo did the same.

Hugo's parents were walkers of average fitness, and liked to chat. Mrs Geddard stayed with them, but Mr Geddard and Ashten pulled ahead. Hugo walked with them and noticed a curious thing. They each watched the other. Ashten's glance flicked in his own direction as well. Hugo quickened his pace. So did Ashten. So did Mr Geddard. Wait, thought Hugo, I'm in a race with them. Why? He left them to it.

Hugo caught up with them at a cairn. Mr Geddard had his map spread out and was turning it to align his compass. Ashten was sitting on a rock, drawing in a notepad with a stub of pencil.

Hugo knew Ashten had noticed he'd arrived. A millisecond pause, then Ashten drew two flamboyant strokes on the page.

Behold, I'm making art. He deserved to be ignored, but Hugo couldn't. He felt a provoking kind of attention coming from him, like a radar beam.

Hugo's parents and Mrs Geddard arrived, puffing. Remarks were made about the view. Hugo's mother noticed the artist diligently working his pencil. 'Oh, let me see,' she said. Don't, thought Hugo, as Ashten put on a show of weary reluctance that was also incredibly smug.

She leaned over the page. 'Oh, that's different.'

Hugo hadn't wanted to look, but he had to because the sketchbook was in his mother's hands and she was passing it to him.

Ashten had drawn a mage-like figure holding a lantern on top of a rocky cliff.

'Ashten is so talented,' said Mrs Geddard. 'He does all this from his imagination.'

It wasn't a bad drawing. But Hugo knew Ashten hadn't invented the image. It was the centre gatefold of Led Zeppelin's fourth album.

Every dead person's house had a record collection. Instead of pocket money, Hugo was given the music from the houses they cleared. Much of it was ancient, scratched and unlistenable. Or sentimental, crooning and unlistenable. But some of it was tempting, like the collection of prog rock that had recently come to him. And even the rubbish could be sold on, at the second-hand music shop in Shrewsbury or record fairs he went to on the bus.

Ashten received the adults' attention without apparent reaction. But Hugo saw something insufferably aware about his indifference. Especially in the way he took the book back and added a signature. While they watched, he inscribed each letter with careful style, as though his name was itself a work of art. There was further praise for his talent and imagination.

'Show them your other pictures, Ashten,' said Mrs Geddard. Ashten handed the sketchbook over, his expression blank, as if he was submitting to examination by a schoolteacher whose approval he disdained but was very pleased to have.

Hugo's mother gasped. 'Oh look at this, Hugo.' Hugo did. There was a striped lawn with a mob-capped figure playing croquet (Genesis, *Nursery Cryme*). A close up of a giant face with golfball eyes, cavernous open mouth and punchbag uvula (King Crimson, *Court of the Crimson King*). Hugo had to check his mother's expression. She surely had seen the albums in his room. Perhaps she was just being nice. But how could Ashten's parents be so square to not recognise any of them, not even the computer-digits portrait of The Police from *Ghost In The Machine*?

Ashten, to his credit, was growing irritated. He knew that impressing a parent didn't count. But he was looking at Hugo with new interest.

The adoration of the sketchpad finished. The walk resumed. Hugo bent to fix his bootlace. When he stood up, Ashten was waiting for him.

The parents had gone ahead, walking in a row through the heather, which made them look like a four-piece folk ensemble. They pointed at the view. The Shropshire plain spread out below: mostly flat like a sea bed, with the odd hump of a hill. The kind of landscape that would be in a child's picture book.

Ashten muttered to Hugo. 'Look at this boring place. They bring you up here and tell you you can touch the sky. But it's really so you can see you've got nowhere to go.' He picked up a stone, slotted it into a forked branch in a sapling and twanged it into the void.

How was Hugo supposed to answer that? The remark was like throwing a stone to see what happened. Would you tell him he was awesome?

Hugo had never met anyone like Ashten. All the other kids he knew – at school, at the farm next door to their house – seemed happy to do their schoolwork, their Saturday jobs, support the required football teams, watch the same TV shows, listen to the same music, until they became old enough to work the land or the family business, or teach in the local school. Hugo didn't dislike them, but he spent a lot of time on his own.

Ashten threw another stone. 'What is the formative event of your life?'

Hugo didn't understand. 'What do you mean?'

'The event that's made you who you are.'

'I don't think I have one.'

Ashten looked into the distance. 'I saw a car accident when I was five. We were driving in America. Have you been to America?'

Hugo said he had not.

'We were driving and we came across a family. Their car had gone off the road and they were bleeding to death, lying in the road, their chests going up and down and they were gasping. A whole family. I felt their spirits leave their bodies. I saw them die.'

Hugo sucked his cheeks in, very hard. Under no circumstances must he laugh. Ashten had just described one of the infamous events in the life of Jim Morrison, front man of The Doors.

This was another test, but what of? Whether Hugo recognised it? No, Ashten's eyes burned with sincerity. He wanted to be believed. Certainly if Hugo had been told this by anyone at his school, he would have pointed out, in a kind way, that he knew the story's original source. He might also have added that Jim Morrison's own parents said the event never happened. But Ashten's preposterous fib and ferocious delivery was the real test. Are you with me or are you ordinary?

That was far more important than the small business of whether the memory was genuinely his. Hugo liked it.

But Ashten shouldn't get away with everything. 'The covers you drew,' said Hugo. 'I've got those albums too.'

It was as if he had spoken a secret password. Ashten looked again at Hugo, re-estimating him. 'I saw them in the library. Any good?'

'Come round and have a listen.'

..

Even if Hugo hadn't found common ground with Ashten, he was destined to see him frequently. His parents mocked the Geddards, gently, but they also admired them. Mr Geddard seemed supremely satisfied with being a shopkeeper. He talked of stock control and payment terms as though he was conquering the world. Hugo's parents poked fun at his over-serious manner, but nevertheless, they started to use American-sounding terms like 'bottom line'. They gave their shopfront a lick of paint, and paid Ashten to design them a new logo to paint on a sandwich board and reproduce on business cards. Hugo thereafter hid his copy of *Trick of the Tail*.

Mr Geddard sent Ashten to the local private school, and Hugo noticed his own parents seemed excited by that. He knew they worried that he spent so much time at the piano, because, they said, most musicians starve. But they seemed relieved that he didn't take to farming like the kids of the next-door neighbours, riding the fields on tractors, cutting hay late into the summer evenings and stumping ankle-deep through muck to move the cows around in winter. As a friend, Ashten was parent-approvable. He went to a feepaying school. He was steeped in an atmosphere of stock control, orders and turnover, from clean, indoor work that involved a visible exchange of money. The Geddards represented a welcome widening of horizons.

Hugo knew his parents believed that friends infect your dreams. But it struck him that the Geddard house had no room for dreams. The dining table was permanently stacked with invoices and ledgers. The shop itself was like a quartermaster's store for the end of civilisation; a crowded space of cagoules, hiking boots and tents. Indeed, Ashten seemed keen to escape from both house and shop, and did so into Hugo's music collection.

They would connect two sets of headphones and whack the volume up. The music seemed to give Ashten a new, more brilliant skin. He would sit religiously still as the sounds thudded and swirled into his ears, though Hugo noticed he could not tolerate any track that was longer than four minutes unless he had his sketchbook.

He always copied something; usually an album cover. Hugo said to him one day, as he shaded a sketch of the melting face on Peter Gabriel's third album: 'You should draw something of your own.'

'Don't you think this is good?'

'Don't you want to say something yourself?'

'What should I say?'

'I don't know what you should say. Only you know what you should say.' Hugo lifted the black disc off the turntable, balancing it by its edge so he didn't touch the shimmering grooves. 'What shall we have next?' He swiped the sleeve off Ashten's knee and put the record away.

'That album cover is good art, isn't it?' said Ashten. 'So why not draw it?'

He was such hard work when his ego was challenged. 'Because you could make your own art.'

Ashten tapped the end of his pencil on the drawing. 'This is a good picture.'

'Yes but don't you ever look at them and think...' Hugo picked up Camel's *Snow Goose* and pointed to a bird on the cover design. 'That blue bit could be bigger... or red instead of blue. The bird could be the other way around.' He didn't know anything about art. This sounded lame.

'It looks fine.'

'Okay. Forget about art. But don't you ever look at the track names, and realise when you hear them that you imagined they'd be different?'

'Why would I think that?'

Hugo picked up the guitar propped by the wardrobe and sat on the bed. 'Look, I never liked "Rhayader Goes To Town". This is how I hoped it would go.'

Hugo had never talked to anyone else in this way. Ever.

..

The next day, Ashten bowled into Hugo's bedroom, dropped a folded piece of paper onto Hugo's maths homework, then went to the window, still in his painted sergeant jacket, and looked out as if the muddy tractors over the fence required his concentrated supervision.

Hugo unfolded the note.

He was expecting a drawing. It seemed to be a poem. No, a song lyric.

'*My name is Ray, short for Rhayader. Let me be your love invader.*'

Hugo held his hand to his mouth and pressed it tightly so he wouldn't laugh. Ashten had written a song lyric. Invented something. What should Hugo say?

Ashten snatched the paper. Hugo did laugh then, a pig-honk that was louder for being stifled.

'No it wasn't bad,' said Hugo, though it was. 'Give it here. Let's work on it.'

Ashten gave him a look of contempt that was so vicious, Hugo regretted all the times he'd been tactful instead of saying what he really thought. Especially about the fibs Ashten told to make himself seem remarkable and dangerous. He'd climbed into the lion pen at a zoo on the Isle of Wight when he was nine. At the age of six he'd seen a murder through the window of a hotel room in Scarborough and nobody had believed him. Hugo simply wondered which book, film or famous person he had borrowed them from.

But he also recognised these lies came from a place of truth. Ashten felt he was made for great deeds, a noble purpose that he had to find. There was a phrase he liked: 'get back to ourselves'. They borrowed camping gear from the shop and hitch-hiked to the Brecon Beacons because that was where the SAS trained. To Snowdonia because that was where George Mallory trained before climbing Everest. They went for walks to the top of the Long Mynd, looked at the imprisoning jigsaw of farms that promised you'd get nowhere, hurled stones at it and planned what they'd do next to get back to themselves.

..

Hugo arrived at his piano teacher's house. He passed a girl in the narrow hall, on her way out. Remarked on her music case because he'd spent several evenings repairing it, a few months before.

The girl paused. Surprised.

'It's from our shop,' said Hugo. 'It's quite old, I think.'

She lifted it and showed him an ink stain in the leather, tracing it with her finger. 'I like this. It's got history.' The light through the door's stained glass made her intriguing. It put illuminated shapes on her face, lozenges of lilac and yellow. Hugo had never taken much notice of girls, but she looked like the cover of an intimate acoustic solo album.

A car horn summoned her. She shot him a goodbye smile and hurried out.

As he sat at the teacher's Chappell upright with his sight-reading exercises, he saw a book of grade two pieces was already there. Was it hers? He moved it and a slip of paper poked out. With Ashten's jagged, territorial autograph.

That was annoying, slightly. But Bonnet was so small that everyone met everyone. She might be at Ashten's school. So what had Ashten drawn for her? Most likely the she-bat creature from the back of Kate Bush's *Never For Ever*, which he'd been practising. Yes, Ashten practised.

It wasn't a drawing. It was a stanza of verse. Hugo recognised it. 'Hoping Love Will Last' from Steve Hackett's *Please Don't Touch*. So romantic, yearning and brittle. Ashten had presented it to Laura (that was her name) with his own signature.

Hugo did not concentrate well in his lesson. This offended him, on a level he could not explain. He wasn't especially bothered about the girl, but he was very troubled by the lie. Music was the most honest thing Hugo knew. Ashten had found a lyric from an album she was unlikely to know, and claimed it as his own tender work.

The Geddard shop was on Hugo's way home. Ashten was stuffing packs of laces into a display rack. He looked relieved at the surprise diversion.

Hugo set the slip of paper on the counter. 'You're busted, Romeo.'

A bewitching, twitching grin. 'Good song.'

'You made out you wrote it.'

'No, I copied it out in a beautiful fashion and signed it. She loved it.'

'Because she thinks that's who you are.'

Ashten turned the rack of laces. Still the smile, pleased to see this confirmation of his genius.

'But they were not your words.'

'I like them. They were what I wanted to say.'

'But you made her think that's who you are.'

'It is who I am.'

Ashten could not see it.

He loaded more laces into the rack.

'Did you tell her your formative experience too?'

'You're too uptight. Seize the day. Stop being so quiet. Let people know what you've got inside you.'

What he'd got inside him? 'Jim,' said Hugo. 'Morrison.'

Ashten gave him a confused look. Why are we now talking about Jim Morrison? Hugo held his gaze. You work it out. Your fucking formative experience, which I allowed you. But now I'm telling you: I know.

Ashten began to catch up. Hugo saw it in his face, a hostile blaze, as if his entire inner temperature had changed. The Morrison story wasn't just a show-off fib. It was a deep, unquestionable foundation of his self-narrative. 'Just fuck off.'

Hugo was already fucking off. To the music shop, which was a much better place to spend his time and breath.

As he pushed in through the door he saw a card in the window. *Urgent: temporary pianist wanted for Mutt and the Harpoons, resident band at the Castle Hotel. Must be able to improvise.*

On any other day Hugo would have read the advert and decided it was not for him. He was a schoolboy. His music was a private game.

Today, Hugo was not himself.

He copied the phone number, and that also seemed the act of a person who was not him.

..

Mutt and the Harpoons invited him to their rehearsal, on the Thursday evening. They used the hall of Hugo's school, which was convenient as he could cycle there, but he still needed an excuse to go out. 'It's for my grade five exam,' he lied, and his parents were happy.

The band was a double-bass player and a vocalist. The bass player was called Pemmican. He was fat and shaped roughly like his instrument, with a complexion like corned beef, which explained his name. The vocalist wore a blue trilby hat and a checked shirt. His microphone was tricked up to look like a wartime radio announcer, with the word Mutt where the BBC logo would be. Hugo looked at these two eccentric figures in his empty school hall. He might be in bed, having a dream. Strangely, that helped.

Mutt said: 'How old are you?'

'Eighteen,' lied Hugo. He went to the upright Broadwood which he had heard every morning of his school life, and which he had never touched. Brace yourself, he told the piano in his mind. We're not playing hymns.

Pemmican twanged a rhythm. Hugo loped up and down the keys. Pemmican and Mutt grinned. They were off.

Nobody minded how old anyone was.

..

'You want to play in a band at a wedding this Saturday?' said Mr Bird.

'It's through my school,' said Hugo. He didn't like lying, but that wasn't a total fabrication. He couldn't tell them he'd joined an exciting hinterworld that wasn't connected with shopkeeping, farming or exams.

'What do Ashten's parents think of this?'

They assumed everything he did must be led by Ashten. They adored Ashten.

The second lie came easily. 'Ashten's doing it with me.'

It was agreed. Ashten was the passport to everything.

The hotel was a strange spinsterish place at the foot of the Long Mynd, with fairy lights and false crenellations. It looked like it had been left after a Disney film. The band played jaunty romantic favourites that Hugo would have hauled straight to the secondhand dealer, with red face and apologies. Stevie Wonder's 'I Just Called to Say I Love You' was requested and played several unbelievable times. But it didn't matter. Absorbed in the job of playing, Hugo was happy to honour the song, no matter how trite. He went to bed on Saturday night a musician.

..

Hugo surfaced half out of sleep. It was early morning. Cockerels, chickens and cows were hollering the dawn from the farm next door. They didn't usually disturb him, so why was he awake now?

He heard voices. His door swung open. His father was already dressed.

'We had a call from Ashten's mother. Mr Geddard has had some kind of breakdown. Come on.'

It was not yet six. As they drove the empty streets to the Geddards' shop, his mother told him. 'Mrs Geddard caught Mr Geddard smashing up the shop. She and Ashten found him with an axe. It's a dreadful mess.'

A fire engine was outside the shop. Its chrome was bronzed by the pink light of the dawn. A rack of waterproof trousers was on the pavement. Two firemen in yellow overalls were throwing them onto a tarpaulin. A throat-clenching stench of petrol came from the building. Every window in its two-storey frontage was open as the rooms gasped for air.

'Oh lord,' said Hugo's mother. 'He must have tried to set it on fire. Mind the broken glass.'

Inside was a scene of violence. The cabinet with the water flasks and other apparel of walking was a smashed wreck of glass and wood. The posters, of handsome men smiling on rugged hills, were ripped off the walls. The floor was heaped with sand, to soak up the petrol.

Through a narrow corridor, Hugo could see to the back yard. Ashten was out there. The camo jacket had gone; he had grown too long and bony for it. Now his naff-off garment was a roadmender's donkey jacket with leather shoulders, painted, of course, with Jimmy Page's Zoso symbol. A scarf covered the lower half of his face. He was spreading a pile of Aran sweaters over a washing line.

Hugo went back into the shop. Everything carried the oily smell, though the fire brigade had taken the hazardous material away. Hugo and his mum brought stuff from the stock rooms and carried it outside. Ashten hung it up, not looking at either of them, pulling the scarf up so it hid his face.

Other neighbours arrived. They gathered armfuls of stock and looked for goods that could still be sold. Swept up the broken glass. Carried the wooden skeleton of the smashed cabinet out into the yard.

There were functional conversations about where to put what and what to do next. And other, quieter remarks.

'At least he didn't take the axe to the till.'

'The men break before the women.'

It was very strange. As they put their honest backs into helping, there was something enlivened and satisfied in the way they talked.

'She'll have to keep him away from here. He'll snap again.'

Hugo had a terrible feeling of the walls moving closer and

trapping him. And these people, kind and plodding, were the jailers, and would ensure these bleak predictions were fulfilled.

He took an armful of anoraks outside.

The florist was there, talking to Ashten. 'When you've done that,' she said, 'your mum says to bring everything from the store room. We'll get you a stall in the market so you won't starve.'

Starve. Hugo heard in the word a double-edged gleam. She meant to be heartening and helpful. She was also excited, and strangely happy. She busied back to the gloomy doorway, where Hugo saw her deliver this same sentence to the butcher. A stall in the market so they won't starve. She landed on the word with heavy relish, loving how important and desperate it was.

Ashten was standing nearby, watching her too.

Hugo spoke, over the anoraks. 'Where do you want these?'

Ashten looked properly at him. The scarf had slipped. His expression was thoroughly sickened. Want them? I don't want them. I don't want any of this.

'I've got some Fripp,' Hugo said.

...

The Geddards' shop was repaired. The family fitted once more into the tight clamp of routine. Ashten helped there when schoolwork allowed, in holidays, and on Saturdays. When possible, he escaped to Hugo. They made noise. They went to the Brecons and Snowdonia again. Ashten wanted to sleep in the open, without a tent, because there were too many tents at home. Hugo made sure they had a tent, torches, a map, compass, a weather forecast. And packs of expedition rations because Ashten was saying they should strangle their dinner with their bare hands.

Every Saturday, Hugo played with Mutt and the Harpoons, serenading the start of a couple's married bliss with Stevie Wonder, Chris de Burgh and more Stevie Wonder. Hugo turned sixteen. Then seventeen. They tried a female singer. On her first gig, she got in a funk of stage-fright and forgot the words to 'Feelings'. She made up nonsense verses that went *we aren't knowing what we're singing*, then forgot the tune too. Hugo improvised and Pemmican caught his vibe. They surfed for a while, playing tag with the

melody while the vocalist sang every line as '*babadoo*', until Hugo
brought the song to a rumbling, rippling finale.

...

The following Monday, Pemmican came into the Birds' shop.
Hugo, sanding ten layers of paint off a bedside cabinet, thought how
the man's double-bass body looked unbalanced without its compan-
ion instrument.

'Hey kiddo. We need a talk. I'm firing you from the band.'

Hugo stopped sanding, stopped breathing, shocked. 'Was it because of "Feelings"? Sorry about that.'

'No,' said Pemmican. 'This is killing you. You don't need to play
this shit every Saturday.'

Hugo knew the music was dire. But that wasn't the point. 'I don't
mind about the music. You're a good band.' He'd auditioned for
other local bands and they were rubbish.

Pemmican opened the satchel that rested on his ample hip. He
slid a folded newspaper to Hugo, stabbing it with a calloused finger.
'This is a scholarship to study music in London. It pays an allow-
ance for living expenses and books, so your parents don't have to
fund it.'

Hugo's future was still a frightening void he preferred not to look
at. He was studying A levels and his parents and teachers were
pushing him towards teaching or accountancy. He vented by writing furious songs about the adult world, about people who sleep-
walked through deadening existences. Ashten performed them in a
despising spoken-word snarl. Hugo saw a dressing-table come into
the shop and recognised it as one he helped his father restore many
years before. Now it was back, battered at the end of another life,
so puzzling and sad. He wrote about it. Ashten sang the song with
naked desperation that filled him with fear for the future and also
a sense that they were uncovering a truth the world didn't want
them to know. Meanwhile, Ashten was repeating GCSEs at his
expensive school. He wasn't academic.

But this scholarship? Hugo could study music? He hadn't
thought that was possible.

He got the letter in August, just after his A-level results. He'd won the scholarship. His parents were astonished. His noodling hobby was something he could be paid to study, alongside real musicians. That day, he took books and clothes to the village's charity shop. As he carried boxes into its fuggy-smelling store room, he heard the conversation of the two volunteer staff.

'It's rheumatism. We've got it because it was so damp when we were children.'

'At night the bed sheets were transparent.'

'They've gone too far the other way now. People have no idea.'

'We used to sleep two to a bed. Top to toe.'

He set the box on the floor. The letter from the college crackled in his pocket. It warmed him. He was leaving. Leaving this dreary place that liked to smother young people and watch their souls shrivel. Until this day, he didn't know how much it troubled him. You couldn't survive here if it troubled you. People would know. They reached out with their long minds and watched for ambition and dreams, or signs that you thought you were better than them, and they'd make your life even worse. They liked to keep you here, suffocating. They did not want you to think you might go to London to work in the arts. But now this future was being given to him; it really was.

'You know, it's loneliness that kills old people now. They die of depression.'

'And if they go into a home it's not good.'

'Oh no, they aren't nice in there. They kill each other.'

He walked away from the shop laughing. He was leaving and they could get on with killing each other. Ashten would think it was brilliant.

..

Ashten didn't come round at his usual time. Hugo went looking for him. The blinds of the shop were down, but he could hear the till as it rattled through its nightly tally, counting the little sales that made the sum of the day. Hugo knocked.

Footsteps. A jangle of keys as the lock was turned. The door pulled back, enough to show Mrs Geddard's peering eye. She flinched suspiciously when she saw him. Fingers around the door, not opening it further. That was unusual.

'Are you looking for congratulations?'

Congratulations? He didn't think anyone had been told. 'Thanks.'

'Your mother gave us the news.'

Heavier footsteps. Ashten's father. Without a word, the door was closed and locked again.

The following morning Hugo heard it from his mother. Ashten had left home. Mrs Geddard thought he had probably gone to London, but she didn't know where. Mr Geddard wasn't speaking to anyone.

Hugo's family was never welcomed in the Geddards' house again.

22

Steve dropped Hugo at the studio, safely away from the hostile vibes of Elza, then asked Nigel, the driver, to take him back to the townhouse. Oliver Jared had sent a text.

How well do you know Elza? I think she needs to talk.

At the townhouse, Elza ran down the steps, her shoulder bag clamped under one arm, her face pinched. Steve buzzed the car window down and gave a builder's wolf whistle. Elza glared, ready with an acid word. He leaned and opened the door.

She looked at the seat. 'It's not far. I can walk.'

'I know a great short-cut,' said Steve. Nigel was primed to take them on a long loop until Steve said otherwise.

Nigel touched a switch on the dashboard. A glass screen rose behind him.

Elza climbed in.

The car moved out into the traffic.

Steve could see Elza was noting the smoked glass screen. The suited back of the driver.

'Like the old days, isn't it?' said Steve.

She didn't answer. But he could see her mind was hammering.

'I'm sorry about that earlier,' said Steve. 'We needed to do some band business.'

She did speak then. 'Here's some business we need to do. You and Hugo are having a jolly reunion. That's great but I don't need to be there.' Her voice was clipped, as if explaining a simple fact to an infuriating child.

Steve put both hands up. Surrender. 'You're right. I should have checked.'

'I do my bit when it's important. But I'm not a member of the band. And I'm not a popstar's girlfriend.'

She looked away, out of the window. The suspension loops of Chelsea Bridge glided by, made grey by the glass.

'I presume we are at some point going back to my house?'

Steve asked Nigel to take her home.

Steve looked at his phone. An email from Oliver Jared.

I feel bad about the way we left it with Elza. I think I should write to her. Something like this. Any thoughts?

'Dear Elza, it was such a pleasure to meet you today. I probably didn't handle it well, but I was thinking as a star-struck teenager and in those circumstances I don't give my best. I'm deeply privileged to be in a position to help Ashbirds make the album, and I understand that people have sometimes been tactless in involving you. I have no idea whether this new album pleases you or dismays you, and I have no right to ask about that or presume I understand. Let me apologise for anything I've done that may have added to this burden. Yours, Oliver Jared.'

Steve handed the phone to Elza, the email on the screen. 'Pax?'

23

Robert had doubts about the lyric they were working on.

Hugo had arrived, singing a hook. '*For he is prince of silence, and you, you are queen of pain.*' He paced the live room, stepping over leads, singing lines as he scribbled them on a notepad, calling out chords, improvising, until he had three completed verses and a bridge. Verse one set the story. A woman whose lover dies after a brief, grand

111

romance. In a tragic accident, no less. Verse two described the man –
a philandering egotist who'd have dumped her within weeks. In verse
three, many years have passed and she still pines. The end of each
verse was a knife-twist. *'For he is prince of silence, and you, you are
queen of pain.'* Not subtle, but not a bad start.

Now Gil, at the desk behind the glass, played it back while they
listened. Paul at the Steinway. Robert on a Gibson ES-355 guitar,
and also singing harmony with Hugo. Hugo tapped a Biro on the
notepad, thinking.

Gil paused the music. Hugo had his hand up.

'Robert's flat,' said Hugo.

Robert thought he sounded okay. 'Am I? Gil, can I hear my last
vocal?'

Gil said, through the talkback: 'Robert, you're not flat, but your
tonality jars with Hugo's. So he's doing you no favours. I'll try
something.' He glanced at Robert. 'Sorry.'

The track resumed, with Robert further back in the mix and
softened with chorus. Hugo raised his hand. 'No.'

Gil said: 'Hugo, you could sing both lines.'

Hugo closed his eyes. 'I want two voices. For the dynamic.'

If Gil looks at me again in that apologetic way, thought Robert,
I will nut him.

'Gil,' said Hugo, 'what's your voice like?'

'My own mother says it's like Fozzie Bear impersonating
Michael Caine. Shall we get a singer?'

Hugo turned away. 'Everybody out.'

'Well that's not going to be a single,' muttered Paul to Robert as
they walked away from the recording suite.

'Let's work,' said Robert, still wearing the Gibson.

When they reached the kitchen it was a mess. A band called The
New Surface, who were now making a dim racket in the other suite,
had had a party.

Robert and Paul swept broken cupcakes off the sofas. They laid
a tea towel over a gateau that was studded rather disgustingly with
cigarette butts. Paul stayed on walkabout, looking in cupboards,
scatting ideas for lyric hooks, while Robert sat with the Gibson and
wrote down the useful ones.

'Some Like It Hard,' called Paul.

'That won't be a single.'

Paul pulled a DVD out of the cupboard and held it up. Robert glimpsed bare thighs and black straps, like horse harness on a naked person. The title was *Some Like It Hard*.

Paul looked into the cupboard again. 'Ooh, vicar, do you take sugar?' He held up a saucer with a small crystalline heap that wasn't sugar. 'Don't mind if I do,' he said, but Robert noticed he put it back. He'd like to be wild but couldn't follow through.

Gil came out of the studio. 'Guys, we're done.'

Gil sounded knackered and a bit serious.

'Is he doing all the vocals himself now?' said Robert.

'No. He deleted the track.'

Paul was so surprised he stopped exploring the cupboards. Robert looked closely at Gil, because he might be joking. He wasn't; not with his mouth in that pained line.

'He told me to drag the whole thing to the trash.'

The track was gone. It had come together with such thrilling synergy, so immediately nearly flawless. Sure, they'd need to revise the lyric. But to junk the whole thing?

Paul said: 'He'd have had to pay Sting for that line. Queen of pain.'

'No,' said Robert. 'It's from a Victorian poem. Not in copyright. But Gil, there are backups, right?'

'Trashed too. It's gone. I've never known anyone do that. See you tomorrow.'

Paul closed the cupboard. 'He doesn't change, does he?' he said. He didn't mean Gil.

Hugo was running true to form. He'd pushed them out of the studio and deleted their work. Just like old times.

24

Hugo entered the house. The glass shutters were closed, as always. Elza Jones's Havisham clock guarded the stairs, striped like a white film noir in the early morning light. The clock disagreed about the hour. Hands at five to twelve, pushing to midnight and fairytale mayhem.

Oliver Jared's voice called. 'Up here.'

Hugo followed the voice up to one of the first-floor rooms. It had one piece of furniture – a long decorator's table for pasting wallpaper. It was heaped with opened envelopes and their unfolding contents. Oliver Jared was organising them into piles with such focus that he might have been splitting the atom. Hugo glimpsed publicity pictures from their touring days. Excerpts of lyrics, presented like prayers. Scans of artwork based on their album covers.

Jared gave his big, marvelling smile. 'I thought we'd get the fans involved. I ran a competition on the album website.'

Hugo didn't know there was an album website. He said so.

'Haven't you seen it? We're collecting email addresses so we can keep them updated about the album.' Jared leaned his meaty hands on the table, put away his smile and said, heavily: 'So. I'm worried. I haven't heard any tracks. Is there anything you need to sort out?'

'Oliver, it's not like building a house. It's an organic process.'

'Perhaps your organic process needs fertiliser.' Jared pushed a heap of envelopes towards him.

Hugo kept the comparison to himself. Fertiliser and manure. 'Are you really going to open all of those?'

'Just enough for a collage on that wall. These are the fans who paid on Kickstarter for the chance to have their work included.'

A Kickstarter page. Hugo didn't know about that either. It sounded tawdry. 'Included in what?'

'Fans love to be acknowledged,' said Jared.

And Jared was loving it even more, being the acknowledger. He must have been here for hours. It was a bit like the collection of band stuff Hugo had seen at that other house, turned up to eleven.

'This is how we'll build our street team,' said Jared.

'A street team. Are we pushing drugs?'

Jared ripped another envelope with his thumb. 'Hugo, everything's changed since your day. I know fans can be tricky. But if we treat them right, they do the publicity for us. This house can be a hub for the album.'

That certainly sounded tricky. 'You're going to let the fans in here?' Hugo checked the address on the letters. A PO box. Thank God.

'They might not have to come in. They can watch things on webcams.'

Webcams again. Jared had wanted them in the studio. Hugo refused.

Hugo picked up a letter.

'*I like the first side of* Hush *but not the other side, the concept thing. I could see you thought you were clever because you called it* The C Side, *but your other songs are better. I don't like it when bands try to be different and new, it does not please your people who like you as you are. So please make the new album like* The Switch *and* Surface Tension. *Those were good albums. Thank you.*'

He passed it to Oliver Jared. 'Street team?'

'Hugo, look at all this love. All these people who are pleased the band is back. Now consider something. We offer the chance to write lyrics. Just a few lines. Or whole tracks. Your choice. How much do you reckon we should ask for that?'

Hugo picked up another letter. He read it out. '*I wrote to ask you for an interview for my podcast. You never answered. I bought all your albums and you were happy to take the money for that, but you won't give me half an hour of your time.*' He dropped it back on the table. 'Don't involve the fans, Oliver.'

'I'm just worried that it's taking a while. Don't over-think this. Just make the album like *Hush*. And by the way, I love *The C Side* so another of those would be great.'

'You'll hear something soon. I've got to go.'

Hugo left, the clock catching his attention again. Forever at five minutes to mayhem.

Making up lies about time.

Hugo held that thought and took it to the studio.

25

In the control room, the lights were off. Robert and the rest of the band were lying on the floor, listening to a rough cut. It was called 'Making Up Lies About Time'.

On the dimmed ceiling, the effects racks made a beating light-show of red and green. The bass made a fidgety, timber-shaking snap. The guitar and vocals sliced the top, a little bit menacing, a little bit warning, a little bit knowing. A synth cruised in the breaks, classy as a top-end car. On it went, bossy, spare and silky, into the final silence.

Gil spoke. 'Awesome. Don't take this the wrong way, but I'd swear that Ashten was back. It's just what he'd write.'

Ashten writing? Robert, sitting up, glanced at Paul. Paul's face was amusingly mobile. The glistening tip of his snake-tongue moved in his mouth with opinions about Gil's remark. But Gil didn't know how those other albums were written. He didn't come in until the songs were ready.

Hugo stood up, reached for the notebook, riffled to a fresh page and began writing.

'Just needed to find my way. Gil, let's have a beat for this.'

26

In December 1989, Hugo had not seen Ashten for four months. He was near the end of his first term at King's College London, writing out a composition in his room while students passed the window friskily and noisily, when Ashten walked in.

No hello or how-are-you or long-time-no-see. Ashten walked in, without knocking, as if he had popped away a mere few minutes before to buy cigarettes. Closed the door, looked for the record collection, always his first interest, and let Hugo stare.

Of course Hugo stared. He also knew this was what Ashten expected. He'd be pleased by it.

How instantly Hugo's understanding of him came back.

So what did Hugo notice when he stared? Ashten was thinner. His hair was long, a tousled crop that skimmed his shoulders. His cheekbones were so prominent he looked female. Or was he wearing make-up?

The grooming was less polished the closer you looked. His jeans were smeared with several shades of white paint. Accidental smears, not the look-at-me daubings of the naff-off jackets. His boots had steel toe caps that poked through the worn leather. A bit boy-feminine artist, a bit construction worker, a bit robot.

'So I've got a place to stay at Christmas,' said Ashten, as though they'd already been talking about this.

'You're not going home for Christmas?' That was what Hugo intended to do, though he didn't particularly want to.

'I've got a place,' repeated Ashten, 'and we can spend the whole time playing. Rent free.' He selected an album by Yellow Magic Orchestra and sat on the bed as though he came round all the time. 'What's this like?'

..

Ashten was working as a building labourer. He was also trying to get unpaid intern work in a recording studio. Meanwhile he was caretaking a half-built house in a moneyed part of Surrey.

On the twentieth of December, Hugo arrived at a railway station in twilight and followed Ashten's directions. Past the barber shop, which hummed with buzz clippers. Past the Chinese takeaway, closed but smelling of heated oil. He crossed a roundabout and climbed a long hill. A few lights twinkled from behind high hedges, hiding from the traffic. Then the directions seemed to abandon him. There were no more houses or streetlights, just a lane up a tunnel of darkness.

Hugo did not find this amusing because he was bringing the music gear. A Roland keyboard in a padded flight case on his back, which felt like carrying a sideboard. A trolley with a Tascam Portastudio, which appeared portable until you picked it up and realised it was as dense as a neutron star. Also on the trolley was a Marshall busking amplifier, a Yamaha effects unit and a multi-block for all the plugs. Everything was taped into bin liners in case of rain. He couldn't see the bumps in the pavement, but the un-wieldy trolley found them all and kept trying to overturn. His wrists burned from fighting the twists. He wanted to straighten and ease his back, but when he did, the edge of the keyboard came too low and tipped the trolley over. Even his coat was weighted. In one pocket was a microphone and all the leads. In the other was underwear, a toothbrush and metal cassette tapes for the far-too-unportable Portastudio. Around his wrist was a roll of Gaffer tape, worn like a bangle.

Gradually he saw a light behind a lacework of tree branches. If this wasn't it, sod Ashten for ever. He was going back.

He came to a construction fence with an entry buzzer. Jabbed the button. A gate was pulled back. Ashten stood there with his surprising, longer hair, breathing mist.

Hugo followed him in. He made out the shell of a huge house, big as a cliff face. An arched front door. A great tented roof reflected a faint glow of moonlight. A little way away was another house, less finished. Walls and black voids, waiting for windows.

'Mind the hole,' said Ashten.

Hugo stepped over a trench where floorboards had not yet been laid, and bounced the trolley into the main hall. The kit was probably trashed by now from all the bumps.

A huge staircase rose at one end, the banister and handrail wrapped in polythene. On each side of the hall, doorless openings led to further rooms. This would be somebody's home? It was as big as a public building.

'They've had break-ins,' said Ashten, 'so they're paying me to live here until New Year. So long as we scare everyone away we can do what we like.'

Hugo had been hot from walking up the hill. Now, as the sweat in his clothes cooled, he realised it was freezing cold. Ashten opened a door. The only room that had a door. A blast of warmth came out with a fiery sound. Inside was a gas-powered heater shaped like a jet engine, which glowed flickering orange-blue.

They unpacked Hugo's gear. They found extension leads in the tool store and an arc lamp on a tripod. They balanced the keyboard on a carpenter's workbench, made a podium of breeze blocks for the Portastudio, taped heating pipes together as a stand for the microphone. Ready to play, but the jet engine heater roared over everything like a bomber.

They turned it off. The house was a waiting cavern. No furniture, no carpets. You could hear the dust playing hide-and-seek.

Hugo punched up a beat on the synth's sequencer. Life jackhammered into every corner, exciting, urgent, mind blowing. Ashten stood at the mic, took a breath and howled, long and animal, a king-of-the-planet hello.

They smoked joints. They stopped time. There were no street-lights outside and the winter dark was endless anyway.

Hugo heard a buzz. Had a lead fallen out? He stopped playing, waved Ashten to silence.

No, not the purring yawn of a separating electrical connection. The buzzer at the gate.

Ashten checked his watch. Swore. Sucked on the joint, though it was dead.

'I'm back in a few hours.'

'What?' Was he going somewhere?

'My other job.'

Hugo heard the front door. The scrape of the gate. The boom of music from a car. Voices. The gate closed. They'd gone.

It was nearly midnight. What kind of job started at nearly midnight? Still, Hugo had plenty to do. He went back to noise.

After many more hours, Hugo wrapped the keyboard and Portastudio in plastic and put them in the tool chest, with a breeze block on top. Remembering there might be thieves. He bedded down beside the engine-burner, in his sleeping bag, like the sole survivor of a nuclear holocaust.

..

A torch strafed the room. Ashten was back. Hugo, inside the sleeping bag, felt warm and boneless. In the clammy smell of curing plaster, he caught another smell as Ashten fumbled his boots off and slid into a sleeping bag. A musk of aftershave. Ashten hadn't been wearing it when he went out.

..

In the morning, Hugo explored the kitchen. The builders had plumbed in a freezer, sink and cooker, still cocooned in the manu-facturer's plastic with holes cut so they could use them. He found instant coffee and mugs in one of the cupboards.

Ashten came in, muffled in jumpers.

'So what's your second job?' Actually, Hugo noticed something else. Ashten's eyes looked curiously defined and smudged, like a hungover lion. 'Are you wearing eyeliner?'

Might be, said his shrug.

'Is it a job in music?' Ashten had said he was getting to know music people. Hugo wanted to know them too.

Cupping a steaming mug in his hands, Ashten went to the door. 'I'll show you around.'

Was he hiding something?

It wasn't hard to be suspicious of him, after situations like the piano lesson girl. And his appropriation of Jim Morrison, who he now looked rather like.

'If you're letting people hear our songs, I want to meet them too.'

'Sure. Next time they come.'

They walked through the upstairs rooms. The master bedroom suite was waiting for a window and a balcony. It was open at one end like a garage dropping away to nothing. There was a steep, tumbling view over frosty fields with valleys and hedges, bubbly boundaries that curved down the hill. In the distance was the steeple of the church in Dorking, a needle in the roofs of the sleepy town.

They returned to the kitchen, found pizzas in the freezer, started the oven. Hugo played some new sequences he'd made, loops of rhythms and chord washes that whipped around the echoing room. He sang a melody line. Ashten picked up the mic and sang it back. No words. Words seemed to interfere. The meaning was there already, coming up from the roots of the earth, through the machines and Ashten's singing. Just them and the music. Every atom in the house, every cell in themselves, alive with the power of sound.

Then they ate pizza and jammed, from memory, the entire score of *Rocky Horror*.

..

In the middle of the night, Hugo made a trip to the bathroom. The bathroom was not yet tiled. The white porcelain stood on bare cement. God, he was stoned, and this house with its vacant, rudimentary spaces was like arriving at a place too early in the continuum of time, or too late after all the life had gone. He crossed the hall, with its banisters lit by moonlight, eerie struts in a polythene chrysalis.

The front door rattled.

A hard, deliberate rattle. A gritty scrape on the step outside.

He tried to blink away the dope in his brain. Was this burglars? The burglars they were here to scare?

That sound was definitely boots, moving about.

He couldn't hear any talking. If it was a burglar, there was only one.

An escape of breath, sounding exasperated. Again, a rattle at the door.

On the floor by the foot of the stairs was a pile of copper pipes. He could grab one. He stepped carefully backwards.

A rapping of knuckles on wood.

Burglars didn't knock.

A voice. 'Ashten! I can see you. Open the door.'

It didn't sound threatening. It sounded upset. Near to tears. Also, female.

'Wait,' called Hugo. He found the key.

A girl stalked in. She had mud on her elbows and knees. She must have crawled through the hoarding. Or over it. A woolly hat was pulled down to her eyebrows. A scarf up to her mouth. Together they made a kind of balaclava that only showed her eyes, which were furious.

'Where is he?'

Hugo went to their room. Ash was still asleep, unaware.

At some point in the days they had been here, as they stopped using words, his name became just a syllable. Ash.

Hugo shook Ash until he woke, complaining.

..

The next morning, the girl's woolly hat poked out of the top of Ash's sleeping bag. Ash was not there.

Hugo sat up, offended. She was in their space.

Where was Ash? He went to the kitchen. He climbed the wrapped stairs.

In a bathroom on the upper floor, Hugo found him. Ash had

improvised a bed in the sunken tub, lined with plastic, cardboard and a wad of yellow fluff used to insulate the roof. Elaborate lengths to avoid her.

'Has she gone?'

'She's downstairs in your sleeping bag.'

'Can you get rid of her? I can't talk sense into her.'

Hugo's mind was heaving with music. He needed to work, not talk to a stranger. But he could see that Ash was going to hide until she had gone.

'You haven't got her pregnant, have you?'

Ash let him know he hadn't.

Hugo went downstairs. He found the girl in the kitchen, discovering that the cupboards had no shelves. The bobble hat cupped her head, covering her ears, forehead and the nape of her neck, so she looked like a knitted pixie.

'I'm Kate,' she said, with an emphasis that implied he should know who she was. I'm *Kate*. He didn't know Kate. Kates were not the kind of thing he and Ash talked about.

'I've come all the way from Shropshire. I had to see him.'

Hugo made instant coffee. Apologised for the lack of milk, though not for the lack of Ash. Last night's dope had given him an epic appetite. He took a loaf of sliced bread from the fridge and made toast. He hoped the smell would rise up the stairs to punish the cowardly fugitive.

Kate didn't eat anything. She stood hunched over her mug, hollow with sadness.

'He's not gay, you know. Very definitely. In case you think you've got him to yourself.'

Hugo ate toast.

Kate put one hand over her face. 'It's been hell. I thought he might be dead. Please could I have one of those cigarettes?'

Hugo passed her the pack of Silk Cut, which they used for making joints.

Kate picked up the lighter on the worktop and touched the fag to the flame. Sucked on it, breathed out, studied the burning end. 'I'm sorry. We did everything together.' She took a tissue from her pocket and blew her nose, which was red from crying. 'You can't imagine.'

Hugo couldn't imagine; that was true. He hadn't had serious relationships. He didn't have time. And he'd seen several people on his college course have romances that turned into all-consuming turmoil. It seemed insane to risk that situation, considering what they needed to achieve. Some of them failed their year. If Hugo failed, his scholarship would be gone.

Hugo was sure that Kate had good reason to complain. Ash wouldn't be a considerate boyfriend.

He asked Kate if she'd known him long.

'He worked for my uncle's building firm. I was with someone else but Ashten just swept me away. We were living together, from the start. Then he didn't come home. I had the police out; everything. Eventually, one of the guys from our building firm told me they'd seen him on a subcontractor's job down here.'

This sad, fickle history didn't surprise him. Hugo wasn't fluent in talking about relationships, but he could see Kate needed a guy who took them seriously. It would not help to say that.

He was still stoned. But maybe he could make her see something positive so she could move on. He said it was terrible their relationship had ended, but it hadn't disappeared now that they were no longer together. It had still happened, it still existed at its own point in time. He was surprised he was able to be so sensible and profound.

'You don't know what it's like,' she said.

She continued to talk.

It seemed she wasn't looking for solutions or even replies. She was giving voice to the feelings that would not lie quiet inside her.

He began to find her captivating. Music was still snowing from his sleeping mind. Her words fell into it, a free-form aria. This love affair was the most staggering, mysterious thing that had ever happened to her. She had waited for it her whole life. She was saying these things about Ash, who told tall stories about seeing spirits leave dying bodies on a highway, and yes she related this incident to Hugo without a shred of doubt. Also, the lions and the hotel murder in Scarborough. He knew they weren't true, but her sorrow made Ash into someone transforming, someone who knew what things really were, who made you crave to belong with him, in his remarkable world. Every morning she had feared she didn't deserve him, but he would be there, sleeping beside her, which proved she did deserve him after all. Hugo began to feel dizzy with it, and humbled, as if witnessing a force that made humanity helpless, like violent weather.

Gradually she talked herself dry. Checked her watch. 'I'd better leave.'

She shouldn't go out alone. 'I'll walk you to the station.'

'I've got a car.'

He walked her to the door, warning her about the hole at the threshold. Unlocked the gates for her. In the road outside, tilted on the kerb beside the hoarding, was a white Mini with a fluffy fish tied on the rear-view mirror.

'People like you have turned his head,' she said tartly as she put the key in the ignition. Hugo hadn't heard a phrase like that since Bonnet. He thought it very ungracious, considering all the listening he'd done.

She drove away up the frost-speckled road.

Hugo went to the keyboard.

..

Ash came down.

'She's gone,' said Hugo. 'You could at least have talked to her.'

Ash picked up the mic. 'What are we working on?'

Hugo swapped the output from his headphones to the amp and unleashed the sound. He taught Ash the song. 'Girl In The Night.'

Ash sang. If he recognised that Hugo was writing about Kate and what she'd told him, he didn't care. He sang with all his substance.

The sun came in through the plastic-covered window. It glowed in the steam off their coffee mugs, in the clouds of their breath. They were drenched in hard, howling sound and it was amazing.

Then they made mini-Stonehenges out of cigarette packets.

..

On Christmas morning, the bells rang out from the little needle steeple in the valley. Hugo and Ash set their own roof ringing. Ash seized whatever Hugo wrote and sang as if it magnified his life, made him significant. It made Hugo significant too.

It was so cold. They wore coats. Hugo found a Stanley knife and sliced the fingertips off his gloves so he could wear them as he played. They made the freezing house sweat with sound. Later they lit the roaring burner and lay in the sleeping bags, close together for warmth in a languor of dope, devising harmonies until they turned the heater off and let its scorching glow fade to black.

..

The buzzer sounded on the evening after Boxing Day. Hugo was returning, at a shivering run, from the cold cement bathroom.

From outside came voices. Music. An idling engine, deep and throbbing. Ash's other masters.

Hugo skipped across the trench by the front door and went out.

Waiting outside the gate was a stretch limousine. A wedge of reddish light came out of its open door. A guy was stamping his feet on the icy pavement. Hugo disliked the look of him. His eyes were prominent, like a greedy amphibian.

The guy opened Hugo's coat with one hand. 'Are you coming too?' He grasped the front of Hugo's jeans.

It was sudden, obscene. Hugo shoved the man away.

'Ooh,' said the man. 'Skittish.' The music throbbed, lewdly.

Ash stepped out from the gate. 'Are you coming with us, H?'

Hugo backed away, unable to speak. Did nobody think there was anything unusual in what just happened? Had Ash seen what the man did to him?

Ash's eyes had a Mata Hari intensity. He was wearing eyeliner. He climbed into the red interior. 'See you later.'

The door closed. The limo glided into the dark. Hugo was cold to the core, but he continued to watch the car, bothered by it, its retreating rear lights like red mocking eyes.

..

The next day, Ash and Hugo walked down the hill in the winter sunlight. To buy groceries and cigarettes, visit the laundrette.

'You really think that guy will get you a record deal?' said Hugo.

'The lyrics to "Later" suck,' said Ash.

The days were short. The nights were long. The December darkness fixed them in their ice-cold, polythene-wrapped, moon-illumined, cement-walled, jet-roaring cathedral of sound. No one else came to disturb them.

They lay in their sleeping bags, hazed with dope. Hugo thought how neither of them had any money, but at least he was set for a qualification. He could teach music while he tried to make other things happen. But Ash?

'You don't have to live like this. You could go home.'

'Says the guy who ran away to London. Anyway, I'm meeting people.'

A frog-eyed man leering and groping in a perfumed limousine. 'Is that your best hope? Those people?'

'Do you know it's January the second?' said Ash. 'We went through New Year.'

27

May 2014. The fourth Ashbirds album was going well. In the control room, Robert watched Paul at the Steinway.

Hugo said: 'He's good. And he's been out of music until now?'

'I guess we all have wilderness years,' said Gil.

Paul played to the end of the track, lifted his hands away and let the instrument spread the final echoes. He had the certainty of his art.

Hugo flicked the talkback. 'Fantastic, Paul. I'm happy if you are.'

Paul came into the control room. Hugo high-fived him, gripped his hand.

'We were just talking about our wilderness years,' said Gil. 'Where did you spend yours?'

'CallMe.'

Blank looks.

'CallMe,' said Paul. 'Call Me please I'm gonna be a star. Call Me please get me out of this cubicle. Call Me please I'm not like the others. Call Me because nobody ever does.'

'Christ,' said Hugo. 'You're well out of there.'

They continued on the new song, 'Sun and Air'. Hugo then taught them some fun songs to keep behind the scenes, which they used to sing on the tour bus. There was an a cappella arrangement of Kraftwerk's Trans Europe Express album. Hugo directed them to imitate the robotic burbles of Kraftwerk's synths, in stacked harmony and German accents. They were mischievous, meditative and moreish. He also taught them the highly secret and unreleasable 'Turned His Head', subtitled 'The National Anthem for Bonnet'. Paul improvised another napalm verse, on the spot. He'd got very comfortable with Hugo suddenly.

..

Robert walked out of the studio afterwards with Paul.

' "Turned His Head" is a great lyric,' said Paul.

Robert waited for the kicker. Something snide, sneering.

Paul sucked cigarette fumes into his lungs .'Take the swearing out, write it properly and it'll chart. He should release it. That melody is so hooky.'

What happened to the Paul who had a low opinion of everyone but himself?

'Well,' said Robert, 'you've always got CallMe.'

'No, this is good. We're cooking now.'

'Until Hugo changes his mind and we no longer have jobs. Tomorrow he might erase it or record a heap of crap we can't use. Me, I'll be okay because I've got other contacts. You've just got to think what you'll do.'

Paul did go quiet then.

28

Elza received a picture by email from Oliver Jared. The white hallway of the townhouse. The Havisham clock, in the banded light of the shutters.

He included a note.

Dear Elza, I hope all is well. I still have these shutters. The clock loves them. I am thinking about more art to go with them. Would you be available for a meeting? If not, I understand.

No, she wasn't available to make a work for Oliver Jared. She was preparing to paint a portrait of the principal of a private school.

She finished the email to the school, explaining what she would need for the sitting.

Oliver Jared needed a reply. Her reply would be no.

But if she said no, he wouldn't stop wanting an artwork. He'd commission someone else. *If not, I understand.* That sign-off said so.

She should visit him, to see what he had in mind.

..

They met at the townhouse. In the kind, striped light, Oliver Jared laid his laptop on the bleached floorboards and gave a rambunctious hand-clap like an eager games teacher, which made her want to duck.

'First, the basement room. Something like this.' He clicked a file: a stock photo of Everest at sunrise, its tip glowing orange. A white valley with an avalanche.

So far, so predictable. Just like her juvenilia sketchbook and the stuff fans posted on the internet. But this was how she would find out what he wanted. She asked her standard questions. Was this artwork to be a painting? How was the room to be used? For games, as a den?

'A temporary public gallery. While the album is being made. What about a mini-theatre with a screen, with a day and night on Everest. Lots of ideas. Whatever you want.'

Whatever she wanted. Did she want it?

If she didn't, another artist would, and they would decide what they wanted.

There were also practical questions. He was going to let the public in? Did he know about liability insurance and fire exits?

'I used to have a café. Steve will be my security consultant. We'll make everything white. The seats, the walls, everything. We give people white robes to wear. They become part of a glacier.'

He might rethink when he saw what was and wasn't possible, or what it might cost. So red tape might kill it, and at least that would mean she had not.

'I can't start properly for about a month,' she said. 'I have a portrait to paint.'

If Oliver Jared was impatient to start immediately, it couldn't be done.

'No problem.' He climbed the stairs. 'Come up. I've got another idea to show you. Oh, and the boys are playing a gig here in about three weeks.'

'In the house?'

'In the house,' replied Oliver. 'I can't wait.'

A gig in the house? Red tape might kill that too.

..

Red tape did not kill the gig.

Or the artworks.

So when the band played the gig, Elza was in the townhouse, starting work in the room on the first floor, which was to be a gallery of fan tributes for display on the website.

The fan tributes were letters, drawings, CDs of home-made cover versions. Delivered in grey postal sacks. Enough for ten rooms. Ten houses.

Right now, the gallery room was a hideout for the band. Robert Speed was pacing, playing an imaginary bass. Left hand making agile patterns on the fretboard, right hand plucking strings. A broad guy with a grey ponytail and a waistcoat was playing a round rubber pad on the table, very fast, like the woodpecker that wouldn't stop pecking.

Hugo Bird was reading lyrics silently on his phone, taking swigs from a plastic cup and gargling.

A guy with a squashed-up face was playing fast scales on a keyboard that made no sound. He looked like he was tickling it, with a very serious expression. He'd parked it on a stack of fan letters. The letters were inching over the edge of the table, like the arcade machines that push coins towards a gulf where they might drop but never do.

Steve put his head in. Two minutes.

The guys stopped rehearsing. They formed a circle around the ponytailed drummer, who held his sticks in a cross shape. They touched the sticks, murmured some ritual words, then filed out in silence.

The room was hers again.

Elza lifted the keyboard. The letters avalanched onto her feet. She bent to pick them up.

The letters were to be a collage of the public's affection for the band.

Oliver Jared had sorted them, culling anything crazy. That was one of her conditions. But the first letter she picked off the floor was written in silver ink in a shape like a gravestone, bordered with flowers. *Do not mourn, Elza. We keep him alive with our breath. We play him every day. There isn't a day we don't miss him. He is as alive as ever.*

She and Oliver would have to chat about definitions of crazy.

If she opened the blinds she would see a street full of waiting fans, fans who had queued for hours, not minding the heavy June rainstorms, and might write letters like that.

From the room below came an amplified shiver. The band were plugging in. Outside there were gasps. Cheers. Applause. A voice shouted: Ashbirds.

Beneath her feet, the music began.

Her phone flashed a message. Gina, in hysterical capitals. *I'M LISTENING ON THE RADIO. THEY'RE MAKING HISTORY!*

Elza thumbed a reply: *I know. I'm sitting on top of it. Hate people who play loud music while I'm trying to work.* A smiley, so she knew it wasn't too serious.

Obviously she wasn't in the best spot, acoustically, but the music didn't sound great to her. Brash and rattly, as if it was being played on kitchen pots.

..

The set was over. The band were climbing the stairs, noisily, coming back to hide. A safe exit was as important as the performance, Steve always said.

Robert came in and hugged her, which was something he never did. He wasn't in his usual mind. The scrunch-faced keyboard guy hugged her as well, which was less welcome because there was something slavering about him, like an Alsatian dog that has seen meat. By the time Gil and Hugo barrelled in through the door, she made sure she was standing behind a chair.

They were all talking with one triumphant voice, about acoustic difficulties with the room, and the couple who won tickets to sit with them and kissed ravenously through the whole set. They all moved and spoke with an unmistakable strut that was indeed like having Ashten back, except multiplied by four, which was far too much.

29

The next morning, Oliver Jared breezed into the control room wearing red braces like a stockbroker clown, praised everyone for the gig, listened to 'Sun and Air', then shared his next genius idea. Robert had warning prickles before he even spoke.

'Hugo, have you looked at the fan poetry in the Glacier House? They've reworked some of the hits. You'd be surprised how good they are. We could offer a very special Kickstarter with revisited versions.'

A ghastly suggestion, but exactly what Robert was used to.

Hugo spoke. 'Let's have a break. Fifteen minutes.'

Paul left. Furtively. He wasn't doing so well today. His face had a dragged look. His eyes looked like tiny nail holes in a slab of wood. How much had he drunk to look like that?

Hugo moved close to Robert. 'Get some coffee into Paul. He's wrecked.'

Never mind Paul. They needed to straighten Oliver Jared. 'I'd better stay,' Robert replied softly. 'I'm experienced with these situations.'

Hugo looked meaningfully at the door. 'Paul needs a chat. You know him better than I do. I want him ready for this afternoon.'

He turned away, closing Robert out.

Cheers, thought Robert. Plonkers like Oliver Jared have been my daily grind for years. You've no idea what you're dealing with. But you want me to be the babysitter.

..

Robert found Paul in the break room, sagging into the sofa. The New Surface had left presents again. A silver bowl of white mischief. Paul was lining up a cigarette with his lips, but his desire was in that snowy heap. It had already blown holes through his brain. He should just get it done.

Robert pulled a bottle of mineral water from the fridge. 'Had a hard night?'

'I quit CallMe. Yesterday.'

'Is that wise?'

'CallMe is Heartbreak Hotel.'

And now you're in Terrified Towers. So am I, nannying your needy nervousness. Instead, I should be in the control room to stop them ruining the album of my entire career.

'Well don't make it everyone else's problem. Sort your shit out. We've got a long afternoon.'

'A long afternoon of what? It's a funfair for the fans now. That's what he wants. A tribute band.' His spitting laugh. 'No, the tribute bands are more real than we are.' He crouched over the bowl. 'Come on. A quick one. We need it.'

His eyes had a flirtatious gaze.

I always knew you'd be slippery, Paul. You could be writing songs with me. Two of us against one Hugo; together we could put our mark on this album, launch ourselves as songwriters. That's why I brought you in. But you saw the drugs and that was it; you looked for an excuse to dive in. And I've sussed what you do. You don't want to sink alone. You'll drag me with you for company. I can't believe I worked so hard to get you here. Now I'm stuck with you, playing addicts' mind games, when I should be in that control room where the band's future is being made. My future.

A gout of smoke escaped from the dark hole of Paul's mouth, like something evil rolling out of a cave. Robert went to the door. 'Perhaps check what that stuff is before you take any of it.'

He returned to the control room.

Hugo and Jared were shaking hands. All fine, a misunderstanding. Continue as you are, it's great. And my helicopter, do borrow it. Say the word.

God knows what Hugo said. Robert had been out of the room for just five minutes.

30

Gina stood in front of the bride and groom.

The bride's dress was dark green. The rest of the party wore the same green in a scarf, a waistcoat, a tie. In it together.

As Gina began the ceremony, she had a view that no one else did; every face, ready for her. At this moment, they were open with their feelings. Sometimes there were less positive emotions. Unease, which could be about anything. Perhaps about the couple's decision to marry. Perhaps their choices for the occasion. She never found out.

Her role at this time was to unite them all, smooth their differences, sweep them into the significance. A couple were making their commitment. Witnessing it was an honour.

But sometimes a doubter would not let go. Gina could see it now. The groom's brother wore the green, but did not join the smiles, the laughs or the applause.

She wrapped up the ceremony, shook hands and wished them well, the only one who had seen it.

She knew that unease very well. It couldn't be won round. It was too complex.

Robert also had it. He was always fighting inside. She wondered if he'd eventually find a political cause, because fighting seemed his natural state, but he had no interest in politics. His sense of wrong wasn't about world injustices. It seemed interior, about himself.

She used to try to talk to him about it. What's wrong? If work is the problem, what else could you do in this business? You have so much experience. He sensed her intention before she even started. He turned the shower on and locked the bathroom door, a decisive, excluding click. They never locked the bathroom door. Then later he came to find her. Put his arms around her, tilted his stubbled head on her shoulder, his usual greeting. She sometimes joked it was the way a billiard ball would say hello. Now it was hello, can we start that again? It's not you, he said.

If it's not me, what is it? Sometimes she said that. She didn't expect an answer. He probably didn't know.

Right now, they needed to renew the render on the house. Gina tried to discuss it as they were going to bed. Let's give the builder a start date. I can't think about it, he said, and went out with his bike. In the middle of the night.

He did that a lot. She'd see him going to the front door fastening his helmet. He hadn't even said he was thinking about going out.

After the wedding ceremony, she answered some emails, then met a friend for lunch. Harry, who she'd known since they trained as registrars. In a pub with brick arches and workbench tables, they shared a sticky slab of cheesecake served artisanally on a slate roof tile. Harry liked to change career every few years and was now in a niche of education she couldn't quite grasp. He'd also had a recent cancer scare, which came as news to her.

Harry had had cancer? God, they'd been bad at keeping in touch.

Usually she and Robert held regular dinner parties, but right now, if Gina suggested a weekend to invite people, Robert said he might need to work. But the band kept office hours, so why? Still, that was the mood he was in. Builders couldn't be booked and neither could weekend guests. So when Harry said he was in town for a training course, Gina nabbed him for lunch.

And what did she find? Harry had had cancer. While you wait for life to be less busy, your lovely friend who bumbled from one profession to another, did them all well and dressed like an eccentric home-knitted time-traveller, has been locking eyes with his own mortality.

He was in the clear now, thank God, so there was a lot of laughing.

'You know when they give you an MRI scan,' he said, 'they ask your favourite music so they can play it to drown the noise of the machine. But do you want your favourite music ruined by the most terrifying time of your life?'

Gina asked which music he chose to ruin. Harry mentioned a novelty pop group based on a children's TV show. Gina gasped. 'Robert works with the guy who used to be their drummer.' So she explained what Robert was doing.

Harry put down his spoon and stared like an owl. He'd heard the gig on the radio yesterday. Seriously, Robert was there, playing in the actual Ashbirds set?

Seriously yes, she said. She ate three mouthfuls of sweet lactic gloop while Harry asked the question from all possible directions.

'You know what?' said Harry. 'Sue is organising the school's summer concert next year.'

Harry's wife was head of science at an expensive school in Cambridge.

'We've got Dream Report this year because the lead singer's son is in the juniors. The school is paying a cut of ticket sales to the British Heart Foundation. Would Robert get us Ashbirds next year? It's much more the parents' era than Dream Report. They'd go wild.'

'Ah, he can't do that.'

Harry looked confused. She wasn't surprised. People often didn't get this.

'Robert's not actually an Ashbird. He's a session player they've hired. Ashbirds was two guys. Well, one guy now, obviously, and he's retired. He climbs mountains. He's come back to do one album and that's it.'

Harry still looked confused. 'But isn't Robert in the band? You said he's working on the album...'

'It's all work-for-hire. Like a carpenter who builds a kitchen in one house, a bookcase in another. He turns up, does what they tell him, goes to another job. So by next summer when your concert is, Robert will be working for someone else, writing music for air freshener again or whatever comes along.'

Harry looked at her with concern. She must have sounded so weary. She dug another spoonful and said brightly. 'And in a few months we will be back to normal. Get your diary out, let's sort a dinner date.'

31

In 1991, Hugo and Ash were making their second album. When ideas wouldn't come, they drank vodka martinis in a club called Fire in Regent Street, a basement full of red glowing steam like a spaceship emergency, where bands and producers played demos of tracks they thought were possible singles. If Hugo and Ash were lucky, a beat or harmonic colour would send them urgently back to the studio with ideas. If they weren't, they had monstrous hangovers the next day.

Or Hugo did. Ash claimed he never had hangovers. Hugo didn't believe him.

They recorded videos in wrecked warehouses and rusted gasometers. Ash prowled, singing, through angled shafts of sunlight, wearing a floor-skimming coat that made him look like the last survivor on a Byronic battlefield. Hugo stayed in the shadows, swaying at a piano or ripping a rhythm out of a guitar.

You couldn't put a guitar on Ash. He had no chemistry with it. He held it like a plank. You couldn't video Hugo if he wasn't playing an instrument or he looked like he'd been caught with no clothes on.

They got used to interviews. Hugo didn't like them. Ash liked them a lot. He made journalists feel like they were meeting royalty, even though Ashbirds had only made one album. He invited them to a private room at Ari Markson's club, which was full of brash art that suggested the members were adventurous in their tastes and dripping with wealth. Ash ordered drinks for them, talked about whatever they wanted, and was never reluctant to flirt.

Hugo had no patience with interviews. He told Ash what to say about the song lyrics and left him to it.

Hugo didn't read the interviews. He had no idea what Ash said in them. One day in the studio lounge, Ash walked in, talking on a mobile phone.

Hugo was thinking with a notebook, trying to nail a lyric.

'Yes, we're proud of that one,' said Ash, obviously talking to a reporter.

Hugo needed a break. Which song was Ash talking about? Ash mentioned the title. 'I Found Your Letters.' An album track. Another ambitious one he had to draft about a hundred times, but eventually it came right. You just had to trust the process. At the end of all that frustration, if you did your job, a critic would be telling Ash how much he liked it.

Ash said, on the phone: 'It's about someone finding their old letters.'

What? No it wasn't. Hugo waved at Ash.

Ash sat down, spread his arm across the back of the sofa and looked away from Hugo. 'Yeah,' he said to the journalist. 'After an old romance.'

Hugo slapped his notebook loudly on the glass coffee table. It didn't put Ash off. Hugo stared, demanding Ash's response. What are you doing?

Ash did look at him then. A nod. I've got this.

No, Ash hadn't got it. 'I Found Your Letters' was inspired by his parents' shop in Bonnet. The letters and photos that were never claimed, the saved memories that no one now cared about, left for a stranger to throw away. It was a human tragedy, an entire life vanishing unnoticed into time. Ash's explanation made it tepid and average, a sentimental self-indulgent woe-is-me whine.

'I found some letters from a girlfriend I was with in my teens,' said Ash, 'and that's how the song happened.' There was a tender, confessional edge in his voice now, no doubt encouraged by the reaction he was getting from the reporter on the other end. He was working her.

Unbelievable. Hugo had to leave the room.

...

They met American record executives in a hotel in Tottenham Court Road. We have a title for your new album, said the Americans. Radio stations have gone nuts for bands from Manchester, so we want to call your album *Manchester*.

'We haven't named the album yet,' said Hugo, 'and we're not from Manchester.'

'We're from a place called Bonnet,' said Ash. 'In Shropshire.'

'ShropshEAR,' the execs repeated, looking uncertainly at each other.

Hugo and Ash left Ari Markson to sort it out. They were due on stage in east London.

'There are press outside,' said the hotel manager, and unlocked a door to a service corridor.

'I thought you were showing us to a bedroom,' said Ash with a wink. Because not enough people had adored him in the past five minutes.

The manager looked like her legs would buckle, exactly as Ash intended. 'I'll come with you and show the way,' she said.

'No thanks,' said Hugo, we're fine. People were always trying to follow them, spend longer with them.

A lot of old city hotels had secret corridors. They refurbished, divided rooms, moved walls, colonised adjoining buildings. The leftover gaps became a warren of hidden passageways for staff to use as room-service short-cuts or to smuggle a dead guest to a back door. These corridors were always full of noises. Glassy chinking, squeaking trolley wheels, voices shouting in several languages, which mostly sounded like hysterical arguing.

Ash and Hugo walked, imitating the way the Americans pronounced *ShropshEAR* and other words, until Ash said: 'Is this the right way?'

They'd been walking for a while, past unpainted plasterboard walls and dim light bulbs, which were going on for ever.

'Maybe the other way,' said Hugo.

They went back to the door. It was locked. They nearly didn't find it because the wall was made in sections that were all roughly door size.

They walked on. Hugo pushed random panels with his hand. Anything might be a door.

'We could have let her show us the way,' said Ash.

Hugo pushed a section of wall and it opened. At last. A set of spiral stairs, scuffed in a way that suggested they hadn't been painted since wartime. A breeze came from above. Bird feathers and crusted guano; it must go to the roof. Hugo saw a fire door, down below. 'Here we go,' he said happily, and ran to it. They were practically outside now.

The door was trussed with a chain. Hugo yanked the lever bar and shook everything, but nothing opened. 'They can't lock a fire door,' he said and ran back up the stairs. He glimpsed Ash's profile, backlit by a stingy bulb. He didn't look at Ash's face as he passed him.

'We're on in an hour,' said Ash. 'We've still got to get across London.'

Hugo knew that.

Back among the sounds of rattling china and multilingual strife, they set off again.

'We won't miss our gig,' said Hugo. 'They know we're coming.'

'H, the manager knew the way out.'

'If I see her, I'll ask her,' snapped Hugo. It was time for Ash to shut up about that. 'The venue will bump our spot to later. We'll call them from the car.'

On the other side of the wall, two voices were having a pelting row in Brummie accents.

Ash said: 'I don't understand why you didn't let her come with us.'

Because. A whole truckload of because. Because Ash wanted everything to be a cabaret, and to be the biggest light in the room. Hugo said: 'It's just another person who wants to bother us.'

'You don't have to talk to them.'

Well maybe he should talk to them. After what Ash told that journalist about the song.

'I said,' repeated Ash, 'you don't have to talk to them. I do that.' Ash couldn't stand it if someone didn't connect with him. If they held back. He smelled it. He'd charm and claw to the small locked space where you were hiding from him. That was his talent. 'H, why are you in such a mood?'

Jeez, that tone. So hurt, so suddenly sensitive, as if he'd been unjustly told off.

'I told you what to say about that bloody song.'

That song?

Hugo had to explain. The interview. Which interview? Most conversations with other people seemed to be like interviews. Hugo reminded him, so he was exactly clear which interview and which bloody song.

Ash began walking again, fast. 'I know what that song's about.'

Hugo pursued him, with a backing chorus of yelling Brummies. 'It was not about you. And now you've made it into trivial mush. Think about it. *"All your moments, I'm your only witness."* How does that line make any actual sense if the song is about you?'

'Don't tell me what I should say about a song.'

'You don't mind being told what to sing. Or taking the credit for writing it. You'll hijack Jim Morrison's life to make yourself sound cool. But you can't be arsed to listen when I tell you what a song is about.'

A piece of wall opened. A broad-shouldered guy stepped through and asked if they'd seen a Dalmatian.

That was a security code. He was their driver for the night. They knew that already, before he ever spoke the password. They could tell when a guy had been sent to find them.

Hugo said hi. Ash muttered a surly hello. Normality was returning. Strangers popped up to do things for them, ask them if they needed anything. Smuggled them into hiding places, led them out of labyrinths.

Hugo and Ash followed the guy through the wall, down another wartime staircase, to a fire door, which wasn't padlocked because the guy's job was to know that. They walked out into a yard that smelled slimy and citrusy, past dustbins as big as coal sheds. Behind them, the door closed. It was a piece of wall, a section of brick on a hinge, which they had come out of like a secret entrance. Exactly the sort of sudden and ridiculous thing that happened to them all the time. Hugo nudged Ash to look at it, and Ash laughed, as Hugo knew he would.

'These hotels are a nightmare,' said the guy, and opened the back door of a black Merc. 'I used to work security here. A lot of the staff don't know all the short-cuts. By the way, my name's Steve.'

Hugo shook his hand. 'Nice to meet you, Steve.'

32

August 2014. Steve was with Hugo on the patio of a farmhouse that overlooked the Shropshire plain. Instead of a garden it had a tumble of bare heath and a vast view of sky and distant fields.

The Long Mynd, the high plateau of moorland near Bonnet, where Hugo grew up.

Steve felt privileged to be invited. Hugo didn't let many people into his family patch. After Ashten died, the press sniffed their way to the village and tried to whip up a feud between the two guys' families. Once the courts allowed the death certificate to be issued, the Geddards moved to New England with the money from Ashten's estate and the press got tired of Shropshire.

In the distance, a helicopter, supplied by Oliver Jared, wheeled through the sky, a buzzing black tadpole high in the clouds. His pilot, Ian, was taking Hugo's aunt and two uncles for a ride.

Inside, the farmhouse was smart and modernised. Walls of lime plaster and bare brick. Steve could see the influence of Hugo in a wall hanging and a woven rug, with a design of wide-eyed dragons and geometric Nepalese insignia.

From the kitchen came the swoosh of a tap and the snap of the kettle lid as Hugo made tea. On the wall was a display of framed pictures. Now Steve saw why Cassie, Martin and Tom had been so thrilled to be offered a whirl in the helicopter. They were sky junkies. Most of the pictures showed a family member posing with a glider or paraglider, or sitting in a contraption of struts and canvas. Did they really fly in that? It looked like a tent with its clothes off.

There were a few pictures of Hugo, which broke the aviation theme. One at a gleaming black piano, with downy short hair and intense brows. He looked as young as a fawn. Steve recognised the shot from *NME*. Another was typical of recent years – in a padded parka on the summit of a mountain, eyes and smile scrunched against the sun, a crumpled tinfoil sea of blue and silver mountains behind him.

The beat of the helicopter came closer. Steve glanced out of the window and saw its black body descending to the grass. The runners skimmed along the ground. He saw hands at the cabin window, waving like excited children, then the craft lifted upwards. Ian was showing off. Hugo's folks were loving it.

Later, Cassie, Martin and Tom had a barbecue on the patio. The conversation was easy. News about other relatives. Who had started a new career or business; whose children were entering secondary school; who was divorcing; who was remarrying. Escapades from running the gliding club. The club Christmas party the previous year. Hugo replied in kind with amusing anecdotes about recording the album, climbing, the weekends spent running marathons for the avalanche relief fund. Steve was begged for stories about getting Hugo out of trouble and everyone laughed themselves into helpless, eye-wiping gulps.

In their faces, Steve could see Hugo's strong nose and take-no-shit gaze. The resemblance was close, even their yen for deathtrap hobbies. But as they matched his stories about narrow escapes and daredevilry, Steve could see another conversation. You've been away for so long. Isn't it time you settled back here with your clan? And he could see that Hugo, although he shared so much with them, did not fit here at all.

33

Elliot called at Oliver Jared's townhouse to collect Elza on his way home and was faced with the sham clock they got rid of five months earlier.

The first time he saw it here, Elliot had been surprised. That thing is part of the installation?

It's important to the client, Elza told him. She'd said that a few times in the eight weeks she'd been working here.

Now, her voice called from a room on the first floor. 'The basement's finished. Go and look.'

The basement was a wide space, hollowed out from a cellar and part of the garden. It had skylights that Elza had sealed with blackout material so the only illumination came from the stairwell. Elliot could see items hanging from the ceiling on threads. Gloves. Some climbing gear, savage-looking clips and pins. The floor was a mirror, so the objects reflected downwards like a very still pool. Several familiar sounds scratched at the edge of his hearing. The soft jetstream of computer fans. The ruminating mutter of hard drives.

Elza pattered down the stairs, her tread fast like a tapdancer. A run-by kiss. 'Stay there.'

Her reflection walked upside-down as she crossed the room. She bent in the corner, opened a laptop.

Gina arrived as the magic began. The light became soft and pearly. Images appeared between the hanging gloves and crampons. Ice axes, like extravagant, curve-toothed hammers. A blue rope, stretched through the hanging objects like a travelling snake. A fleece, its arms forever flying as it fell. An antique climbing boot. More metalwork, some of it bent or snapped. All moving between the suspended objects like slow fish.

'Elza, that's gorgeous,' said Gina.

Elliot wasn't sure what he thought. Or what he was expecting. Perhaps he hoped Elza would make a work that was a personal statement. This was slick and polished, but about as personal as her standard comments to *Hello* magazine. Compare it with the mural of night road signs they'd stripped off her kitchen wall. That seemed torn from a real piece of her.

From the laptop, she added a further layer. Rings, necklaces, pebbles, rosebuds. An earring made of a peacock feather. Pages from a calendar. Appearing, disappearing in a ghostly mirage.

Beside the doorway was a wishing well and a sign. *Deposit items here for the People's Glacier.*

'That's lovely,' said Gina. 'The People's Glacier.' She looked at Elliot. 'You don't seem so keen.'

How sensitive Gina was to unease and ambiguity. Disconcertingly so. 'I'm sure it will play well in the newspapers,' he said.

'Oliver Jared called it the People's Glacier,' said Elza. 'When he announced it on the website. So I'm stuck with the name. We'll have to be careful with the stuff they leave. Today we were sent two pulled teeth.' She closed down the projection, leaving the hanging objects on their strings in the semi-darkness. Walked back across the mirror, on stilts of her own feet.

Back in the hall, Elliot heard voices from the upper storey. A chair scraped on the wood floor.

'Is Robert up there?' said Gina. She ran up the stairs, in wiggly hops because her tight skirt didn't allow her to stride. 'I love this house!'

Elliot didn't love the house. Perhaps Elza didn't either. But that wasn't something she would say, even to him.

34

Elza was back at the Glacier House the following lunchtime. The weather was drizzly, but still a small clutch of journalists and photographers kept watch. They called her name in a mash of accents; probably from agencies in Europe and America. She smiled. Otherwise they'd use the pictures they had already taken, when her face was not connected to her brain and she looked like a haddock.

Steve came out with a bin liner for their coffee cups. She knew he also wanted to check she was okay.

She was. When this happened all those years before, she'd been so tender and afraid. Their shouted questions, the pictures they snatched when she didn't expect it. They always shocked her, seemed to put her on trial. C'mon, luv, prove you deserve Ashten Geddard. But today, these guys, with their damp hair, wet faces and their gear under plastic bags, seemed to come in peace, to take a nostalgic story all over the world.

Oliver Jared's press agent was getting placements with pictures from the house. It wouldn't be officially ready for another fortnight, but the previews were starting. This morning, she saw a picture of her glacier on the news, followed by a report about people who had their dead bodies frozen in case they could be revived in the future.

There was a blogger who reviewed the gig. *After I heard it I felt so sad. I know they won't ever be together again, but … I don't know. I haven't yet figured it out.*

Elliot also said he couldn't figure it out. Hugo could have come back at any time in the last twenty years and made an album. Why now?

Hugo is not like the rest of us, said Elza.

Hugo walked out onto the landing. He was checking his phone, stepping backwards, trying to look at messages and at Oliver Jared, who he was talking to. Elza thought, he's going to walk into that banister. She watched him do it, as bewildered as she sometimes felt. He still dressed as though he might get the urge to leave all this and hike into the sunset. Shorts with pockets for holding maps. Walking boots.

She took off her coat, shook the dampness off and hooked it over the post at the foot of the stairs. She remembered Gina the day before, trying to hurry up them faster than her skirt would allow, calling 'I love this house!' That was how Gina ran at life, with a giant seizing embrace, giving it a chance to be wonderful instead of worrying about it.

Had she ever been like that herself? She didn't know. Like the blogger. *I haven't yet figured it out.*

35

Gina leaned into the band's trailer at the Forever Summer festival
in Hyde Park and spied on Robert, turning the tuning peg on his
bass. In his element, deaf to everything but the hoarse, unamplified
twang of the string.

Gil was pacing in a nervy strut, rapping his sticks on the walls.

A small guy with a scrunched face was playing scales at a
dummy keyboard.

She left them to it. She walked past trailers, broadcasters' vans
with dishes pointing to the sky, stepped over cables as thick as
pythons. Beyond the buzz of generators, the Hyde Park darkness
crackled with the crowd's anticipation. A restive shout. A why-are-
we-waiting whistle.

Steve passed her, talking to a headset, and pointed. She turned
and spotted Elliot, looking around, as though he feared he shouldn't
be here. She hugged him. He looked relieved to be seen, shocked to
be grabbed. He wasn't a hugger.

At the band's trailer, Steve gave the knock. Robert stepped out
carrying his bass, a glow in his face, as if going into a fight he knew
he would win. Then came Gil and the other guy. Hugo stepped down
from another trailer.

Gina put her arm through Elliot's, whether he liked it or not,
and followed them down a tent-tunnel to the stage. Elza grabbed
him from the other side. Steve overtook at a jog, talking into his
headset. Robert, Hugo, Gil and the short guy, silhouetted by the
tunnel lights. Black T-shirts. Black jeans. Sleek and striding, like a
staged photoshoot. Towards the crackling crowd.

Steve opened a door. They climbed a metal staircase that shook
with their footsteps. At the top, everywhere was black and big as a
cavern. It smelled of sweat. It prickled with the hum of live leads
and listening microphones and the rapt attention of a wide ocean of
people. Gina glimpsed the slender stalks of instrument stands, the
chrome trim on the drums, the white piano keys. All gleaming and
ready. She held back with Elza and Elliot. The skin-tight figures
padded onto the stage.

The stage was suddenly drenched with light. The drummer clicked four times. The sound plunged in. Beat, piano, bass. Swift, powerful, thrilling. Light, clicks, go.

Oh *yes*. This was it.

36

Elliot had never heard anything like it. The melody rolled out over the crowd. They sent back a roar of approving noise that shook the floor like a demolition.

Hugo stepped up to the microphone.

His voice soared. The audience howled again, a sound so savage that Elliot flinched. He didn't know how Hugo stayed in front of it, let alone how he sang, and with such angelic control and pitch. He must have astounding nerve. This wasn't a crowd. It was a vast linked consciousness of feral emotion.

The band played.

The crowd settled. By the first chorus they were gentled, swaying in the spell of the sound. Hugo's singing carried it all. Elliot had never heard better, not even in a classical concert. So strong and pure. Like hearing light.

Elliot was just twenty yards away from the four figures on the stage. This was Hugo, who he had met in Elza's Glacier House, and Robert, who he'd had dinner with on many occasions. He hadn't understood who they were at all. He knew they were talented and remarkable, but no description was equal to what he saw here.

After four tracks, a piano solo began.

The crowd, still applauding, became mystically, breathlessly silent.

Elza moved closer to him and stood rock still. On his other side, Gina did too.

There was probably not a person in the land who could not identify this song. Or a moment where it was not being played, somewhere in the world.

'Hurricane.'

Hugo began to sing.

Elliot thought he knew 'Hurricane'. It always seemed poignant and epic, but so overfamous that it barely held his attention. But Hugo, singing over the lilting, tumbling piano, made it startling and urgent. He walked to the front of the stage. Faces gazed up. Tiny stars swayed into the distance; a twinkling galaxy of phones. All were in thrall to his agile voice, which brought this song that belonged so personally to all of them and so indelibly to Ashten. Elliot was in thrall too, to the music, to this night, to this breathing sea of spellbound souls, to the enigma of Elza and all her people.

After the second chorus, the piano took the melody. Hugo stepped back and Robert blew a searing descant on sax. Elliot had forgotten to let his breath out. Just as he did, Hugo's voice returned, frayed with emotion yet still flawlessly on note.

The song chorused, faded, ebbed away. The audience was silent. Then it erupted in a thunderclap of shrieking, stamping noise. Gina exploded in a jumping frenzy of joy, hugging him, hugging Elza, waving wildly to Robert on stage. Robert couldn't possibly see her, his arms hanging slackly by his side as he let go of his instrument, gasping like a runner. An image of Ashten Geddard's face appeared on the back wall. The crowd screamed.

Elliot came back to his senses. He pressed Elza against him. She seemed stunned, then she pulled him tight.

On the stage, the drummer sat on his stool, his hands on his thighs, puffing and grinning. Hugo fastened the microphone onto the stand. He was looking down, away from the shrieking, shrilling faces that wanted more. He raised an arm in salute, first to them and then to Ashten's image behind them all, then jogged towards Elliot and the girls in the wings. The others left their instruments and followed him. Steve handed him a black towel and he hid his face in it, then hurried down the stairs.

Robert reached them. Gina grabbed him. He looked handsome, luminously happy. Elliot had never seen him like that, so open, with no suspicion or brooding ambiguity. Robert peeled off his sweat-sodden T-shirt and threw it at Gina with a grin that was a bit provocative and a bit ravenous. She caught it and chased him down the stairs.

37

Hugo stood in the shower. He closed his eyes, felt the rush of the water and its needle jets. The concert had gone by like an out-of-body experience. He had not stood on a stage for twenty years, yet it was familiar. Except he used to sit at the keyboards while Ash commanded the wildness at the front. This time, he had the front.

At first, he needed all his courage to stay there. Delivering his words and music directly to those eyes, mouths and reaching hands. Receiving their naked need and gratitude.

He showered for a long time.

He didn't know what to do next. He should be bickering with Ash about the mistakes. Paul missed a cue and Robert covered. Paul played a fill they axed in rehearsals and Gil soloed an extra twelve bars to cover another slip. He himself had fluffed some lyrics. No one in the audience would guess, but Ash, who was with him in his mind, expected better. And there were no mistakes to scold Ash for because Ash was not here.

Hugo would need a post-mortem with the band. But not right now.

That was why he'd claimed a trailer to himself.

He came out of the shower, finally. Dressed. Checked his phone. A missed call that had gone to voicemail. It was his aunt Cassie. 'Hugo, we saw you on TV and we're so proud of you. Lots of love from us all.'

He also had an email. He didn't recognise the sender. Charmian.

He read her message. *I have a present for you. I have a body.*

Who was Charmian? A groupie who'd got his personal number? He'd have to find out how to block her. Now his rock-star transformation was complete.

No, wait. The sick climber on the mountain in Argentina.

A body.

He began to understand. A body. From the ice.

I have a present for you. I have a body.

Charmian. Sneaking pictures of him, fishing for confidences by telling him confessional stories. A bit too eager to be intimate. No doubt she enjoyed being able to write the innuendo.

There was a second email from her. A picture.

He would have to look at it.

It was all pale. Pastel blue jacket, a white blare of snow. But definitely the shape of a head and shoulders.

Now what?

Hugo had forgotten the routine for this. The sad processes he used to know. His senses were still surfing on darkness and sound.

Look at the picture properly. Enlarge it. This might all be settled in a few seconds.

He sat down with the phone. Crept all over the picture, slowly, with a hammering heart, waiting for the hangman's drop of recognition. What could he see of the face? It was encased in ice, like white, wet glass. The outline of goggles was visible. That seemed a mercy. It hid the pit from brow to cheekbone, often so sunken and skullish. It also covered bone structure that might be identifiable.

There was no helmet. The hair was bleached white. The down jacket looked bleached too. It could have been there for twenty years or twenty days.

Was it Ash? The body was not wrapped. That meant it was still on the mountain, in the place where it was found. Perhaps it couldn't easily be moved.

Still, was this Ash?

Impossible to tell.

While Hugo was playing the set, this news had stolen into his phone. While he was out there, sending a cyclone of sound across the summer night, to all those faces, putting his breath into their music again. Was that real? This used to belong to both of them, him and Ash. Had that been real? Shuffle the years like a pack of cards and here he was, doing it without him.

He heard the thump and shimmer of distant amplified music. The Vaudeville Butchers were clashing through their hit 'Did You Do That Thing'. The crowd belonged to them. Ashbirds were gone already.

This picture on his phone. This was real. This picture was now.

He checked the time. He should reply, but Kathmandu was

nearly five hours ahead of London, so Charmian would probably be asleep. It could wait.

And besides, he didn't know what he wanted to say.

38

Elza rushed Elliot out to the backstage area. This wasn't his world, the sweaty thrashing of rock. Elliot preferred live music to be served by a choir or in an opera house, in formal dress, with music read from staves and guided by a conductor.

She told Steve: we're going home.

Wait for a minder, said Steve.

No need, she said.

Wrong answer, said Steve.

So now they were in the back of a black cab, accompanied by a squat-built earnest-faced lad from Steve's gym, who was wearing a phone earpiece with a glinting blue light.

'I'm not really a gig person,' said Elliot, 'but that concert was pretty awesome.'

'You liked it?'

'I don't think I could go to many, but I hadn't realised how good those guys are.'

The bodyguard, beside Elliot, found this amusing. His gaze patrolled the windows, left, rear, right, with a twitching smile.

Elza's phone trembled. She opened her bag. A message. From Steve.

Room 101, guys. We're meeting at the Glacier House.

She closed the bag.

She needed a few moments. Studied the podlike ceiling of the cab.

'What?' said Elliot.

She let him see the phone.

'What does that mean?' said Elliot.

'They've found a body.'

'Wow.'

Elza zipped the bag shut. 'Phenomenal timing, isn't it.' She laced her fingers into Elliot's, gripped them. Gripped hold of this moment, swaying against his shoulder as the cab cornered, with a pleasant homegoing tiredness, which they didn't have to change if they didn't want to.

'We can go straight there,' said Elliot. 'What number is the house? Thirty-four?'

'Perhaps we won't see the message until tomorrow.'

A confused look.

'I'm not doing this tonight. I've had a nice time and now I want to be in our bed. Besides, think who'll be there. The band who just played the world's biggest comeback gig. They will not be talking sense.'

The bodyguard grinned so widely that a gold tooth glinted beyond his canines.

'Our friend here says I'm right,' said Elza. She turned to the bodyguard. 'I never got your name.'

'Colin,' said the bodyguard. Colin closed his gold smile and concentrated on the amber-lit streets.

Elza leaned on Elliot's shoulder. 'I saw the guys after the Glacier House gig and they were high as whistles. We'll pick up with them tomorrow.'

The taxi stopped at their house. Colin watched from the back seat, a Buddha silhouette with a cyber-earpiece, as they opened the door. Elza waved him off, he saluted, and the cab pulled away.

Elliot didn't come in. 'Shall I go anyway? I'm wide awake now.'

'It's up to you. But we don't have to go to a meeting in the middle of the night. They're not thinking straight.'

'I'm a bit deafened. I need to freshen my head. I'll take a walk that way.'

39

Elliot walked out into the quiet streets. Elza was probably right that nothing useful would be decided, but Steve had asked them to come. Perhaps there was something to discuss. Circumstantial facts that someone might confirm one way or the other.

He couldn't sit at home, wondering.

Elliot pressed the bell and was buzzed in. The street light threw amber stripes through the frosted shutters. The projectors were silent. There were voices. He climbed the stairs, listening. If they were partying he'd wave, say congratulations, and leave.

'Our stock has never been higher, guys. The video of your set is on Radio Two's Facebook page and it's going bananas. Hell of a time for a body to pop out.' That must be Ari Markson, the band's manager. Elliot had met him once.

It didn't sound like a party.

They were sitting around the big table in the room where Elza made the collage of letters. Robert, Steve, Ari Markson, Oliver Jared, the guy who played the piano.

Robert was across the room in just two big strides, grasping Elliot's hand with a grip as strong as a fireman, pulling him to a chair. Oliver Jared radiated pride in his twinkling eyes. The event had left a glow on them.

Ari Markson had his arms spread across the back of two chairs. With his tailored suit, tan and open-necked shirt, he looked like a tycoon on a yacht, about to order cocktails. 'Elliot,' he called, 'what did you think of the gig?'

This wasn't a genuine wish to know his opinion, simply a way to say hello. Elliot said: 'Very impressive.' How insipid that sounded.

'The reviewer in *London Arts* said it made him feel ill,' said the pianist, who was introduced as Paul. Paul laughed. Nobody else laughed. Paul could not keep still. He jigged his foot nervily against the table leg.

Elliot's eye was drawn to a phone on the table. He knew it was Steve's because of the case, which seemed to be made from the tread of a bicycle tyre. On it was a picture.

Steve nudged it to Elliot for a proper look.

A picture. A face covered in snow. Whoa, that was a bit raw. No, last time there had been a picture. That's how this was done.

The face was covered. A relief. Also a shame. There would be no quick answers. Elliot studied it, in case he'd see a detail that would help, though what detail could he possibly help with? He suddenly noticed the hair. It was bleached white. As if the man's ordeal had turned him old before it killed him. Enough.

'Poor guy,' said Elliot, and passed the phone back.

'Did Elza go home?' said Steve.

Elliot nodded. 'It gets a bit much sometimes. I think she'd like it to be over. The bodies thing.'

'She's had a few this year,' said Steve.

'It's about time this was it,' said Robert.

'That,' said Ari Markson, still in cocktail position, 'would be bloody perfect. With the gig, the album, this house... completely perfect. So where is Hugo, by the way?'

Elliot realised Hugo Bird was missing.

'He's booking plane tickets,' said Steve.

'Listen, people.' Robert leaned forwards. His black leather jacket and the certainty in his posture made Elliot think of a virile, sleek gorilla. 'This isn't just about pleasing the fans or hitting the sweet spot. We need it to end, don't we, Elliot?'

Elliot was shocked to hear his own name. And shocked by Robert's direct eye on him. He felt slightly hypnotised, as if he was still at the edge of the stage, watching them in territory they ruled, accepting what they gave.

'It's nothing really to do with me,' said Elliot.

'Look at this,' said Robert, and stood Steve's phone up with the snow-masked face. 'Who's to say this isn't Ashten?'

'I suppose it might be,' said Elliot, though again, of all of them, he was least qualified to offer an opinion.

Ari Markson stretched his arms further across the chairs and said 'Keep the faith, Elliot', in a tone he probably used with a musician who had lost a deal.

Elliot didn't lack faith, and he didn't think he needed a pep-talk, though he was grateful for their concern. 'We'll see, won't we? I just want what's best for Elza.'

Robert placed a hand on Elliot's shoulder. It was a curious gesture; dominant, shepherding. He looked around the room. 'People. Elliot needs his life back. He and Elza need to move on. There will never be a better time for Ashten to be found.' His eyes checked each face for comprehension. 'We can make that happen. Are you with me?'

What was he suggesting? Elliot didn't dare ask.

A sharp laugh from Ari Markson. 'You mean we identify this guy as Ashten? You guys are legends. I knew you wouldn't disappoint me.'

Perhaps Ari Markson wasn't taking it entirely seriously. Or perhaps he was taking it exactly as seriously as he took the rest of life.

'Let's cut the bullshit,' said Robert. 'Forget rock-n-roll stunts. I'm speaking as a man who has a wife. You all have your families.'

Elliot didn't think he'd heard Elza mention that any of them had families, except for the drummer who had a son. The drummer wasn't here, Elliot now realised. Paul raised an eyebrow ironically, as if he also disagreed with Robert's assertion about families. But Ari Markson and Oliver Jared watched Robert with complete belief. No one would contradict him. He had the invincibility of performance.

'Elliot and Elza deserve a new start,' said Robert. Still keeping his hand on Elliot's shoulder, he laid the other hand on the table next to the phone. 'This body is Ashten Geddard. It ends here. We have found him.'

Surely someone would crack a smile, admit it was a joke. Elliot was waiting for it. But nobody spoke.

Elliot said: 'Doesn't that depend on ... well surely Hugo Bird will identify ...'

More weight went into the hand Robert kept on Elliot's shoulder. Like a gaoler's hand. 'No, Elliot. The people who have paid the biggest price are you and Elza. Twenty years is long enough for her to wait. Do you want another twenty? You need to see this finished.'

'But I wouldn't ask that you –' Elliot dried again. 'Ignore me. You all dazzled me a bit tonight. It was great.'

Get them talking about the concert again. Not about helping him.

Paul squinted at the picture on Steve's phone. 'This could be a woman.' He gave a high snort-laugh. White dust appeared in a bloom on his upper lip. He ran his finger over it, popped it in his nostril, ran it round the rim, put the finger in his mouth and licked it. Elliot blinked hard, but too late to blink that away.

Robert released Elliot's shoulder and patted it. 'Stop worrying, Elliot. Let us take care of you.'

Perhaps they'd all taken the white dust.

Oliver Jared stood up. 'Elliot,' he said. 'You should see this.' He left the room and unhooked a white rope across the entrance to a further staircase.

They all climbed the stairs.

The ceiling on the top floor was folded into slopes by the roof above. Oliver Jared stopped at a door and tapped a number into the keypad. Inside was a storage area with stacked cardboard boxes and heaps of bubble wrap. He high-stepped over a box and reached for a black portfolio case. It was a style that Elza used. He unzipped it and laid it flat.

Elliot recognised the black and white portrait on the top of the file. It was one of the body pictures Steve had sent from Kathmandu back in February.

Oliver Jared spread out the pictures in the portfolio case. There were many of them. All portraits. Like the first one.

'Elza made these, Elliot,' said Oliver Jared. 'Did you know?'

Serene, hollowed faces in black and white. Some had closed eyes and open mouths so that they seemed to be singing a secret back to the living world.

No, he didn't know Elza was making them. He said so. He felt he was being asked more. How well he'd taken care of her soul.

It's not what I would do myself. Her standard phrase about the art she made for clients, which had started to become maddening. Well this is what she made herself, portraits of the men found in the ice. She had made them for years. Was still making them, spending hours with their detail, reckoning with them, and he hadn't known.

Robert crossed his arms across his chest. 'I hadn't seen these.' His tone was grave.

'She shouldn't have to make any more,' said Oliver Jared. 'I think we're all agreed about that.'

They were all still hyped, gods in command of thousands.

Far down in the house, Elliot heard the front door close.

Ari Markson called out. 'Hugo, we're up here.'

Hugo Bird. Thank goodness. Hugo wouldn't agree to any of this.

Ari Markson said: 'How many of these men were eventually identified?'

Steve recognised the question he was really asking. 'Not all of them. Sometimes you can identify them by their clothes but that won't work for Ashten because he kept swapping his gear with climbers who wanted clothes he'd worn. You know what a tart he was.'

'It won't be a problem to make a convincing picture for the press,' said Robert. A sweep of his hand said *We can use these.*

Ari Markson scratched behind his ear. A cufflink glinted in the half-light. 'If we tell the press it's Ashten, they'll run it. No questions.'

Elliot felt the eyes of those dead pictures on them. It was like a horrible dream of a pact. Or swearing on the Bible. Again, he thought of Hugo, whose footsteps were now approaching. 'But let's be sensible. We can't ask Hugo to –'

Robert's hand on his shoulder again. The anchoring hand. Looking after him. 'We'll work it out. You go and rest.'

He should protest more. But those pictures challenged him. Face after face after face. How many more would there be? He didn't want this deception, but he also saw a glimmer of release. They picked that up with their rockstar insight, where all that mattered was what you needed, and nothing was too dark or bizarre. And now they would talk all night about how to make it happen.

Elliot heard Hugo arrive, step into the room. Saw him turn away from the portraits.

Oliver Jared spoke. 'Hugo, it's time we gave this guy a break.'

Elliot had to get out. They would start trying to convince Hugo, and use him as the reason. And if they asked him if he wanted it, he wouldn't be able to hide that he did. He excused himself, went down the stairs and into the street.

40

In the Glacier House, they talked, trying to get Hugo on side. Hugo refused to discuss their plan. They wanted to all come along, to Nepal. He'll never agree to that, thought Steve, and Hugo told them why they couldn't. They blustered, began to tire, like toys winding down. Time to stop, thought Steve.

'Hugo, my car's here. Want a ride to the airport?'

Yes, said Hugo's face. The others followed them out, staying close around them as they locked the front door of the house. Ushering them to the car, patting its roof as they said goodbye, wishing it luck, sending Hugo into battle.

Steve liked driving at daybreak, gunning through streets that were stirring to life.

'I've known Elza a long time,' he said. 'This has been hard on her. Especially these last months.'

The mention of Elza didn't thaw Hugo's mood. He took a glug of water. Crumpled the bottle with a harsh crackle.

Steve tried again. 'Markson and Jared are being crass about it, they're just looking at money. Rib's bonkers but he's also right. Elza needs to leave you all behind. She's got a good thing with Elliot.'

'I know that,' said Hugo. 'But I'm not going to lie to anyone.'

'We won't lie to anyone. We'll explain to Elza. We'll find a way. This can't last for ever. It's a bit of a mad season.'

'Our entire lives are a mad season, aren't they?'

Steve saw the ramp to the motorway and floored the accelerator. 'Speak for yourself, mate. I'm not the one who clings to mountains with just my toenails.'

41

All countries have their own smell. As the plane doors opened at Tribhuvan airport in Kathmandu, Hugo recognised the aroma of home, a lifetime ago. Dust, spices, car fumes, cooking oil. Heard the distinctive music of its language, felt its different air temperature, warmer than London. It would be familiar soon but now he noticed only how it was not.

He'd spoken to Charmian. She told him the body's rough location so he could plan the expedition. Just above the Western Cwm. She kept the details vague. Protecting her knowledge so he would need her.

In the same way, he protected his own territory.

The others had thought they could come with him. Robert and Ari Markson wanted to accompany him from London, then fly from Kathmandu to Base Camp in a helicopter. Indeed, why not go there with Oliver Jared's pilot and hire a helicopter, do it all themselves?

The discussions about it had been exhausting. Hugo explained Jared's pilot had no licence to fly in Nepal. Still they refused to see why it was so difficult when Steve could fly to Kathmandu at the drop of an email. Because, said Hugo, Kathmandu was a city. Sending Steve there was like sending him to Bristol. Whereas this was a search-and-rescue climb on the mountain.

So then they started talking about the climb. Robert was gym-fit, couldn't he join the expedition to the body? Hugo explained about acclimatising, and how he'd need to trek to Base Camp to build tolerance for the lower levels of oxygen. I don't mind getting out of breath, said Robert, which proved he had understood nothing about oxygen and altitude. Hugo told him it was not possible to get him a climbing permit. Won't you need a climbing permit too, said Robert, suspecting Hugo was cheating him in some way. I've still got my permit, Hugo said, from April.

Hugo would also have to relearn the mindset for climbing there. He'd been away for five months. He'd used a climbing wall several times a week, but that kept him in training for rockfaces. Not for the rope skills, navigation and decision-making needed on a big, glaciated Himalayan peak.

He did not want a macho idiot on this trip.

Or any of those people.

At Tribhuvan Airport, Hugo queued for a flight to Lukla, the airstrip nearest to Base Camp. The day before, there had been no flights because of visibility. The terminal hall was dark, except for a long window facing the dusty, sun-drenched runway. It was crammed with trekkers in hiking boots, sitting on their luggage, staring out in the hope of escape, annoyed that the loos had no soap, that there was nowhere to buy food or drink except the two small news kiosks. Hugo chatted to a couple of girls who had been waiting for two days to fly. The delay wasn't unusual.

He sipped a Diet Coke, which tasted flat because he was taking Diamox, a drug to help him metabolise oxygen faster at high altitude. It helped a little, but wasn't a quick fix. However, Robert, Jared and Markson had been thrilled to learn a drug might speed things up. It would not – at least it wouldn't produce an instant miracle, among the many they were hoping for.

They were also hotching with impatience when he told them his walk to Everest Base Camp would take ten whole days.

He could imagine how they'd react if they could see him now, waiting for a flight that might not happen until the following day, or even the day after that. He was probably the only person in the sprawl of exasperated, fidgety passengers who did not mind the wait at all.

42

A warm evening. Elliot and Elza were at Gina and Robert's for a barbecue.

After a week of work, the discussion in the Glacier House now seemed unbelievable to Elliot. It belonged in a night of temporary hysteria, all part of the astonishing concert. Today, Robert was a guy in his suburban garden, bending over the hissing coals, and Elliot was taking him a platter of sausages, and, to his relief, finding that the conversation flowed easily. The sun was low behind the trees, making spear-shaped beer o'clock shadows.

They talked about how *BBC Breakfast* were scheduled to film in the Glacier House. Exciting for everybody, and Elliot said: 'Elza's never had this kind of publicity for her work before.'

Robert replied: 'I think great things will be happening this autumn.' His voice was quiet and very assured. Sit tight and it will all work out. Somehow warning, too, as he was when they were all shown Elza's portraits.

Robert took a tea towel off a tree branch and wiped his hands, scrunching the striped material in his fingers. The nails were trimmed and manicured, the fingertips calloused like the pads of a wolf. Groomed and wild. Like the duality of his persona that made Elliot unsure how to talk to him.

'It'll be good,' said Robert. Exactly like the night of the concert.

Elliot felt like he was on trial. To see if he was still on message. What could he say? Only one answer seemed possible. 'I never mentioned anything to Elza. I don't think I should.'

Robert took the tongs from Elliot and turned one of the sausages to inspect the underside. 'It would be easy to misunderstand. If you weren't there.'

159

Laughter came from the kitchen, loosened by wine. Elza and Gina were assembling a pudding. An ensemble of spoons chiming on bowls, knives clacking down on boards.

'I don't think Gina would understand it,' said Elliot, 'would she?'

'No, she wouldn't. I'll find us more beer.' As Robert stepped into the house, he put his hand heavily on Elliot's shoulder. A fixing weight. Anchoring the bargain. This time, his touch wasn't without warmth. Perhaps it contained gratitude for understanding, for helping to make everything easy.

Did Robert think the coming weeks would be easy too? Elliot didn't. He thought it would be the bumpiest ride of their lives. But at least at the end, there would be a new start.

43

In the basement of the townhouse, Elza was kneeling on the mirrored floor, installing a wire column to hold donations from fans. In the reflecting depths at her feet, it was a downward-growing chandelier of a hundred metal keys, some as small as fingernails, some as big as bell-pulls, some from suitcases, some from cars, some from doors, the partners of locks that had gone for ever.

Oliver Jared was standing in the doorway. He was scrubbing his hand through his dandelion clock of hair as he considered a message scrawled on the wall. 'Have you seen this graffiti?'

Elza had seen it. *Malaysian Airlines Flight 370. 239 souls lost, March 2014.*

'It's on theme,' said Elza. Also, it was courteously done, in red ballpoint pen, and impeccably punctuated. 'But do we want to let people write on the walls?'

'Have you been to Romeo and Juliet's house in Verona? The walls are covered in love messages. People could do that here. Write to loved ones who have gone missing. Or is that depressing?'

Loved ones who had gone missing. Many people might hesitate before saying that to her, or say it, then flail in apology. Even Elliot sometimes hesitated or flailed, and he must be used to it all by now.

But Oliver Jared didn't hesitate.

'We seem to be getting a lot of gloves,' he said. 'And a picture of

Marc Bolan the other day. Did Ashten like Marc Bolan?'

Oliver Jared was the only person who didn't seek special sanction to utter Ashten's name. Did Ashten like Marc Bolan? He thought it; he said it.

'I've no idea if he liked Marc Bolan. What have we decided about the graffiti?'

44

Day by day, Hugo crossed the landscape that used to be his home. Bare earth paths, scrubby trees, steel bridges spiderwebbing over the gorges, tattered prayer flags fluttering like forgotten washing.

He walked alone, with plenty of company. Trekkers were everywhere. Clustered on hills, their shoulders heaving with the effort of breath, turning their iPads and phones to catch a 3G connection. Stopped on bridges taking pictures of the chasms that plunged beneath their feet. Debating whether the silvered peak in the far distance was Everest, Lhotse, or Nuptse. Exclaiming as porters marched past at an impressive pace, despite crates on their backs as big as washing machines.

Hugo made steady progress, letting his body relearn the thinner air, ignoring the headache from the altitude change. The landscape made him feel atom-tiny, simplified.

At dinner in the guesthouse, everyone sat together. Sometimes a trekker asked what he did in the other world. 'I travel,' he said, and they understood to leave it at that. Others talked only about this place they were in, and other places they had trekked or climbed. Existing in the present, with as much past as they wanted to give. Or as little.

Sleep was in an unheated room, his sleeping-bag on a plywood bed with a foam mattress. And then the morning, walking again.

The time in London seemed distant. The theme-park shrine of the Glacier House seemed impossible. So did the people who belonged to it; Robert, Gil, Paul, Oliver Jared, Steve, Elza Jones, always wanting things from him that were so unreadable and intricate. Here, you could share a dinner table with a stranger and they'd let you stay a stranger. In London, at the climbing gym one day, a person had recognised him and asked for his mobile number. 'I won't use it,' she said. 'I just want to feel I have it.'

The only relief had been the studio. A low-lit haven where nothing mattered but sound. He had taken a while to get used to it. It folded back in his mind onto an older time. Was that uncomfortable? He didn't know.

He hadn't expected it to finish so abruptly. But now it had.

Here, the awareness of breathing and walking put him back in his body, cleared weight from his mind. One foot and then the other. The way he had lived for years.

He saw shrines, painted white like snowmen, with startling colour-lined eyes. Towns in a jumble of roofs. The guesthouse called Rivendell after Tolkien's *Hobbit*. Forests rising up the valley walls. Mani stones offering prayers for travellers. The view up the Imja Khola valley, with the Nuptse-Lhotse wall at the far end and Everest's summit pyramid behind, circled with a plume of cloud.

At Pheriche, Hugo found people he knew: staff at the rescue centre and doctors at the hospital. They had seen the concert on a satellite channel. They needed beer to get past that and remember the Hugo they knew. Then they talked as they always had, about life here. The April and May climbing season had been cancelled. The money that Hugo raised from walks, marathons, interviews and the Ashbirds name had helped families who depended on guiding and portering. It kept their children in school. After more beer, Hugo decided his mission to find the body of a dead popstar was obscenely irrelevant. He would stay and build fences or work in the hospital.

The next morning, in the fumble of their hangovers, they all decided he must carry on. Find your dead guy. Use his fame. That will help more.

A teahouse kept a padlocked trunk for him. He hauled it into the sunshine and spread the contents out to air. Thermal layers, down jackets and salopettes, hooded sleeping bags, waterproofs, carabiners, cords, harnesses, ice tools, boots, gaiters. He chose what he would need. Inspected the clips and ropes. Practised putting the gear on, finding the zips and buckles while wearing padded gloves. Awakening old routines. Everything was more snug around the middle and looser on the shoulders. Although he'd kept in shape, it was not the same shape.

..

He reached Base Camp. In April, it had been a vast tent city. Now it was a bare grey hollow with mountains on three sides, scattered with crumbs of rock and prayer flags.

A woman was lying on the lower helicopter pad in the sunshine, a book propped on her bent knees. She must have been watching for him because she sat up tall, her hand forming a peak over her eyes. Charmian.

'Hello, rock god.'

She got up, being careful of one leg, walked to him unevenly.

'You're injured.'

'I'm not. I had a knee operation a few years ago. It gets stiff when I've been sitting for a while.'

She led him to her tent. Put water on for tea. They ate apple pie, looking at the view. A few people arrived, wearing light daypacks. Everybody here looked the same, in fleeces, leggings, jackets, backpacks and boots, souvenir hats and scarves bought en route. No clue to their nationality until they spoke.

'You look soft,' said Charmian.

'No mountains in London.'

'Are you fit for this?'

'If I'm careful.'

She didn't bother to make encouraging noises. In London, people would tell you you'd succeed if you believed in yourself. She did not.

'What state is the body in?' said Hugo.

'Whole.' She kept shuffling her feet as though trying to reposition a piece of grit inside the sock. A sign of old frost damage.

'Can it be moved?'

'We'll see.'

He heard a ringtone. On Charmian's sleeping bag was a phone. 'Duty calls.' She answered.

'Hi darling. Yes, how was your day?'

Her voice became bright, as though she was angling for laughter and smiles. 'Yes, lots of material for the book. How did they get on at school?'

He remembered their conversation over the sunrise on Aconcagua. Her rules and regrets, and her emphatic French lilt that made them somehow beyond question. As she talked, her feet were in motion, the discomfort she kept out of her voice. Two Charmians. Family Charmian and the Charmian under the domestic wrapping, who was all hurricane.

Hugo crawled to the tent vestibule and set more water on the gas to heat. He checked his own phone. There were messages. Steve. Oliver Jared. Robert. Even a message from Elza Jones. *Let us know when you have news.*

All waiting for the neat ending. Should he reply? And what should he say?

Charmian chatted. Children were being put on to talk. Three times she said hello, asked about school.

When she finished, Hugo said: 'How did you find this body?'

'I was here in April. I found him on a practice climb.'

'Who else knows?'

'No one.'

That wasn't possible. 'No one besides your team?'

'No. Totally no one.' She folded down a panel of her rucksack and lifted out her camera. 'I found him in a photo.' She thumbed the buttons. Passed the camera to him, balanced on her palm. 'It's only luck that I didn't crop him out. Look on the right-hand edge, then zoom.'

First he saw a speck on a high ledge, a pale blue flaw in the white snow and grey granite. He closed in and the image jumped bigger, became a soft-edged shape, creased into the snow, like a sleeping-bag left out overnight. Or a down suit.

'It was just after the avalanche, when they were still recovering people. I was going to report it, but then I saw the colour of the hair. Look closer.'

The picture was now at the blur limit, but a second colour was apparent. If you were thinking in terms of a body, it could be very bleached hair. He remembered the photo she sent. How the hair was phantom white.

'To look like that, he might have been out for a long time. Maybe meeting you on Aconcagua made me think of it, but anyway, I had to go and look.'

'You went with a guide?'

'No. I went alone. Totally alone.' Emphasis now. You keep asking. Believe me, I went alone.

A scamp grin. 'I came looking for you first, but everything was chaos. When I found your team they said you'd already left. So what choice did I have?'

What choice? Most people would choose not to go. And worse, to get to that part of the mountain, she must have climbed through its most treacherous region. The Khumbu Icefall, a landscape of dizzying crevasses spanned by narrow ladders, and ice towers the size of skyscrapers that seemed poised to topple. Sometimes they did.

'And you climbed by yourself through the Icefall.'

'All the ropes and ladders were still there. Scariest thing I've ever done. I'm not doing it again. You'd better have a helicopter.'

Yes, he had a helicopter. And news that she would not welcome. 'I hate to say this but the body is not likely to be him.'

'Why?'

'Because of where he fell. He's much higher up.' Hugo named a location.

'I know where he fell. It's on the Himalayan Database. And Wiki.'

'So how could he be here?'

She shrugged. 'He was in a glacier? Perhaps it broke off in the avalanche? Became exposed in the spring weather? I didn't climb through that Icefall just for kicks.'

Hugo didn't push. There was a further explanation, and he was grateful she had the delicacy not to mention it. After everyone left Ash, certain he was beyond help, he might have struggled on alone. Hugo had always known that was a possibility.

'Do we have a helicopter?' said Charmian.

Hugo picked up his phone. 'We do. But I'm in charge of this expedition. You don't take so much as a step unless I say so. No heroics.'

'Agreed.'

Hugo sent a text to Oliver Jared.

Jared replied instantly. *You're using the helicopter? Does this mean it's him? What's this about a bribe?*

When Hugo arranged the helicopter, he was told nobody was permitted to fly up the mountain right now. Hugo kept asking until a price was agreed.

He deleted the reply from Jared.

On the stove in the outer vestibule of the tent, the water hissed slowly to the boil. A noise of home. Other noises also told him he was home: a constant rumble and shirr, the tides and drifts of snow and ice in the mountain's upper reaches.

Charmian passed him a mug. Her hands were rough and thickened, like his own. Her snow tan had a pioneering gauntness. Her bare arms and shins were like a hardwood frame, with the wiry firmness of a life lived by sinew. She was a creature of this place, with her shoulder blades shifting under the fabric of her fleece, the ladder of her rib bones in her greyhound flank. This was how he was used to people looking.

Tomorrow he would walk on ground that was made on the whim of snow, sun and wind.

Hugo felt real at last. Surging with fear and life.

45

Robert sat in the control room with Gil and Oliver Jared. Paul was at the Steinway, lost in his headphones and travelling hands.

Oliver Jared was talking strategy. He'd got news from Hugo, who had reached Base Camp. Was on target to confirm the body was Ashten Geddard, perhaps in the next twenty-four hours. The PR agency from Bowie's comeback album was primed. So was the art director who did Bowie's comeback cover. Both had written NDAs in the blood of their firstborns. Everybody would be made by this. No more giant fur suits, Gil. No more cat food commercials, Robert.

Why, thought Robert, are you telling me to count my blessings?

'It's time to pull together. Put everything in the pot to get this done.'

'Well you're the one who has the pot,' said Robert.

'This is crunch time,' said Oliver Jared. 'We can all make this happen. Our salaries for this month can go into the rescue.'

Gil eased his headphones fully off. He'd also been listening for a sting.

Robert leaned back in his seat, clasped his hands behind his head. 'Run that again, Oliver?'

'The thing is, we've got a lot of people to hire and pay. This rescue is big bucks.'

'So you'll go without dinner at Claridges and we'll put our salaries in?'

Oliver Jared studied his fingers on the desk and chuckled, as if he'd always expected people would object, but he was sure that would change when he enlightened them. 'Guys, think what's coming. Hugo is about to report the discovery of Ashten Geddard's body. That will transform everything.'

Gil spoke. 'Oliver, isn't this assuming a lot?'

Of course, Gil didn't know about the deal to identify the body. Robert could explain, which might help Jared argue his case.

Robert didn't feel like helping.

In the live room, Paul worked the Steinway, a softness in his goblin face as he did his stuff. His bloody good stuff.

Robert slid his phone off the mixing desk, stood up and put it in his pocket. 'See ya.'

He saw a hop of anxiety in Oliver Jared's eyebrows. 'We should talk about this. How much do you need right now? Gil, I could pay your son's extra tuition this month. How about that?' Gil's son had learning difficulties.

'We need the wages you agreed to pay us, Oliver.'

'We're so close, Robert. The situation is temporary.'

Robert paused, hand on the door. 'My absence will be temporary if you look in your pocket fluff and find my salary. It's probably next to the last place you saw your bollocks.'

Gil laid his headphones down. 'Sorry, mate.' He leaned over the talkback to stop Paul.

Oliver Jared put his hands up. 'I'm sorry, I thought we were all loyal to the project.'

Loyalty. Next he'd say they shouldn't need pay at all because they were having a good time.

'Look, I'm sure I can make savings somewhere else.' Oliver Jared gathered his car keys and phone. 'I've got a couple of meetings.'

'I'll walk with you,' said Robert.

Oliver Jared gave a clenched smile. He did not want Robert to walk with him. He wanted to escape. Tough.

Outside in the corridor, Oliver Jared tried to explain himself, looking at his shoes like an ashamed schoolboy.

'Hugo's just bust the budget big time. We had a helicopter booked, which is two thousand US dollars for every hour we use it. Hugo was supposed to climb to the body, call the helicopter to collect it. A short trip. But now he's using the helicopter both ways. He's flying to the body instead of climbing there. And he's had to pay a massive bribe because of some local ban on flying helicopters. Thousands of dollars burning away every hour. God knows how many hours.'

A few thousand dollars? And how much did this guy have? If he was skint, he should sell the Glacier House, which was just a toy. But a toy he still enjoyed. The band was a toy he was tired of.

'Oliver, I'm glad you mentioned costs. I'm worried too. While Hugo's there, he's not writing for us here.'

An exasperated sigh. Good, Jared was irked by that too.

'I think,' said Robert, 'there's a way I can help. I have four extra tracks we could work on.'

A new keenness in Jared's eyes. 'You do?'

'Four tracks, written and ready. So Hugo's absence won't delay us.'

Did Jared remember the demo in April, which he told Ari Markson he didn't like? Actually, in his new austerity mindset, he probably didn't give a millicrap.

'You could start recording them now?'

'Straight away, Oliver.'

'Yes. Get them rolling. You're a genius. Thanks, Robert.'

Right. Now he had to clear the *Superstring* songs with Markson. And get it done quickly.

..

Robert talked to Markson. Hugo's sent news. He's about to view the body. Today or tomorrow. We could be getting the announcement. So we need you to check something, urgently. And you might not know this but... Robert explained. Four unreleased songs written with Ashten in 1993.

No need to mention the demo, he realised. With Hugo about to find the body, four unreleased songs written with Ashten would pop anyone's lid.

It certainly popped Markson's. By the time Robert said can you dig into the paperwork and confirm we're allowed to use them, Markson was promising an answer within an hour. And the answer? No contractual restrictions, Robert. All fine.

..

At the end of the afternoon, Robert went to the changing room with a feeling of pleasant, productive exhaustion. They'd got a rough cut of 'A Shebird'.

They played their rocks off. Though Paul nearly didn't. He was so excited he needed some toot in his tank but the kitchen cupboard was bare. He made jittery mistakes, blamed everyone else for them, took breaks every ten minutes until the receptionist arrived with supplies.

If Paul could be kept fuelled, this would come together.

Robert opened his locker. His cycling skins were on a hanger, airing after the morning's ride.

He was still using the Sirrus Expert, the bike he'd had to take when his own was stolen at the BBC. That must be nearly a year ago now. No, he didn't do any radio interviews last year. It was... Christ, the year before. Nearly two years ago.

..

Robert met Gina at the bus stop for the Glacier House.

She squeezed close to him. 'I thought you were coming by bike.'

'It got stolen.'

He knew she'd be shocked. 'Whoa. What?'

'Someone screwdrivered the locks. Several were taken. It happens.'

Taking the Sirrus Expert had been a temporary madness. At the time he'd been so swamped in crapstorms that he let it drift. He couldn't sort out another bicycle. It was hard enough just to keep moving. But today, on his way out of the studio, he felt able to deal with it. He stayed in his work clothes, wheeled the Sirrus to the police station and reported that he'd found it on the abandoned building site.

Now here was Gina, worrying too much about it. Asking if he'd been to the police, if they thought he'd get the bike back. He tipped her chin up, looked in her searching green eyes. 'Gina, it's just a bike.'

Her answering look asked a fresh question. Do you really mean that? Yes, I think you do.

He had a further surprise for her. Headphones. 'I've got a track here. See what you think.'

Smiling, she untangled the wires. 'Me? You know I don't know squat about music. How do I start this thing?'

She made happiness seem so easily possible, free of complications, though, unfortunately, she had no critical judgement. All her family were like this. Christmases and weddings were a mob of smiling aunts and cousins who were star struck just because he played on albums and wrote music that was on TV. They talked about his success. He explained about real success, which was being a musician whose name and songs people actually knew. You'll get that recognition too, they would say, so certain, so naive. They might as well be monks chanting gormlessly for world peace. They admired what he did, but what was the value of their admiration if they had so little taste? Or were they saying what he wanted to hear? That was possible.

For the same reason, he was careful what he shared with Gina. When he got praise from her he wanted to deserve it, not get it as a matrimonial duty. But this track, today, he wanted to share with her.

He found the file with the song. Played it.

..

They stopped for a short time at the Glacier House to check in with Oliver Jared and play him the demo. Gina then took Robert to the basement, where Elza was working, and they played it to her too. The evening was warm, still very much summer. It beckoned you to stay outside with the buzz of traffic leaving the city, drink a beer in a pub garden, bask in the pleasure of kicking off the day.

'Don't get me too rat-arsed,' said Gina. 'It's a school night.'

They ate Thai starters that were nothing like real Thai. They kept ordering anyway, because there was so much to talk about.

He explained about the song she'd just heard, and the others he'd written with Ashten. He'd never told her this because her supportive outrage would be automatic. And useless. Now he told her, because this might really be their time.

She speared a miniature fishcake. 'This is an amazing story. What does your PR agent say? What about Markson? Could he get a label involved? No, wait. You don't need a label. You've got that agency collecting fan addresses and emails from the letters.'

Usually he didn't talk business and publicity with her. Like the rest of her family, she couldn't tell a workable idea from a chocolate flamethrower. But she was right to be juiced about this. With the fan data they were collecting, they could sell everything from their own website without a middle man. The album, merchandise, tickets, spin-offs.

She kept putting down her fork and staring, overcome anew with the wonder of it. 'People will love this. You wrote these songs with Ashten Geddard, just the two of you.'

'With a bit of Paul.'

Paul. A squinch of her left eye asked who Paul was.

Robert mimed playing a piano.

'Oh! The guy with the face.' Gina did the face, scrunched like a toothless cockney music-hall comedian. Robert, aiming a wooden skewer of satay into his mouth, nearly did himself an injury.

46

Slightly sleepily, Gina registered a birth. She and Robert hadn't been very responsible about school-night drinking yesterday.

Something significant had changed. Robert's bike had been stolen, the kind of setback that would usually bring armageddon. But he had filed a police report and shrugged, as if it was nothing.

And he'd played her a music demo. He hadn't done this since

April. She had not heard any of the new Ashbirds music from him. Only the tracks that were publicly released.

Perhaps it was the Hyde Park concert. It put him on the map, made him understand what he was part of. And she hadn't known he'd written songs with Ashten Geddard all those years ago. Half an album, he said, and all of it discarded because of band politics.

This business wrecked people. And he had gone back and worked with those same guys who had cheated him. No wonder he found it so tough. Now, perhaps he was letting the world be kind to him.

And this was why, last night, beers turned into margaritas. She should have said no, but not when she saw him bring two flared glasses, rims sparkling with salt. Two! He so rarely drank alcohol. And the candlelight glinting on a fine silver chain he was wearing, just visible in the open neck of his shirt. It gave him a potent strength, trickling across his shoulders, kinking in the notch between his collarbones. She hadn't seen it before.

'I like that chain on you,' she said.

A spark in his eyes. This man who fought mysterious loner battles, refused help, refused to surrender, was independent and unconquered, true to himself. And completely with her.

Now, Gina stood ready with the groom and groom. They wore sober suits, as if they had nipped away from one of the nearby solicitors' offices. No guests. This was a quickie, a formality. The proper ceremony was happening at the weekend in a castle in Wales. They just needed the legal bit.

She began. By the time the guys spoke their vows, she had them. Locked nervously on each other's gaze, hands gripped as they uttered the words they thought they'd trot through routinely. This was not a bureaucratic tick-box, a form-filling before the real transformation. This was the transformation. A transformation for a new start, for the good things that were ahead.

47

Hugo leaned out of the helicopter's open door as the downdraft stirred loose snow into clouds. He jumped out, waited for Charmian as she came after.

The pilot watched them, a face assembled from a helmet, goggles, headset and oxygen mask. Hugo signalled they were clear. The helicopter rose and rattled away down the valley, to wait at Base Camp. The white on its doors looked drab and scuffed against the luminous purity of the snow.

Above, the sky was violently sapphire blue, the true hue of the heavens.

The snow was deep after the monsoon. They went on skis. Nuptse rose on the right, swept smooth like a dream. The west shoulder of Everest was on the left, rockier, daunting. Lhotse was straight ahead, its tip gleaming in the sun.

This place, the Western Cwm, was also known as the Valley of Silence. The journey became a meditative task in a world of just their own sounds. The rasp of their breathing, the poles piercing the snow, the rhythmic swish of the skis, changing tone where the snow bridged a crevasse. White clouds hovered above at the grey peaks. Everything was so still. Their forward gliding strides were an endlessly repeating moment going nowhere.

He heard a murmuring crack higher up the valley. A small avalanche, from the same area as the avalanche five months earlier. The stasis of this place was an illusion.

Ahead was a cliff of ice. From time to time, Hugo had another thought. Their purpose. What they were here to see.

When time eventually brought them to the ice cliff, it was glistening with meltwater in the sunshine. They stowed the skis and poles on their backpacks. Roped together. Chose their tools. Charmian jabbed her way up first, on the picks of her axes and her cramponed toes.

The top of the cliff was a shelf, wide enough to walk on. On one side, the wall continued upwards. On the other, it dropped sheer into the valley. Hugo followed her.

The shelf began to slope. She clipped onto a rope by a shadowed area of rock to keep moving along. Hugo did the same.

She spoke, on gasps. 'In there.'

He looked. The shadowed area was dark. Deep. A cave.

He began to see a shape.

A jolt of shock. He knew what they had come for, but his brain flashed a primal warning. The shape was, or might be, human.

He had to look away.

Far below, the snow seethed with his sudden alarmed heartbeat. The shape in the shadows was upright, like a person standing.

Charmian inched further along the rope, legs angled like a steeplejack. To let him go closer.

He breathed, a deep in-out. Took the skis off his back so he could enter the cave. He turned and looked in.

Yes, he was seeing it now. A figure.

He couldn't see the face. The figure was short; shorter than he was. No, it wasn't fully straight. His eyes traced the outlines, worked it out. It must have originally been lying down with its legs bent, like a child asleep on one side. Now, pulled vertical, it seemed arrested in the act of kneeling.

'He was out on the ledge,' said Charmian. 'I moved him in there.'

Hugo was getting used to what he was seeing. He could begin to think. For instance, it was smart of her to move him into shelter. She was probably right that he'd become exposed in the warmer weather, and when the monsoon came, the snowfall would have hidden him again. Standing him up was smart too. If he was lying down, he'd be impossible to dig out.

Hugo stepped closer. The figure had a harness over its torso, including the arms. Ropes held it to metal anchors driven into the rock at the back of the cave. It was faintly disturbing. He tried to understand it.

No, first he needed to see the face.

He knelt beside the body. His hands were like paws in the big gloves but he managed to grasp the hood.

'I pulled his hood up,' said Charmian.

Would the body fall if he touched it? It didn't. It was rooted wide and solid, like a mature tree. Snow had blown in and fixed the lower half in a pedestal of ice. Hugo folded the hood backwards.

The hair was stark white, bleached by the sun and the glare of snow. In the picture Charmian sent him, the surface of the face was obscured in ice. Now, up close, it was a hard mask of opaque white, like a weathered face on a cathedral, looking out with the blank serenity of aeons. Hugo brushed it with his padded glove. The surface was marble hard. He knocked it with the handle of his ice tool. Not the pointed pick – this was a face. The ice did not yield.

But even through that masking, Hugo felt an answering recognition, immediate and certain, that he'd never had before.

Of the details he could see, nothing was in doubt. The width of the face. The contour of the lip. After so long, he'd wondered if he would know.

Hugo seemed able to see through everything, through the pedestal of ice to the astronaut-like boots, to the folded legs. This kneeling person looked so vulnerable. All these years he had been out here, through avalanches, days, nights. Perhaps in the first of them, he was still aware and fighting, before he became a passenger on the mountain's mysterious currents. And all that time, also, in the inmost currents of Hugo's mind.

The harness around the body. It was improvised from a rucksack, put sideways. It went over the arms. It was ingenious. It was also like a lynching.

'This...' Anger surged in him. 'Charmian, why have you done this?'

'To stop him freezing into a wall. How will we dig him out otherwise?'

Hugo reached for Ash's rope.

'Don't –' The catch in her voice made him turn. She was pressed tightly into the cliff, holding up a camera. A big lens and her wind-varnished smile, pleased with the angle. In her goggles Hugo could see his reflection. The stripe of the noseguard. His stubble-gritted chin, deep lines bracketing his mouth. His face wearing all the years he had come through. Beside him, Ash's kneeling figure, in his shell of snow. It was like the reunion pictures made by the newspapers, but with a grotesque twist even they never imagined. Trussed with his arms pinned. Like a prisoner bound for execution. Hugo unclipped the rope and threw it away.

He was suddenly loose, plummeting downwards. His mind was a terrifying streak of speed. If you fall, there is no you any more, this place has no need of you. He smashed at the ice with his pick and crampons.

The dreadful rush stopped. The world became still, solid. He lay, his breath roaring, his heart battering against the ice. He was vertical, dug into a face.

He called Charmian's name. He looked up. Waited for her head to appear over the ledge.

It didn't. He called.

The mountain laughed his words back. No other living voice existed but his.

She must have fallen. Christ.

Could he see her? He looked down and all he could see was the jumbled, cracked ice they had crossed in the helicopter, jagging downwards into the valley.

No, was that a noise? His own breathing was so loud. He held it in, listened. Yes. Definitely a human sound. Below.

Charmian was on a ledge, further down. Thank God, quite close.

Her goggled face was tilted up towards him. One leg was folded wrongly.

Hugo called. 'Can you get back up?'

'No.' A plain sound. Not asking for anything. Just stating a fact.

'Are you secure where you are?'

'Yes.'

'I'll call the helicopter.'

He chop-toe-hauled his way back up to the ledge. Ash's presence in the cave stopped him all over again. The ropes now hung slack, although the harness still bound his arms. The prisoner, trussed and kneeling. Hugo snatched the harness off.

As he did, he saw what had happened. The rope he had clipped to, which had let them walk along the ledge, was rigged to one of the ropes that held Ash's body. When he released it, their safety lines had gone.

It was so stupid it was almost a booby trap. Why do such a risky thing? No, remember how he'd first met Charmian, sick because she hadn't understood about altitude. Then how she'd come here on her own, through the riskiest part of the mountain. And pulling Ash into the cave must have been exhausting. What state was she in by that time? Hell bent on securing the body, neglecting to secure herself.

And Hugo wasn't blameless. He shouldn't have trusted that everything was safe. She was tough, but a classic loner. Cutting corners, overconfident because she thought she had control. He should have checked her ropes before he unclipped one.

Charmian's camera had landed on the ledge. He zipped it inside his jacket.

Without the harness, Ash now had dignity.

Hugo wanted to give him more. Cover him with rocks or lower him into a crevasse where he'd never be disturbed again. But he was still fixed upright in the cave, his legs encased like a chess piece.

Possibly that solidity had anchored Hugo's rope, stopped him falling any faster.

Charmian's voice called.

He called back. 'Still here. Getting ropes.'

He looked down. Charmian was still in her fall position. Her leg twisted under her. He heard a new, rhythmic noise, alongside the slippery skitter of falling ice. She was tapping her helmeted forehead on the ice wall to beat away the pain.

Hugo felt overwhelmingly alone again, a speck in the white wilderness. He had to think for two. He studied the area where Charmian was lying. He could lower her off the cliff, down to the flat plain of snow where the helicopter could pick them up. If the helicopter couldn't get close, he could pull her on a stretcher made from her skis and poles.

He was beginning to recognise a pain of his own. A repeating stab in the side each time he took a breath. Years ago, he'd cracked a rib. Sometimes the tissues tore again. As if this rescue wasn't arduous enough.

He called to her again, then radioed the helicopter.

Hugo gathered the spare ropes from around Ash's body. He pulled a fleece hat out of his pocket, smoothed it onto Ash's face. A black mask, another layer to keep him hidden. Under Hugo's gloved fingers Ash's flesh was marble hard, colonised by this place, transfigured into a substance of cold geological time. Hugo packed more snow over the mask. Pulled the hood up. Packed that in snow too. There couldn't be enough snow. Within hours it would solidify. He'd still look like a body, but a body that would be even harder to interpret. Then Hugo left him again.

..

The helicopter touched down at Base Camp. Hugo collected their gear from Charmian's tent while the medics stretchered her to another helicopter with the range to reach the hospital in Kathmandu.

He strapped into a seat. Charmian lay slack beside him, sunk into sedation. With each sign of her debility he felt responsible. The needle taking morphine and fluids into her thin wrist. The blanket covering her body. The splint that held her leg straight. The yellow padding that protected her head and neck. The sweat that streaked her face under her helmet and goggles.

He hadn't asked before he unclipped the ropes. A basic check. Ash's body, Ash's actual body, had made him forget everything.

Hugo sat back. Tried to let the whine and clatter of the chopper take his thoughts away.

It seemed important to think over how he had covered Ash's face, packed it to freeze again. Put him away. Leaving him in that unnatural upright position. But at least he wasn't chained as if he was a possession. He might hold there or he might break away again. As nature decided.

Hugo thought of the people waiting in London. Their request to bring back an Ashten regardless of who it really was. They were like children, with their white house full of white things, playing a game in the safe and warm, looking for an ending to a fairy story.

They knew nothing.

The helicopter sped over the valleys. The ant-armies of trekkers on the spiderweb bridges. The cheerful roof-jumbles of the towns. Busy, benign.

Hugo looked at his phone. Elza Jones's text was the most recent. Waiting for an answer. *Let me know when you have news.*

The news. This was the news: Ash, made of ice, in a cave, looking out over the white emptiness. How do you find the words to give that news?

∴

At the hospital, the medics took Charmian into surgery to pin her tibia and ankle. They checked Hugo's rib and told him not to climb for a while.

He sat in the canteen with coffee and something that was sold as a hamburger, though he wasn't sure what the meat was.

He had Charmian's camera. The screen was cracked. It wouldn't turn on. He had a battery that fitted. Her camera came to life. He scanned through the pictures, the pictures of Ash.

Many were blurred or harshly shadowed, the details swallowed by the harsh contrast. In some you could see the mask of ice over Ash's face. Hugo enlarged them. It could be anyone.

Hugo was in some of the pictures. In his puffy climbing suit he seemed comical, a grub made of orange nylon. Charmian had sneaked a sequence of his face, in close-up. No surprise there, after Aconcagua. He found the delete button. He studied each one before he sent it to oblivion. His eyes were blanked by his goggles. His mouth gave nothing away. Did it not show, the transforming shock of those moments?

Hugo had his laptop in his bag. The next step would be to transfer some pictures and email them to England as he had all the other times. And what should he say?

From the cash register came a dance of beeps as a customer paid. A steady tinkle of cutlery and china from the service area.

He looked further back through Charmian's pictures. Was there anything he could learn about her? What made her world go round? Climbing, it seemed, and little else. Here she was with three buddies. Sun-fierce faces; lifted mugs, backlit tent fabric. Here were a couple of summit pictures, chubby in a climbing suit, the earth curving away, the mountains a low horizon of peaks in the distance. Here was a picture of a man kneeling in the opening of a tent. His face was intense and communicative, as if he had held that expression for a long time, gazing at her, and did not mind that she saw. There were several of this man. The haircuts varied, as did the beard growth and depth of tan; they went back many years, kept permanently on her camera. In one shot was a pair of alpine boots. From what she had said about her family, these boots did not belong to her husband. She kept no pictures of anyone else on this camera.

Perhaps Hugo would learn more from the phone in her rucksack. He woke its screen up. It asked for a PIN. Never mind.

Hugo looked at his own phone. The last message. Elza Jones.

He might as well get it done.

'Hi Elza. How's it going?'

Her voice came, over the distance. 'That's what I should be asking you.'

This was the moment. He should say what he'd found. Tell everyone who was waiting, back in the garden, so they could go on with life.

'There was an accident. I had to bring the other climber to hospital.'

'How bad?'

'Everyone's alive.'

'So was it him?'

Her tone was so routine. As if she was asking: 'which day is the photographer coming', or 'what's the time?'

He could lie. He could say he wasn't sure.

He didn't know what to say.

'It was him,' he said.

Silence. Like a gulf in time. In the service area by the till, the trays rattled around the carousel back to the kitchen.

Eventually: 'Was it?'

Her tone was so amazed, lost. It winded him, like a punch. He had never heard Elza Jones sound like she wasn't in charge, or ironically judging him.

She said: 'What will happen?'

'I don't know.'

Silence.

'I don't think I'm ready,' she said.

'I don't think I am.'

He had never trusted anyone with what he thought, and certainly not her.

'No,' she replied. It sounded like Yes. Yes, I am not ready.

Her monosyllables seemed cautious. Was she in a place where she might be overheard? She said: 'Your other...'

He helped her. 'The other climber?'

'Yes.' It sounded like Go on.

'She fell. We had to rescue her. We couldn't bring Ash down. I don't know how much she saw. I'm in Kathmandu now, in the hospital.'

In the serving area, crockery chattered. The cashier's fingers made a beeping hopscotch on the till. But Elza Jones's alert, thinking silence, far away in London, was louder.

She said: 'Pictures.'

'I have her camera.'

'Don't do anything.'

'I won't.' He added: 'You've got people there?'

'Robert and Gina.' She said the names quickly and quietly. Afraid she might alert them?

'Okay.'

'Don't do anything.'

Yes, that was good. To do nothing for now. Until he could think. 'I won't.'

48

Elza, in her studio, looked at the phone in her hand. From the kitchen, at the other end of the passageway, she could hear Gina, Elliot and Robert. An amused, animated babble.

Robert was talking about a house in Kent that was for sale. Gina was talking about commuting time if they moved out of London. She seemed surprised by Robert's interest in the house. Perhaps they hadn't fully discussed it. Perhaps they were pushing the subject far further than they had taken it in reality, so they had something to talk about.

Robert and Gina weren't really going to move out of London. They were waiting for her to come back and say what she would say.

She could pretend the call was a client.

She couldn't. She said it was Hugo Bird when she ducked away to take it.

Thank goodness she had taken the call in private.

Now she looked back down the passageway. She could see them, sitting on the bar stools at the kitchen's island unit. Gina's tall spiky heels tilted up as she rested her toes on the stool's lower rung. Robert's slim-fitting leather lace-up shoes. City shoes.

They would want the news.

But did she expect this news?

Her phone was still in her hand.

Elliot's voice from the kitchen. 'It was expensive but it'll see us out.' He was talking about the carpet on the stairs, which they'd replaced a few weeks before, and was not worth talking about.

And replacing the carpet seemed to have happened to another person. All the ordinary events of her recent life had been pushed behind a door and only that phone call existed, through the device she held in her hand.

The mouth of a Prosecco bottle tipped into the glasses in front of Robert and Gina. Elza had never seen Robert drink alcohol. Gina and Robert raised their sparkling glasses and chinked them together. Heavens. They had forgotten themselves.

Elliot looked in her direction at that moment. Stop me, said his face, I'm talking about carpet.

The others went quiet. They had noticed his glanced communion with her. Knew she was now available to talk.

She placed her phone on the shelf where she kept things away from the creep of paint: a couple of postcards about gallery openings; a bulbous pottery vase from their holiday in the Lake District. She left her phone there, away from everybody, picked up her glass and returned to the kitchen.

Robert spoke. 'Has Hugo seen the body?'

He was too eager.

'No,' she said.

'No he hasn't seen it or no it wasn't Ashten?'

She hadn't mentioned Ashten's name yet, and here was Robert trying to grab it. Tear pieces off it. 'It wasn't Ashten.'

'It wasn't Ashten?' Robert repeated her words. As if checking she was sure.

Elliot spoke. 'I thought they were certain this time.'

Why would they be certain? Because they wanted it? Robert looked annoyed with her. How dare he. Gina gave Robert's arm a supportive squeeze, as if applying a brake.

Why was this even important to Robert, or Gina? What could it possibly mean to them?

'It seems the body wasn't Ashten,' said Elza. A second coat on the lie, because the truth needed protection. Not from Elliot; she could talk to him later. When she'd had a bit of space.

'Oh well,' said Elliot, 'Here's to the next time.' He fetched the Prosecco bottle from the fridge, so they could loosen up and forget about it. Robert capped his glass with his hand: no more. Gina took a refill and asked about the carpet, that damned carpet. Elza knew she was trying to steer the conversation back to an easy place. Elliot took the cue because he liked harmony. 'That carpet will see us out,' he said, and Gina looked pleased. Elza thought of years unravelling along the same stretch of Axminster grey.

Robert said: 'So is Hugo coming back?'

Hugo. Robert might phone him. That was outrageous. She had to get to Hugo first.

'I don't know if Hugo's coming back,' said Elza.

'One of us should tell the press,' said Robert. He looked at her, seeking permission.

He couldn't wait?

Well if Robert told the press the body wasn't Ashten, she could reverse it with just a few words, whenever she wanted to. She nodded.

'Happy to do it,' said Robert.

Elza picked the empty bottle off the counter. 'I think we'll need more of this.' She went to her studio, where the recycling crate was.

She needed to talk more to Hugo. She had had to be so oblique.

She sent a message. *The press are being told. The body isn't him. Call me when you can.*

49

Robert went up the stairs as Gina kicked off her shoes.

He knew, by the pause in her movements, that she was watching him. He closed the bathroom door.

Inside, he stripped off. Pulled cycling shorts and shirt off the airing rail and put them on. Gave Gina a squeeze as he came down the stairs, said not to wait up, said yes he'd ride carefully, go get some sleep.

Wheeled his bike – hired today while a new one was on order – out of the front shed into the slumbering street, swung on, pumped power down the pedals, felt the gears launch him forwards, the breeze on his muscles through the fabric.

They should not have let Hugo go alone to Nepal. All that guff about permits and their lack of climbing experience. It was obvious he didn't want them watching him, keeping him with the programme.

Oliver Jared shouldn't have been so tight. He could have sent two people.

If Oliver Jared knew how Hugo used his precious money, he'd have sent a second person. He'd have sent a prison guard. The studio time spent on joke songs. The spite-ballad about Elza – that was an entire day of work they couldn't use. But you don't tell outsiders what goes on in the studio. Like *Fight Club*.

To them it was like *Fight Club*. To Hugo it was fuck-all.

This would have made them. How many vintage rockers were relaunching right now? The press were calling them comb-over comebacks. Ashbirds was just one more unless they did something phenomenal. Like bringing back Ashten Geddard, right now, after the Hyde Park concert and with an album about to drop. They could announce an arena tour and pre-sell every seat in an hour. If Hugo had done what they'd all agreed he should do.

After twenty minutes Robert was in town, blazing towards the City. The trellis-gated entrance to Chancery Lane Tube station, the leaning liquorice stripes of the Old Holborn building, the giant red edifice of the Prudential headquarters. All shuttered and finished for the night, except for his speeding presence. Still here, still with much to do, too much to do, too much he might never do. Fuck.

Ahead, a limo had braked at a red traffic light, its black windows and bodywork like a bullet of polished granite. It had to stop and wait, even though no one was there. But Robert didn't have to wait, and couldn't because nobody gave him that luxury. He stole past its gleaming flank and left his handprint, hot and cloudy, rode hard away. Give them something to wonder about, when they finally got out and noticed.

..

Robert was in the studio lounge as Paul dragged his feet in and fell gracelessly onto the sofa, like a shot albatross crashing from the sky. 'What's going on?' he said. This was his routine way to say hello.

Robert had quite a lot to explain, about what was going on.

Paul stared. 'But we all agreed.' His voice rose; an offended bleat. 'We certainly did agree,' said Robert.

Paul protested, staring at Robert as if he held him personally responsible. But they were on track for amazing PR. They were going to use Bowie's cover artist. What about the tour?

Strangely, the more Paul blamed and complained, the calmer Robert became.

'Our tour,' said Paul, beginning all over again. 'What about our tour?'

Paul was now on his feet, making his own tour. Of the kitchen cupboards. In case the cleaner had tidied a bowl of snifter alongside the cornflakes and ketchup.

..

Robert made a dignified statement to the BBC, which was on their site within the hour. *Everest body not Ashten Geddard, band says*. He made the statement by email so there could be no misinterpretation, and no risk of a wormy journalist wriggling between the cracks.

His online search for Ashbirds news also pulled up something else.

Paul had made a friend on a tabloid.

Dear God. He might have told them anything. The redacted songs. Their plan about the body. Especially if he'd had a deep breath of white devil, to paraphrase an Ashbirds song. Robert felt a feverish tingle. It might all be out there.

Jared might see. He might discover how thoroughly Hugo had made a fool of him, every last detail.

The article was interrupted by adverts, pop-ups, videos. It took a while to get through the text. With each new paragraph, Robert's pulse surged for a fight, a big change.

Paul had talked exclusively about himself. About his lost years after the boy band split. His drugs hell, of course. His triumphant return to Ashbirds. What? He wasn't an Ashbird until Robert personally hauled him out of the Loser Street call centre. Robert could have co-written the fourth album with Hugo by himself.

Paul made a small mention of creative strains in the band and affirmed his dedication to music.

It was not armageddon. Not yet.

50

Approached from the car park, Tribhuvan University Teaching Hospital in Kathmandu was a squat, square building with bare red bricks and ribs of concrete. Hugo had found a hotel nearby so he could visit Charmian. He was carrying her rucksack.

His phone rang.

Oliver Jared.

Right. This had to be done.

He dodged past the taxis waiting at the entrance. A driver beeped his horn. You want me? Hugo shook his head. No.

He answered the phone. 'Oliver, how are you?'

He could already guess how Oliver was.

'I just saw the news online. Hugo, why do I hear it this way?'

Hugo put Charmian's rucksack by his feet. He sat on a wall next to a municipal-looking flowerbed of yellow blooms. 'There was an accident. A lot to clear up. The accident took priority.'

'And where are your priorities, Hugo? You were supposed to identify him. This money you've blown on flights and helicopters and bribes and this junket; it's coming off the piece for your charity.'

A junket. 'I fell off a mountain, Oliver.'

'Now the album has no publicity, I hope you realise.'

Hugo did realise. It hardly seemed important. 'I need to go back there.'

'Go back there? What? If you're not bringing Ashten back, what the fuck are you talking about?'

Shit. What was he talking about? He wasn't himself. 'We found a body. We don't have to bring him back. But he deserves a proper burial. Just fly me one way. I'll get back on my own.' Christ, he sounded like Charmian now.

'You should have done your rituals at the time, Hugo. I'm not paying another cent. And where are the pictures you were going to send? I haven't seen any.'

Hugo had not sent pictures.

'The other climber has the camera,' he said. 'The climber who was injured. The camera was injured as well.'

Injured. A deliberate choice of word. Because Jared was sounding thwarted and entitled, and talking too much about his investment.

'Your buddy had better have good travel insurance. I'm not paying for their rescue. And we need a picture for the press. There's always been a picture.'

A picture. Thank you for the reminder. Anyone would think you'd been doing this all your life.

'What about the picture we saw before you went?' said Oliver Jared.

The picture Charmian sent. Which they all inspected in the Glacier House after the concert. No one had recognised it as Ash. Even he hadn't.

'That picture,' said Jared. 'You can send me that picture?'

'I didn't keep it,' said Hugo. Actually he had, but he wasn't giving it to anyone. 'I'll be in touch.' He ended the call.

Hugo scrolled through his emails to Charmian's picture of Ash. He was sure the face was well obscured, but he checked again.

He looked into the distance. The view was characteristic Kathmandu. Power lines gridded the sky, pulled taut between the buildings. One of the blocks was painted a scorching shade of fuchsia. The concrete on the hospital was the colour of powdered ginger. The taxis were white and battered. None of it remotely like London. Hang up the call and their hassle was gone.

This morning, many hours before the sun came up, he talked to Elza Jones again. It began with a text.

Robert played us some new music. A ghastly song called 'A Shebird'. I think he was trying to be clever. He says he wrote it with Ashten.

Hugo was awake. He phoned her immediately. 'I know that song. Oliver Jared played it to me. A Shitbird.'

From her, an instant snicker of laughter. Surprised, wicked, from her guts. He'd never heard her laugh like that.

He heard a car pass, far away in England, where she was. She must be outside.

He was in his hotel room, looking out over the sleeping city. A corrugated roof that was pale grey in the streetlights. The close geometry of the blocks around the hospital.

'So what happens now?' she said. 'Did you get the climber's pictures?'

'I got them. I deleted them.'

'Okay.' Relief from her. It calmed him too.

There was the roaming noise of another car. It sounded curiously solo, as if she was in an empty place. Kathmandu was nearly five hours ahead of London. 'What time is it there?'

'Late. I'm in a car on Wimbledon Common. When I need to be alone I go for a drive. If a journalist follows me, I can keep driving until they give up. If I want to make a phone call, I know no one can hear me.'

That was smart.

'How much did your climber see?'

'I don't know. I'll talk to her later today.'

'I suppose you have to go back up the mountain.'

'Not yet. Another trip will take a bit of organisation. And fundraising. I must have burned twenty grand with this trip. Oliver Jared will bust me for it.'

'Don't rush back up there. I'm sure everyone can wait.'

He was sure of that too.

'I'd better go,' she said. 'Before Elliot thinks I've been kidnapped.'

'Be careful about texts,' was the last thing he said.

'I know. I won't do that again. I changed my password.'

Steve had rules. If you don't want it in a newspaper, don't put it in a text, email or voicemail. It's all stored somewhere. If you receive anything that might make a story, change your password immediately and pray that nobody had the previous one. And don't keep anything.

She knew Steve's security rules. Of course she did.

Now, in the hospital car park, Hugo looked at Elza's text again, about Robert's song. It was dynamite. Steve would say it should never have been sent.

By Steve's rules, he should delete it. He usually deleted messages he'd read, for tidiness. But he didn't delete this.

Hugo stood up, looked along the ginger-coloured building for the entrance. Time to visit Charmian.

Her private room was decorated in muted green, as if to look like a hotel, not a hospital. She was leaning back on wide pillows.

As Hugo closed the door, she looked up. Reached to pause her iPod, winging her arm out sideways to avoid tugging the drug line in her hand.

Her leg was in a cast, elevated by a hoist so she seemed to take a bold stride into the air. She wore a hospital gown of papery blue. The white bedcovers formed a rumpled sarong around her hips. Her uninjured leg was bare and muscular. She looked darkly tanned against the bleached white of the hospital linen and the plaster cast.

'How are you?' Never had a conversational gambit seemed so absurd.

Her tough smile. 'The drugs are wonderful. But my down suit is dead. I've had it for ten years. They cut it off me.'

Was her voice slower? She must be on something strong like morphine.

Drugs and the shock of the accident might make her memory unreliable.

'I brought your things.' Hugo looked for a place to put her pack, but everywhere was tubes or injured parts. He put the pack on a chair. 'Is there anyone you want me to contact?'

'You haven't snooped in my stuff, then.' The question was serious. Aggressive. It suggested she had no problem with lucidity.

She folded her arms, threading around the drip in her hand. 'So was it him?' She played with a smile. 'Your secret is safe, rock god. I'm not sharing it with anyone else.'

Hugo said: 'What do you remember?'

'No, no. You don't get out of it like that.' The words now seemed to come slowly. Was that a lag from the drugs?

She slammed her hand decisively on the bed. 'Where's my camera?'

She'd lost the tread of her earlier question. Was it Ash. Had she forgotten she asked?

Or did she think he had confirmed it by evasion?

Would she remember this conversation?

Hugo fetched her camera from her rucksack. 'I put a new battery in.'

She worked the buttons. Beeped through the stored pictures. 'You've deleted some.'

Hugo said nothing.

Her expression grew fixed and anxious. She scrolled. Checking for the keepsake pictures of the man with the lingering gaze?

Hugo asked. 'Who is that guy?'

'Just someone.'

'Your husband?' He knew it could not be.

She said a name. Hugo recognised him as a French climber who had won the Piolet D'Or award for a pioneering ascent. 'He fell.'

Hugo knew that too, now he was reminded of the name. The death had made the national headlines.

'Does your family know him?'

'Is this blackmail, rock god?'

Blackmail. That was sudden. And belligerent. Had she beaten back the fog of drugs? Did it indicate she was thinking of blackmail herself?

She might remember this conversation; she might not. But at this moment he had to take it seriously. And he might have an equal hold over her: her family. Did they know about the French climber who looked at her with such possessing affection?

She said: 'That body is Ashten Geddard, isn't it?'

He owed her nothing. And she, meanwhile, felt she owned Ash. She had trussed him into a grotesque trophy to assert that ownership.

'No, it's not him. I told you. He's in the wrong place. You said you've done your research. You know where he fell. How can it be him?'

She tunnelled him with her expression. 'Don't lie. You do it so badly.'

She still had her wits. He should never drop his guard with her.

'So what are you hiding? Did you push him or something?' Said with a roguish challenge. You know I don't think that, but what's the story?

The story? 'We weren't as strong as we thought we were. He fell. Nobody could reach him.'

She was quiet. Perhaps that answer was more honest than she expected. Perhaps, for all her bluster, she respected the difficulties of the situation.

'I need time,' he said. 'Time to finish a few things. Have they said how long you'll be out of action?'

'Six months. But doctors don't know. I heal when I move. And where that body is hidden, it's not a difficult climb. This is the biggest thing I've ever done. No one will ever repeat it. This will always be mine. Four weeks, and I can get back up there. Wanda Rudkiewicz didn't let a broken femur stop her on Annapurna or K2.'

'Wanda Rudkiewicz was an elite climber,' said Hugo. 'And she died.'

The same roguish challenge. 'You can come back with me to get him if you want.'

No, he did not want to climb with her. And no matter how determined she was, or how quickly she ditched that plaster cast, the Icefall wouldn't be navigable until next spring, when the ropes and ladders were fixed for the season. She might charter a helicopter, but that wasn't within her means or she'd have done it this time. However, she might be able to persuade a publisher or newspaper to fund it if she could convince them Ash was there. That wasn't impossible.

A nurse brought in a small tray like a child's tea-set. On it were several pots with coloured pills. Hugo stood up to leave.

'Four weeks,' said Charmian. 'This is mine.'

Her emphatic manner, reinforced by her accent, implied he owed her a moral obligation. His mind lashed back. Is that right? This is yours? So many people think that.

The nurse studied the chart at the end of the bed.

Charmian picked up her camera. She was done with him, or perhaps had forgotten he was there. Her aggression suddenly softened sometimes, like a slap under water. Was that the drugs? Now she was checking through the pictures, her breaths deepening. Agitated about the ones that had gone. Relieved for the ones that were still there.

Hugo walked away down the green corridor. Four weeks. Morphine talk? In all seriousness, she surely could not be back on the mountain in that time. But he'd already seen her determination knew no limits.

He checked his phone. Hopped through a few recent texts until the message from Elza, relieved to find it was still there.

51

So many times Hugo had made the statement about how Ash died.
'He fell. We couldn't reach him.'

In 1992, after their second album, Hugo and Ash went on tour. Travelling without knowing where they were going. An aide booked everything, got them to the airport in a blacked-out car, rushed them off the plane and through the city in another blacked-out car to a hotel whose lobby was cleared of other guests, took them to the rehearsal studio, the radio or TV interview, to the gig venue, then back to the hotel and then the airport. They couldn't drive a car themselves in case someone jumped in front of it or crashed into them and sued for the injuries. They were loaned private jets by rich playboys. It had been months since either of them bought groceries or boarded a train.

In New York, Ash's hotel room was broken into. Nothing was stolen, but the rumpled, stained sheets showed his bed had been used. The manager and security team were distraught. Ash hid from their apologies and promises in Hugo's room. They leaned on the balcony, glared at the imprisoning grids of concrete and glass and talked about how everything was rubbish.

'I met a guy who said he can take us up Mont Blanc,' said Ash.

'I was going to say we never did Ben Nevis,' said Hugo.

'Ben Nevis? What would be the point of that?'

Hugo spun a beermat down into the inching, squealing traffic. 'Mont Blanc would be cool.'

In the middle of the tour, they had a fortnight's break. They went to the Alps. White days. Indigo skies. Abundant silence.

Space. Solitude. Clothes that were a new uniform for a new kind of task, transformed who you were. Tools, ropes and harnesses, which transformed how you moved. Lessons in new skills and all day to learn them. The clean slice of an ice pick into snow. Peaks folding blue into the distance. 'That was easy,' said Ash as they stood on the summit. 'We should do something bigger.' It had not been easy, but Ash liked to breeze through achievements that others found hard.

They resumed their tour. They were smuggled across cities, state lines and continents, not knowing what was beyond the windows of the car or the tour bus. They saw each other for most of their waking hours. The music press treated every utterance as gospel while also sneering at them. Interviews were edited so the two of them agreed on everything, as if they were clones. Or edited as if they fought, as if each was the other's gaoler. A *New York Times* journalist asked for Hugo's opinion on a book written about the band. Hugo didn't know about the book. People wrote books about them all the time. In this book, Ash said he wrote all the songs. Hugo put the journalist right. Ari Markson told Hugo that Ash wanted to file a lawsuit for the sole songwriting credits. Until that moment, Hugo didn't dream that Ash had actually said it.

Ash dropped the lawsuit but told *NME* that Hugo had left the band. Hugo hadn't, but after that he did.

He wrote albums for other artistes, living with them at luxury studios in the middle of a desert or on an island. Windsurfing or camel-riding by day. Recording by night.

Ash stayed in London and began a relationship with a dancer, made the paparazzi adore her and announced that his first solo album would be for her. He told *X* magazine that Hugo was a session player hired by the record company. He told the *New York Times* that Hugo held him back and made him repeat the same old work. *Wonderstuff* magazine got viciously into the spirit, and reported that Ash had had a malignant growth removed that had been crippling him for years. Then Hugo wrote 'Hurricane' and an album to go with it. On the first side, every song began with the first two letters of his name. Ash sang them, either not noticing or not caring. Hugo didn't care that he didn't notice.

They forged each other's autographs on photos. They spoke to journalists on separate phone lines at the same time, both pretending to be Ash.

Ash said it again.

'Let's get away from this rubbish. Back to ourselves. I've found someone who can get us to the top of Everest.'

Hugo argued several reasons why Everest was probably not as 'easy' as Mont Blanc, but knew he would agree. It was a trick Ash had: the 'come with me' moment. He could make you take his emotions, make you want what he wanted. Hugo could never resist.

..

Ash engaged an elite guiding company and a trainer, Natalia, to get them fit. Natalia looked like she was sculpted of tough rubber. Her abs, which she displayed a lot, were corrugated with muscle. Even her jaw looked muscular. It seemed to be constructed of triangular planes, like origami. They went for training runs. Ash turned each run into a race, staying at a just-faster pace than Hugo and Natalia. Which was certainly getting back to his essential nature.

'Listen,' said Natalia to Hugo. She gave him a white plastic bottle of tablets. 'When you get to Kathmandu, start taking these.' The bottle looked innocent enough, like aspirin. The label said dexamethasone.

Hugo knew about dexamethasone from their pep-talks about altitude acclimatisation. Climbers could get sudden, fatal accumulations of fluid on the lungs or the brain, and their guides would carry emergency jabs of dexamethasone to stabilise them while they were airlifted to hospital.

'Take a couple of these tablets a day,' said Natalia. 'Or that guy's going to kill you.'

..

Hugo and Ash flew to Lukla and began the trek to Base Camp. Treading the slender bridges over the gorges. Gasping at the effort to climb the steep cobbled villages, while porters overtook them, carrying massive loads. Even the local children walked faster than they did. Ash watched them with wonder, wheezing in defeat. 'Fucking amazing place.'

Back in London, or indeed anywhere else on the planet, Ash would not have laughed as a ten-year-old in a pink hoodie bounded past him up a hill.

As with the Alps, the new territory erased everything they knew. It erased Hugo's ability to talk to Ash.

In most aspects of life, he now found Ash hard to take, especially the way he treated people. Hugo still sometimes thought about that Christmas when the distraught girlfriend tracked them from Bonnet to the half-built house and told him about the promises Ash had broken. At the time it seemed like a sad muddle, but Hugo saw Ash repeat that muddle with everyone. Girlfriends, musicians, aides, personal trainers, healers, voice coaches. He would declare an all-consuming need for a person or their expertise, woo them to work for him. Sometimes they left other jobs. Just as abruptly, he'd tell Markson to fire them. He chose them. Then he un-chose them.

Also, there were their own rifts and reunions. Hugo was accustomed to those, after a fashion. He might even have set the pattern himself, when they were teenagers and he joined the weddings band to send Ash a message. Ash never forgot a message.

Their true language and culture was studio, song and sound. That culture was in every meaningful word Hugo thought to say to Ash. Even their escapes were part of that purpose, to retune their souls, help them make better art. Now, here, without music, Hugo had nothing to say to him.

From their earliest years, music was their secret power. A bolthole for both of them, away from parents, teachers, normal life. It was their source of true meaning, their rebellion against the oppressive disappointment that life seemed to force on them. Their sacred space where they made the world they wanted. And forgot the things they disliked about each other.

Who, actually, were they now? When they weren't touring or recording or training to come here, they had entire lives they never shared. Hugo played in jazz clubs, incognito. Ash had a show-off affair with a gawky dancer, Elza Jones. What was she? Hugo would like to ask Ash about her. Was she a soulmate to settle down with? A novelty dalliance? A tactic to keep him on the front pages?

Now, in this place, with no limos or assistants or appointments or areas specially emptied for them by security, Hugo felt like a pit pony released into paradise. Walking all day in daylight, mountains, gorges and dust. He had been rebuilt with an overwhelming new set of senses, where nothing tasted, smelled or felt like it ever had before. They could share this.

Ash, meanwhile, was giddy with new people. He talked to them, not to Hugo.

They walked separately.

In some of the hostels they stayed in, they had to share a room. Hugo, exhausted, crashed into oblivion long before Ash came to bed. At breakfast and back on the trail, Hugo spotted clues that Ash's night had been lively. A trekker rolled up her sleeves and Ash's artwork was on her forearm, a phoenix drawn in marker pen. Another trekker had the Ashbirds logo on his bald head, like a tattoo. Did Ash even sleep?

The land became higher, bleaker. One morning, Ash didn't come to breakfast and still wasn't out when the group was ready to leave. Hugo went to his room.

Ash was still lying under the covers, on his side, his hair straggled over closed eyes and a sleep-slackened jaw. Hugo would not call his name. Ash had stopped talking to him. But everyone was waiting.

Hugo threw Ash's backpack on the bed. He threw it hard, hating to make that bid for his reaction. Ash did nothing. Hugo threw boots. Forced out some words. The guides will leave you behind.

Ash turned, opened his eyes and watched Hugo, as though he couldn't understand.

Sorry if you're tired, said Hugo, not sorry at all. We are all tired. We're now going.

Ash did walk that day, in a mood that changed the temperature of the air. People walked beside him, tried to chat, then moved away, not comfortable to be near him.

They walked close to Hugo and muttered. Is he ill? Is he suffering from the altitude? Has he had bad news? They seemed to think Hugo should know.

On a long, webbed bridge across a gorge, Ash stopped walking. Trekkers from other parties edged past him, annoyed, getting stuck with their bulky backpacks, but still he didn't move. Vertigo, said more than one person, to Hugo, giving the problem to him. For God's sake, get him to cross or he'll cause an accident.

Hugo went back to Ash. Ash stared down into the tumbled boulders far below at the bottom of the rift, his elbows propped on the handrail. Was it vertigo? That seemed unlikely. They'd crossed countless bridges like this with no trouble. Hugo jogged Ash's shoulder and didn't stop until Ash turned his head and looked at him.

There was something dark and different in Ash's eyes. Not fear. A catatonic stillness.

Years before, Hugo had gone with his parents to clear a house that had belonged to an elderly lady. Her husband was there. He sat in a Chippendale chair, so bleak and still that it put a frightening sorrow in Hugo's own heart. Now, looking at Ash's expression on this bridge, Hugo felt it again. He asked: Is something wrong?

'Just leave me here,' said Ash.

A porter in collapsing sandals led a yak onto the bridge. Its horns and panniers took up the entire width, which forced Ash finally to the other side. He walked on, wrapped in warning silence.

The following day they reached Base Camp. A sprawl of nylon colour across the foot of the mountain, busy with people. Low tents like coloured bubbles for sleeping in. Marquees for meeting, dining or showering. The mirrored tiles of solar power rigs flashing in the high light. All strung with prayer flags, the national karmic bunting.

Ash and Hugo's expedition had their own enclosure, surrounded by a tall windbreak in turquoise fabric. Getting there was like crossing a crowded beach, stepping around tents and generators, passing people crouched beside stoves or sunbathing. A man about to enter a shower tent saw Ash, turned and grasped his hand, staring, his towel over his arm. A woman setting out her climbing kit on a rock saw him, gasped, and threw her arms around him.

The effect on Ash was like daylight on a flower. He opened and warmed, seized people's hands, saying, 'Isn't this place amazing, aren't we lucky to be here?' Hugo pulled the peak of his cap down and his hood up, wanting to disappear.

At their enclosure, Hugo called to the camp manager. 'Don't let him invite them in.' The camp manager bolted the gate as soon as Ash was through.

Inside, Hugo went for a long, solitary shower. When he came out, Ash's rucksack and walking jacket were thrown down by the gate.

'He's gone out, hasn't he?' said Hugo.

'He has,' said the camp manager, worried.

Hugo explored. The communal area had a hi-fi and a small library. He spent some relaxing hours engrossed in a travel book by Paul Theroux. Ash came back.

He was carrying an acoustic guitar.

'Really?' said Hugo.

They had a policy of not playing random improvised concerts. Someone would make a bootleg and sell it. Every fluff would be itemised and analysed. And many of the climbers here did not want to be made to hear music anyway.

Ash took a chair, sat down and placed the guitar on the table. 'I've told them it's just today. One special night. Tomorrow, we're just climbers like everybody else.'

This was the old Ash, full of their unique mission. Come with me. Let's be extraordinary.

'Weren't we getting away from this rubbish?' said Hugo, happily, reaching for the instrument.

Rifts and reunions. That was what they did.

They jammed a few songs outside the biggest dining tent. A crowd gathered, bringing chairs or sitting on the ground. As darkness fell, Hugo could see attentive faces through the entire tent city.

'What shall we finish with?' said Hugo to Ash.

' "Hurricane"!' called one wag. Several other people called 'No', in genuine and superstitious alarm. Nobody here joked about the caprices of weather.

'Dido,' said Ash quietly to Hugo. He meant the aria from Purcell's *Dido and Aeneas*, which they had performed recently for a charity concert.

'On guitar?' replied Hugo, doubtfully. He originally accompanied it on the cello, and it needed a legato instrument with long sustain. But Ash was already preparing, turning his face away from the microphone with lowered eyes, seeking the mood. The audience hushed. Ash's grip on the mic tightened. Ready. Hugo gave him the introduction, in spare, solo notes. Ash opened his eyes wide and sang.

The sound was spellbinding. The aria was written for a woman, but Ash managed the range easily, in a soaring, otherworldly counter-tenor. Hugo played a minimalist accompaniment, like a lute, while Ash sang his soul into the mic he held between his two hands, as if he was drinking from it and it was drinking from him.

The lyric was a plea for wrongs to be understood and forgotten. As Ash sang, he seemed to have self-knowledge, as though he fully knew he was ruled by savage and reckless emotions that punished everyone around him and would always master him, as if his very nature was a tragedy. Damn, thought Hugo, I wish I'd been Henry Purcell and had written this for him. It fits him completely and he knows it. '*Remember me*,' Ash sang to the sky and the moonlit people and the silvered, eternal peaks, and Hugo thought I will. I will always remember this.

..

They began acclimatisation sessions. Short ascents to higher altitude in thinner air, then back to Base Camp to recover. Training their bodies. Training their nerve, too.

One ordeal was the Khumbu Icefall.

It had to be crossed before dawn, before the sunlight made it unstable. A landscape of tilted walls and towers as immense as cliffs, like a city after an earthquake. Many had a Daliesque beauty, sculpted by the sun and wind into fins and hollows. There were cracks in the ice. Some could be stepped over. Some were wide gulfs that were crossed on bridges made of aluminium ladders, which tilted and flexed, and felt as if they would crease like hairpins and carry you careering down. Each crack, big and small, gave a glimpse of endless black depth, as if the whole region floated on a swallowing null. The null sang with music from the waters that ran underneath in the darkness. The sky echoed with sudden, heart-freezing crashes, as a tower came down.

Hugo's body did not like the altitude. His head hammered with pain. His stomach slithered like a restless worm. Ash was full of strength, as if he was still in a performance, radiating energy and joy.

His energy charmed the people who had loved the concert and irritated everyone else. Ash fed off them all. He worked to keep his supporters believing in him. He took pleasure in annoying the others, climbing past them when they were tired, mastering the ropes and tools after just one demonstration, crossing every nerve-quaking ladder with focus and calm. The star who deserved his followers. The upstart show-off oik who was better than he should be.

Back at camp in the evenings, Ash decorated the main tents with his thick pen, putting his mark everywhere. Hugo lay on his sleeping bag, too nauseous to speak, worried that with his heaving senses he would make a fatal mistake with his footing or clip onto something that wouldn't take his weight.

Hugo went to the camp doctor, who made him do star jumps, listened to his heart and lungs, said the sickness would clear and passed him as fit to carry on.

Hugo showed him the bottle of dexamethasone he was given in London by the fitness trainer Natalia. 'Should I start taking these?'

The doctor saw the label. 'Jesus no. That stuff is proper nasty. It will stop you feeling altitude symptoms but you won't know if you develop something dangerous. It's meant to be a rescue drug to keep you alive while you get off the mountain. Who gave it to you?'

Hugo handed it to the doctor. 'Keep it.'

'I bet you were charged a lot for it too.'

Hugo didn't know what he was charged. He didn't deal with the bills.

..

They moved to a higher campsite. That night, Hugo came across Ash sitting on a rock in the darkness, away from the lighted tents.

Hugo sat down next to him. It was mesmerising, a crystalline view into the far distance of the universe. Tiny speckle galaxies, fine as dust. More substantial stars and planets closer to. A travelling light that was probably a satellite.

Hugo remarked that it could be a spaceship.

'It could take me away,' said Ash.

His voice was quiet and small. At last, his batteries were empty. And not before time. 'Have you eaten anything?' said Hugo. 'Come on, let's get something.'

Ash said nothing. His silence had a shut-down quality, as if he had reached a point beyond exhaustion. Hugo offered Ash his water bottle. To make contact.

Ash took no notice of the water bottle. He said: 'It would be good to go out there and disappear.'

'You mean, not go back? I can't imagine going back either.'

Eventually Ash spoke. 'There's nothing I want to go back to. I'm just making a noise to keep away the silence.'

At that precise moment, the mountain's splendid silence was sundered by a consumptive, spasming cough. It went on, obviously past the point where the cougher wished it would stop. They would probably all develop this, they were told, because of the altitude. The outburst would have been funny after Ash's remark about silence, if not for the pain that was starting to spread like a red pressure in Hugo's head.

Ash was still staring into the darkness. Hugo jogged his shoulder. 'We're all trashing ourselves up here. Come on. Drink something. Eat something.'

Ash did not move. His stillness was blank, like the time on the bridge. Hugo had a sudden feeling that he had badly misjudged something. What had he misjudged?

Sitting out here wouldn't help. Hugo stood up. 'It's this place, Ash. Come on. Come back to the tent.' Ash remained where he was sitting.

Okay, he wouldn't move. No use trying to make him. Ash didn't have a headtorch. Hugo gave him his own. Ash wouldn't lift his hand to take it, so Hugo put it on his lap, pressing it into place as if Ash was a stubborn child. 'Don't fall off anything. Remember we were told about the guy who walked off the side of the mountain when he went for a leak.'

Ash spoke again. 'You keep pouring your words onto me. Like I'm a vessel, waiting for you to fill me up.'

Where did this come from?

'All your tidy lyrics,' said Ash. 'Your catchy hooks. You need me

201

to sing them. Nobody will listen to you if I don't.'

Oh, right. He was starting another sulk cycle. Except he didn't have a newspaper to perform it to. He only had Hugo. Well Hugo wasn't having that. Not with this headache.

'Stop that right now.'

'They should remove my brain so I'll be your puppet. All these neat songs. Then everybody would be happy.'

The strange thing was, he sounded sad. He wasn't fighting or ranting. It was like a drunk person, soliloquising their inner misery. And not caring that they smashed up their home while they did it.

'Those songs don't say anything, really. Not what I'm really feeling. There are things I want to say and you have no idea what they are. You bury me. You suffocate me. With all your words and melodies.'

'And you're pouring petrol on everything, just like your father.'

Silence. If they ever referred to this event, it was with camaraderie. *Things could be worse. We could be like your father.* Hugo never used it the way he used it now, to strike a mortal wound. He was shocked at himself. What would Ash do?

Ash said nothing. He had no fight to send outwards. Only inwards.

But Hugo had fight. 'So, Ash, what do you want to say? I'm interested.'

Silence.

'You don't know what you want to say. But you're being held back? Great. I'm being held back too. Do me a favour? Don't dick me about like last time. Let's not make any more lawyers rich. Oh, and write down that fine speech you've just given me. You'll need a seriously sorry-for-yourself song to launch your solo career. I mean your second solo career. Though if you get stuck you could see if I'll write something for you.'

Ash didn't look at him, even when Hugo had to touch his knee to take back his torch.

Hugo went to bed.

..

The following morning, Ash wouldn't get up, like the day on the trek. Hugo grasped Ash's sleeping bag at the toe and stripped it off. The cold would surely force him up. He didn't move.

They had to get going. Hugo pulled off Ash's beanie hat. Mashed snow into his hair. Ash sat up slowly and stared into the gap between his socked feet in a way that tuned Hugo out, and was so vacant it frightened him right to his heart. Hugo went out and cadged hot water from another member of their team and came back with a cup of tea, which he put in Ash's hands. His headache blared like a siren every time he straightened up or bent down.

Ash said: 'You find it so easy, don't you?'

'Yeah,' said Hugo, 'this is where you stop being a spoiled popstar.'

..

The higher they ascended, the longer everything took. Getting undressed and dressed while agonising cramps locked their leg muscles. Fastening boots, gaiters and crampons when the cold made their fingers numb and alien. Even the simplest task required a trance of patience and commitment. Chopping snow; starting the burners to melt it. Hugo's thumb was grated raw with the forty or fifty strokes it took to get a flame from the cigarette lighter. He would pass the lighter to Ash, who would make a few listless tries, then lie back on his sleeping bag, dropping the lighter beside him in the bedding so Hugo had to finish the job.

Ash became one of Hugo's personal chores. Making sure he wore dry socks when he said he didn't care if he got frostbite. Checking his crampons were secure when he stared at them without interest.

Hugo persevered in a fire of bloody-minded refusal. Refusal to accept his own exhaustion. And Ash's laziness. 'You made us come here,' he said. 'This is something we will finish.' Everybody developed the cough.

The night before they summited, they were allowed to sleep in oxygen masks. Hugo crawled into the tent. Ash was lying on his back, wearing his mask. A black rubbery cover for the mouth and nose, a small silver tank of gas and a red pipe. He pulled it aside and spoke. 'Get some of this stuff. It's bliss.'

He sounded alert, contented.

Hugo put the mask over his head. It smelled of rubber. He opened the flow. The first breaths were a sweet gush of freedom that loosened a tight band from his throat all the way down his ribs. He sank onto his sleeping bag, beside Ash. They breathed. They laughed. When had they last laughed?

Outside, the sun was setting. Hugo could see it spilling scarlet over the snow. He nudged Ash with his foot. 'Fab sunset out there. Go and take a picture.'

'Nah. Got a headache. You do it.'

Hugo couldn't be bothered either. They lay still. The colour outside the tent deepened to an astonishing, luminous crimson, like a sky of Turkish delight.

Hugo pulled his mask back. 'Looks like a good one.'

'Yep.'

Hugo started to laugh again. It was incredibly funny, witnessing a sunset in this rare place, and lying like a pair of wasted old-timers in rocking chairs.

Ash also laughed. The oxygen masks hissed and muffled the sound, and that was all the sillier, and also made them look a bit like elephants, and the oxygen itself made it inebriating, after so much starvation, which made them laugh all the more.

It was Ash's last sunset.

..

Summit day began at nine that evening. Hugo was woken by a torch. Their guide's bearded face was in the tent opening, his headtorch a cyclops light in his forehead. 'Get going, guys.'

Two hours later, they set off into darkness. Other teams were already on their way. A path of head torches, inching upwards, a glimmering chain into the night.

They crossed a wide snowfield, a plateau of blue in the light from the stars.

They passed an old camp. Tent fabric shredded by the wind. Foil food wrappers, brittled by the ultraviolet light.

The sun arrived as a blush over Tibet, opened into a streak of flaming orange, as if the blue icy land was tilting into a sea of lava. As the sky formed in the darkness, so did the valley below, a slanted infinite depth that skewed Hugo's balance like the heaving deck of a ship. He stopped, unable to move. The void was magnetic. It wanted to pull you in.

Someone bumped into him. Hugo turned and saw Ash, his eyes over the oxygen mask gunning for Hugo to get going. Hugo let him pass. There was nothing wrong with Ash's motivation today.

They changed to fresh oxygen cylinders. Hugo was already exhausted. He should have been noticing when they were on the Balcony, the South East Ridge, notorious places on the summit route that they'd been learning about for weeks. Instead, he was in a trance where nothing moved except the determined lines of climbers chopping into the snow with clawed feet, pulling themselves up in lurches. People in padded suits like coloured spacemen, risen from their sleep to climb to the crown of the world. They walked a knife-edge shelf along a drop into a distant snaggled valley of white ice and black rock, then climbed a vertical face, the Hillary Step, past old ropes decayed to ragged tatters, like stranded seaweed.

Finally, they stepped up onto a small sloping shelf of ice. Planted in the middle was an alloy pole; the official marker for the summit.

They couldn't stay long. Hugo and Ash lowered their masks. Renchi, their guide, took pictures. Various markers were fixed to the summit pole. Buddhist prayer flags, snapping in the wind. A Japanese flag from one of the other teams. A football scarf caught on Ash's spiked boot, then on Hugo's too, binding them like a three-legged race. 'Look at all this shit here,' said Ash as he and Hugo untangled, stamping and bumping in their burly suits, fumbling to grip in the fat gloves. 'We've left hotel rooms in a tidier state.'

The descent was quick. Now, in full daylight, the ridges had horrifying depth. The fixed ropes were like impossible questions. Each time Hugo clipped on for a descent, he anticipated the rush of terrifying, swallowing speed. He clung to the idea that the camp waited below. He just had to keep his wits until then.

They changed to new oxygen tanks at the South Summit, where they had seen the sunrise. Renchi, their guide, was helping another climber who was looking at his tank in confusion.

'We did it,' said Hugo.

Ash screwed a bottle into his regulator. 'Where are your pills?'
'Pills?'

Ash snapped the mask back onto his face and sucked in a breath.
'I've used all mine. You'll have to give me yours. I'll never get to the
summit without them.'

Ash still had his sense of humour. Hugo was too wiped to laugh.
'I'm going down to get warm.'

Ash seized Hugo's arm. An immobilising grip, like a citizen's
arrest. 'You're giving up? Because you're a bit cold?'

Ash still had the energy for banter? Hugo could only think about
his tent, where he could stop worrying that he would die. He waved
wearily at Ash. Whatever.

'I'm not giving up,' said Ash. He pressed his grip on Hugo's arm.
Wanting an answer.

'Ash, we've been up.' Hugo felt dumb. He was the person who
was too tired to tolerate the joke. He laughed a bit, to show he
wasn't a moron.

Ash wasn't laughing. 'The pills. Come on, hand them over. We'll
soon be at the turnback time.'

Was Hugo wrong? Ash was so convinced. Had Hugo dreamed
they summited? Every decision seemed life and death. If they
hadn't been up, he didn't think he could do it now.

Three climbers came past. Windscreen goggles. Elephant masks.
And, like elephants, they took slow steps, following the leader in a
careful line. Going downwards. Like everyone else.

'Ash, you've already summited. We both have. Renchi took pictures.' Hugo saw a strip of blue wool on his boot. From the football
scarf they stepped on by the summit pole. 'Ash, look at this. We got
that at the top.'

Ash shouted. 'People, what's wrong with you? Am I the only one
who'll climb this mountain?'

He truly didn't know.

In training, they'd been told to watch each other for signs of
confusion. Ash might need help. Hugo looked for Renchi.

Renchi was busy, kneeling over the other climber, who seemed
to need him more.

Ash's confusion might have an easy explanation. His oxygen
might be blocked. Hugo had had this already himself. He thought

he'd run out until Renchi switched the gas on. Hugo had turned it off by mistake.

'Ash, show me your mask.' Hugo reached for the regulator.

Ash volleyed his arm aside. 'My mask is fine. I'm going to summit this mountain so give me the fucking pills.'

'Ash, we've been up-'

'I know Natalia gave you pills. Give them to me.'

'We've been up already.'

Ash demanded the pills again.

Hugo pulled his mask away from his mouth so his voice would be clear. 'I haven't got the pills. I gave them to the doctor at Base Camp. I think something's wrong-'

Most of Ash's face was obscured by the mask and his padded hood. Just his eyes were visible, through the goggles. They radiated a dangerous-looking darkness, like a photo turning black in a flame. 'You gave them to the *doctor*? What the fuck?'

'You're not supposed to take them like... How many have you taken?'

'I'm going to summit. You're in my way.' Ash raised his ice tool. Its claw flashed in the sunlight. Hugo flinched backwards. Then he stopped. Christ, he'd moved without checking where his feet were. He was half a step from plummeting into the white valleys where nothing could ever be found.

When he had his wits again, Ash was at the vertical rope. Four climbers were coming down, slowly, carefully. Ash threw his hands up, pulled his mask aside to shout at them.

Hugo called to Renchi.

Then Ash was a speeding shape, going downwards. He fought it instantly and impressively, chopping into the ice.

Just as suddenly, he stopped. A small, sprawled figure on a narrow white shelf, lying very still, a long way below the ledge where they all stood.

No one spoke. Every face was looking down, unsure what they were witnessing, fearing they already knew.

Ash's shoulders quivered. Hugo's heart gave a painful jolt.

Ash might be okay. He might be trying to move.

It might be the wind on his suit.

Then, incredibly, Ash did move. He twitched, as if jerking himself alive. Took some heaving breaths, folded back on his haunches like a sprinter, paused for more breaths, then stood. Looked upwards. Lifted both arms, saluting the faces who looked for him. Face unmasked, a bare unvanquished smile. Sunlight gleaming in petrol rainbows on his goggles. I'm still here.

Hugo would remember that shape for the rest of his life.

The ice beneath Ash's feet collapsed.

There was no noise. Just a flash of sunlight on his oxygen tank as he fell.

..

Hugo came untethered from his own world.

He returned to London. The accident shouted at him from the front pages of newspapers. The sudden, unbelievable loss of Ashten Geddard, who was so alive and young on their TVs, turntables, posters, news cuttings, tapes, discs.

Ashbirds music howled out of shop doorways, thudded out of passing cars, ticked out of the headphones of strangers passing in the street. Every hour of every day the world seemed to take possession of Ash, to wonder that they had his voice and his image but not the real heat and breath of him, to share the staggering shock of his loss.

Hugo did not want to share it. He did not want their music played, to hear it used. It belonged to just them. A private conversation.

There was hate mail, dealt with by an agency. So many people who asked why. Hugo knew he should not answer questions, but he wanted to. People wanted answers. They blamed him. They should blame their ignorance. They did not know how small their warm world was, what went on in the places beyond. Places that could take away your air and then your mind.

He was worried by the teeming bustle of people walking through a London street. The cities with their plentiful oxygen, dependable ground and benign temperatures. It was all a lie. Stepping-stones floating on darkness, like the Khumbu Icefall. He preferred to be near the edges, where the truth was, where he could keep an eye on it.

Hugo gifted his royalties away. To medical research. Humanitarian organisations. Clean water charities. He hardly knew what he was giving them to. He gave a song to whoever needed it. You need a rescue? Please, please take this song.

He went to live in Namche, a town on the trekking route to Base Camp.

He helped families with their farms. Tilling the soil or building fences. It was soothing, and in his soul, he knew its rhythms. Like the work he used to see long ago on the farms in Bonnet. An old way, as old, at least, as his time on this planet.

Ari Markson sent him recording and writing offers. Hugo told Markson he was not making music any more.

But his mind still made music. It came from the daily toil. The routine moves of sowing a field or digging a potato crop suggested a beat. The movements were a metronome. Sounds and tones crossed and coincided and started a melody, like when he wrote in the studio. In his mind Hugo built the music of the new place he lived.

They were sounds of protest. High, brittle, like a bird cawing above a roof of glass, a shadow in the slowing cold. Hugo didn't like them.

These sounds were wordless, until words started coming. He didn't seek them; they landed from nowhere as he built fences and the music built itself. They were not the kind of lyrics he used to write. The person who needed those lyrics had gone, and so had the person who wrote them. It was music that spoke for their stranded ghosts. It was not to be shared, not with anyone.

He had nightmares. About people waiting in the Khumbu glacier. Deep in the ice, suspended like stopped angels. Tumbling out of avalanches, gloved palms facing the sky to say *here I am*. In crevasses, looking patiently up.

Namche had a hospital nearby. He volunteered there. He learned to treat injuries and illnesses. He learned about altitude medicine for the climbers. What the elevation and airlessness did, how it could burst arteries, block lungs.

He found scientific studies about the pills Ash had taken, dexamethasone. A strange word, a word he had not seen or thought about since the day Ash fell. Now, here it was again.

He read the studies. They were dense analyses that meant little:

an enigma of cohorts, double-blinds, confounding factors. He understood one statement in ten. Still, seeing these facts made dexamethasone more knowable, though he couldn't explain what they helped him know.

Then he read this. If dexamethasone was taken regularly, it drastically changed a person's behaviour. First, there was euphoria, then a crippling payback: a profound, intractable depression.

Hugo knew Ash's mind must have broken. But he thought it happened on summit day.

He realised he'd been seeing it happen all along, through their entire trip.

Trekking through the villages, staggering in the thin air, Ash high-fived the locals who outpaced them. Just a week before, in London, when they trained, his main pleasure was to show he was strongest and fastest. 'I've never known a guy so competitive,' said Natalia. 'He's always been like this,' said Hugo. 'If you open an envelope at the same time as him he wants to get it done first.'

Ash was always so compulsively, pointlessly competitive, until Nepal, when he started races with children, had to let them beat him, and sportingly cheered them for it.

After days of this, there was the morning when Hugo couldn't get him up. And in the higher camps later, when he hadn't the will to fasten his boots. It fitted the pattern exactly.

Here, documented in the textbook, was every inexplicable quirk Ash had shown. So exactly described, it was as if the book's writer had been with them. And Hugo had not noticed Ash was not himself? That he was getting worse, every day? He'd not thought Ash needed help?

When the crashes came, Hugo whipped him to continue. He thought Ash wanted to give up because he was bored. People even asked him if Ash was all right. He's just being Ash, Hugo said.

Had Hugo understood this correctly? He raised it with his tutor at the hospital. He changed the circumstances. 'I was offered dexamethasone while I was training for my climb,' he said. 'What would have happened?'

The tutor confirmed the symptoms Hugo had read about. She called them manias. Just like the book, she described what happened to Ash, correct in every detail, without Hugo telling her a single thing. Everyone seemed to know that Ash's behaviour was a known malfunction of mind and body, as obvious as a broken leg. The tutor added, with a questioning inflection: 'A doctor who supplied those drugs could be sued for malpractice.'

Hugo hadn't witnessed Natalia giving Ash the drugs. He couldn't testify about it for an official inquiry. He didn't volunteer more details.

'How many were you given?' said the tutor.

He could answer that. Two hundred tablets.

The tutor rocked back in her chair. Two hundred tablets was a shocking quantity. 'Still, everything turned out all right. You didn't take it.'

Ash must have been given the same amount. He'd taken them all.

Hugo had known from those earliest days that Ash wasn't himself.

But they barely knew each other any more, except in the studio.

But Hugo was the only person on the expedition who knew Ash at all. Ash didn't quit. It wasn't in his character. He aced all the practice climbs, glorying in it and irritating the tits off everyone, then he suddenly gave up?

But no, if he lost enthusiasm, he had a way of quitting abruptly. Especially with people. One moment you were his shining saviour. Then you were destroying his life and art. If you were working in the studio and he didn't like a session player or an engineer, he walked out. He went to the kitchen and played ping-pong until the person had been fired. Sometimes Ari Markson did the firing. Sometimes Hugo did the firing. Sometimes, Ash fired Hugo. With a remark in a book, or the music press, or a lawsuit.

When Hugo started the third album, he was waiting for Ash to fire him again. Firing Hugo was now in his dramatic repertoire. They finished the album without Ash firing him. They trained for Everest without Ash firing him. Ash fired Hugo, eventually, on that mountain ledge looking into the stars. *You suffocate me.*

No, Hugo sensed Ash was different by that time. The way he looked at people. His gaze was usually a heat-ray, seeking to stir up your molecules. Instead, he looked fragile and dimmed, as if he carried a preoccupying sadness, like a person who is bereaved but finds themselves still stuck with life. Hugo noticed and it made him curious. It made him feel strong. You brought us to this mountain, Ash. This was your quest. Now it's breaking you? You want to quit? Like you want to quit me? You don't do that here.

Hugo made him go on. It became a grinding ordeal that he hated. But he didn't stop. Ash took more drugs and slipped further into the black sinkhole.

But Ash was so exceedingly self-involved. His emotions were the most important thing he saw. If he was tired, he wanted to make the world tired too.

Then there was an appalling interview in a paper, where Elza Jones, who didn't know a thing, said Ash's death was Hugo's fault.

..

Hugo began to work as a guide. Training people from Sherpa families so they could work safely and get a better deal from the mountaineering industry. Some of them were eventually lost on the mountain. Red monks glided through the villages for the funerals. He should have kept more songs to rescue them.

Hugo shepherded climbers. He gave talks about mountain sickness. On one expedition, he saw a climber fade. He jabbed him with an emergency needle and saw him jolt alive again. He saw people imagine they had invisible companions climbing alongside them. While Ash circulated in the mountain's emptiness, in everyone's fantasies, in his own repeating dreams.

Now, twenty years on, here it was, the return the world was ready for. Desperate for.

And here was Elza Jones, in his phone, the only person who was not ready. Except for him.

52

Elza was in the room of fan letters, with scissors and a can of Spray Mount, laying out a design. Gina leaned in through the door, pulling a hair-tie out of her blonde ponytail and flaring her fingers so it snapped onto her wrist. She asked for something silly and lovely to read.

Elza did not read the fan letters when she worked with them. She chose them for the size and slant of the handwriting, the shade of the paper and the shape of the margins. She piled up pages that said *My first love, keep him alive, he went far too young* and she trimmed them, outlined them in colour, tinted them with an airbrush.

Gina settled at the table. 'I've had a vile day. Oh, here's a sonnet. It doesn't scan.'

Gina read out its fumbling lines, and made it silly and lovely. Elza cut a blue letter diagonally across.

'Here's a letter from a fan claiming she owned the ring that Ashten gave you, because it was stolen from her in Berlin.'

'Ashten never gave me a ring,' said Elza.

'You were wearing it in the *Sunday Times* interview,' said Gina. 'So it says here.'

'I didn't give an interview to the *Sunday Times*,' said Elza. 'Not this century anyway.'

Elza looked up. She didn't know what made her. It must have been something ordinary, perhaps a footstep, or a change in the light.

Hugo Bird was back.

Elza had a bisected blue letter in her hand and couldn't remember what she intended to do with it. Hugo Bird was here. Standing in the doorway. How long had he been there?

The sound of a person coming up the stairs. Two spectacle lenses made oval glints in the dark hall beyond the open door. Oliver Jared.

'Hugo,' he said. 'A word.'

53

Hugo followed Oliver Jared up the stairs and into the small attic room with the peaked ceiling and high window sill. 'I'm selling this house. I've had two good offers. The time is right to sell it.'

Hugo suspected he was being told this for a reason. 'Congratulations,' he said.

'In sales, timing is everything. This album's used up too much of my money.'

His tone was so personally disappointed, as if to say 'I thought I could trust you'.

'I didn't want you to be in any doubt about the costs,' said Hugo. 'To make a good album takes time.'

'But this trip...'

'Climbing has never been a cheap sport.'

Oliver Jared leaned against the window sill. The light from outside put him in silhouette. He ran his hand around his chin as if scrubbing away a thought that Hugo shouldn't see, or the words that came out wrong. 'Oh it's not about the money, Hugo. You broke our deal, my friend.'

My friend? Jared was not his friend. 'I'm sorry.'

'We all agreed. In this house, after Hyde Park. We agreed.'

Hugo had not agreed. He said nothing.

He heard a chair scrape in the room below. The blocky track of hard shoes across the wooden floor. Talking. Some of it Elza Jones.

The way she reacted when she saw him. Shocked and even affronted, as if she wanted to be better prepared. Or not to see him at all.

'It's not too late,' said Jared. 'We can issue a new press statement. Bodies are found all the time, aren't they? Where's that picture you showed us? The picture of the body.'

'I deleted it,' said Hugo, not for the first time.

'But I was never given a copy.' *And I had a right to it*, said the rise in his voice. After all that money.

'It's gone.'

'Don't be too sure. Phones can be hacked.'

Hugo remained silent.

Jared spoke again. 'I could have... we could have... made history.'

Interesting. Jared was trying to pretend he hadn't made a threat. Then he said 'I' and realised he should have said 'we'. These people were all the same. Parasites.

Jared scrubbed his face with his hand again. 'We could have made a beautiful ending to the story. Don't you think?' Conciliatory now. Don't be nasty. We're friends.

'Let me tell you a beautiful story,' said Hugo. 'The money men thought they'd get rich if Ash was found now, so they planned to identify him falsely.'

Jared raised his hands and shook his head. Like a preacher who would hear no evil.

'It's a sensational story,' said Hugo. 'I can think of five scumbag journalists who'd bid five figures for the exclusive. That would pay back all your money.'

Dealing with Charmian has prepared me for people like you.

Voices coming down the stairs. Robert's wife sounded upbeat, cheerful. She always was. Elza Jones sounded quiet.

Jared spoke. 'This is a pity, Hugo. You and I used to get on well. There's all this love around, right now. The fans are giving it all back. Some of them write every day. They hear one of our songs on the radio and they email about where they first listened to it, what it's seen them through, what it reminds them of. All these people are waiting for the album. I could fill twenty houses with their messages.'

So now Jared was trying to make him feel guilty? Jared didn't have the slightest idea about guilt.

'We could have given them a beautiful story,' said Jared. 'We could have made that for them. They love us so much.'

They love us so much. Our songs. The man thought he was in the band.

Hugo heard the front door. Elza Jones had left.

Hugo took a breath. 'Ash and I did a lot of good things together. Let's not make this into a money-grubbing circus. There are people in Nepal who need help, and I don't want the charity to feel it has to refuse because of a scandal that brings them into disrepute.' Subtext: I won't tell anyone if I don't have to. He smiled.

Jared smiled back instantly. Monkey smile.

'And my phone won't be hacked.'

'No no no, that's unacceptable.' Now Jared was pretending he hadn't threatened it.

'So what's going on with the house?' said Hugo.

'I'm taking sealed bids. The next few weeks. But look, why don't you visit your folks again while you're here. Take the helicopter.'

Take the helicopter? How much did a trip cost in that? Jared was no different from the record company execs in the old days. When Hugo asked for more studio or publicity money, they'd tell him they'd gone over-budget. Ash would ask and they paid immediately, and gave him a limo for the weekend.

Just now, Oliver Jared told him off for wasting money. Then offered him a helicopter.

54

Gina was pulling the cork out of a bottle of Shiraz.

'Tell me I'm being silly. But I had real vibes that we were going to find Ashten Geddard this time. I don't know why. Do you ever get that?'

Robert was slicing tomatoes for a salad. His knife passed into the globe of red flesh. The fruit fell apart in slices. He wasn't talking much. Gina knew she was talking too much, because she could see a locked room inside him again. And what was she doing now? Trying to talk it open, like a hostage negotiator? But she couldn't stop herself.

'Everybody seemed so ready for it,' she said. 'Elza especially. Just think of how long she's had this. Hugo arrived at the Glacier House while I was there, and there was such a weird vibe. She looked angry with him. I felt there was an awful lot she would have said if I hadn't been there.'

Robert arranged the tomatoes on two plates and turned the pepper mill over them. 'Did you ask her?'

At least he had answered. She wasn't talking entirely to herself. 'No. I didn't get the chance to ask her. But I wouldn't like to be in Hugo's shoes. I don't think anyone's pleased with the news he's brought back. Talk about killing the bringer of bad tidings. What do you think it will be like in the studio?'

'We'll find out tomorrow.'

Gina got the cork out, tidied the ragged foil on the neck of the bottle and reached under the counter for two glasses. She held one up to Robert. He refused.

She wasn't surprised. But she was disappointed.

55

Elza sat in a red velvet seat watching Dvorak's *Rusalka*. Beside her, Elliot was listening with careful attention. She still didn't warm to opera, but after the Hyde Park show, she felt she owed him an evening of dignified sopranos and big-browed baritones.

Opera. Are you sure? he'd said. Shut up and choose, she said.

While Elliot had his edges soothed, Elza needed to think. Hugo Bird was suddenly a substantial person, leaning in a doorway. Not just on a phone, as distant as the mountain, a voice that existed only to her. He was here, carrying a small injury next to his eye and looking thinner, to prove he had been real all the time she was talking to him, and so had all the things he said had happened. And now he had brought them back.

The soprano was starting an aria, a sound of sad, piercing oddness that seemed to be speaking for her. It seemed Hugo had come because she had commanded it, and she had no idea what to do.

56

Elliot sat beside Elza in the dark.

He knew Elza was not sensitive to opera. She was rarely moved by a film, either, or if she was you never knew it. They'd seen many movies where he might be blinking away tears, but she would be dry eyed. If something moved or upset her, she would make sure you never saw her cry. She didn't want to share it. But now, in the light from the stage, her face was wet. He felt ashamed he had seen it. She would not have liked him to.

And it surely was not the opera.

It must be this latest body from the mountain.

Elliot was so certain this would be over. A moment's sober thought should have disabused him of that. How could Hugo Bird be expected to go along with the plan made in the Glacier House? But Elliot had hoped he would, and that it would work because something had to. And now, beside him, Elza was in pieces.

He should take her hand. But she was facing straight ahead, not looking at him, not wanting her distress to be noticed. Elliot sat like that, watching the singers, glancing at Elza in her fortress of thoughts until the finale, the curtain, the applause, the bouquets.

They walked out into the autumn night. He put an arm around her. 'Okay?'

She was grinning now. 'Overblown tosh. Was it good for you?'

'Not the opera. I really hoped it would be over this time.'

'Yeah,' she said. 'Come on or the Tube will be hell.' She ducked away from his arm and took his hand, pulling him through the mob of shoulders coming out of the theatre, which stopped the conversation.

..

The following morning, Elliot's route to the bus stop took him past the Glacier House. Three press photographers were there, snapping lots of angles. Why were they interested in it again?

They were photographing an estate agent's sign. *Sold.*

Not even *For sale*. Already sold. That was Elza's gallery. Did she know?

He tried her phone. Got voicemail. Should he leave a message? No, that would sound panicky. And voicemails weren't allowed in Steve's rules.

He had a meeting at nine. He absolutely hated being late. But Elza shouldn't learn about this from a newspaper's website, or a journalist nibbling for a quote. He turned back for home.

He probably didn't need to do this. He'd tell her and she'd give her shruggy smile and say, effing galleries, who needs them? If she told him to bugger off to work, stop being a worrywort, and she looked like she meant it, that would be brilliant.

..

He found her at her computer in the passageway next to her studio. Silhouetted by the sun through the studio skylight, peering at the screen in a chin-poking hunch that would horrify the IT ergonomists he worked with. He told her about the Glacier House.

She loaded the browser.

'Well there it is. On the BBC. Nice of you to tell me, Oliver Jared.'

'You didn't know?'

She reached for her phone. 'I'm on it.' She waved her free hand at him. 'Scoot. You'll be late.'

57

Elza listened for Elliot leaving the house, the closing of the front door, the confirmation that she was alone again.

Elliot had turned back to tell her this. Elliot hated being late. He got them to dinner parties early, so that they had to kill time strolling the streets nearby or looking for a place to buy a last-minute gift of chocolates. But he had risked being late for a work meeting to tell her this news about the Glacier House. Or had he noticed how she was going to great lengths to appear normal? She felt everything was off kilter, right now.

She called Oliver Jared.

'Elza, I'm sorry you saw it like that. The press are bastards. That sign only went up this morning. They must have been watching.'

'Watching is their job, Oliver. Why didn't I know it was for sale? It's my gallery.'

'An offer came along, so I thought I'd test the market. And you do realise I've been financing the band? It's time for a conclusion. Everything is taking too long.'

'Well yes, it is taking a long time,' she said. 'I would like a conclusion too.'

She hoped for an ashamed hush. Instead, Oliver Jared said: 'It's been great having you display there. Really great.' Because Oliver Jared didn't hesitate in territory that was difficult or tactless.

'I can find you somebody to help dismantle the gallery,' he said. 'You can keep the keys until then.'

'I'll arrange the dismantling.'

'And we'll still get lots of letters,' said Oliver Jared. 'It's still a work in progress. You can have the letters. They're really to you.'

Those letters. 'No,' she said. 'I don't need the letters, thank you.'

He gave some other, practical details. The new owners were aiming for completion in five weeks. She rang off.

Five weeks.

She needed to talk to Hugo Bird. She hadn't yet. Now he was back, everything seemed to be on a countdown. Did he know about the Glacier House?

She cursored to his number.

He answered instantly. 'Elza.'

No need to ask 'how are you', or 'is it nice to be back'.

'You sound busy.' She could hear a drumbeat, smart and stirring. He was in the studio.

'I'll be finished at five.'

'Did you hear what Oliver Jared's doing with the house?'

'I did. We could meet there?'

'Yes.'

58

Robert was with Hugo in the control room. A guest engineer from Jodrell Bank Generation was in for a few hours, remixing a song for a trance Balearic album. Robert and Hugo guided him through the tracks on the master. He made notes on a wide paper chart he spread across the controls and asked for the piano solo in a more trippy style.

'Sure,' said Robert, and got up.

Hugo, grabbing his phone to call Paul, who hadn't been booked today, looked surprised and said: 'Do you play keys, Robert?'

'You play the piano, Robert?'

Oliver Jared also said those words when he came by at lunchtime to hear the mix. Robert knew it wasn't a compliment about his playing. Oliver Jared's glasses, twinkling with the light from the computer monitors and the glow-worm dots from the mixing desk, were like the display of a two-screened calculator, parsing numbers in the brain behind. Doing money sums.

'You know, I'm wondering about personnel. How many musicians do we need?'

Hugo also caught his real meaning. 'Stop that, Oliver.'

'We don't need two keyboard players if one guy can do both.'

'Robert's playing just for today. Paul will be back tomorrow.'

'He's back on Monday,' said Robert. 'Tomorrow's Saturday.'

'Is it?' said Hugo.

'Guys,' said Oliver Jared, 'how many hours does Paul sit around with nothing to do? Robert, how many instruments do you play? And how many does Paul play?'

'It's not an office, Oliver,' said Hugo. 'We're a band.'

Welcome to my world, thought Robert. We've had these arguments already, when you were away. Jared was already sore, and now you've come back empty handed.

The argument continued. Hugo told Jared what was what. Eventually Jared dialled a number on his phone and exited the control room, telling someone he was on his way.

Hugo stared after Jared's wide back as he went down the passageway past the gold discs.

'What else are we doing today?' said Robert.

'Oh,' said Hugo, vaguely, 'you could help with some new ideas.' He sounded distracted, as if it was a surprise that they were there to get a job done. Jet lag? Add that to the usual Hugo reality lag, and no wonder Oliver Jared was at the end of his rope.

...

Robert and Hugo moved to a smaller studio.

Hugo had a title: 'Come Back'. He sat at the Nord piano to block through a melody in stiff three-note chords. He sang. 'We carry the past inside us. It is a man, a man, a man in a glacier treading back, slowly.'

The lyric was not yet in tempo, but Hugo's pure voice made it like plainsong from a mountain monastery. The chorus was already perfection, as if he had had it prepared for years. 'And until it comes, til it comes, we will not ever rest.'

Robert took over at the Nord, cycling through the chords, directed by Hugo. Hugo wrote another verse that was rough in rhyme, true in gut. '*Guilt haunts you. Things that are not done right. Untruths stacked in your attic. Days you should have seized. Peace you should have made. A man in a glacier is bringing this to you, all your life, back to you. And until it comes, til it comes, we will not ever rest.*'

After a few hours they had a melody and lyric on Hugo's laptop.

'Nice work today, Robert. We've been wasting you.'

No kidding, thought Robert.

Hugo set his laptop on the floor and came to the Nord.

The bench was long enough for two. Robert gave Hugo the middle C position.

Hugo roamed through a sequence of chords. He had no dexterity but he still knew how to think through the keyboard.

'Look,' said Robert, 'just between us, do we need other musicians?'

'Don't worry about that. Oliver Jared doesn't tell us who we need.'

'I wouldn't say this in front of him. But Paul... He's a talented player, but I don't think he's always got the right sound. On the keys he's great. But he's not always in...'

'The right spirit,' said Hugo. It wasn't a question. So he already thought Paul didn't fit.

'I hate to say this because Paul's a mate of mine,' said Robert.

Hugo repeated the chord pattern. Something was taking shape. 'Paul's a good player. It's brilliant working with him. But those songs you've been doing with him...'

So Hugo had heard them. Robert's heart glitched. Yes, Hugo. What do you think of my songs?

Hugo gave a taut laugh. 'Just no.'

There was no pretending after that.

They worked. Robert played the melody Hugo had just developed. They tried a muted counterpoint in the left hand. Robert said: 'I was worried about those songs too. I'm glad you've said that. Paul hasn't got the Ashbirds vibe. Those are not Ashbirds songs.'

'They definitely are not.'

As if there was any doubt what Hugo thought.

They played the new melody again. Hugo took the top line, Robert the accompaniment. It was solid. It would hold your attention as a verse.

'We'll get Paul back for the tour,' said Hugo, though he sounded like he doubted there would ever be a tour.

'Yes of course we will,' said Robert.

59

Hugo saw the moment Elza Jones recognised him. A startled stiffening in her body as she walked down the street towards him. She transmitted emotion so easily. What had she been like as a dancer?

She looked away just as abruptly, nervous of the contact.

60

A couple of fans were outside the Glacier House. A girl with a jacket in a tropical shade of green was standing on the top step, while a guy filmed her with his phone.

Elza said hello as she passed them with Hugo Bird. The guy who was filming looked a bit amazed and also shifty. The girl gave a smile that was fierce and fixed, as if they had ruined everything and she hoped they'd go away soon.

Elza and Hugo entered the house.

Inside, with the door locked, they were alone, invisible to outsiders. In the chamber with the striped shuttered light.

When they were voice to voice, text to text, she talked easily to him. Like her own private ghost. Now he was here, she saw details that were not in her mental picture and made him a stranger. His tight-strung climber shoulders, his slightly damaged way of walking.

And those fans were outside, doing whatever they were doing.

She should take charge of her space, keep him busy. 'I've been itemising what I need to do. Dismantle the exhibits. The projectors and sound units...'

Hugo didn't speak. He put his rucksack on the floor, took out a speaker dock and tapped something into his phone. A beat punched the air, fast and feisty. Guitars rattled a reply in fidgety funk.

What was he doing? Elza asked. He handed her a clot of black wires, unfolded another and put it on. A wireless headset with a microphone and battery pack. Like singers use in concerts. When she got hers in position, the thundering music receded to the far distance, as if sent behind thick doors. Hugo fiddled with another box that had an aerial.

His voice sounded in her ears, close as a whisper. 'Testing?...'

'Steve's rules?'

'Yes, and Oliver Jared made some threats about phone hacking. He might have webcams here. And there's also our fanclub outside.' Hugo went to the front door. Looked through the spyhole.

He beckoned Elza.

The woman in the green leather jacket was standing on the step, twitching to the music that was playing in the house. Elza felt suddenly wild. What power they had. And a colossal secret. They could do anything.

Elza drew back from the door. 'Come and help me with the artworks. We'll need a ladder.' Wait; didn't Hugo have an injury? 'If you can carry a ladder.'

He followed her anyway.

She descended to the basement. Past the room with the giant mobile of glacier debris, which hung in darkness. She unlocked another door beyond it, hit the light, clambered past a vacuum cleaner, guided a ladder out. Hugo took the end. Like the time, not so many months ago, when he came to her house with Steve and she didn't know what to do with him, so she made him move the Havisham clock. Now she moved this ladder up the stairs with him, avoiding the paintwork, and she still didn't know what to do with him.

She directed him to the front room, which showed a film loop of sunrise and sunset over Everest. There was also a tent, fixed to the floor, which she had daubed with jagged graffiti based on something Ashten once scrawled on a guitar case. Oliver Jared's idea.

Hugo rested the ladder against the wall, for her to climb to the projector shelf. Elza leaned on a rung to test the stability. 'You think Oliver Jared would tap our phones?'

'Did you know what they all agreed?'

What they all agreed? What who agreed?

Hugo put a hand on her arm. It was the first time he had touched her. 'Before I tell you, you'd better have both feet on the ground.'

Elza sat on the ladder.

On the night of the concert, he said, before he flew back to Nepal, there was a meeting.

She listened.

Who was at the meeting, she asked.

Everyone, he said. Oliver Jared. Ari Markson. Steve. Not Gil, the drummer.

Elliot had also gone to the house. 'Elliot as well?'

'Elliot was leaving as I arrived. I don't know what he heard. He looked...' Hugo seemed to have trouble deciding how to describe Elliot. She guessed. Bemused. Bewildered.

'Do you think Elliot tried to change their minds?' she said. The thought was so hopeless, helpless, that they laughed.

The music thumped and jiggered, far off, as if it was several houses away. Was that really covering their conversation? Elza tweaked the earbud aside. The sound yelled in, loud as a nightclub. She replaced it and the sound shrank to the distance. She heard Hugo's breath in the earpiece. He sounded close. As if he was in her mind.

'I didn't agree to do it,' said Hugo.

'And look what we've done instead.' They laughed again.

Hugo sat on the floor. Elza eased off the ladder and sat beside him. Backs on the wall.

She asked what he knew about Oliver Jared.

'Steve did a few searches. He's a property developer.'

'So we're being fitted for concrete pyjamas?' They continued to laugh. It seemed so desperate.

'But even if Oliver Jared isn't in league with the Kray twins, there's something demented about him. Think of the money he's spent on this.'

'What about those fan letters? Why does he keep opening them? I'm sure he thinks they're written to him. Don't tell me you haven't had that thought.'

Yes, said Hugo's face. He'd thought exactly that.

'I think we're a superfan's exclusive toys. I don't think the album will be enough. He wants to find the body too.'

Hugo said: 'Everyone wants to be the person who finds the body.'

'How well is Ashten hidden?'

'You have to know where to look. It would be better if he stayed on the mountain and was never found again. I wanted to go up again and drop him into a crevasse. Do it properly. But I can't get back there.'

Elza noticed again the cut on his face. Close up, he had an older scar that showed a whitened line at the outer edge of one eyebrow, like thread under the skin. She had not known anyone who had so many scars.

'Did the climber know it was him?'

'I think she did.'

'Will she tell anyone?'

'She's a possessive sort.'

'You said she's broken her leg. How long will that stop her for? When I was dancing, if I got injured I'd do everything possible to be back on my feet.'

'The good news is, she wants to keep it to herself. She won't try to go again until she's fit. And she'll need help. And money. That gives us time.'

It gave them time. They wanted time.

What did they want this time for?

'What did he look like?'

'Elza, he's been there for twenty years.'

'Will you let me be ridiculous? I thought he'd be beautiful. Preserved. With all that cold.' She knew this was naïve. The cut on Hugo's left eyebrow said so. It showed the brutal, battering reality of that cold place. 'You knew it was him, though.'

He did.

'Would I know it was him? Have you got the picture?'

'Not here. I deleted it from my phone and saved it to a drive with a password.'

'You think I shouldn't see it?'

'His face was covered in ice. I honestly couldn't see much.'

A random thought landed in her head. 'Ashten and I talked about a wedding. He wanted a dress code. All the guests barefoot.'

She saw Hugo's thoughts racing, in the many darting movements of his eyes. The left eye creased more than the other when he was thinking. 'What is it?' she said.

'Do you think you'd have ended up married to him?'

'Whoa, you don't mind asking the big questions.' She looked at a scuff mark on the pale wooden floor. Tried to shift it by rubbing with her finger. 'No. I think when he talked about the wedding it was like planning a concert or a video; just a way to make people do stuff. Though he made you feel like everything he said was the truest statement in the world.'

'He did,' said Hugo. He rubbed the mark on the floor as well. Trying to help her with it. 'Speaking of weddings, what about Elliot? Any plans?'

'More big questions,' she parried, and laughed. Then, not laughing: 'We've never discussed it.'

'We haven't got very far with clearing up, have we?'

'You like to talk in metaphors, don't you?'

..

Elza slipped the key into the Yale lock. The front door opened. The deadlock was off. Elliot was home.

She dropped her door keys into the bowl, on top of his. Coming home had a sequence of habitual moves, each with its signature sound. The tumbler click of the turning lock; the snap of the latch as the door closed; the percussive jink as the keys landed in the bowl. She must have made them hundreds of times, yet she had never noticed how they followed a pattern, like a tune. The soft clatter of a keyboard in the kitchen as Elliot cleared through emails.

Entering the kitchen, slipping into his hug was also routine.

'How did it go when you talked to Oliver Jared?'

About what?

Was that only this morning? It felt like a week ago.

She talked about how she would have to dismantle her work. Elliot listened with a look of concern. He thought she was putting on a brave face, but dismantling the installations hardly mattered. She said: 'It's okay, the show had run its course. The visitors started taking stuff. Steve caught a fan unscrewing a door handle the other day.'

It was like making small-talk with a stranger, about subjects that were unimportant.

'Look, do you have to hang around with these people any more?'

She didn't need him to worry about this. 'It's nearly over anyway. I have to dismantle the installations, then I'm out of there.'

'Can't someone else dismantle the installations?'

'No. I have to.'

Elliot closed his laptop. Pulled her hand. Wanting her to sit down. 'There's something I have to tell you.'

He told her about the band's pact to identify Ashten, after the concert. Yes, he had been there. He heard it all. Knew about it from the first.

Layers of the day printed over each other. One person and then another saying Elza, sit down, I'll tell you what they wanted to do.

'I didn't tell you before. I thought it was what you needed. Then I realised they were doing it for their own reasons.'

'It's okay. I know about it.'

'I'm sorry,' said Elliot. 'I should have stopped them.'

'You couldn't have stopped them. It's okay.'

Elliot stood up, abruptly. The chair scraped noisily backwards, as if he had shouted. He went to the dishwasher. Grasped the cutlery rack, took it to the drawer. 'I've told you what they did. How can that be okay?'

'They're a bunch of guys with big talk. That's all.'

'Haven't they sucked you in enough?'

Sucked her in? Where did this come from? 'I'm not sucked in. It's just work. I'll deal with it.'

Elliot placed knives, forks and spoons in their drawer compartments. He said nothing. The dropping cutlery had less restraint. It crashed harshly into the drawer. He slid it closed and kept his hand on it, everything becoming still. 'I'll never keep anything like that from you again.'

She took dinner plates from the dishwasher. Stacked them in the cupboard, placing them with care so they did not make a noise. To calm the edge that was sharpening in him.

'They shouldn't have involved you. You didn't have a choice.'

'You aren't angry about it. You're not even surprised.'

'It's just what they're like.'

They returned to the dishwasher. She took wineglasses and he took china, while they carefully discussed whether she should be angry and tried not to be angry with each other.

61

Robert, reaching for the Gibson on the guitar rack, recognised the melody Hugo was blocking out on the Nord electric piano.

A surprised shiver. 'Prince of Silence, Queen of Pain'.

'We're really using that?'

Hugo sang. *'For he is prince of silence ... and you...'*

The angry anti-ballad that Hugo had junked a few months before. Now, Hugo found new lyrics and chords. It was no longer accusing and specific. It was universally puzzling, as if we were all princes of silence and queens of pain, full of misunderstandings. The melody was roaming, unresolved, full of hanging harmonic questions.

A guitar wasn't right for this. On the rack was a Travis Bean fretless bass. Robert tried that. Its looser tuning added an ambiguous texture; tender, mysterious. As Robert played, Hugo caught his eye. He liked this combination.

Before, working with Hugo had been a battle. He was so exact about what he wanted. So bloody exact, actually, that he would infuriate you by not hearing an idea you contributed. But now it was just the two of them, working without egos.

Robert put down the Travis Bean. 'Retro Mellotron harmonies?'

'Yes, let's try that.'

..

Later, Robert left the studio for a breath of fresh air and to make a phone call. A figure was coming towards him down the unmade track through the building-site badlands. Scrunch backed, crumple faced. Paul Wavell.

Robert's heart flipped like a landed fish. What did Paul want from him?

'Hi Rib,' said Paul. 'Gissa job.'

A job? Robert didn't owe Paul anything. And neither did Hugo, who was in the studio, working, and wouldn't appreciate being disturbed or made to feel bad about Paul.

Robert had to get Paul away. 'Let's have coffee,' he said, though where would they go? The only nearby place was the burger van for the builders at the tower block development.

Paul laughed. A cheeky light came into his eye.

'I'm here to work with Rolling Drunk Monk. Hope you've kept our powder dry.'

Robert watched him push in through the front door and speak to the receptionist. He continued to watch. In case.

A mourn-faced, sleepy-eyed guy with a monk tattoo up one arm came to collect him.

Little fucker.

Robert looked back out over the wasteland, clearing Paul from his head. A car turned in from the main road and crept closer, bonnet nodding in the potholes. A bizarre car. On its roof was a bar of lights, like a mobile disco or, no, actually like a police car, because Robert could now see the word *Police* on its doors, and a crest. Not British police; American, like from a 1980s TV show. Black body, white roof and LAPD emblems on the doors. What the fuck?

No, more bizarre even than that. It was a Bentley, sprayed as a 1980s American cop car.

It braked. And, oh lord, Oliver Jared put his head out of the driver's window, pleased as a kid, hand resting over the steering wheel, which was white leather. 'I just picked it up. You like?'

The cost of that thing could probably send them on tour. And the Bentley, with its square, grandmotherly styling, looked like a brick trying to be Concorde.

··

Robert and Hugo were due at the Glacier House for a photocall. Oliver Jared took Hugo in the cop car to record a short TV interview first.

Robert went for a blitz on his bike. He arrived at the house. Looked for a place to prop the bike in the hallway, though the white-wedding paintwork was now so scuffed he didn't have to be careful. The fake clock certainly showed the strain. Visitors had decorated it in sticking plasters on which they had written messages, to the band, to their own lovers. They readily confused the two. Oliver Jared took it as a personal compliment for his house. Gina, when Robert showed her, said it was sweet and funny.

A quick change to non-sweaty clothes in the basement, then Robert climbed the stairs. He could hear Hugo. His voice had an orating quality, as if he had an audience.

'All this... heating, colours, light... We don't notice it. We even distract ourselves with music and books, because our environment doesn't give us anything to do.'

In the room, a reporter was nodding as Hugo talked. There was also a guy with a video camera on a tripod, another guy in headphones watching the sound levels.

Oliver Jared beckoned to Robert with a look of pride, as if he had invented Hugo himself and wanted Robert to come and look at him.

'But,' said the journalist, 'it must be beautiful there.'

'It is beautiful,' said Hugo. 'It is white. It is vast.'

Every musician had their interview patter. This must be Hugo's. Robert hadn't heard it before. Hugo was working them, and they knew it, but he was rock aristocracy and that was what they wanted.

The journalist laughed. 'What about the cold? I'm not good with cold. I'd be a complete wimp.'

'It's cold like you've never known. It shuts you down. I've trekked for two days over a glacier, sometimes on my hands and knees because I was so exhausted, testing every step with an axe. These places don't care about anything you've done before.'

Robert walked in. 'I've seen attack ships on fire off the shoulder of Orion.'

Hugo immediately creased with laughter. The cameraman scowled and noted the time code.

'We can cut that,' said the interviewer, and gave Hugo his most earnest stare. Please continue.

Hugo, to his credit, couldn't. He gestured at Robert. 'This guy rides a bike in London traffic. I'm not man enough for that.'

'I fell off the other day,' replied Robert, and this time they all laughed.

The interviewer decided they'd got enough. The sound engineer unclipped the mic from Hugo's T-shirt. Wrapped the wire around the battery pack. The interviewer stepped forward with a camera and asked them to stand along one of the walls, making them sidestep until he liked the light.

While they faffed with angles, and Hugo apologised for the shadow caused by his crag of a nose, Robert glanced at the letters on the table.

I would like to work in the music industry. Advice from you would mean so much. I have written every day.

He knew they had written every day. Gina had told him.

Please love each other. Hugo, look after Elza. You're the last, you two, both of you. More fans who imagined the band personnel were an incestuous love-in. Some of them sent fanfic about it, which was eye-popping. He and Gina tried reading some, for saucy mischief, but stopped in extreme embarrassment.

Hugo was now having the hair over his eyes rearranged by the photographer.

The photographer said: 'Is it true you wrote the *Eye Music* album for VidalVine?'

Hugo said he did.

'And even heavy metal? Like *Metrognomicon* by Thirst?'

Hugo said he wrote the *Metrognomicon* album for Thirst.

'Is it true you and Ashten Geddard stole a piano from the Royal Festival Hall?'

Yes, he and Ashten persuaded a posse of tourists on the South Bank to help them wheel a nine-foot Bechstein out of the theatre and onto Jubilee Gardens, where they busked until security arrived. Because no one will refuse when a handsome, famous-looking man asks you to hold a door open, or if you will help push. The interviewer already knew this piece of band lore, but Hugo understood the power of telling it personally for them, like performing a much-loved song. Ashten and I. We were it; never forget. And what an exquisite put-down for Oliver Jared, who was watching Hugo, chuckling as if he'd been on the South Bank himself that rascally day, and deserved a smidge of credit. You weren't there, Oliver. Don't pretend. You can buy an album and a vulgar fancy-dress Bentley, but you'll never be us.

Robert wheeled his bike down the steps and swung on, threading north.

He took pleasure in the movement, judging the traffic and lights so he never had to stop, like a flowing sequence of yoga, reading the junctions and pedestrians, weaving between lanes and into side routes. Random moments surfaced from the day. The transformed song in the studio with Hugo. Watching Hugo tell legendary tales to an awestruck room. These moments raced alongside him as the body-bike gestalt enjoyed the game of uninterrupted motion. It was a good day, one of the best so far.

He felt a sudden catch in the mental flow. It seemed to say, there's something you haven't seen. Rewind. Something's wrong, look again.

No, this happened to him sometimes. He'd carried so much worry these past months. The band was on a tightrope. Paul made it worse, which Robert hadn't realised until he'd gone. Seeing Paul today was awkward. Perhaps he was processing that. And actually there was no need; Paul had gigs. This worry now was nothing. Aftershocks, a sign of too much strain. Ashbirds was him and Hugo and it was smooth as this ride. This was a good day. More were coming. No need for this anxious hitch in his heart.

62

Gina's sister Meredith was in town. She was bringing her kids to London for a day's drama and movement course at the Guildhall drama school in the city, and thus Gina had no excuse to not meet her for coffee.

Meredith had twin five-year-old boys and a life of mumsy exhaustion in Bedfordshire. She seemed worried by people who weren't yet mothers and was on a mission to convert them.

This was why Gina made excuses to not meet her.

It didn't help that Robert enjoyed Meredith's twins. Gina thought he might shrink from their blurting, blaring energy, but they seemed to warm him up. He exhausted them with games, plucking tunes on a ukulele and stopping when they were most likely to fall over, to their shrieking delight. 'He's ready, honey,' Meredith would say. 'Ditch the pill and jump him. You don't want to be the oldest mum at the school gates.'

'People still have kids at forty,' Gina would say. And she wasn't that old yet anyway.

Meredith's real question was always this. What's the problem?

There wasn't a problem. Simply, Meredith did not know their world. Meredith's husband worked in the legal department of a bank and had a predictable career ladder. A safe, organised life. The very opposite of her and Robert.

Right now, it wasn't a good time for her and Robert to discuss family and future. A week ago they'd been close to it, researching towns they might move to. Now everything was unsettled with the album, he was a loner again, going out on the bike late at night to ride it out of his system. It would pass.

Ditch the pill, Meredith? There were times when Gina would, in an instant. After some of the births she registered. Not because of the babies; no, it was the parents who won her round. They introduced the baby with care and surprise, sometimes helping each other get the names in the correct order, not yet used to them. When you asked how old the baby was, they told you in days, hours and minutes. There were also the blasé parents who brought their second-born and quipped that they'd been breeding again. All with such trust and shared purpose. But then, Meredith, there were the single mothers. Faltering as they spoke the father's name, or spelling it out defiantly, as if to a higher power of justice. I never intended to do this alone. I thought I had a partner. Not just for this, for everything. When you've seen a few of those, Meredith, you don't jump your guy into surprise fatherhood.

Now, Gina saw Meredith arrive, with shopping bags that showed she'd made the most of her time in town. They talked about this and that. Meredith soon mentioned holidays. Holidays were all she did, really. 'Why don't you take the house in France?' The house belonged to their aunt. She had renovated a cottage as a holiday home and was keen for relatives to keep it ticking over. 'She's installed a pool which is a death trap for the kids, so we can't go until she gets a cover for it, but you still could.'

No, Meredith, Robert would not want to go on holiday to France right now. The question chafed Gina on the special channel of their shared DNA. What Meredith meant was this: is everything going well? Is Robert a suitable man to settle with? He's an adventurous choice of husband, and I know you think we are dull, but honey, the results speak for themselves.

'We can't get away at the moment,' said Gina.

'What a shame,' said Meredith. 'The weather will still be good.'

'Here's where we're going next March,' said Gina. She showed Meredith a website. 'I'm speaking at this conference in Kentucky. I'm chairing a panel on unconventional weddings. Robert will fly out afterwards and we'll take a road trip. And – ' Another website. 'This is where we're going tonight.' The Groove Awards, a party in Mayfair with all the headline acts of the music business. And, Meredith, my husband, my untamable husband, has an invitation.

'You two are working so hard,' said Meredith. She made that sound like a criticism. 'Shall we share a cake?'

'Not for me, thanks. I've got to get into my dress. Here, I'll show it to you.'

63

Hugo had set up the music in the Glacier House. Instrumentals from films, not dance tracks. Elza told him the dance tracks made her feel she should put on leggings and do three hours of splits and pirouettes in a studio.

She was working in the Everest sunrise room. He was in the room with the glass shutters and the Havisham clock, scrolling through his iPod, making a playlist. He'd been invited to guest on a radio programme about early '90s music.

'So how many songs have you chosen for the programme?' Elza spoke in the headset, close as a whisper, though her body was the other side of the wall.

Hundreds, he said.

'How many are you allowed?'

Ten.

'Give the list to me. And a pin.'

She was reinstating the Everest sunrise-sunset film loop. Oliver Jared wanted to auction one of her artworks at a charity event this evening. It was the tent she had painted with Ash's lyrics. She was making a video to show at the sale. So that the tent wouldn't look too laughable.

'Could you help me move this?' she said. 'Then we'll fix your playlist.'

He walked into the room. The mountain on the wall was a scarlet blaze of sunset. Powder galaxies glittered at the pointed peak as the sky darkened. Elza was kneeling at one corner of the tent, slotting a power driver into a screw. The tent was nailed to a board, which was screwed to the floor.

'Hold this down,' said her voice in his ears, while the drill spun a screw upwards out of the wood, making no sound, as if it was happening behind thick glass.

Hugo knelt in the mouth of the tent. The Everest sunrise glowed through the walls. Ash's lyric made leaping loops across the nylon.

He felt the board slip as the last screw released. 'Stay there,' said Elza. She had a camera ready on a tripod. She bent behind it, considering the image. Her voice stayed with him. 'Move the tent back towards the wall. More, more, stop.' On the video, the stardrifts rose again above the mountain.

'God, that's so meta. Look at the camera.'

Did she just take a picture?

'Is that for the auction?'

'It's for me. It looks amazing. Hold that.'

She took another. The Everest sunrise coloured her with the pink beginnings of a new day.

'I think I saw an image like this once,' she said, 'in a picture he sent back. Or maybe in a newspaper. Of course he might not have taken it at all.' She turned a ring on the lens. 'How did it go with the journalist today?'

'The usual. You answer questions and wonder how they'll twist it.'

'Yeah. I used to feel like I was caught in a game and was trying not to get it wrong. Took me years to realise they didn't care what I said. They just wanted stuff to print. Don't speak. Sorry. It'll spoil the shot.'

A pause. Colours shifted. She said: 'I can barely remember the real things we did. Me and Ashten. It all got overwritten and confused. One journalist who interviewed me cried the whole time. I was talking about my boyfriend, my dead boyfriend, and she was crying. She didn't print a word I said; the whole article was sentimental gush about her own thoughts. That's all we were to the media; performers for the article they'd already written.'

She studied him as she talked. Took more shots.

'The only thing they couldn't mess with was the music. Whatever they invented about me or him or us, the Ashbirds songs were pure. From his voice to my ears. They were the truth. Wow, this light. You won't believe how amazing it looks. I'm going for some close-ups.'

Yes, the light was amazing. Night warming to dawn, brightening to a white dazzle, ebbing to gold then red, blackening down to night, colouring blue again to dawn. She twisted a screw on the tripod. Looked again through the lens.

'If it was like that for you too,' she said, 'no wonder you stayed away. Wasn't there anyone to come back for? Family?'

'It wasn't a friendly time.'

'No it wasn't, was it?'

'I needed to get away. From the music.'

Night, dawn, white, then dimming through the golds and reds to night.

'I found the music helped,' she said. 'Even songs that weren't Ashbirds. They played a piece of time where Ashten was still alive. As if that time mattered enough to be preserved so we could still go there. All the posters I saw around London after he died... for a while, they were shows or movies that were on while he was here. I remember the day I saw a poster announcing a new festival. It shocked me. It was like losing him again. He'd been removed. Made irrelevant. That probably sounds crazy.'

'It doesn't sound crazy.'

'He was writing with Robert Speed, wasn't he? That's where that awful song came from. God, Robert really trampled on Ashten's style. There was nothing of Ashten in that song, not like the others he wrote with you. Oh, that smile's great. Hold that.'

The songs. Did she not know?

'Everything is chemistry, isn't it? If Ashten wrote with Robert we got Shitbirds. If he wrote with you we got "Hurricane".'

She didn't know.

'I've never seen you smile like that. I'm used to you on moody album covers. God, I sound like my mother.'

Hugo said: 'Ash never wrote anything.'

Everest came out of darkness, grew bright and brilliant, grew red, grew dark, began to dawn again.

'Ashten said they were his words. Actually, his whole heart. That's what he said.'

'They weren't his words. We said I wrote the music, he wrote the words. It looked good for the fans. And the press.'

She was quiet, bent over the camera.

He said: 'It was the game.'

Silence. She truly didn't know. Night, colours, night. Days, years, like history speeding through the sky.

She stayed bent over the camera, hair flopping forwards, face hidden. She might have been taking pictures. She might have been just looking, thinking. He couldn't tell because the shutter click was in the noise of the room, which he could not hear, and not with her breathing, which was everything.

She spoke. 'Oliver Jared needs this video. You can get out of the tent.' He stood up. Another breath, long, hesitating. It made him hold his breath too. She said: 'Ashten didn't write "Hurricane"?'

'Ash never wrote a single chord or a line.' Hugo touched the tent, where the cursive tail of a y curled into the corner. *My world world world.* 'Except that.'

64

Elza had the camera in a padded bag on her shoulder. The tripod was in a case across her back, like a quiver. Both of them bumped against her as she walked from the Glacier House to home.

They bumped the afternoon against her too, the things she had thought could not be changed, and in fact had.

She wasn't finished with it either. She had to transfer the video, tidy it, then upload it to a secure site for Oliver Jared in time for the awards ceremony this evening.

She had just been staring down a lens at the man who wrote her songs. He was still alive. Like one of those wrong dreams where Ashten walks in. She asks where he's been and he says, oh, just out, sitting on the roof. Or he gives her a birthday present when it's not her birthday. Sometimes they celebrate her new birthday and sometimes she says it's too late, and proves it by opening her eyes where Elliot lies beside her, in a warm cat-soft sleep. Sometimes she wakes violently, as if thrown suddenly backwards, to the very beginning.

Now, she wrestled her gear into the house, past the table with the framed photos. There she was, with Elliot. She looked so contented. Sitting against a rock in the Scottish Highlands, her face gleaming with rain. There was Elliot posing with a sheep. He wasn't an animals type. His face was touchingly trusting. You tell me this sheep won't bite me. I believe you, but do hurry up.

The pictures didn't save her or wake her reassuringly. Nothing was the same. Nobody was the same. Nothing she relied on was true. These pictures on the table seemed naïve. Like pictures taken in the unsuspecting years before a world war.

Elza sat at her computer and connected the camera. Up came the other pictures, the kaleidoscope of Everest from the memory card. Many of Hugo beside the tent, because no moment was like another, that bewitching light kept changing. The voice of the songs was not the voice of the songs. It came from someone else, and he was looking at her now, like one of those wrong dreams, where someone arrives in a part of your life where they have no business to be, like an error in the fabric of time, and kicks everything over.

..

When Elliot came home, she said: 'Come with me tonight.'
He didn't believe her. 'Come to the awards?'
'I'm serious. Come with me to the awards tonight.'

Now Elliot did hear her. He still seemed to wonder what the catch was. 'Me? No one wants to see me.'

'This is 2014. They should see you with me.'

65

Elliot was ready long before Elza was. She stood in front of the mirror, putting on a dress, studying how it hung, deciding it offended her and peeling it speedily off, putting on another until she looked quite angry.

'If it's that bad, we don't have to go.'

'I want to go,' she said, with an impatient snap.

This at least seemed to make her decide. She pulled on a dress without checking again what it looked like, then held her hair up, let it flop down, looking queryingly in the mirror, held it up again and stared, as if asking it: who am I?

'Wear it up,' he said. Again this seemed to make her decide. She twisted her hair into a chignon, snapped a band around it and hurried past him down the stairs. There was something defensive in the way she did that, as though he had intruded on something she didn't want him to see.

Now they were putting on coats, in silence. She said she wanted him to come, but she seemed very uncomfortable about it. He had the feeling he would be in the way, indeed was in the way right now.

66

To understand what it was like to attend these awards, Robert thought, imagine a formal dinner staged on the passenger concourse at Waterloo Station. In rush hour. Making your way out for the loo was mayhem. Once you reached the edge of the room, you saw the swish view shown on TV – orderly lines of tables, white circles on an inky background. The throng of humanity seemed to disappear as all those black dresses and dinner jackets melted into the dark carpet and walls. Around the room, hanging screens replayed highlights of the evening so far, including the auction where Hugo and Elza helped a Radio One DJ auction a tent for £25,000.

The bathroom was a chamber of green marble, like a Mafioso's mausoleum. A band called Dream Report were partying in there. They offered him a line, or whatever you call coke when it's inhaled through a twenty-pound note stuck into a lily from a bouquet.

As he came out, a laughing, female voice called his name. An arm hooked his elbow. A perfumed cheek snugged close to his chin, nudged his face towards a camera at selfie level.

A tabloid gossip columnist. They waited in ambush at the bathrooms. Robert knew what was needed. Smile. Say you're having a great time otherwise they'd write how stroppy you were.

'I'm such a fan,' bubbled the reporter. 'You should have won something, Robert.'

So kind of you, he smiled, hoping she wouldn't tread on his feet. Her bayonet heels would leave stigmata.

'Robert, I need help with something. We've been offered these pictures from the backstage area and we're trying to confirm the story behind them.'

She thumbed through her images and showed him.

It was Hugo, in his dinner jacket. And Elza. Just the two of them. Elza was in back view, her hair coiled in the nape of her neck, a strict stripe of zip down her spine. Hugo was half-facing the camera. He had his bricklayer hand on her, where the dress zip serpentined over the outward curve of her sacrum. The tilt of her head suggested she was very alert to this. But he might not have been touching her at all. It could be the angle.

The reporter scrolled through more pictures. Seen quickly, like a sequence from a movie, Hugo turned away from the camera and Elza's face became visible. Their expressions had an interesting intensity. They crackled with awareness of each other, a silent conversation. Enough to stir the imagination if you were on the sniff for celebrity shenanigans.

'So where's Elza's boyfriend this evening?'

'Elliot?' said Robert. 'He's sitting at our table.'

'You don't think he minds that Hugo's trying to pull his girlfriend while he just sits at the table?'

'We are all dear friends,' said Robert. 'Thank you, great to see you, hope you're having a great night.'

A figure came lurching out of the loo and put an arm over the reporter's shoulder. The rap star Hobemian, whose cuffs were pierced with jewelled studs the size of matchboxes. The reporter said she was a big fan and took a selfie.

..

The auditorium was in darkness when Robert returned. A beat was playing, with a deep twanging bass, a Roland handclap, and seductive, beckoning vocals.

Robert had that feeling again. An inward gasp of anxiety, like a heart-rattle after too much coffee. But he hadn't had coffee. The feeling vanished, too soon to identify the cause. He passed a table. The mourn-faced guy from Rolling Drunk Monk was brow to brow with Paul Wavell as if wrestling through mindmeld. Was Paul the cause of this feeling? A lingering guilt, though he had no reason to feel guilty?

No, it was not Paul. Thinking about Paul didn't make it suddenly clear. It remained elusive and maddening, like something he dreaded but did not know about, something he feared he'd left undone. He had to throw random answers at it, like dice, until he rolled the correct number and the feeling stayed.

When Robert reached their table, Gina sprang up and pulled him to dance.

Around them, the floor was rammed with the industry's slickest movers, shoulder popping, moonwalking, holding arms high to show taut waists and shimmying hips, twirling so that skirts and coat-tails spun out wide. Robert and Gina settled into a space where she danced a simple side-step, her face lit with admiration for the dancers around her. Elza was suddenly with them, performing an elegant swinging salsa step, an intense smile showing her joy of the beat, while Elliot held onto her hands and stared at his shoes, trying to copy her steps. He looked like a jerky puppet. He had no rhythm at all.

After a few tracks, Robert and Gina returned to their table. Hugo was there with Gil. They were banging coffee spoons around the glasses, bottles and table-top in an ebullient, chiming percussion. Behind Hugo, Elza was still dancing, working the same beat with mobile grace, and Elliot was still taking dithering, mistimed steps with his face screwed up in uncertainty, not getting any of it.

Robert felt that catch again, unmistakably. Like a thorn, stuck deep in his soul. Hugo. Elza. Their unknowing synchrony was right in front of him.

The pictures on the showbiz columnist's phone, the jumped sequence of turning backs and the raw pull in their expressions.

Really? Were they? No, it had all been suggested by the columnist, who was simply prospecting for muck.

But Hugo was reworking the malice ballad. Not a scrap of malice in it now.

Maybe Oliver Jared put him up to that. Hey Hugo, if you can't bring us the real body, do this instead. Write a song to give the fans a thrill. Look at all those letters in the Glacier House. *Please look after each other, you two, you're the last.* Look at the sticking-plaster messages on the fake clock. We know what they want. The fans don't want Elza to be with Elliot; they want her with the other purebred Ashbird. Good idea, Oliver, I have just the thing.

It was all fake, of course.

Fake or not, Robert had found the trouble. A persisting, churning twist in the gut, clear and sustained now, like a stab wound, and not easing. Hugo and Elza.

..

In the taxi coming back, Robert was deep in thought. Gina dozed against his shoulder, her high-heeled shoes on the seat beside her, her face in neutral, her snub features like a koala bear. It didn't take much wine to make her sleepy.

The roads would be quiet and open. He could take the bike over the river, around the centre of town, own the city along with the other night prowlers. Ride the sting out of his system, and maybe it would stop.

67

Hugo pushed through the station barriers with the morning commuters, bought a coffee in Costa, put it on a table and a red gloved hand grasped it and carried it away.

He jumped up, barging the chair backwards. A woman in a smart coat was leaning on the glass door to butt it open, holding his coffee. He called out, to say she'd made a mistake. She turned with her phone and snapped a picture of him, then completed her exit and hurried away across the marble concourse.

Hugo stared after her. A commuter in a grainy herringbone coat, a leather satchel bag swinging from her shoulder, on her way to an office, holding his coffee with one (red) hand and her phone with his surprised photo in the other.

He sent Elza a text. He had to meet her later to deliver the tent. The buyer had increased his bid if they would give him some personal pictures and a couple of handshakes.

You won't believe what just happened, he wrote to Elza. *What time are we meeting?*

...

Hugo arrived at the studio, hung his jacket over a chair, and was aware that Gil and Oliver Jared were regarding him with ill-concealed smiles, as though they knew a very good joke about him.

'What?' said Hugo.

'Seen the papers?' said Gil.

Oliver Jared gave a chuckle.

Robert was at the far end of the desk, concentrating on something in his headphones. He raised a hand to say hello, then looked down, as if he was doing something that demanded all his concentration. It was too deliberate. He was as involved in the joke as Jared and Gil were.

Oliver Jared passed Hugo an iPad. It showed headlines from several papers, with pictures of him and Elza standing close to each other at the awards.

Spotted! Bird makes move on Ashten's girl

Elza and Hugo's secret moment

Hugo ceased to breathe. Oliver Jared and Gil were clearly amused, and if Robert thought anything, he looked embarrassed. Hugo found it offensive and violating, but that was not a reaction he could show here. Even the tabloid reporters saw it as harmless saucy fun.

He hadn't wanted to make a public appearance with Elza, and certainly not after the things he'd just told her. He hadn't ever thought about whether to tell her, but if he had to, he should have picked a better time. Not done it before they both had to attend an event full of paparazzi.

There were more headlines. He might as well see them all.

Ashten's girl has new love... his best friend

Ashten would knock your block off, Hugo

You couldn't take it seriously. Like the kidnapped coffee this morning, you had to shrug it off. He looked again at the pictures. Their supposed clinch was in the backstage corridor before the auction. Anyone would think they had sneaked deliberately away. In reality, they were alone together for only that brief time. Otherwise, she was with Elliot, Robert and Gina. He was with Gil and Steve. One picture made it look as though he had his hand on her back. He didn't. They didn't usually hug or touch, although last night she air-kissed when they arrived at Grosvenor House. He tried not to show his surprise and then spotted a reporter, so she must have done it in case anyone was watching for hostility or a feud.

In other pictures, they appeared to be having an involved conversation. In truth, they hardly exchanged a word. Who goes onto the stage first? You first. No, you.

But now he saw that accidental, surprising proximity again, he saw what he was really looking for in that moment. He was checking if what he'd told her about the songs was all right. Cameras try to read minds. He forgot that.

Oliver Jared picked his car keys off the desk. 'Hugo, I'll pick you up at the station later. Text me when you're on the train.' He left.

'You're very quiet, Hugo,' said Gil. Robert, despite his headphones, seemed to be listening and gave him a long, strange voleish look.

'Hangover,' said Hugo. 'And someone at Costa stole my coffee. I'm going to get another. Does anyone else want one?'

68

Elza was at her computer. She had a new client to email, a waste management company that wanted a set of paintings for its boardroom. She pasted together a standard email about her process. *We will establish a brief and I will prepare roughs. I have produced commissions for Stevens Hotels, The Friendly Bank, Who Computer Systems. My work is discreet and modern and well suited to the corporate environment. I can tailor it to include your company colours and emblems.*

She wondered about the person who would read it. Had they ever hoped for a job where they could commission art? And if they had, did they hope it would be real art that might be important to future generations, not art that was themed for a waste management company?

Her mobile. Steve.

'Have you seen the papers?'

She opened a browser.

God, what was this?

'Perhaps,' said Steve, 'today should be a duvet day.'

It couldn't be a duvet day. She had a photocall with that ridiculous tent. And with Hugo.

Still on the phone, she paced to the front of the house and nudged the blind. Outside, a man pointed a long lens at her and stole her image through its tunnel of glass. She pulled the blind further open and waved. Nothing to hide. The photographer gave a salute but he didn't leave. He was wearing a many-pocketed vest like a fishermen's waistcoat. The pockets hung in heavy bulges. Batteries, energy bars in case he got the munchies. This is what they did for a long-term stake-out.

She ducked back into the private spaces of the house. 'The press are here.'

'Is it a problem?'

No, she could cope.

'When were your bins emptied? Don't use them. If you need anything disposed of, put it in a bag and I'll collect it.'

'Sure,' she said, 'they'll learn a lot from onion peel.'

Steve gave more advice. Don't do anything where you can be seen. Don't send texts or voicemails. Remember the court cases about phone hacking by newspapers.

She knew all this. But she still had to meet Hugo.

Go by car, said Steve.

He didn't ask if the press reports were true. Nobody even gave that a thought. But she wanted someone to. So she could say it was definitely not.

What did Hugo make of this?

No, she should not phone Hugo. She phoned Elliot. 'Darling, don't look at the papers.'

She heard the scamper of keys as he did precisely that.

Seconds passed. Quiet enough to hear the mouse rolling on his desk. He was reading. Click. He was reading another.

'It's just tabloid hi jinks. Not what it seems.'

'I know it's not what it seems.' He sounded surprised that she felt the need to say it. Even, a little insulted.

'I might have to go to Guildford later for a meeting,' he said. 'Where are you taking that tent?'

'In that direction, actually. Somewhere near Farnham. I'll have the car. What time will you finish?'

If they were both going on business journeys, they always checked if they could coincide. If they could travel some of the way together, it felt like they had won bonus time. They compared schedules. Agreed to call. It was nice to arrange that.

'Don't worry about the papers,' said Elliot. 'Don't let them waste your time.'

The client had replied to Elza's email proposal. *Yes, my CEO says that sounds very suitable. He would like to arrange a meeting.* In the world of waste management, this morning's gossip made no difference to anything, and that was also nice.

69

Hugo waited for Elza at a railway station in Hampshire. He didn't realise she'd arrived until a very straight-backed figure hurried across the car park to the ticket machine. Then, the dark glasses and woollen beret were no disguise at all.

She went back to a small black car, put the ticket on the dashboard, locked it, then walked towards him on the steps. Her expression was masked by the dark glasses but her stride faltered, as if she needed to prepare for meeting him.

They didn't say hello. That hesitating step had already said it.

He said: 'You came by car?'

'Steve said to.' The rest of the sentence was in her inflection. Steve said to, because there is such a mess.

Obviously the papers were a mess. But what he'd told her about the songs. Was that also a mess?

What else did they need to discuss? He couldn't think.

A gleaming Bentley radiator crested the hill then turned, revealing the white door with the Protect and Serve badge.

Had Elza seen the car before? She hadn't, by the way she sucked her lip back against her teeth. Whether it surprised her, appalled her or amused her, she kept it to herself.

Yesterday, or before yesterday, she might have discussed it with him.

..

Oliver Jared drove the car through sunken lanes rusted to autumn colours. He told them about the guy who'd bought the tent. The owner of a premier league football club.

'It's a present for his wife. Just shake everyone's hand, pose for pictures and you're done. And that's a few extra grand for your charity!' As usual, Oliver Jared sounded faintly patronising when he talked about Hugo's charity. In Jared's world, philanthropy was soft-headed.

Jared turned at a pair of gates and waited. They glided open onto a wooded valley. Jared took the car down a winding drive to a long house with black Tudor woodwork, as if it had been built from ornate dominos. A man came to greet them, wavy haired, bristle-chinned, bare-footed, wearing a loose shirt and shorts. He had a Robinson Crusoe toughness. You'd believe he could light a fire from anything. He grasped Hugo's hand and gaped a big smile. More people came out to meet them. Two youths who would surely turn into this guy as they got older. They had his frame. Others of their age without the resemblance, probably their friends. A woman, obviously his wife, well advanced in pregnancy.

Robinson Crusoe led them to a terrace, where a young woman, also of sturdy Crusoe stock, was waiting with a camera on a tripod. Elza shook out the tent fabric to show the lettering and the Crusoes gasped and applauded. That was the first picture. Elza and Hugo each took a corner of the tent and held it taut like a sheet. More pictures. Mr and Mrs Crusoe then stood between them.

Hugo's eye was drawn to a gold figure in the shrubbery. It was a naked woman with a pendulous pregnancy. He realised, with embarrassment, the statue was a cast of Mrs Crusoe, who was standing next to him, in clinging chiffon so that she was all bump and buxom curves. He looked away but his eye found another naked gold statue, with a shorter hairstyle, again unmistakably Mrs Crusoe, pert nippled, her arms cupping another advanced pregnancy.

She'd had more than two pregnancies. He didn't dare look any-where else.

Elza, at the other end of the tent, faced the camera and held up a glass of champagne she clearly didn't intend to drink.

The Crusoe who had the camera moved the tripod closer and called to Hugo. He looked into its lens, exactly like the day before when he looked into Elza's lens, with the tent, under the speeding Everest sky, the magic rush of days and decades.

'I'd give you a lift back,' said Oliver Jared, 'but I've been drink-ing.' He twisted the wire off another bottle.

'That's okay, we'll find a cab,' said Hugo.

He walked up the drive. He realised he'd got ahead of Elza. She was looking back over the house and its valley. The tent was now pitched, with poles. It looked scruffy without its prismatic sky, after the months it had spent being mauled by visitors who traced their fingers over Ash's writings. Just a grubby tent. One of the Crusoes sang a line from 'Hurricane' in a brisk squaddie roar.

Elza caught up with him.

'I'll call a taxi,' he said.

'I don't mind walking.' Her stride was laboured. Her voice defeated. How he felt too.

They walked. He found a footpath. They climbed over a stile and followed a sheep groove across a field. It made him think of the paths in Bonnet. He told her of beginnings there.

She told him of hers. A childhood in Australia. Open spaces with a big sky where her parents imagined she'd get a free run, as if she was a brumby or a kangaroo. She volunteered as a reporter on the local paper, to be involved in important events, but hardly anything important ever happened. She joined the amateur dramatics group, to play in tragedies and epics, but they preferred musicals and parlour plays.

Over another stile. Into a wood where the bracken was turning brittle and brown.

Hugo told her of emptying the houses of dead people in Bonnet. He told her of music, of Mutt and the Harpoons, of Ash. Everyone like walking dead, with long minds to interrogate your secret hopes and murder your rebellions. You've heard the mountains have a death zone? Well you can find the death zone without ever going to the Himalaya. It's right where you're growing up.

She told him of hitch-hiking hundreds of miles to Brisbane and Victoria and Sydney to audition for drama schools, dance schools, art schools. Any artform would do. She was untrained, but maybe she'd get ahead with sheer energy. She fell in love with a guy, not because she liked him but because he was going to London, which sounded exactly the place she needed to be. She worked in bars to save the fare. Put leaflets through doors. Cleaned schools. In London, she split up with the guy. Lived in a squat where the bath was in the kitchen and a pet rabbit had its own bedroom. Got tips about dance auditions from a flatmate, who taught at Pineapple. Worked as an artist's model. Met Ash, a bigger adventure than she'd ever bargained for, the adventure she'd always known she had to find.

Hugo told her of escape to London. The half-built house, filled with winter and roaring with their music, where they began to make their amazing futures, when anything was possible.

70

Elza collected Elliot from the station in Guildford. The rush hour had thinned. They glided through the town past superstores and car showrooms closed for the evening, looped the roundabout onto the six-lane A3 back to London.

They discussed the day's adventures, big and small. Elliot's meeting. Elza's tent delivery. Oliver Jared's police car. The enormous Tudor house. The golden statues of naked people. One, to her embarrassment, was of the man, the football manager, barely covered by the rhododendrons. Who would do that?

She described it with such gaiety. But she didn't feel gay. She felt fragile and emptied. She wanted to talk about that, but she seemed stuck in an entertaining persona that was determined to make it a mad, marvellous caper. I stood there, she said, I was trying to look into the camera, and in my sightline was this football manager, naked in gold, full frontal, his hose on view for everybody. I held up a glass of champagne so I wouldn't have to see it.

She changed lanes to avoid the filter to the M25.

'Our bridge isn't far from here,' said Elliot. 'Let's stop.'

...

A footbridge over the A3. They leaned on the handrail, looking into the lanes of traffic that raced below.

This was a place they often came to. They liked standing here, watching the rapid river of movement while themselves being still. Surrounded by trees and pylons. The carriageways vanishing into pinstripes in the distance, sunset burning above it all, the soothing constancy of the traffic.

'I don't know what's going on,' said Elliot, 'and I'm not asking, but I think I'm in the way.'

'You're not.'

She said it as a reflex.

He was silent.

'It won't be for much longer,' she said.

'You can't know that.'

She did. Ashten's body was coming. The thought kept catching her unawares, as if she was balanced on a ledge and a great weight was yanking her into frightening freefall.

'It won't be for long,' she said again. But then again, it might be. It might take months. If she thought that, she felt steadier.

'This is what I mean. You've lived this life. There are things you understand that are simply too difficult to explain. I'm not asking you to explain, but I feel it all needs to go on without me.'

No, she wanted to say. That was a reflex too. She swallowed it.

Red tail lights chased back into Guildford and the sunset. White headlights went up to London and darkness.

'I think if I stay here,' said Elliot, 'people will start telling me lies because that will be easier than the complicated truth, whatever it is.'

..

They drove back to London. They parked the car. Elliot would stay with his parents in Sussex. He could commute into town. His files for work were in the cloud anyway.

When he told her that, it gave her a jolt. Of course he must have thought about this beforehand. But weren't they making the decision on the bridge, together, in those moments? No, he had planned it, perhaps over the last few days. Of course he must have. Arrangements had to be made. She'd driven him to that.

While Elliot packed, Elza loaded the dishwasher. She didn't have to do it at this moment; but it would keep her occupied and out of his way. She could hear him upstairs in the bedroom. The sliding of drawers. The click of the wardrobe door. How long would he keep taking things? Or should she help? Find essentials that were still in the airing cupboard?

He came downstairs with the small travel bag he used for short business trips and weekends away. Not a big bag; that was a relief.

No, it was evidence that he was going.

When he closed the front door, walked down the path and out of the gate, she felt the house pause in silence.

She had never lived here alone. It had always been theirs. Each item in the house represented a lively negotiation when they decided to join their lives: lamps and pictures that pleased both of them; chairs and dinnerware that one adored and the other suffered with grumbles; awful ornaments and furniture that were kept only if they stayed in her studio or his study.

Now it was all here around her, selected and ordered for their shared life, full of their rules and culture, and he had gone.

71

Steve was happy to be back in Shropshire, at Hugo's family's house on the top of the Long Mynd.

He was also happy to be sitting on a chair. He had spent the morning inching up a limestone wall in a quarry strung with ropes while Hugo patiently schooled him through a headset.

Steve wasn't sure he was cut out for climbing, but lunch afterwards made up for it. A gossipy gathering with Hugo's aunt Cassie and uncles Martin and Tom. It was Tom's birthday. Hugo didn't have family gossip to share, but he kept them amused with anecdotes about the guest lodges on the Everest Base Camp trail and having his coffee stolen at Victoria Station, which had them in uproar. It surprised Steve to see this raconteurial side to Hugo, which he never saw at any other time.

Now, Cassie, Martin and Tom were enjoying another ride in Oliver Jared's helicopter while Steve and Hugo lounged in deckchairs with the view over the Shropshire plain. The tweedy rumple of purple heather, the yellowing fields stretching into the distance.

Hugo was quiet. The quiet that suggested a fretting mind.

'Spit it out, H. I can't possibly guess what you're not telling me.'

Hugo gave him a letter. 'This came to the Glacier House.'

Dear Mr Bird

I am the former husband of Charmian Maurice, who I believe you

*met in the Himalaya. I understand you brought her to safety after
her injury. I would like to thank you for this and ask if you could
rescue her one stage further.*

*She might listen to you as your music has long been special to her.
The doctors say she shouldn't climb again because her lungs and
brain have been so damaged by extreme environments. Charmian
has struggled with more injuries than most of us would face in a
lifetime. Although I am no longer married to her, she is the mother
of my children. Please, for our sakes, don't let her climb again.*

It wasn't unusual for them to receive this kind of letter. There
were always people who wrote asking for miracles. Please help me
get started in the music business. Please send life advice because
my friend worships you. Please send best wishes because my mother is ill or dying.

'The things people think you can do,' said Steve.

In the distance, the helicopter drummed.

'And what else do you need to tell me, H?'

'You need to know about Charmian,' said Hugo. 'And a few other
things.'

By the time Hugo had finished explaining, Steve's head was
rattling.

'So that picture was actually Ashten?'

'It was.'

'All this time we thought a picture would be enough to recognise
him.'

And now Hugo and Elza were keeping the body a secret. Jesus.

'So it probably won't be long,' said Hugo, 'before we all meet
Charmian.'

Just half an hour before, they had been talking about a cousin's
wedding plans and the laying of the new terrace, which had nearly
caused family meltdown when Martin couldn't split one of the
stones.

'So what about those newspaper reports? You and Elza?'

'No comment.' The helicopter underlined his silence. Then Hugo
said: 'Ash would not have made Elza happy. Though he might have
mellowed as he got older.'

That, in a way, answered the question about the newspaper
reports.

'H, Ashten would never mellow. Everything was about power to him. That was what he did well. Music was power. He kept people on side if he needed them, but he didn't like needing them, because they might go away. He fired you, didn't he? He hated that he had to depend on you. He didn't understand that you might feel loyal to him or be his friend. Loyalty wasn't possible for him. So he tried to get other people to replace you, which they couldn't, which made him hate you even more. Meanwhile, you were the only idiot who'd help him. I don't know how much longer that could continue.'

Hugo looked offended to be called an idiot, but didn't seem to disagree.

The helicopter dipped and buzzed. Steve thought about the people in it, their warm clan, their carnival of family ups and downs, nesting and nurturing the generations. They would probably never comprehend the complicated partnership he had seen between Hugo and Ashten.

What did they notice about Hugo? Were they baffled by him, as Charmian's family was baffled by her? Distressed, even, by his life choices?

'Ashten must have liked Elza, though,' said Steve. 'Six months, wasn't it?'

'I think Elza gave him an interesting role to play.'

Steve didn't argue with that.

'I knew you wouldn't stick to that agreement about identifying the body.'

'I didn't make an agreement.'

Steve was still holding the letter from Charmian's ex. He gave it back. 'Sounds like that climber's in a bad way. I think your relatives worry about you.'

'I'm careful. I'm not like her.'

Steve laughed, and Hugo looked surprised and said 'What?'

'What you had me doing today in that quarry wasn't my idea of careful.' And look at Hugo, now. The hand with the tendon strain still wasn't right. He constantly hitched and fidgeted the fingers, checking he could still move them.

The helicopter was heading back. Hugo stood up. 'Let's get the cake.'

Steve checked his phone as he followed Hugo to the kitchen.

It was livelier than he expected. Several missed calls. From Robert and Gina. And finally a link.

'H, check the news.'

A weary, must-I-really look, then Hugo felt in his back pocket, found no phone, and went out of the door.

Steve skimmed the headlines. Was it just the BBC website? No, all of them had the same story. A body had been found.

Some details matched what Hugo just told him. Some didn't.

He found Hugo in the hall, impatiently scanning his phone.

Steve said: 'Is that her? Charmian Maurice?'

'I don't know.' Hugo was swiping windows, trying to make sense of it. Then he looked startled.

'What?'

Hugo shook his head warningly. Don't distract me. He made a sequence of swift movements. Then talked. 'Charmian messaged. So I just changed my password.'

'And?'

'She says someone knew I took a helicopter up the mountain. I don't think I covered my tracks very well. Another team thought that was a good reason to go there themselves. They're bringing him to Kathmandu.'

'It's him?'

'It's him.'

72

'Another body?'

Gina knew that tone of Robert's. It made her want to bite something. It said, you can't give me news like this. How can you know something like this? You must have misunderstood.

No, Robert, I haven't misunderstood. And I know that face you're pulling, even though I'm on the phone and can't see you.

'Look at the news,' said Gina.

'Which news?'

Any news you like, she said.

He went quiet for a moment, reading the facts she'd already told him. Then he said: 'The body hasn't been formally identified,' as though that meant he was more right than she was.

'I didn't say it had. I just thought you'd like to know.' And now I'm sorry I bothered, because I have work to do.

She turned her phone off. She had white roses on the desk in front of her and on the stands in each corner of the room. A couple arriving shortly to be married. They deserved a calm, romantic Gina.

She opened her file of notes about the couple, reminding herself of names, their discussions about the ceremony, facts from their history that could personalise the wording.

She went to greet them. A bride, groom and two women of a parental generation who would give them away. Formal suits for everyone, even the bride, but glitter-painted talons. So a more spirited celebration was planned for later on and this ceremony would be the formality. She felt like telling them, don't dismiss any of it, not even this paper-signing legal bit. Relish every moment you are so truly in step. Don't save the joy for later. You don't know what later will bring.

How dare Robert doubt what she was telling him.

How dare he suggest she didn't appreciate how important it was.

73

Outside Elza's front window, in the lamplit street, a man with a press pass was holding up champagne. Lanson. Proper stuff. His greedy grin said, cor it's happened, can I come in?

Sure, she could think of nothing nastier. What she did was give him a wave, then she closed the curtain and went to the kitchen.

On the TV, the news channels were delirious. Hugo and Steve had identified Ashten by video link and would confirm officially when his body arrived at Heathrow.

Ashten's face was on the screen. A series of monochrome studio portraits. She never usually bothered to look at pictures of him. They were overfamiliar. She knew them as well as the cupboards in her kitchen, and besides, they weren't really him, just part of the show. Now she imagined how others might see them. This one where he wore a high-necked brocade jacket, open on a bare chest:

exotic, original, insolent. This one, all about the texture of his skin, milk-smooth and feminine, a dimple in his chin, a rugby-player's brawny throat.

The news report gave the practical details. Two climbers from Canada had found the body. What about the French woman Hugo told her about, who originally discovered him? She wasn't mentioned. Did she know these other climbers? Had she sent them? Had she talked to anyone about her expedition with Hugo?

Elza watched the news coverage. In case tough questions were coming.

Now she was seeing the airport in Kathmandu, where it was nearly midnight. A ground crew at work beside a plane. They were positioning a long box on the flat bed of a hoist to lift it into the cargo hold. It looked so routine, with the reflective strips on their uniforms flashing in the floodlights, and then she realised the box was a coffin. Of course, why else would a piece of cargo be filmed for the news? An oblong box with a bevelled lid, wrapped in plastic like a cabinet being shipped from a furniture store. Secured with straps to a metal tray. Ashten in a coffin, now being loaded into the hold of the plane.

She tried Hugo.

Voicemail.

In newsland, it was like Christmas. Rejoice, the wait is over.

Elliot had called earlier. He'd heard. How were things? Things were fine, she said. And this proved his point exactly: nobody would tell him the truth.

If she muted the sound on the TV, she could hear the reporters in the street. A satisfied laugh. Laughing as they anticipated the goodies to come. They would stay all evening, taking selfies to fill the time, posting pictures of her closed door on social media, talking to camera about how long it had been closed, because this was the place to be.

The house had blackout blinds, but she felt watched wherever she went. She put on all the upstairs lights so her movements would not be betrayed by a changing glimmer. She spotted a glow along the lower edge of the blinds in the front room. It was flickering. They must be candles. What if one was knocked over and started a fire? Or someone put a candle through the letterbox?

She had a lock on the letterbox. But night thickened and so did the vigil glow.

She phoned Steve. He told her there would be another post-mortem when the body arrived tomorrow. Just routine. Then the body was theirs and plans could be made.

He was sending someone to deal with the candle-people.

She thought of the road bridge where she and Elliot had talked. It felt safe. Spacious. Private. She wanted to drive there now, but the pack outside would pounce. Literally. They'd jump on the car bonnet with cameras, or into a seat when she unlocked the door. They'd chase on motorbikes. She'd heard at least one motorbike outside. Big, thrum-engined; it sounded like it could beat a Ferrari. She was safer staying where she was, alone in big rooms.

She watched more news. So many channels were showing Ashten, like a national takeover. A video clip of him singing, savage, tender, and incredibly confiding, as if it was not a performance to an audience, but a private revelation to a person who needed to know they were not alone. She remembered the fan who wrote that this song was going to be their wedding vows. Another who told her it was going to be their suicide note but they had overcome their depression. Everybody's anthem for who they were, or who they had now become.

The house phone rang, showing an unknown number, and it wasn't the first. She didn't answer.

When she'd seen enough news, she put a movie on at loud volume. She went upstairs and up a ladder, into the loft above the bedrooms. Dusty lagging, a bare light bulb, a basket hatching of rafters along the house from back wall to front. The bare brick bulk of a chimney breast running up from the rooms below. A space that the watchers outside, with their eyes on the windows, would not know existed.

She felt safe to phone.

Hugo answered immediately. 'I didn't know whether to call you. Steve said you were surrounded.'

You couldn't mistake his voice. It had the spirit of the songs, their cadence; their understanding of your soul. Suddenly the songs belonged to her, every syllable.

Hugo was hiding as well. There were reporters outside his flat, so he had walked to the studio where there was an abandoned building site and found a way in. She imagined him climbing a fence, or worse, a scaffold gone loose with neglect. 'Don't get arrested.' Or hospitalised.

Steve knew everything, he said. Charmian, the French climber, was on the plane with Ashten's body. Steve had had a number of conversations with her.

'What mood is she in?'

'Fighting. These other climbers think they discovered the body. And her family are protesting.'

It couldn't be simple, could it? 'How are they protesting?'

'Her family are saying she found him first. She must have told them. Steve's kept a lid on that but something will have to be done.'

More people would be told. About their lie.

The loft of the house was cold. Like a cave. Elza caught voices outside. They couldn't possibly hear her, but she was aware of them there, not so many feet down, looking up, wondering which part of the house she was in.

'Is it illegal, finding a body and not telling anyone?'

'I don't know. No, surely it's not illegal.'

'It's not as if we obstructed the law or concealed the fact that he was dead.'

'Or killed him.' They both laughed.

In the street below, she could hear footsteps. The simmer of conversation. The searchlight of attention. She's in there. People who would be very interested in what they had done, even if it wasn't illegal.

'Damn! I thought you said no one could find him until you went back.'

'I did everything I could. But they knew where to look.'

'Can we say we didn't know? How does anyone know you found him, and came back and didn't tell anyone? We say it was an honest mistake. You fell off the ledge. In all the snow and ice you didn't see him properly.'

'Charmian knows.'

It all came back to Charmian.

'Can you talk to her? It's just her version and your version.'

'It's not. The other climbers will want to know why they can't claim the glory.'

'The glory? What glory?'

'Lecture circuits. After-dinner speaking.'

A flare of disgust. 'That's revolting.'

He came back, also irritably. 'That's what people do. It pays well. And they write books.'

Yes, the books. There were so many books, sniffing for sensation and scandal. Hasty patchworks of unproved newspaper gossip. Untrue confessions by opportunist rentagobs. Mostly dismissible. But this.

'If someone wrote a book about this...'

'I know.' Tartly. Let's not speculate about that yet.

She heard an engine start outside. Too bare and low to be a car. One of the motorbikes?

'I think some of the reporters are going home. I wish they all would. I feel like they're going to break down the door and shine lights in my eyes.'

'How's Elliot?'

Did he know about Elliot already? He did. His tone said it. Elliot isn't there because you wouldn't be talking to me for this long.

She told him about Elliot.

She heard a metallic sound. Footsteps at his end.

She said: 'Are you all right there? Please don't fall off a rusty scaffold.'

Boots on a ladder.

'Hugo, I can't get out and you can't get in. Stay where you are.'

'You shouldn't be there on your own.'

74

Robert expected exciting changes when he went to the meeting with Steve, Gil and Oliver Jared, especially as Jared had booked a private room in his Soho club.

He was totally unprepared for the situation Steve explained to them.

So that's why Hugo wasn't here. Because Hugo was the problem they needed to discuss. The godmother of all problems.

Gil listened to Steve with little visible reaction. Just the occasional cocked eyebrow and forgiving nod, as if all was amusing and harmless.

Amusing and harmless? No it bloody wasn't. Robert told them.

'Hugo knew what we wanted. He sees the body, sees it's actually Ashten. But he doesn't identify it. He says it's not him. Fucking unbelievable. It would make a huge difference to the sales of this album and he tried to cover it up?'

Oliver Jared poured water from a carafe. He also looked surprisingly mellow. He couldn't be hearing this for the first time. If he was, he'd need something stronger than water.

'So now,' said Oliver, 'we have to decide what we tell the press. You'll have to say you didn't want to reveal it was Ashten because the album wasn't ready.'

'Why do we have to hide this? Who's going to care?'

'Think of the band.' A defensive rattle in Jared's voice. 'This morning, Markson told me the first album is at number one. Lemon Demon want to record an album of Ashbirds songs unplugged. Chinless in the Roses want Hugo to guest on one of their tour dates when they perform "I Found Your Letters". The fans are only just accepting Ashbirds without Ashten. Hugo found Ashten's body and didn't tell them. What if Paul McCartney had somehow concealed that John Lennon was dead?'

'So he's McCartney now is he? Oliver, you've spent too much time with fanmail.'

'No, I've spent too much damn money on helicopters and bribes.'

In the street below, a drill rammed through asphalt. Sunlight slanted through the window and deepened the shadows on the baronial public-school panelling.

'I was actually sitting in Elza's kitchen when they were plotting this,' said Robert. 'I was even drinking Prosecco. How long was he going to cover it up for?'

'Perhaps Hugo was in shock,' said Gil. It was his first comment. And what a surprise, he was trying to apologise for Hugo.

Steve spoke. 'I think he was in shock. He wanted to come to terms with it before the madness started.'

'And what about her?' said Robert.

'So did she.'

And what about other reasons, such as the affair they were surely having? Which wasn't important or anyone's business, except that it made them lose their minds and behave like self-absorbed teenagers.

'What about this crowdfunding page?' said Gil. '*Ashten Geddard funeral campaign*. It says it's been set up by Elza.'

Steve's eyes bulged. He snatched Gil's phone. It was the first time Robert had seen him actually give a damn.

Steve read. '*Please help me pay for his funeral. All donations gratefully received.*'

'She wouldn't do that, would she?' said Oliver Jared.

'Of course she fucking didn't,' said Steve. 'I'll get it taken down, then this is going to the police.'

..

At the studio, Robert found Hugo in the small room, working at the Nord electric piano, caught in the task of music, no cares at all.

Right, time to talk. Robert dragged the other chair close to the keyboard.

Before he sat down, Hugo spoke. 'Good meeting?'

Seriously? We just heard everything you've hidden from us. And you ask how the meeting went?

'So you're a sly horse,' said Robert.

Hugo gave a small, acknowledging smile. As if to say, I know people will find it difficult.

'Why?' said Robert.

Hugo set the bassline on a loop. A growl of low notes, big-footed, like the thoughts of a Russian bear. Rising to the minor third, then the fourth, then a jazzy, trip-up swerve that surprised you cleverly back to the beginning. Rise, rise, swerve, start again. He shadowed the pattern on the higher keys, thinking about the melody. And not about Robert's question.

'I think we deserve to know why,' said Robert.

'Sometimes there's a thing you simply do. You know what it's like.'

Was Hugo stuck on a planet where everyone spoke in heroic lyrics? No, Robert didn't know what it was like. What would make any reasonable person hide the discovery of Ashten Geddard's body?

On Hugo's forearm, below the pushed-up sleeve, was a long, bloody graze. 'Been in a fight?' said Robert. Did someone thump you? Because I'll be thumping you next.

'I fell off a roof. Trying to find somewhere reporters couldn't follow me.'

At least someone had given him a hard time. Robert was blazing for a showdown, but he couldn't get it started. He might as well try to provoke Yoda.

On the table was a newspaper. Photographers had been at the airport when the plane arrived at dawn. They'd seen when Steve walked out of the arrivals lounge with the woman climber who'd originally found the body.

She was interesting-looking. Handsome, hard.

'How well do you know this Charmian?' said Robert.

'She's tough. Markson will have to talk to her. About her publishing contract.'

Her stare in the picture was full of appetite. And something ruthlessly self-preserving, like a lion. 'And that will work, will it? A little chat about her publishing contract. What fucking publishing contract, by the way? Is she a journalist?'

'Markson will find something she wants. He'll surround it with non-disclosure agreements. He got Ash out of trouble a few times.'

Nothing was impossible for Hugo. He'd buy the silence of this woman, who looked like she would never respect anything he cared about.

Hugo continued with the bass sequence. He slowed the speed a little, a little more. It was suddenly intriguing, gangly, full of hypnotic space. Hugo listened, opened more reverb, flashed Robert a look that said, this is cooking now. More alive to his work than to their discussion.

A rap on the door. Gil leaned into the room. 'Ready.'

Hugo was clearly expecting him. He saved the track, stood up. Beckoned Robert too.

'What are we doing?' said Robert.

Gil walked ahead of them, down the corridor, to the studio. 'A video for the album's YouTube channel. We'll light a candle in the live room and film it while we play "Hurricane" over the monitors.'

Hugo turned to Robert. 'Or do you think it will look naff?'

Now, all of a sudden, Hugo, you want my opinion?

'Sounds okay to me,' said Robert.

You'll do what you want anyway.

Gil said: 'People will take it for what it is; a spontaneous gesture.'

'You're sure it's not sentimental?' said Hugo.

'You mean, is it more sentimental than the crap all over the internet or on the walls of that house?' said Robert.

'Or should it be "Hush"? Less obvious than "Hurricane"?'

Shut up, they said. Be obvious. Do 'Hurricane'.

Hugo, who never heeded an opinion if it wasn't the same as his own, took their advice and went to the live room, saying: 'Pray we finish before the smoke detectors notice.'

Robert helped Gil set up the camera and sound in the control room. 'Must be a relief that this is all over,' said Gil, dropping a CD into the player. 'It's taken years off him.'

Something certainly had. Hugo was invincible, easy in his skin, confident beyond all reason, even playful.

They watched Hugo in the live room place the candle on the Steinway, light it, back out of shot, join them in the control room. They stayed quiet as 'Hurricane' played on the monitors, line by lilting line. Still epic, still kicking the heart. It made Robert feel he had missed something. Been a fool, been on the wrong life path, and now it was too late. He thought of Hugo and Elza, so full of their shared secret, like he'd seen in those pictures. The song made you want to give everything for a bare, bold moment like that.

No wonder Hugo didn't care a crap about anything else.

The last round of choruses was beginning. Gil nudged Hugo's chair. 'Blow the candle out as the track fades.'

Genius, said Hugo's face. He sprang up.

'Hugo.' Gil said Hugo's name again. With a grave tone that made Hugo look back, startled. Startled Robert too.

'You could have told us,' said Gil. 'Trusted us.'

Hugo paused, his hand on the door, then pushed through, crossed the live room, bent over the candle.

Kudos, Gil. You made him think.

75

'Elliot, it's Gina.'

She thought he sounded pleased to hear from her. After some catch-up conversation, she said: 'Steve told me about you and Elza. I didn't want you to think we didn't care. I know the others are all behaving like a zoo, but … you know what rockstars are like.'

He seemed relieved she'd mentioned it.

They chatted about it all.

'How do you cope?' he said. 'You seem like a normal person.'

'I guess my work keeps me grounded. Did you know I used to be a management consultant?'

He was surprised by that. Most people were.

'I was on a graduate training scheme,' she said. 'After six months I was signed off with exhaustion and all I could do was sleep and watch TV. I got hooked on reality shows, especially the ones about ordinary lives. Long-distance truck drivers. A couple who ran a building company. Just people, trying to make a good life. I saw a show about a register office and thought, I want that to be me. Does that sound bonkers?'

A laugh. 'Not at all. You have an origin story. I think we should all have an origin story.'

He was easy to talk to. He made you feel like you were good company. She could see why Elza took to him. 'I think all our origin stories are the same. We might be complicated in our own ways, but the things we want are simple. A place to belong. People to belong to. Ha, can't you tell I'm used to giving speeches?'

'Do you know where I think it went wrong?' said Elliot. 'I think they all lost their marbles when they made the plan about the body…'

A plan?

'Do you know about the plan?'

She didn't know about a plan. Robert had made a plan?

'I swear this is true,' said Elliot.

What he then told her sounded like the plot of an espionage movie.

No, Robert had never said anything about that. He'd have known what her opinion would be.

Tell me how they did this, she said. Because she needed to grasp it. From all angles.

Elliot described how they assembled in front of a set of portraits made by Elza, in the attic of the Glacier House. 'Think of Dorian Gray. With a side order of *The Omen*. These guys were ... they were high, really, off the concert. And I thought it would never work, but I also thought if we didn't do something this would never end. And it went to pot anyway because Hugo Bird wouldn't play along.'

'And then look what Hugo did,' she said. 'He can't claim the moral high ground.'

Elliot was very quiet then.

She meant only that Hugo lied about the identity of the body. But of course, Elliot had other, more personal reasons to be sensitive about the subject of Hugo. She hadn't thought. 'I'm sorry. Just tell me to mind my own business.'

A long, fatigued sigh. 'She's always had this in her. It's like she has a broken leg but doesn't want anyone to know, but it's bloody obvious she's broken her leg. She somehow made it a thing no one could talk to her about. She's got to work things out for herself. No one else can do it.'

God, thought Gina. You and I should form a support group. Robert going out on the bike late at night. It's obvious he's got issues, but he doesn't want me to know.

'I never thought I could be with a guy who didn't tell me what was on his mind. And look who I'm with. We don't choose them, they choose us. Like rescue pets.'

Another laugh, thin now. 'I think Elza needed something I couldn't give her, but she didn't want to tell me.'

She shouldn't have started Elliot thinking like this. You could go mad with questions. Change the subject.

'Elliot, this will pass. Don't be a stranger. Not all of us are rockstars. Let's meet for coffee sometime and not talk about them.'

'Thanks, Gina.'

She rang off.

Dear God. This explained why Robert was so happy when Hugo went back to Nepal to view the body. If they passed it off as Ashten, with the album coming, it was ideal. Never mind whether it offended all possible considerations of decency. No; they were, as she said to Elliot, just being rockstars.

No wonder Robert was so stirred up when it went wrong. But Ashten had now been found, properly and officially. Robert might calm down. Thank you, Elliot. Thank you for telling me about their plan. This makes everything so clear. And perhaps we can all now breathe.

76

Robert arrived at the Glacier House. The press gaggle were setting up in the main downstairs room. Robert glimpsed lenses, press passes, the wigwam frames of tripods. Badges from Fox, Sky, Euronews, ABC, BBC, CNBC, CNN. All the alphabet of the news world.

Steve waved him to the upstairs room.

Around the big table, Hugo, Elza, Oliver Jared and Gil were seated, silently and separately, heads bent over documents.

Ari Markson gave Robert a copy, like the start of an exam, and he sat down and read. The official, agreed story of how Ashten was found. An NDA about everything else.

Elza finished reading, took her papers to Ari Markson, leaned over the table and signed.

More footsteps on the stairs. Steve stepped into the room and held the door with his outstretched arm. A slight, muscular figure pegged her way in on crutches, in a grey yoga top and baggy tracksuit bottoms that showed a slim leg on one side and the broken one on the other, the fabric clinging to the bumps and rods of an orthopaedic frame.

Charmian.

Robert had no difficulty recognising her. She was made of the same material as Hugo. Hard, physical. Her manner, too, was similar, bemused by the comforts and clutter in the room, by soft, indoor people.

Hugo introduced her to everyone. She stripped off her yoga top. Robert's heart nearly flipped right out of his chest. Underneath she wore an orange vest. Her pectorals and biceps were unexpectedly plumped, like an out-of-condition trapeze artiste. He could envisage her doing pull-ups from her hospital bed.

Busted and unconquerable all at once.

When she shook Robert's hand, her smile showed ice-white teeth. Her grip was like knotted rope. He couldn't look away from her face. Long months in goggles and sunglasses had left the area around her eyes untanned, which gave her a luminous look, as though lights shone from within her. Hugo looked like that too when he came back from the mountains.

Robert resumed reading his NDA. He heard Hugo tell Charmian he was sorry about all this. She said why? I've still got a story I can tell. I'm getting top private treatment. And two sponsorship deals.

The other climbers arrived. The two Canadians who had brought the body down and thought they had discovered it. A tight-muscled man who moved with gymnastic looseness. A woman who was strong boned, as though her skeleton had been assembled from a horse. Their eyes had that same luminous angel light.

They each read and signed a copy of the document, in which they gave away their piece of history for a silence payment and a lesser story they were allowed to tell. Just as, years ago, Hugo and Ashten had quietly erased the music Robert had written for Ashbirds and made him play session roles.

This man and woman didn't look like they minded being silenced. They didn't look like they worried about anything.

The business done, Ari Markson stacked the papers and laid them in his briefcase. The exam mood lifted. With so many climbers in the room, that's what they talked about. Where should they go while they were in the UK, said the Canadian climbers. They were interested in sea stacks. Try Old Harry in Dorset, said Hugo. Twenty-five metres.

Robert quickly googled sea stacks. Christ, there was a picture of a narrow, high pinnacle of rock like a tall chimney, marooned in the middle of a crashing sea, no other land anywhere, three guys standing on top.

I want to do the Needle at Hoy, said one of the Canadians. Best in summer, said Charmian, when you can abseil from the main cliff into the water, swim across, then climb.

They lived so totally for their bodies. They had the same slightly stooped posture, as though they were unused to having roofs above their heads. If you could do what they did, signing a hush-money agreement wouldn't bother you at all.

There was Elza, slender Siamese cat among these muscled tigers. Hugo standing close to her, very close. As though they had no personal space of their own, but just one, in which they were tightly joined.

'Ready?' said Steve.

And they went down and told the story to the press.

77

Sunday. Gina and Robert were hiking in Suffolk with Pennie and Sam, friends who'd made a big move out of London. They didn't see each other often, so there was always a lot to catch up.

The last time, two years ago, meeting Pennie and Sam was quite a trial. They had become solar panel tycoons, winning eco-awards and hiring staff for a growing empire in Norfolk. Gina, at the time, was trying to be cheerful about a job that choked her in admin. Robert was recording covers of chart hits for a fitness company, and trying not to admit it was artistically treasonous. On the train home afterwards, she and Robert gave themselves a good laugh. Pennie and Sam must think we're schmucks. Because laughing was all you could do.

But today, as they walked the grassy dunes with Pennie, Sam and Pennie's brother Will, Gina could tell them she had a job she loved and Robert had truly exciting news, something that matched the majesty of this landscape. This year had been phenomenal.

After climbing to the top of a high headland, Gina and Pennie sat at a picnic bench, overlooking a bay of tumbled rocks, eating ice-creams while they waited for the guys. The guys had gone off piste, just because.

Gina and Pennie had time to explore a Napoleonic gun emplacement before Sam and Will came striding over the rise, jackets unzipped to cool off. Robert wasn't with them.

'Where is he?' said Gina.

Sam laughed, on deep breaths as he recovered from the climb.

Oh God, what had Robert done?

'He's coming the long way.'

'The long way?' said Gina.

Sam glugged some water. 'We went up something that looked like a path. I said we were lost and Robert said it would connect if we climbed a bit. Then I slipped down it on my backside and that was enough. It was a cliff.' The side of Sam's jacket was plastered in wet sand.

'It wasn't a cliff,' said Will, whose elbows and shins were caked. 'More like a lot of bushes on a very steep slope.'

'You couldn't walk up it,' said Sam. 'We were using tree roots as handholds. I could see that if I went up any further I wouldn't be able to get down again. Robert looked like he was enjoying it, so we left him and came up the steps instead.'

Gina tried Robert's phone. Left a message. 'We're at the top and we're hungry. Move your arse.'

Robert joined them some minutes later, looking like he'd crawled through a sandpit on his hands and knees.

'Did you discover a lost village?' said Gina.

After more trekking, they began to discuss a pub they'd been to the previous time. No one could agree on its name. Gina looked at her map app but her signal was at zero. Robert had a signal but couldn't be bothered to look, so he gave her his phone, while he and the others had a conversation about kitchen gadgets they never used.

Gina searched the unfamiliar screen. Fergodssake, Robert, where do you keep the map? Email notifications streamed annoyingly along the top. Swiping them away, she opened Gmail by mistake.

She hadn't intended to read any messages. But one was visible and the first paragraph stopped her like a slap.

Thank you for your enquiry about the Everest expedition with Once In A Lifetime. To help you achieve your goal, we should schedule a call with our training team, who will recommend next steps and put you in touch with a personal trainer in your area.

She was so surprised she called his name. It flew out of her mouth. 'Robert, what's this email?'

He didn't hear. He was further down the path with the others and they were talking about coffee machines.

The email remained on the screen. Everest? Was Robert thinking of climbing Everest? Surely not. For one thing, they didn't have that sort of money.

'Gina, have you found that pub yet?' called Sam.

'Wait a minute,' said Gina.

Should she delete the email? No, he couldn't seriously be thinking of climbing Everest. It wasn't what it seemed.

'I've found the pub,' called Will, turning back to face her, holding his own phone high. The sun flashed off its surface. 'The Anchor.'

..

As Gina and Robert walked back from the station, a rain shower turned into a deluge, swirling in the gutters and turning the roads into rivers. They squelched in through the front door, peeled off windcheaters and boots, raced up to the bathroom and into the shower, where they shivered back to a human temperature, then grappled feistily in the steam for a while.

As they dressed, she thought how skinny Robert was now. His waistline used to bulge slightly. Not that he was ever overweight, but now he was lean as a fish. She'd thought it must be the bike rides. What if it was something else?

He might be in training to climb a mountain.

No, there could be many reasons.

She should have deleted the email about Everest. She could have. She had the phone in her hand. He wouldn't have known. And why not, when he hid so much from her, as if she wasn't on his side, couldn't be trusted to help or understand. Like Elza and Elliot, it had to stop sometime. And now Elliot had told her about this insane plan with the body. That had evaporated harmlessly, but what other crazy thing might Robert do?

Actually, in those moments she had Robert's phone, she'd had ultimate power. She could have set up a redirect to copy future emails to her own inbox. That's what the newspaper hackers did. She'd learned a few things from Steve. No wait. That couldn't be done from the phone app. It had to be from a PC.

Anyway, that was theoretical. She hadn't done those things.

They threw their wet gear into the washing machine. She kept noticing his leaner proportions. The blue shirt he was wearing looked taut around the shoulders. Not from bike rides, surely? Or did his shoulders look bigger because of his tighter waist?

They made Bolognese. It popped and bubbled in the pot. It seemed alien with its red ingredients and potent smells, a game with dangerous substances.

..

Later, photos arrived from Pennie, Will and Sam. Heads crowded into the camera, hair wisping upwards in the wind, the sky behind, seabirds and a red fabric kite flying in the clouds. Then a picture that made her blood stop still.

Robert half-way up the cliff.

Will was in the foreground, pointing with a look-at-this-idiot expression. Yes, it really was a cliff. No exaggeration. Gina zoomed the picture, inspected it all over. Perhaps it wasn't all that it seemed. A few scrubby trees poked out of the boulders at the bottom, but further up was sheer rock with hardly any handholds. And Robert was on that rock, well clear of the trees, clinging with his fingers to nothing. His gaze was upwards, intent on the top. Even if he'd done it to tease Will and Sam, then climbed down when they left, he'd gone a long way up. A broken neck if he slipped.

She could hear him in the other room, on his PC. The dash of fingers across keys, the downbeat of the space bar and carriage return. He sounded busy, on a mission.

A quick google. How much did it cost to climb Everest? It was impossible money. Of course it was. Look it up; stop this worry.

She found an article from the *Telegraph*. Prices started at £6,500. A wave of nauseous panic. Then anger. That must be a misprint, a silly, misleading mistake. She was sure she'd read that Ashten Geddard's Everest expedition cost nearly ten times that.

Rockstar wages. And that was twenty years ago. But here it said £6,500. How were they calculating that? Had they separated out one element, like how much you pay a guide, a theoretical minimum that would never be enough in actuality? She read on. No, the price was all in. Everest could be climbed for £6,500.

Further down the page, she came to a picture that nearly stopped her heart. A Sherpa guide in hospital after the avalanche earlier this year. A face on a white pillow. An oxygen pipe in his nose. Eyes closed. Sleeping or more deeply shut down? A wound on his cheek was covered by a bloodstained plaster. Other lacerations were still wet on his dark skin. The wetness made him look babyish, as if he had recently been crying.

So very broken. By Everest.

..

She woke early, after not much sleep. Robert was up already. She listened while he moved between rooms. Shower, back to the bedroom, ready for the bike in lean Lycra. She put on a dressing-gown while he gathered work clothes, followed him to the front door, hugged goodbye. All was usual, but his sleeker body was unsettling to her now. She watched him pump away around the corner, waking fully into his physique, fittened for a purpose he was keeping from her.

She went to his computer. Put her hand on the mouse and woke it. Just that move felt like it might crack the fundaments of hell. He was sure to know, to come crashing through the front door. She went to the email settings. Opened a private browsing window so he couldn't follow her trail. Found the steps for a redirect. It would be easy. If she needed to do it.

Sitting here now, with everything ready, maybe she didn't need to. A night of fret and counter-fret had suggested many things she should check. Other messages in his email, the browser history. There could be another explanation. Heavens, one email wasn't exactly a commitment.

The Everest email was there. He hadn't junked it. Not a good sign. It was marked unread. Still being considered.

Other emails had arrived. Nothing similar. Ordinary stuff about offers from Amazon or software companies.

Okay, the browsing history. It loaded.

She had to grip the chair arm for a moment. Last night he'd spent a long time on a forum about climbing.

Think. Find what he was looking for.

Impossible to tell, so many pages, so many threads. Was he a member of the forum or just an observer? Was he posting questions of his own?

He might have a login name. She started another private window, copied a link, checked the top bar. He wasn't logged into the forum. The tight band around her heart eased. Perhaps he wasn't serious enough to have a login.

Perhaps he didn't stay logged in.

She looked away from the screen and out of the window, at the street, at the hedges and gates. People would start to come out of their houses soon, to go to work. Probably every person in this road had a crammed life and wished they had time for something extraordinary too. They might flirt with an epic adventure, become an armchair expert. Then decide it wasn't possible, not without breaking family, routines, their actual futures.

But they weren't Robert. Robert had his own ideas of possible.

There was hardly any traffic on the roads yet. Hopefully he had a clear run, because he was probably bolting like a banshee.

Back to his browsing history. What else was there? So many stops at the climbing forum. Over several days. A lot of seeking and questing. How many hours did this represent?

Occasionally there were other sites. She visited in the private browser. They were rock-climbing magazines. The pictures were terrifying. A man in a scarlet jacket sitting like a pixie on a ledge, looking over a range of crystalline peaks, with no other human or manmade thing in sight. A woman in yellow shorts, ordinary summer clothes, clinging to a sunny rockface with no ropes and not even a helmet, as if it was a thing anyone might do on an afternoon stroll. Like Robert in the pictures taken by Will and Sam.

A newspaper interview. With Hugo Bird. That was worth a read. Robert never sent her links to band interviews, though she knew there had been a few recently.

The interview was about the album, but with a surprise kicker.

'These unkind places give you back reality. On a glacier, the ground under your feet might vanish. Every step might be a coin-toss between life and death. I've trekked for two days over ice, dragging my pack because I was too exhausted to carry it....'

She felt like howling. This was the guy Robert worked for. Did they talk about this lone hero stuff?

'The cold, the ice ... the forces that shift the snow, open chasms and start avalanches... they don't care about anything you've done before. What matters is the next thing you do.'

These bloody men. Hugo was an idiot who might die any day. And didn't care whether he did.

Had Hugo got Robert interested in climbing? It would push his stupidest buttons.

She should check if they'd emailed each other about this.

They hadn't. But Robert had also been looking at a gym in central London, She followed that.

It had a chamber for simulating high altitude. For expedition training.

She put her elbows on the desk, palmed her face and closed her eyes. Her mind howled with one screaming word. Why? Why did he need to do this? If he wanted a grand escape, why couldn't he talk to her? Plan something they could do together? Instead, he said it's me, not you.

Less than twenty-four hours before, when they were walking with Pennie and Sam, they were having a fabulous year. They'd had their ruts and doldrums but now they were out, on fighting form, with great futures to come.

If she hadn't borrowed Robert's phone, she'd still feel like that.

No, she'd be an idiot who didn't know what he planned.

She looked again at the screen. Took a long breath in. Let it slowly out. Robert wasn't telling her what was going on. He might do any crazy thing.

Or he might keep it as a pipe-dream. The album was launching soon. He might fall in love with reality again.

She clicked on the tab with the steps for the email redirect. Pointed it to a hotmail account named so it was obviously an alias. It was possible that he'd spot it, but he'd assume it was a reporter, snooping for secret goss. He'd be flattered.

It was done.

The house was as peaceful as ever. The world hadn't punished her. A lone plane moved over the waking city on its way to Heathrow airport. Its sound had a slow rolling quality, as though the plane had all the time in the world to cross the sky. She checked the browsing history. Don't rush. Don't make a mistake. Remove your traces.

She did. But she couldn't remove the tightening fist of worry in her heart.

78

'I thought you were talking to Radio One.'

Robert was working in the studio when Hugo walked in. He thought they'd have an hour or so of downtime before Hugo arrived. Gil was clicking, thumping, hi-hatting and rolling in a rhythmic daydream. Robert was finger-picking the Gibson.

Now Hugo was here. Early.

Hugo laid his phone on the Steinway, carefully, as if it was fragile.

Gil stopped, breathing like a runner. Asked about Radio One.

Hugo said: 'The coroner just reported on Ash.'

Gil left his drumset, joined Hugo at the Steinway to look at the phone.

Robert could see it too. One of the reputable newspapers. *Broken bones and damage from the cold. How Ashten Geddard died.*

'Oh mate,' said Gil. He touched Hugo on the shoulder, the stick still in his hand.

Hugo nodded. 'Let's work.'

..

They played. All that existed was vocals, verses, chords, choruses, overdubs, fills, the joined meditation of their work. A few hours later, they listened in the control room.

'So are you going to settle here, Hugo?' said Gil. 'With Elza?'

Jeez, thought Robert, no one but Gil would dare to ask that.

Hugo's surprised flinch seemed to say as much. A question too far.

'It's not as if we don't know,' added Gil. 'I feel bad for Elliot but sometimes these things are meant to happen.'

79

Gina had a break in the afternoon. She opened the hotmail divert account. Emails had come from Robert's inbox. She had his life now; it was that easy. Confirmations of meetings. Sales emails from stores he was registered with.

He had email alerts. Several about Hugo and Ashbirds. If he'd set one up for his own name, it hadn't found anything. What a damn shame.

There was an email from someone called Paul Wavell. The name was one she should know. The message might clarify.

I was contacted by your manager who said we have to sign a non-disclosure agreement. Do you know about this? Is it about our songs?

Non-disclosure agreement? That sounded underhand. Were there more dodgy events to cover up? Was this something she needed to know about?

Paul Wavell. Who was he again?

There was a message Robert had sent himself; a link. She knew it; a secure storage site he used for music files. The file was big. More than one song. Her heart gave a gallop of excitement. Was it the Ashbirds album? The actual album?

She clicked. It asked for a login. She knew a likely password. He'd used it on another fileshare site when he sent tracks to her. If it worked, it worked.

It worked.

She listened to one song. She performed a marriage ceremony. She registered a death and a birth, and was glad they were in that order. The song she'd heard clung to her thoughts with a curious and attractive allure, like a fragrance from a stranger's jacket, all through the rest of the day. She felt alight with possibilities and promise, like those days in September when he played her the roughs, so excited to let her hear them. Now the album was done. Finished. She couldn't wait to hear the rest.

When she finished work, she put her headphones in, struck out along a route of quiet back roads that would take her eventually to Victoria station. She wanted proper time with this album, not to get immediately on a Tube. Rain was falling, but she didn't mind. Rain created the perfect solitude, hands in pockets, hood up, ears wrapped in music.

The music didn't disappoint. It was daring, lush. Melancholic, elegiac. Very romantic in places. Angry in others. She liked it a lot.

After several tracks she checked the title listing. How many more before she heard one of the songs Robert had played her? She could come back to the others but she wanted one of his now. She skipped to the next. No, that wasn't one of Robert's. The next.

She skipped on, on. All the way to the end.

She had not heard any of Robert's songs.

Maybe they'd been left off because he'd written others that were better. There were some beautiful pieces here. They got in your blood and made you feel new, like you could do anything. Which had Robert helped to write?

She looked at the album's metadata, shielding her phone's display from the rain. Did it have credits? *Ashbirds is Hugo Bird, featuring Robert Speed, Gil Hustable. Performed and produced by Ashbirds at Hymnasium Studios, London.* Robert was named as keyboards, bass, guitar and sax on some tracks. Hugo was vocalist on all of them. Finally: *All songs written and arranged by Hugo Bird.*

None were by Robert? But he'd been writing, hadn't he? She was unclear on the business aspects but she knew that if Robert wasn't credited as a writer, he would get much less in royalties. And wasn't there some kind of points system as well?

Besides, what about his work as a musician? Ashbirds was everything to him. It was the career he should have had, twenty years ago, if everyone had played fair. And now his songs had been ditched? For a second time?

She ducked into a bus shelter, away from the drenching sky,

shook the rain off her hood, leaned on the bench and searched the credits again. Each squinty little line. She might have missed something.

She hadn't, but she noticed something else. Paul Wavell, that name again, a session credit for piano and keyboards. Of course; the scrunch-faced guy. He and Robert had worked together on song-writing, hadn't they? And now they were emailing each other about an NDA? What was that for? Was it gagging Robert to keep quiet about the songs he'd written?

After all, it had happened before. When Hugo Bird hustled him out of the other album. And now, Robert's songs had disappeared from this one.

She looked out into the rain. Washing the day off the pavement, off the road, keeping pedestrians fleeing, all going fast while she paused in this bus shelter, marooned in the deluge. She was grate-ful for it. She could sit alone and gradually process, clear the fog from her mind.

This was it. This was the enemy Robert wanted to escape. Not their life, not her. When he shut her out of the bathroom while he changed, when he stole out of the house so she wouldn't know or ask where he was going, when she caught him strapping on his helmet and picking up his lights and he made her feel he couldn't tolerate her concerned questions or her reminder to be careful, when he sped aggressively and recklessly away as if she was the problem. She wasn't the problem. He wasn't trying to escape from her. It was those bastards. That aggression of his, the bike frame tipping with each propulsive hellbent downstroke as he fled from her, it was so hurtful. But he wasn't fleeing from her.

Such a relief. It wasn't her.

It wasn't her.

80

Hugo and Elza walked along the Embankment. A row of white globe lights on Victorian posts made a dotted path into the distance. The flagstones glistened, varnished with rain. Joggers passed them, heads down, backpacks bumping on their shoulders. The river splashed and lapped on the other side of the wall.

'I think I should see Ashten,' she said. 'One last time.'

He'd suspected she wanted a serious talk. That was the only reason she'd suggest a walk after dark. If they were at his flat or her home, there were other ways to work through a difficult feeling.

'Do you want to see him?'

'Isn't it what I have to do? Get closure?'

Get closure. It sounded like 'get closer'. At home they'd act on that, like an amusing cue from fate. Get closer – yes, for a moment, for as much time as we can, because this closeness is so surprising. Get closure, she said now, and on they walked in the rain.

'Do you think you need closure?' he said, walking.

'I don't know.'

A cyclist passed, wheels hissing.

'You saw him. That made a difference, didn't it? Before that – be honest, you and I couldn't be in the same room. But then you saw him.'

What he saw. The shelf of ice. He hadn't told her about that. Ash's body tethered in ropes.

He hadn't told her about the pills or Ash's state of mind. Or his own state of mind. He hadn't told any of that, to anyone.

Elza could not be told. For her, Ash was still mysterious. An untamed, thrilling force that had chosen her, defined her, transformed her. Her formative experience, as Ash himself would say.

She did not know Hugo's Ash. Probably no one did.

'You've gone quiet. Is there something I shouldn't see?'

Well, he could reassure her about that. 'It's no worse than any of the other bodies, if that's what you mean.'

'But it's bad that it's him. Right?'

Yes. That was right.

'I should see what you've seen.' Her voice had a quizzical quality. He could not be sure if it was a question or the tilt of her accent.

'Don't do it because you think you've got to.'

'It's a one-time chance, isn't it? If I don't, I'll never know if I should. Either I do it now or I don't, ever.'

Did it have to be so final? It seemed so bleak. Especially out here, among all these people who were running from the hostile weather, hurrying for shelter. Closure. Did she want closure? Did she want him to talk her out of it? 'You don't have to do this. There aren't any rules.'

A curl of blonde hair had dropped out of her hat. She stopped and he did too, pushing it back into the brim, restoring her disguise. Her eyes locked trustfully on his. He noticed another ring of hair, escaping near the nape of her neck, and put that back. 'We decide the rules.'

A person was jogging down the parapeted steps from the bridge. Break away. You don't know what they'll notice.

Hugo and Elza walked onwards.

She clamped his arm, taking tighter hold of her thoughts. 'This will sound mad, but every time I'm away from you I'm afraid you aren't real.'

'You seem real to me.'

'I'm not expecting this to sound logical.'

The jogger passed. Water splashed up from striding feet.

'Well, if you must see the body, ask Oliver Jared for his police car.'

She didn't fail to spot the mischief. 'Wouldn't he love that. Bloodsucker.'

Hugo felt a bit reassured. They were still in tune.

No, it was a cheap test, to check they were.

81

Elza took a train to Surrey, to a hospital. She noticed two kinds of people as she walked through its sprawling grounds. Those for whom the territory was routine and familiar, on their way to work a shift or attend an appointment or a meeting. And those who scrutinised each entrance, reading signs, orienting themselves on maps, uncertain of everything.

There were also two kinds of building. Some with wide windows like a seafront hotel. Some with high blank walls, to hide what went on inside.

The chapel of rest was one of those. A low-rise, windowless building that budded off the end of the maternity wing, of all places. It was surrounded by a garden with benches so that visitors could recover from whatever they'd seen. Or sit and wait for people who were inside.

Elza had not brought anyone to wait for her on a bench. Hugo had not asked if he should come.

She would have felt bad saying no. He seemed to know that.

She had come alone.

She entered. The receptionist was behind a solid-looking desk, like a television newsreader. Elza gave her name. The receptionist checked a list. Asked for identification. Good; her name wasn't her passport. They were doing it properly. They were capable. She needed them to be capable.

Her documents were handed back. 'Take a seat.'

Elza sat. There was a vase of flowers on the coffee table. A box of tissues as well, which she stared at.

Might she need some? They became fascinating to her. They held a warning quality. Are you prepared? Really prepared? The top tissue was pulled into an untidy peak, from the one that had been taken above it. The untidiness bothered her. She saw scrambling, stumbling, snatching fingers, a person made wild by sadness and tears. Were they prepared for that? She took one.

The receptionist called a name. 'Geddard.'

Geddard. It was a shock. She had never answered to Geddard. Restaurants, hotels and flights were always booked in Steve's name for security. Now here it was, used without any precautions. Geddard. Through that double door.

She stood up. She went through the double door. Her heart, her throat, her tongue had become one lavalike substance. She thought the body would be here, immediately, but it wasn't. Of course it wasn't. That wouldn't do, to find it just by falling through a door.

There was a corridor. She was chasing him through a labyrinth and he kept moving, behind one more corner. One more door.

Someone was suddenly in front of her. A woman in a suit. God, she had hardly seen her, she was looking for the body, a horizontal body. Now it was as if this vertical woman had dropped from a hatch in the ceiling.

The woman spoke in a calm, official voice. 'I'm afraid he might not look like your memory of him. He was out for a long time. Let me know when you're ready.'

Elza was expecting he would be changed. Hugo had warned her. And she had made all those pictures, studied the distinction between life and death. Last night, after the walk, she and Hugo went to the Glacier House and sat in the attic room, talking, with the portraits arranged around them.

She was well prepared for this, this day when she saw him. She had even seen some of the actual bodies, in the first months. This would not be so different.

She nodded to tell the woman she was ready. Her skin burned violently in response. What had she just asked for?

The woman pushed open the door. 'Mr Geddard is in here.'

Mr Geddard. Ashten had never been Mr Geddard. It sounded like an old man.

The coffin was plain wood, like a first attempt by an apprentice. It stood across two trestles. A vase of lilies stood on a pillar, like a church. A curtain ran around the walls, like a hospital room.

Ashten lay in the coffin.

How long did she stand there? There was nowhere to sit, but she could not feel her body. She was somehow bodiless, simplified to an essence, a receiving sense, a floating soul.

He did not appear to be asleep, like the other climbers. They had looked as though they were sleeping, but that was because she had not known them when they actually slept. Or when they sucked on a joint and licked ice cream off her fingers and sketched in the window seat and seethed when the phone rang and looked at her across a room at a party in a way that said to hell with all this, all these people, all this nonsense, I'd rather be alone with you.

She began to take breaths again, to come back to the room.

The hospital had dressed him. He was wearing a robe of crimson velvet. Her skin flamed again, all over, a charge crackling within her. Why had they done that? It was diabolical and wrong. Ashten would never have worn such a thing. He would have despised it. He was careful with everything he wore. He knew when a shirt was a centimetre smaller than it should be because it made him appear overweight. Now here he was in this, like a vestment from a priest or the dressing-gown of a rich old man.

His hair was white, which Hugo had prepared her for, but what had they done to it? In life, it fell waywardly over his face, a mussed veil, which his eyes invited you to part so you could be enspelled. Now it was lank and neat, combed away.

'Would you like me to leave you alone with him?' said the woman.

Elza said: 'His hair never looked like that.'

'Would you like to dress it? I can bring you a comb. The robe was provided by the hospital but you could bring him something else.'

No, she did not want to dress his hair. And to bring him other clothes? His clothes went twenty years ago.

Her preparation with the pictures could never have been enough. Death didn't show in a picture, or in the altered colour of the skin, or in the slightly parted lips that were as fixed as putty and never moved no matter how long you stared at them, because your mind could suggest that was like a picture too. Death showed in the clothes they could put on him and the way they could arrange his hair and use his name, because he was not there to know.

Elza walked away, back through the labyrinth, out through the double doors. When she reached the main door, the receptionist was at her newsreader desk. She was looking at Elza. Not the way she had before, as if Elza was a pawn to be sent through her department's process. Now, she was really looking.

'I saw the concert in Hyde Park this summer. I wouldn't have missed it for the world.'

On the desk, a phone began ringing. The receptionist continued to look at Elza.

'Shouldn't you answer that phone?' said Elza.

'I will never forget this day,' said the receptionist.

Elza said goodbye and pushed through the door. On the steps were three bouquets. They hadn't been there when she arrived. Someone always found out.

There was a bench on the edge of the lawn that faced into a clump of conifers. She wanted to sit there, to be still and look nowhere and let the weight work through her, but she might cry, because of not knowing what else to do, and another person might come to leave a bouquet and see her. She glanced over the sprawl of buildings, where she would have to find her way back. The buildings with their two kinds of walls, places of activity and fight where life was not yet over. She might cry if she walked, too, but at least she would not be sitting where somebody might arrive with flowers, or a CD, or all that stuff. She left the bench and walked.

She dialled Hugo. Got voicemail. Did she dare leave a message? 'I did it,' she said. 'Call me when you can.'

She looked back through the texts from him. Texts he'd sent in spite of Steve's warnings about hackers, because sometimes you had to. *I was in Costa and somebody stole my coffee. Just stole it from the table in front of me as I was sitting there. See you later.*

She walked, not knowing where she was going, through the land of the living.

82

Hugo saw her as she walked towards the gates. She'd worn a hat to hide her hair, as usual, and a man's overcoat. The coat must be Elliot's, he realised.

He texted to say he was here, but it was a while before she noticed him. She walked slowly, as though along a deserted shore, seeing only the surge and retreat of her thoughts. She seemed to look at him without awareness, then came back, abruptly and with a visible shock.

It was a wary stiffening he'd seen before. When he returned from Nepal. As if she was thinking: 'Now you're here, what do I do about you?'

'Are we still friends?' he said. That seemed to do the trick. She melted onto him gratefully, hat tipping off.

He had a car. They drove back to the city, through wide freeways edged by suburban semis, keeping to the speed limit because a ticket would be a gift to the papers. They talked about small details of their day.

He told her there had been a meeting about the memorial service. The press agent wanted an open coffin. Steve had said: 'No, mate. You haven't seen him. He's not Sleeping Beauty.'

A soft laugh. 'I will never have to do that again.' She leaned against the headrest, her head tilted back, thanking the whole sky.

Oliver Jared had wanted a red carpet. Then he changed his mind to a white one, and wanted all the guests to remove their shoes.

'That man is like a puppy's tail. All wag, no sense.' Exactly what Hugo thought she'd say, and they were easy and amused again, letting the sluggish route take them, waiting for home to arrive. He saw in her a brittle quality that he recognised. That was how he felt after viewing Ash's body; light as if relieved of a burden, helpless as though the floor had gone.

Later, at his flat, when they were wearing dressing-gowns and drinking wine and roasting a chicken, he caught moments when she faded out to that puzzled trance place. Then she was back with him, talking of ordinary things, or things that were ordinary to them and would never be to anyone else.

83

She saw him wake.

He opened his eyes. Hey, he said.

Hey, she said.

'It's late.' It was phrased as a question. He meant, it's late for you to be awake. What's on your mind?

What was on her mind?

By millimetres, the conversation was starting.

'What happens next?'

He didn't immediately understand. But then, he had just woken, and needed to catch up.

'After the memorial service. You'll go back to the wilderness, I guess?'

'I don't know. I could be anywhere.'

'You'll have to go back to Everest.'

'Namche,' he corrected. 'Maybe. You could come with me.'

'I'm not a climber.'

He hadn't taken her climbing, but just that weekend they'd been for a walk along the Dorset coast and he'd shown her a sea stack. In the summer I climbed that, he said. It was a column of craggy rock, like a piece pulled away from the cliffs and left standing on its own in the heaving ocean. Like a place from a fable where a prisoner might be kept because they'd never get down and no one would ever get up to rescue them. Two guys were ascending it that day, crawling up the side, spread across handholds and footholds. The drop was horrifying, and they were trusting their bodies to just a few ropes and fixings, and the tips of their toes and fingers. Hugo described to her what they were doing as if it was a process as straightforward as building a flatpack desk. First you do this; then this; then be careful of this; and never let yourself do that; then you reach the top and you feel amazing. This is who he is, she thought. Perhaps I can be like this too. Perhaps I can become someone who stays brave while he is out there with all that empty space below and behind him, and kept there just by pins and ropes.

But now she had walked back through the hospital, past all the battles between life and death. She had thought about the ways people ended up behind those walls. The many ways a body could fail just from the wear of ordinary living, never mind this. Walking through that hospital, the future was certain. A kind person would visit and tell her a rock fell and Hugo was now gone, or they had left him in a crevasse, or he had slipped into a void, or drifted away somewhere, alone, in a desolate place. They might bring a picture, like all the other pictures she'd been seeing for years. Or there might never be a picture at all.

The streetlamp outside the window put a steady twilight through the curtains. It deepened the scar through his eyebrow and two gashes on his shoulder he'd said were from keyhole surgery. A keyhole to what? she'd gasped. A giant's castle? And that was just the scars that were visible now, above the sheet. She remembered sitting with him in the Glacier House, the first time they needed to talk in secret, noticing how damaged he looked. That could have been a warning, from a part of her mind that was much more wise and knew what was developing, even though she would swear she had no conscious intention. Back away. He is not for you.

'I'm not a climber,' she said.

'You don't have to be.'

'I'm not brave enough to live with one.'

He reached to hook a lock of her hair behind her ear. Perhaps he meant it to be reassuring. Perhaps it was to help him think.

'I could stay here for a while. My aunt and uncles could use some help with the gliding club.'

She'd met his family and seen the gliding club. His family were sincere and fun, and the scenery was breathtaking, but she'd noticed his clear relief as they drove away. It was the place he and Ashten had vowed to escape. He still kept that vow. That would never change.

'You wouldn't go back to Shropshire. It's been there all your life and you haven't moved back.' She thought of something funny and ironic and wished it wasn't. 'And a gliding club? Flying in a contraption? Isn't there anything you could do that doesn't need a helmet and a safety harness?'

'There are always new starts. We could go anywhere.'

What if they could?

No. The problem was who he was. He didn't want to live at sea level. He could talk through the procedure for climbing a fragile pillar of rock and not find anything to fear.

She rolled onto her back. So she could talk and not see his face, as he offered solutions and compromises.

'Do you know what I remember most about being with Ashten? I was scared that it would end. There would be another girl. Or he'd realise I was timid and uninteresting, as the press said I was, or his manager would find him a flashy popstar who'd make better headlines. It should have been the best time of my life and all I could think was how I was wrong for it.' She felt the bed shift and she knew he was about to say something, but she couldn't let him interrupt. 'I even knew I was thinking that, because when he was away on the mountain, I planned that when he got back, I'd be brave and enjoy it properly, stop being so worried.'

She felt able to look at him again. 'With you it would be the same. I would always be waiting for it to end.'

'But isn't that how we all feel? The tighter we want to hold, the more we fear it slipping away.'

'You can stop the song lyrics now. That's too bloody clever. I'm wrong for you. What will you think of me when I'm saying please don't climb another mountain?'

'Why don't you let me be the judge of that?'

'No. You're trying to talk me round. Don't. Don't. I'm not saying this very well. Not like you would.'

A breath, deepening the mattress.

'Don't.' She turned and lay on her back again. Put her hands over her eyes. 'Don't.'

...

Elza had a meeting at midday in the city, visiting a restaurant that wanted a mural. She measured the wall, climbed a stepladder to check how samples of colour would look in the available light, had a conversation with the manager. It took all her concentration, and now, walking out of the building, she could not remember doing any of it, except that she had notes to prove she had.

She needed to wander with her thoughts. She felt like she had done something reckless and destructive and had to check, at her own private pace, how the world would now be.

Her phone rang. Gina.

'Weren't we supposed to have coffee?'

She'd forgotten. She'd suggested it a few days before, when she arranged the site visit.

'You just walked past the café. Didn't you see me waving?'

She didn't want to see anyone, but here was Gina, in a metal name badge and a tailored suit she wore for ceremonies, walking out of the café with two lattes, one of which she put into her hand. The authority of that was greater than her will to walk away.

They crossed the road. Between the buildings that belonged to merchant banks and investment houses was a little park. It was the kind of place Steve would approve for a private chat. A secluded corner with no passers-by and nowhere for people to loiter without being seen. His precautions were now part of her personality. They might always be.

She and Gina chose a bench. 'Sorry,' said Elza. 'I forgot. Thanks for the coffee.'

'You look like you need it. Have you had any sleep?'

She hadn't. The conversation with Hugo had continued for many more hours.

All the chances he had given her to change her decision. She still could, even now. No one had been told. If no one had been told, it hadn't happened.

Gina said: 'So I assume everything's good'.

This was a moment she could make it actual. Tell Gina.

Except Gina's tone was tart. Accusing. It said while you've been amusing yourself, the rest of us were dealing with something important.

No, I can't tell you when you have a tone like that. I need... what did she need? Gentleness, perhaps.

Gina was angry with her. Surely not because she was late for coffee.

Elza was too tired for puzzles. 'Am I in trouble? You'd better tell me why, because I'll never guess.'

In front of them was a lawn and beyond it, a path. A gardener in overalls and ear defenders was walking slowly along the path with a blower, chasing fallen leaves into a whirl.

Gina looked at the gardener, as if there were many answers to Elza's question and she was picking how she'd start.

'I know about the agreement. After the Hyde Park concert. What you all should have said about that body on the mountain.'

The Hyde Park concert. The night Ashten was found. Barely six weeks ago but Elza felt she'd lived a lifetime since. Had Gina just heard about the plan with the body? Was this what she was angry about?

'I wasn't there,' said Elza. 'I think they were all a bit crazy.'

'Yes, it was crazy, and it wasn't necessarily right. But it would have helped, wouldn't it? It would have helped everyone to move on. You could have considered that. And as it turns out, you didn't even have to pretend. For God's sake, the body was really Ashten. But no, the two of you decided.'

The two of you. She was not ready to hear anyone talk about the two of them. Not anyone, not even Gina. As if she knew all about them. Even, sounding as though she deplored them.

There was so much Gina didn't know. Right now, though, an answer seemed to be required, about the agreement, the body. Elza said: 'It was a difficult time.'

'And Robert, he couldn't move on. You've brought Hugo back here, let him take everything Robert's been working for. This should have been Robert's time. I've heard the new album and none of Robert's songs are on it. Did you know that?'

Did you know? It wasn't a question. It was a statement. You damn well know. In fact, you are partly responsible.

Elza didn't know anything that went on in the studio. She said so.

'You remember those songs we played you in the Glacier House,' said Gina. 'They're not on the album now. They were gorgeous songs, so light and lovely. You remember. And now they're gone. And do you know what? Robert's had to sign an NDA about it.'

Those songs. Oh Elza remembered those.

She and Hugo in the Glacier House, surrounded by the Everest sky, talking about Shitbirds.

Why was Gina hounding her about this? No, she said again, she didn't know what went on in the studio.

'The trouble is, you think Hugo's written the soundtrack to your life. Here's something to consider: my husband was there first. When you and Ashten were first together, the person writing with him was Robert. Not Hugo. Hugo came in and pushed Robert out. Erased the work he'd done. Actually erased the songs. Did you know that? If things had gone as they should have, Robert would have written the soundtrack to your life. Do you know how many times I hear those songs? Weddings, naming ceremonies. Robert could have written those.'

Robert, writing those songs? The idea was laughable. No, it was offensive. Only Hugo could have written them. His mind with perfect pitch and agile timing, the grace of his musical ear, which you heard with every word he uttered. But that was private.

Across the lawn, the gardener was blowing the leaves into a billow, ear defenders on, in a dreamy buzz. This felt like a dream, too. A confusing upheaval dream where a person you had always trusted was putting you on trial.

'Robert's earned a big break. But Hugo's always made sure he never gets it. But Robert has his pride so now he's going to Hugo's world. He's going to climb Everest.'

The last sentence was loaded with aggression and blame. *He's going to climb Everest. What do you say about that?*

What could she say? Elza said: okay, good for him.

'Good for him? I think you're a fool.'

The gardener turned off his leaf blower. Its noise had been

lulling. Now there was just Gina's voice. Tight, precise, prosecuting.

'I want to tell you what it will be like for you with your boyfriend. I want to make sure you know, that you can handle it. After my registrar training, I spent six months in Wiltshire. There were a lot of Army families. Couples would get married as the husband was about to be posted to Afghanistan. The brides were so proud of their warrior men. It's so romantic, that whiff of death. An aphrodisiac like no other. I had never seen such overwhelming love. But then I saw the mothers who came in with a baby to register and no father. Just a young mother and a sister or grandmother, the women of the tribe. Or they brought a maimed man, getting used to a wheelchair, hating himself for being useless, hating them for knowing he needed help. Or they came to register a death. Sometimes there wasn't even a body for the funeral. Their men threw themselves away and broke all the people around them. Can you handle that? I don't think you can.'

A thousand voices screamed in Elza's head. She closed her eyes. She knew she couldn't handle it. Gina seemed to think she was teaching her something, and she wasn't. Elza had earned this knowledge herself.

'You might think you can handle it. Good for you. But now I have to handle it. You have brought this to me. Look what you've done to me, you and your boyfriend. You've made my man throw himself away.'

Elza managed to speak. Her throat was dry as rubble. 'How have we done this?'

'You need to ask? How long have you known us? Robert's difficult. He has a warrior soul. And these strong men with warrior souls, they have a switch, a trigger. You and your boyfriend, who you brought back here by breaking promises and telling lies, and pushing Robert's work aside to wallow in songs about your own selfish story, you have pulled that trigger. And now Robert is going to climb Everest.'

The skewering look again. How do you answer that?

This would be my answer, thought Elza. Stop talking about us. It is not for you to talk about. She held it in.

Gina continued. 'But you don't have to worry about me. Or apologise. I can stop this. I'll have my work cut out, but I can get

Robert back. He's strong. He needs someone strong to ground him. I've pulled him back before.'

Good for you, thought Elza. I hope he likes that.

'But you? I don't know what you'll do. You've got a lot of trouble coming. That all-consuming romance of yours can only end one way, though you can't see it at the moment. But it will. You'd better make sure you've got good friends.'

Friends? I thought you were my friend. And you seem to hope I have trouble coming.

'You don't have anything to say?'

Elza could say no, I won't be in trouble. I could tell you why, and about everything I've seen and done in the last twenty-four hours, and that would tear the stuffing right out of you. You might even say you feel sorry about it, but I don't think that would be true. I think what I've just seen, what you said about friends and trouble, is true.

Gina took a sip of coffee. Her fingers were gripping the cardboard, making creases.

'Don't forget,' said Gina. 'I know what it's been like for you. You won't be able to bear it when it happens again.'

Do not tell me you know what it's been like. None of you know what it's been like.

Sometime towards dawn, Hugo told her everything else. How Ashten died. Afterwards. Seeing the body on the mountain. Many more things that were not for anyone else to know.

'Say something,' said Gina.

This was the most vicious and vindictive conversation she'd ever had in her life. Worse than anything ever said by the press. That would be the first thing Elza would say.

She did not. She checked her watch and stood up. 'Haven't you got a wedding?'

Gina stood up too. 'You should talk about this. You're just making everything harder.'

Elza looked across the grass to the path. Some of the piles of leaves were breaking their tidy order, venturing out on the breeze. We did what we did, Hugo and I. We found a place away from you all, away from your scrutiny, your demands, your babble, your frustrated ambition, your flailing marriages, your resentful friend-

ships, your self-serving concern and your wish-fulfilling navel-gaz-
ing nostalgia. We found a place where we could do what we needed,
with grief, with thankfulness, with love, with meaning. No, she did
not want to talk about it.

Elza dropped the coffee Gina bought her, untouched, in a bin,
and walked away.

84

Gina stood in the panelled room, the leather folder spread across
her open hand, waiting for the silence so she could begin.

The bride carried carnations, surrounded by something bushy and
green that could only be fresh parsley. The carnations were small, not
buttonhole-grade, as you would get from a florist. Had they improvised
with the flowers and herbs from the supermarket down the road? A
last-minute bouquet. A quickie ceremony, not serious.

Gina spoke the words quietly and without fuss. Let them have
their quickie the way they wanted it. Perhaps there would be a
made-up service afterwards with gowns and crowns and hunting
horns. Perhaps not. Perhaps this was it. This was all the hope they
had. By next year they might be doing it again, in some other office,
with new partners. The woman in the blue trilby hat, looking in her
bag at her phone, certainly seemed to think so.

These vows she was guiding them through: the having and
holding and others forsaking. One day one of them would say that
was just words. You weren't the love of my life after all. I think I've
never had that. I need something bigger. I don't know what it is. I
said you were everything but you can't expect that I meant it. How
could you be enough? You don't make me feel the way I need to feel.
I'm going to find it, to find myself. Don't wait.

85

The press photographers were waiting on the steps of the church.
They were all wearing black, as though angling to be invited inside
for the memorial. Not a chance.

Gina and Robert paused for a picture. Then they were inside, away from the racing motorbike couriers and construction drills, in calm stone chill.

They walked to the pews reserved for the band.

In front of the altar, a white guitar stand displayed a photo of Ashten Geddard.

There was no coffin. Steve had said there would be a private cremation for close family only.

Gina and Robert were great now. They were restored. Hugo was leaving the band, quitting music, running back to his mountains. Robert and Gil would carry on Ashbirds.

Elza had finished with Hugo, Robert said, and that changed everything.

Elza had taken Gina's advice. She'd left Hugo.

Gina hadn't expected that. Truly.

They were directed to a pew on the second row.

Elza was on the front row. Steve beside her. Elza, right there. That was a little shock.

Gina hadn't seen Elza since the day in the park. She'd thought she should contact her at some point, especially since Robert's news, though she felt she should wait until she could set aside plenty of time. They'd been so busy recently. Now here Elza was. A word, a breezy hello, and Elza might turn around. It would be that easy.

Elza might turn her head and see Gina anyway. Gina could smile and say how are you doing, we should catch up. Not necessarily today, no rush, but sometime.

Elza was very still. Very composed. Wearing a black dress that clung to her lean arms and shoulders, her usual uniform as Ashten Geddard's nearly-widow. We made it, Gina might say to her. We often wondered if we'd see this day. We've all been through a lot, haven't we?

Hugo was also on the front row. That was another shock. Gina looked away. It might be awkward if she caught his eye.

He was not sitting next to Elza. Steve was between them.

A dig in the side from Robert's elbow. Gil and his wife had arrived. They stood for hugs and sotto voce hellos. Gina scooched along to let them sit down.

She was now directly behind Elza.

Elza might somehow know. Gina looked away, around the church. Then she could turn back and say casually hi, if Elza was looking at her, waiting to talk.

But look, there, at the back. Was that Elliot, in a suit, making his way in? Elliot was here? Would he come and sit with Elza? If they were together again, everything had turned out well.

Robert pressed her arm. 'This is Bill Radford, manager of the Thought Bicycles.'

All the last few days, Robert's phone had been crazy with calls and emails. As Bill Radford went away, promising to talk later, Robert leaned to her, his breath shivery hot on her ear, and made a remark about Bill Radford's purple psychedelic cravat. They were comrades again.

In the row in front, Elza was still as a wand. Not talking to a soul. Not looking for anyone either. Elliot was not sitting with her. Where was he?

Gina's gaze came to Hugo again. Thoughtful, eyes down, not interested in who else was there. Like Elza.

The service began. The minister gave the opening address. They were gathered to commemorate the return of this man to warm earth. While he was up in the ice they had represented him in the world. They had searched for him. They had never forgotten him, and now, finally, they had brought him home.

Gina recognised the minister. He used to be in a band that topped the charts when Ashbirds were in their heyday. Getting him today was a nice touch. Her professional eye noted his understated take on funeral wear; a black stole laid over a suit and dog collar.

The minister took them through the ritual words and a reading. Music began. Echoed acoustic instruments, gently building a melody.

Hugo's voice began to sing. Gina suddenly recognised the song. A version of 'Come Back', from the new album, currently in the download charts.

'Loves you should have fought for.'

The sound startled everyone, haunting and pure, like a call to prayer.

'Days you should have seized. Ruins you have made.'

She risked a look at Hugo, though she was ready to dodge away if there was accidental eye contact. She didn't want that. But actually, he was unlikely to spot her even if she stared like a mongoose because every face in the congregation was looking at him.

'*And until it comes, til it comes, we will not ever rest.*'

How clever to arrange the song like this, mostly as vocals. You'd think it was written for a church. She even found herself liking him. If only he didn't make other guys want to be Tom Cruise or live in hurricanes.

Hugo was veiling his eyes behind his hand, as though he wanted to vanish. Small chance of that, Hugo, love, with your voice tearing everyone's hearts to pieces.

Robert was not going to climb a mountain. There was too much to do here. Pre-release publicity. Talks about a tour, maybe even another album. The things he should be doing. Should always have been doing. He was so busy he'd had to get that Paul Wavell guy to help.

She should probably thank Elza for that. Seriously, in a few weeks or months, they'd both look back and say, Gina you were right to tell me. Someone had to. No, Elza, you were right. What a strange time that was.

Hugo's voice kept circling. An intricate stack of harmonies. It was a persuasive song. Don't be like this. Don't have regrets. Don't make ruins. Hugo, listen to your own words. You nearly left us all in ruins. It wasn't pleasant having to tell that to Elza.

And now they had to worry about Steve. Steve was moving to Shropshire to partner with Hugo's family in the gliding club. What did Steve's girlfriend think of that?

In the row in front, Elza abruptly shivered, violently.

Another voice was swelling out of the mix.

A series of gasps went around the auditorium. Gina began to realise, as everyone did, what they were hearing.

It was Ashten's voice, singing over the new song. Words that everyone knew. From 'Hurricane'.

Gina saw Elza look sharply up at the vaulted ceiling. Were those tears in her eyes? In the front pew, Steve laid his hand supportively on her arm. Gina did too, on Elza's shoulder. The gesture was instinct; she was always a toucher. Let it out, love. We all are. Everyone understands.

Elza did not respond to Gina's comforting touch. She did not move at all.

The voices continued, so in synch. Ashten: *'It's coming. When you hear the roar, it's coming.'* Hugo with the new song: *'Until it comes, til it comes.'* The two guys, demolishing them all.

Under her hand, Elza was unresponsive.

Gina began to feel a chill, mounting in her heart. Perhaps she had made a mistake. Maybe she should not have touched Elza. She should withdraw her hand, but she did not dare. There was a dangerous potential in that stillness, like a cornered animal that might lash out.

86

Near the back of the church, Elliot listened. The bare instrumentation dropped away, leaving the two voices, soaring high and clear, calling and answering across the years. They should somehow be visible in the vaulted ceiling, in the light that slanted through the leaded windows, in the floating fireflies of dust.

Gradually, they faded into silence. The minister gave a final blessing. The congregation began to stand. Shaky, hushed, blinking. Elliot did too. It was as if everyone shared the same mind. There were quiet private sounds as glasses were wiped, mirrors were opened, bags were shouldered, skirts and jackets were straightened and everyone came back to their individual selves.

Elliot had an offer of work in New York. He'd emailed Elza to tell her and she told him about today. Come along, she said.

Now, people were moving out of the pews. Strangers grasped Elliot's hand, told him their names, received his as though they were all one brotherhood. Maybe they now were, after that ceremony.

He saw Elza. She was at the front of the church, suited, aloof and efficient, like a person in a uniform. Her hair was pulled back, which he knew she had done so she would not look girlish and frivolous in photos. He wanted her to know he was here, as promised, but not to feel obliged to talk to him. Since the night on the bridge, three weeks ago, they had not met, though they had chatted a few times on the phone.

She was standing alone, nodding at people in a way that let them know they could leave without speaking to her. Always a master of the friendly hello that said you can go.

Elliot glimpsed a swifter movement at the far end of the church by the empty corner pews. Someone who wanted to leave without being seen or stopped. It was Hugo Bird. He opened an arched door and was gone.

Elza, still alone by the front pew, was watching the closed door, her head laser-steady. She nodded to a well-wisher, then her eyes fastened on the door again.

She had not told Elliot anything very personal when they talked on the phone. Things were fine, she said. He understood. They weren't fine, but she couldn't begin to explain or didn't want to bother him. But the way she fixed on that door, looked through it, was its own explanation. Much was ending as it closed.

He felt the affectionate press of fingers on his arm. Gina, shawled in black, clasped him, patting his shoulder as if she thought he needed comfort. Robert reached for his hand. Elliot prepared for crumpled fingers. Then there was Steve, with wide shepherding arms, also claiming a hug.

The conversation in the church was rising to a busy murmur. Steve asked about New York. How did Steve know he was going to New York? 'I'll email you my special list of restaurants and clubs,' said Steve, with a wink, as if he thought Elliot would be out every evening, painting the town red. 'Use my name and you'll get a table, any time.'

'So what's next for you guys today?' said Elliot. 'A service with the coffin?'

'Not any more,' said Steve. 'Ashten's parents want him flown to their ranch in New England. Just to keep us on our toes.'

'I suppose they want him at home,' said Elliot. 'They didn't come today?'

Steve gave an amused eyeroll. Elliot realised Ashten's parents were a long story.

Someone leaned close and said: 'Thank you for coming.'

It was Elza.

Surprised, he said 'Lovely service'. He assumed she would move on, continue circulating. But she stayed beside him.

Elliot said: 'Steve said you had to change the funeral plans.'

'Yes, that was nice. You don't know about Ashten's parents, do you? They threw him out when he was seventeen, but he didn't leave a will so they got everything when he died. They live on his wealth and his royalties, but when I got the body they chucked lawyers at me.'

It was so grasping, nasty. And she was so unsurprised. Elliot had imagined a normal grieving family.

Elza laid her fingers on his arm, amused. 'You look shocked.'

'I can never get used to your people.'

'Somebody always wants the last piece of you.' She sounded resigned and philosophical, as if this was a life lesson she learned repeatedly. But also, in that touch, she seemed to appreciate that he noticed.

She withdrew her hand and he saw her reserve return. She was preparing to say something that needed distance. 'When do you go? To America?'

He recognised the subtext. We need to sort things out. We'd better start.

'I leave in two weeks' time.'

'So we should maybe talk next week?'

He agreed. Next week. How casual they were able to sound. He wanted to add 'I'm sorry', for rushing her, because of this job offer. No, it wasn't rushing. Better than letting it drift. Months might pass and he might still be giving her space, and she might still be reluctant to bother him with difficult details.

Next week, she confirmed. 'I'm sorry,' she added.

She was sorry? 'Sorry for what?'

She shook her head, as if many answers were possible.

They couldn't talk here, not with so many people passing, nudging each other in greeting, turning to embrace. Any moment someone would interrupt and claim her. He'd already monopolised her for too long. 'Next week,' he said. His throat was tight.

She nodded, turned.

Immediately, another set of arms was waiting for her. He saw her stiffen. She had never liked the casual social hug. He knew all the reasons. Its lack of sincerity; the assumption that it was welcomed; the requirement to reciprocate. Which was why he had not hugged her today, even though everyone else had, because today, with hugging everywhere and so commonplace, it would not mean what he wanted it to mean.

He'd seen everyone he needed to. He should leave.

By the pews and the panelled organ loft, a party vibe was setting in. The mourners were loosening, relaxing. Robert had commandeered the area by the stone font, using it as a desk as he talked to people and added their numbers to his phone. Gina was networking with everyone waiting to speak to him, keeping them animated and chatting, like a sheepdog, to stop them wandering away. Steve was watching them both, as if he thought they needed a minder, a habit he would probably never break. The new Ashbirds.

Elliot should leave.

There was Elza again. Cornered by a shaven-headed man who had both her hands clasped together in front of him as if he was using her as a conduit to say a prayer. She wasn't comfortable; she kept looking at the hands, obviously waiting for release, while the man gazed gravely into her face and spoke. Elliot moved closer, in case she wanted rescue. The guy let go and Elza turned and took a big stride away. Suddenly Elliot was chest to chest with her, or nearly so. He hadn't intended to talk to her again, but here they were, both startled, so he said: 'Everything okay?'

Business as usual, said her composed nod. He stepped aside to let her pass.

She stopped, gasped quietly and leaned close. 'Oh my lord, look at Robert. He's about to make a speech.'

No, really? Elliot turned. Robert was standing beside the font, solemn as a president, staring into the distance. A man wearing a purple swirled cravat was aiming a phone at him.

'No,' murmured Elliot, 'just having his picture taken.'

Muttered: 'He is taking it so very, very seriously'.

For a moment Elliot forgot where he was and why. It was as though they were on their way home, discussing whether Robert had been easy company or how they'd sidestepped the nerve-testing stares and the backhand questions where he tried to trap you into offending him. Grateful to be by themselves again, tired, amused. Always the best part of the evening.

Now would be the perfect time to exit. It could not get better than this. 'Next week,' he said, glancing towards the door.

'You're going? Which way?'

He told her he had a special getaway route, given him by Steve.

A fizz of laughter. 'Which getaway route?'

'Is that a trick question?'

'You've probably got an easy route. Mine is really complicated. Through a private garden and then a solicitors' office.'

'Is that necessary?'

'Probably not. I think Steve just likes to feel needed.'

That made him think of one more thing, which he'd tell her quickly because she'd like it. 'Steve said he'd send me his list of New York celebrity nightspots. I hope he doesn't check whether I've been to any of them.'

Yes, she did like it.

A silence followed, companionable, easy. Around them, the buzz of friendly talking. Life getting on its feet again, finding new directions. Now he would leave. 'I'll email,' he said, meaning about arrangements for next week. He said it on his way backwards and out, don't dwell on it. Next week was next week.

She stepped after him. 'You know what? I keep thinking I have to do another thing today, but I've done enough. There isn't even a funeral any more.'

She began walking away from the party. A second's pause and a glance at him. She was checking that he was leaving too.

'I think my route's the other way.'

'I'm not allowed to do that one. You'd better come with me.'

They passed a pillar of deeply scratched stone. Opened a trellised gate into a side chapel, laid with snowy linen. 'It's bloody good to see you,' she said, and pushed a panelled door into a dark chamber that smelled cold and forgotten. 'I warn you, we're sure to get lost. That was forever happening in the old days.'

Ashbirds discography

The Switch (1991)
The Switch
Girl In The Night
Sacrophiliac
Tell No One
I Had Your Dream
Make You A World Without Monday
I Found Your Letters
In Their Long Minds
Astronomy Divine
Lost in Jewelspider Wood
Arrhythmetic

Surface Tension (1992)
Surface Tension
Air Tigers
The Season
The Witch Mark
The Manchesters
For The Bold
Blood Noise
Deep Breath of White Devil
Ragged
Enfin Unfinity
Embryoyo
She Did Not Turn

Hush (1994)
Hush
Hurricane
Hunger
Hurry
Hustle
Human

The C Side
A book on C
Silent Cs
C creatures
Deep C
C you away
For the Frozen C Inside

Come Back (2014)
Making Up Lies About Time
Come Back
Back/Comeback
Sun and Air
Prince of Silence
E-rhythmetic
Untethered
White Noise
Where In All That Air
Day Before Tomorrow

Never officially released
When I Am Laid In Earth (concert footage 2014)
Turned His Head, The National Anthem for Bonnet

Everlasting thanks

To the experts who advised me on matters mountainous, medical, morturarial and musical: Rachel Atkinson, Jessica Bell, Dr Amani Brown, Sandy Bennett-Haber, Ralph Hoyte, Karen Inglis, Matt Sanders, Brenda Scruby, Andrew Thompson, Vivienne and Nigel Tuffnell, Steve Williams.

To my perceptive, patient beta readers: David Bodanis, Garry Craig Powell, Mark Horrell, Dave Morris, John Whitbourn. To my literary family at Vine Leaves Press. To Robin Austin, inexhaustible photographer of the comfort facilities on the trek to Everest Base Camp. And to his brother, Peter Snell, who never stopped asking when the book would be ready.

If you've enjoyed this book, would you leave a review on line? It makes all the difference to independent publishers who rely on word of mouth to get their work known. Thank you!

About the author

Roz Morris lives in London. From the earliest age she had a compulsion to express herself on the page. After a degree at London University, where she learned more about rock bands than about her academic subject, she worked as a journalist and accidentally became a ghostwriter, hitting the bestseller lists incognito. Then she found her groove with her own fiction – *My Memories of a Future Life* and *Lifeform Three* (longlisted for the World Fantasy Award). *Ever Rest* is her third novel. She also has a memoir, *Not Quite Lost: Travels Without a Sense of Direction*, where you'll find many of the origin stories for her fiction, including the electrifyingly dreary town that became Bonnet.

Roz is also an editor and writing coach, and has presented masterclasses for *The Guardian* and Jane Friedman based on her acclaimed *Nail Your Novel* series.

'Taut plotting and sharp storytelling'

'Classy, stylish ... a profound tale in page-turning fashion'

If your life was another person's past, what echoes would you leave in their soul? Could they be the answers you need now?

It's a question Carol never expected to face. She's a gifted musician who needs nothing more than her piano. She certainly doesn't think she's ever lived before. But forced by injury to stop playing, she fears her life may be over. Enter her soulmate Andreq; healer, liar, fraud and loyal friend. Is he her future incarnation or a psychological figment? And can his story help her discover how to live now?

'Much more than a twist on the traditional reincarnation tale...'

'Stunning... like Doris Lessing but much more readable'

Available in ebook, print and audiobook.

More at mymemoriesofafuturelife.com

Lifeform Three (longlisted for the World Fantasy Award)

'Beautifully written; meaningful. Top-drawer storytelling in the tradition of Atwood and Bradbury'

'I really didn't want this book to end. It's that good'

Misty woods; abandoned towns; secrets in the landscape; a forbidden life by night; the scent of bygone days; a past that lies below the surface; and a door in a dream that seems to hold the answers.

Paftoo is a 'bod'; made to serve. He is a groundsman on the last remaining countryside estate, once known as Harkaway Hall – now a theme park. Paftoo holds scattered memories of the old days, but they are regularly deleted to keep him productive.

When he starts to have dreams of the Lost Lands' past and his cherished connection with Lifeform Three, Paftoo is propelled into a nightly battle to reclaim his memories, his former companions and his soul.

Available in ebook, print and audiobook.

More at lifeformthree.com

Not Quite Lost: Travels Without A Sense of Direction

'Delightful, amusing, gripping and often very moving'
'Move over, Bill Bryson'
In life there's the fast lane, and then there's the scenic route. Take your time getting there and you might meet people whose stories are as gripping as those of any famous name.

In *Not Quite Lost*, Roz Morris celebrates the hidden dramas in the apparently ordinary. Her childhood home, with a giant star-gazing telescope on the horizon and a garden path that disappears under next door's house. A tour guide in Glastonbury who is having a real-life romance with a character from Arthurian legend. A unit on a suburban business park where people are preparing to deep-freeze each other when they die.

But even low-key travel has its hazards, and Roz nearly runs down several gentlemen from Porlock when her brakes give up. She takes her marriage vows in a language she doesn't speak, has a *Strictly*-style adventure when she stumbles into a job as a flashmob dancer, and hears an unexpected message in an experiment in ESP. Wry, romantic, amused and wonder-struck, *Not Quite Lost* is an ode to the quiet places you never realised might tell you a tale.

Nail Your Novel books for writers
Nail Your Novel: Why Writers Abandon Books & How You Can Draft, Fix & Finish With Confidence
Nail Your Novel: Writing Characters Who'll Keep Readers Captivated
Nail Your Novel: Writing Plots With Drama, Depth and Heart
Nail Your Novel: A Workbook

Find Roz

Tweet her as @Roz_Morris
Email rozmorriswriter@gmail.com
Explore her website rozmorris.org
If you'd like to hear about other books she's writing, sign up for her newsletter tinyurl.com/rozmorriswriter

CPSIA information can be obtained
at www.ICGtesting.com
Printed in the USA
LVHW041124250521
688447LV00020B/1457